eling Eighteen Changeling Eighteen Changeling Eightee

Indrek

Vol. II of Truth and Justice – a pentalogy

A.H. Tammsaare

Translated by Chris Moseley
and Matthew Hyde

Vagabond Voices
Glasgow

First published in 1929 as Tõde ja Õigus (Vol. II) © A.H. Tammsaare

First published in September 2022 by
Vagabond Voices Publishing Ltd.,
Glasgow,
Scotland.

Translation © Vagabond Voices 2022

ISBN 978-1-913212-33-9

Printed and bound in Poland

Cover design by Mark Mechan

Typeset by Park Productions

The publisher acknowledges subsidy towards
the translation from the Estonian Cultural
Endowment

EESTI KULTUURKAPITAL

For further information on Vagabond Voices, see the website,
www.vagabondvoices.co.uk

Introduction

Indrek is the second volume in A.H. Tammsaare's *Truth and Justices* pentalogy which can only be defined as monumental, given its size and ambition. It is first and foremost a monument to Estonia, the most northerly of the Baltic States and perhaps more importantly the little sister of Finland both in terms of their proximity and their closely related Finno-Ugric languages. But it is not an equestrian statue aspiring to achieve a place amongst the powerful; no, it is more like Picasso's "Guernica" which, in spite of its name, is about humanity as a whole and the terrible suffering it experiences often inflicted by those who have lost their humanity in a vortex of brutality and intolerance. This is why *Truth and Justice* is a series of five books for us all: it could have been written anywhere, but it was Estonians' great good luck that it was written in their country. It is about Estonia and its historical journey from province of the Russian Empire to independent state (the First Republic), but it is also about the human condition; it is about independence but it is also about the limitations and provincialism of nationalism; it is about the uniqueness of cultures but it is also about the validity and the similarities of all human cultures. Perhaps only a small country can truly understand these subtle realities, and the title *Truth and Justice* is there for a purpose.

However, the reader is not going to get all of this in *Indrek*, where the protagonist encounters the city and its absurdities which differ from those of the countryside he has just escaped from. Towards the end of *Vargamäe*, the first volume we published in 2019, Tammsaare provides us with an unflattering portrayal of a nationalist but the author's desire for independence and acknowledgement of Estonia's language and culture is argued for in a subtle and low-key manner, which possibly explains why the War of Independence (1918-20) does not figure in this pentalogy. The truth emerges not from any particular speech – in fact the speeches are usually satirical – but from the complex totality of the work. And justice – well, that is conspicuous by its absence. It is something strongly desired, which belongs to the eternal as the narrative voice explains in this volume (see quotes on the front flap).

Volume II is an essential transition from the countryside and its unfulfilled hopes following the emancipation of the serfs (Volume I) to the social problems and conflicts of Volume III, and it is to some extent a moment of comic relief in which Indrek's belated adolescence goes through its intellectual and emotional ups and downs. More precisely it is the story of his secondary education in an eccentric boarding school – aren't all such schools always eccentric in literature? It doesn't matter whether they're good or bad, and this particular school is perhaps somewhere in-between those two.

The headmaster, Mr Maurus, is an Estonian and apparently a loyal citizen of the Russian Empire, though this maybe his pragmatic nature as he has no wish to pick a fight with the powerful. He is slovenly, erratic, conformist and strangely attractive, because he is guided by some very watered-down moral strictures which have not kept pace with social change. In a way, he is as lost at the end of his life as Indrek is at the beginning of his. Perhaps it is inevitable that they will clash at the end, but even then Maurus suggests a hint of residual affection of the boy he often calls "the tall one", which in turn is based on his faith in the moral superiority of the Estonian countryside.

The Estonian academic, Piret Peiker, argues that *Truth and Justice* is a "postcolonial Bildungsroman"[1] which is a

---

1   Piret Peiker, "A.H. Tammsaare's Truth and Justice as a Postcolonial Bildungsroman", *Journal of Baltic Studies* (New York: Routledge, 2015), pp. 1-18.

good place to start the difficult business of defining a work which defies definition – one of the signs of great literature. I personally have a problem with the term "postcolonial" because the world is still struggling to get out of the neo-colonial stage, but I understand what this category generally means: it is the need to see the world not from the viewpoint of the West, but from those countries who carry the burden of their experiences as colonies of one particular European empire or another (and in quite a few cases a country can experience more than one of them). If we take the argument that Estonia was a colony to its logical conclusion, then all the peoples annexed by Germany, Russia, Austro-Hungary and the Ottomans would have to be included and thus half of Europe would be postcolonial, which quite possibly undermines the concept of postcolonial studies. What is perhaps not understood is that the heart of empire often includes pockets of dire poverty unequalled elsewhere. For example, life expectancy – excluding infantile mortality (death before the age of one year) – was seventeen years in working-class areas of Manchester in 1850, at the peak of Britain's wealth, and equally in remote rural areas of Europe, living conditions could also be very poor in the late nineteenth century though rarely would life expectancy have been so low. In my introduction to Volume I, I pointed out that land ownership in Estonia, north-west Scotland and Ireland was almost identical at that time. I have seen the excellent Estonian film based on Volume which in English is called *Robbers' Rise* (a translation of *Vargamäe*) and the modest peasant houses are positively palatial compared to the black houses of north-west Scotland (though not that different in design). I have a feeling that this categorisation is misleading because Estonia and its language was typical of many stateless minority cultures around nineteenth-century Europe. In Eastern Europe in particular but not only, cities often spoke a different language from the surrounding countryside. Before the Second World War, still only 3%

of Vilnius's inhabitants spoke Lithuanian (the dominant languages were Polish and Yiddish), while they mainly spoke Greek and not Bulgarian in Sofia, German and not Slovene in Ljubljana, English and not Gaelic in Inverness, and English and not Welsh in Cardiff, though I would expect in most cases that however small the minority it would have been higher than the 3% of Vilnius whose surrounding territories spoke Lithuanian. Quite unlike the phenomenon of the global European empire established principally in the eighteenth and nineteenth centuries but with roots going back to the sixteenth and the seventeenth, Estonia came out of an extremely long period of stasis in the very period covered by this pentalogy. It had been conquered by the Teutonic Knights in the Middle Ages, and they imposed a feudal system which remained in place until well into the nineteenth century. Sweden annexed it in 1561 and Russia did the same in 1710 following its overwhelming victory at the Battle of Poltava. However neither the Swedes nor the Russians saw fit to tamper with the German hegemony in Estonia and Latvia, possibly because they saw it as a very robust power structure. This, I think, is important for the anglophone reader to know because it explains the presence of at least three languages in this volume: Estonian, German and Russian. Estonian was the dominant language of the countryside and it appears from this volume also the towns, but the balance was different: German was clearly the language of culture and also of the landowners, and so an educated person would be expected to speak it. Russian was of course the principal language of the Tsarist Empire. In other words, Estonia was a polyglot society, even in the countryside though to a lesser extent. Polish was also significant in the region since it was annexed in the late eighteenth century (when three empires carved up the extensive lands of one of Europe's most intriguing states: the Commonwealth of the Kingdom of Poland and the Duchy of Lithuania which elected its kings), and the teacher Voitinksi is one of Tammsaare's most exquisitely empathetic and quite bizarrely satirical character portraits in the novel. Hopefully I'm not going too far in claiming that he symbolised the decay of that great and quite extraordinarily liberal culture of a state that took in all the heretics and outsiders who came their way. As for the claim that *Truth and Justice* is a Bildungsroman, it is most definitely true of Volumes II and III but only of those volumes. Writers shouldn't write in order to conform to some template, and this is certainly true of Tammsaare's approach to the pentalogy this volume is one part of.

However Piret's article is useful and somewhat alone amongst academic studies of Tammsaare in English. She establishes Dostoyevsky's influence on Tammsaare (like so many European writers) by linking a quote from *The Brothers Karamazov* and an important event at the end of Volume II in which Indrek finds himself obliged to lie about his beliefs in order to avoid hurting a young girl, having refused to do so during an argument with the headmaster. I'll say no more than that. She also claims that "For Dostoevkii, there is an unresolvable … contradiction between the secular idea of progress and the idea of happiness." Progress is generally considered to be an idea that arrived with the French Revolution and that elusive thing we call happiness as something states and even philosophers should engage with arrived a little earlier with the American Constitution. Surely Dostoyevsky is obsessed with demystifying the dominant idea of his own times: Anglo-Saxon utilitarianism that rejects the concept of moral responsibility to others because this is an interference in the perfect but finely balanced mechanism of the market, and believes that such well-intentioned acts can cause more harm than good. Dostoyevsky was far from being alone in this stance and I'll only consider the English ones: Thackeray's *Vanity Fair*, Trollope's *The Way We Live Now* and much of Dickens's outpourings had already done this, but none of the English writers were political as their literary task was to satirise and also record moral decay, and although Dickens thought that this was reversable, he did not explain how this could occur or what was responsible for it in the first place other than the presence of some pretty ugly characters. Dostoyevsky, who was open about Dickens's influence, went much further: he challenged the philosophy that stood behind these modern amoral attitudes, which have returned in recent times making all these writers very relevant again. He also stressed that the philosophy itself was creating the damage. And Tammsaare clearly follows this lead. Like the Russian, he is also extremely bold in his style and plotting. He does not copy Dostoyevsky here, but he is as bold. His fine discursive prose leads to the considerable size of each volume in the pentalogy, while his other novels are not so long. He is also a modern novelist, but this is truer of his other novels. The pentalogy is a realist work in the Dostoyeskian sense of the word, because when the Russian author was told by some people that his books weren't realistic (perhaps they had a problem with a policeman who philosophises), he retorted that they were and it was a higher form of realism. Extraordinary things happen in Volume II, even more so than in Volume I, and they are extremely entertaining and meaningful. They are not farce, but sometimes they come close to it. Finally on this subject I would say that there is sometimes a degree of looseness to the narration in *Truth and Justice*, which can be found in the late works of Dostoyevsky in a more extreme form, such as *The Idiot* and in particular *The Demons*. I confess that I enjoyed both of those works, especially *The Idiot*, but I can see why some readers may find them occasionally a little directionless. The pentalogy however is tighter, and this sense of balance makes it extremely readable.

Tammsaare's great strength is that he can have quite a few themes running concurrently throughout the novel in the low-key manner I've mentioned, and so readers only become aware of this quite slowly as they move through the story. One overarching theme of this volume and the entire pentalogy is the relationship between the city and the countryside. The city should be the home of rationalism and learning, and this is certainly Indrek's perception when he sets off for the town at the end of Volume I and arrives there at the beginning of Volume II, but very soon he is to be disabused. The intellectual ramblings of the townspeople are all over the place, and they seem unaware of their incoherence. They play with ideas and principally wish to demonstrate their erudition, and they live in a perpetual state of rivalry and envy not entirely without their moments of humanity. As readers of Volume I will know, rivalry in the countryside can be open warfare – brutal and unmediated by "good manners". The town is more nuanced and mendacious, and at times it seems more rancorous and certainly more fickle than anything Pearu was capable of, which is saying quite a bit.

Tammsaare, like his creation Indrek, was born and brought up on a small farm and left his home to study when he was almost grown-up, however I think that it would be wrong to exaggerate the autobiographical nature of this volume or the remaining three volume (Indrek only takes centre stage towards the end of Volume I of the pentalogy). It is worth mentioning that Tammsaare did not name the volumes, but it appears that some foreign publishers (and possibly some Estonian ones) have found it helpful to do so and I think that they are right. Indrek is certainly the unchallenged protagonist of the second volume which carries his name. However we should not assume that the pentalogy is anything other than vaguely autobiographical, because I know enough of Tammsaare's life to know that it does not fit exactly into Indrek's fictional one. Quite possibly Volume II is the most autobiographical of the five, and although I may be making the common mistake amongst readers of attributing autobiographical elements where there aren't any, I can't help feeling that the author's schooling was in an establishment fairly similar to the one described here, but it has definitely been adapted to his literary purposes.

What is certain is that Indrek in Volume II has very different ideas from the middle-aged Tammsaare who created him. He may be Tammsaare's memory of his youth, and at the end events drive Indrek towards atheism (a belief the author shared), but he remains naive though not as naive as when he first arrived at the school. The character who may speak for the author in this volume is, in my opinion, Tiit and it is significant that the author should put his thoughts in the mouth of a peasant, albeit a bookish one referred to in Volume I as "one of the wisest and most respected men in the whole neighbourhood." He was the one who advised that Indrek should study, and in Volume II he reappears to give Indrek a political lecture which Indrek mostly ignores, but it is not lost on the reader. In Volume I, an even humbler character – a cottager or cottar – is the mouthpiece for a dramatic denunciation of religion which is highly complex and produces some of the most stunning passages in the book. Tammsaare is no lover of stereotype, and is always surprising the reader with the hidden resources of his characters as they fight their way through their mostly difficult existences. But in particular, he depicts rural life with its merciless hard work and limited resources in the knowledge that rural society is just as varied as city life, and perhaps even more so. Volume I teaches us this with its vast array of characters, and Volume II does the same from the distance with little bit of help from Indrek's brief return to Vargamäe in the middle.

Indrek, the second volume in this pentalogy, prepares us for Volume III and the new experiences of life in an industrial town in which social tensions are about to boil over. The next volume (*When the Storm Fell Silent*) will bring us a new slice of life in Estonia during the early years of the twentieth century, and Vagabond Voices will be publishing it in 2023.

We hope that our readers will stick with us as we continue on the remarkable journey through a masterpiece that should have been published in English long ago, and Volumes IV and V will be published in 2024 and 2025 respectively.

Allan Cameron, Pitigliano, July 2022

Indrek

Chapter 1

As soon as the train started to move and the carriage wheels clattered in an unfamiliar rhythm, Indrek felt completely alone, forlorn and cut off from all that was familiar for the first time in his life. His past life in Vargamäe seemed to collapse in on itself, as if it had all been a dream or a fairy tale – as if it had never really happened. Everything he'd known lost its meaning, while the future so dazzled him with promise, he could make out no clear details. He felt like a stranger to himself in these surroundings. And total strangers leaned against him, pushing him into the corner of his seat. His only solace was to gaze at the scene flashing past outside the window: telegraph poles topped with white ceramic insulators, standing in open land or amidst bushes which were almost leafless now, haystacks ringed with fences in wide open meadows, forests, marshes, bogs and fields dotted with stooks of grain. Here and there, herds of piebald cows, a herd-boy standing by a fire while his dog chased the thundering train until it was gone, lost in the clouds of smoke that billowed from the engine. But Indrek had seen such sights before – they held no interest for him and left him cold.

A grey apathy overcame him, and yet every fibre of his being wanted to tremble, either from the pain of irretrievable loss or in the hope of some future happiness; who could know?

From time to time he tapped the tip of his boot against the chest which he'd shoved under the seat in front of him, as if afraid it might have gone; that chest was the only thing which he could call his own in this strange new place, and

3

it contained those possessions from his past life which were most dear to him. It gave him a homely feeling of safety to know his chest was still there. It was silly, laughable even, but he couldn't help it. That chest of his, bound up tight with strong ropes, was a more trusted travelling companion than any of his fellow passengers could ever be.

On arriving at his destination, Indrek waited until the very last moment to get off the train, hoping that there would be less of a crush. But as it turned out, he had jumped out of the frying pan into the fire, because now he had to struggle past irate passengers as they shoved their way onto the train.

"Get a move on, young bumpkin!" came a mocking cry.

Indrek looked around, but before he could discover the source of such discourtesy, someone else yelled angrily, "Get yourself and that battered old chest of yours out of the way, and let people pass!"

Those rough words brought Indrek to his senses. There was something strangely familiar in them, something well-suited to him and his simple old chest. Suddenly he noticed the crowd of people bustling around him, and he became fully aware of himself, standing with his chest propped against his right knee to make it easier to pass through the jostling crowd of people.

He soon found himself at the station building. He lowered his chest to the ground to give himself a moment to gather his wits and wait for the crowd to thin out. He was glad that he did so, because it allowed him to see the people walking past with cases much larger and more cumbersome than his own. Taking courage, he pulled his case back onto his right knee, and continued on his way.

By the time Indrek had got through the station building and the entrance hall, most of the others passengers had left. He put his chest down on the floor, and immediately a stocky old man with a straggly beard pulled up his cab, waved his whip in Indrek's face and bellowed, "Hey young man, you need a lift?"

Without answering, Indrek found himself picking up his case and lifting it onto the cab.

"Put it on its side, and then it'll fit in," the old man told him before instructing him to take a seat.

"Where am I going? Where is he taking me?" Indrek thought to himself.

"Are we going over the river?" the coachman asked.

"I don't know," Indrek replied.

"How's that then? Where do you want to go?"

Indrek briefly explained his situation.

"So I was right," said the coachman. "Over the river, there's nowt else for it, to old Traat's place. It's nice and close, and it's cheap too. But I'll tell you one thing, that's a lousy school, really lousy. My nephew went there for years, and he probably would have continued to go there until the day he died, if he hadn't been called up. And so off he went, there's no fairness in this world, it was no help to him that he'd spent all those years kicking his heels around at school. He did go to Pihkva to sit his exams, but no luck there either: he failed them, completely failed. But that school of Maurus's is really lousy. As is the man himself! Keep your hands on your money when he's about, shield it from him as you would your soul from the devil. You heed my words, if you do have any money on you that is. When he hears coins jingling together, that old man is like a bee to honey, otherwise…"

The coachman broke off mid-sentence, punctuating his tirade with a gob of spit. But once they had crossed the river, he came back to his point: "That's a really lousy school! No fairness to be had, and no decent uniforms either!"

After that he didn't say another word; it was almost as if his disapproval of the school extended to anyone who planned to go there. Indrek's thoughts were teeming, and his heart racing. And so he didn't notice when the coachman came to a halt; he only recovered his senses when he heard him speak, "So, we're here – old Traat's place … number seventy-five … go in through the front door and you'll arrive at the dining room. There are rooms for the Germans round the back, pretty nice rooms they are too. But you go right on in … it's not far to Maurus's place from here: just round the corner, and you're there. Old Traat will show you the way, he knows. Everyone knows. But make sure to keep one hand on your money."

And with that he gave his horse a tap of his whip, and drove off.

Indrek dragged his chest in through the front door. Inside, he was met by a young lady, who held the inner door open with one hand, and grabbed hold of one of the ropes on Indrek's chest with the other. If Indrek were later to have been asked whether the girl was dark or fair-skinned, slim or stocky, tall or short, then it's unlikely that he could have answered. But one thing he was sure of was that the girl had smiled, and for some reason that smile stayed with him for a long time, maybe because it was his first time in town and he felt that it was meant especially for him. And he probably would have remembered it for years to come, if he had not encountered that same girl years later in a different place, in different circumstances. Then that wonderous smile was extinguished from where it was hidden, buried deep in his memory, and afterwards he couldn't find the girl anywhere. So much for the first smile of a town girl.

"Can I help you, young man?" asked a man with a red beard. He was slouched against the counter, chatting to a couple of peasants who had their packed lunch open and were eating. "Are you looking for a room?"

"I would indeed like a room, if there is one available," said Indrek, suddenly feeling hungry.

"The small one," said the red-bearded man to the girl, who looked at Indrek and smiled again; then she led him and his chest to the room. "Thirty kopecks a night!" cried the man after them. The words were meant for Indrek, but they flitted past his ears unnoticed.

Left on his own, Indrek undid the ropes from around the

chest, opened the lid, fished out the food he'd brought with him, and began to eat. He did all this in a dreamy, distracted fashion, still dwelling on the coachman's scathing words about the school and its headmaster, whom he hoped to go and see as soon as possible

To get from his room to the street, Indrek had to go through the corridor, or back the way he had come, through the buffet. He decided on the latter route, and he must have been guided by providence, for as it turned out, it allowed him to leave the inn with a lighter heart than when he'd arrived.

Entering the buffet, Indrek saw that the red-bearded man was now alone, although he was still slouched against the counter; it must have been his favourite spot for savouring his pipe.

"First time here?" he asked when he saw Indrek.

"That's right," was all Indrek said, because he was in a hurry to leave.

"Come far?"

"Quite far."

"From Talnamaa?"

"From those parts, yeah."

"To the school?"

"That's what I've come for."

"To Old Maurus's place of course? There's nowhere else to go."

"Who knows if I'll even get in there," opined Indrek, who was starting to take an interest in what the red-beard had to say.

"You can get in – but you have to have money. You can even get in without money. You can get into Maurus's from any place at any time: in autumn, at Christmas or Easter, whether you're eight, eighteen or eighty. I'm not joking! There are a lot of baldies and grey-beards studying there. A few years ago I was supposed to go there myself. I thought, why can't I study too, if others are. I've given enough useful food and drink to people, because beer and vodka are useful

7

drinks, if you consume them sensibly. But not temperance. Up till now I've been useful to people, but now I've started to think to myself: I'll go and study at old Maurus's place. And I did go once to chat with him, but he says to me, 'First shave your beard off, and then come back. You can't get in with a beard, because behind the beard you can't see what sort of man you are, what sort of face you have.' That's what old Maurus said. Well, what do you say to that? I'm supposed to shave my beard off before I even get tested on whether or not I can study! 'No, Mr Maurus,' I said, 'I'm not parting with my beard, especially as I don't even know if there's any sense in studying.' Alright, let's say I get to be a student. What am I supposed to do as a student if I don't have a beard? Do you think a student costs as much as my beard? You should hear what the women have to say about it – I mean about my beard. Ten students aren't worth as much as my beard, when it comes to women. Women like them just like mine. Anyway, once I've got bored with women – because they all get muddle-headed in the end – yeah, maybe then I'll take up that mad thing, shave off my beard and go to old Maurus, because I like that school. All sorts of layabouts from all over the place come together there, no word of a lie! And old Maurus makes men of all of them. If need be, he gives them a thrashing, because there's no substitute for a good old birching. My brother had a son – a whopper of a lad, but a real brat. He put him in the town school – but after a year they kicked him out! He put him in another school – out again after half a year! He wanted to put him in a third one – they wouldn't take him in. 'Take the urchin to old Maurus,' I said, 'and if he doesn't make something of him, get him shovelling manure!' My brother went to old Maurus and told him in private (this is what I told him to say): 'Take whatever it costs, but make a man of my son, a proper man. Make him a student, so he can wear a coloured cap.'[2] 'Sure

---

2   *a coloured cap*: worn by members of university fraternities.

8

we'll make a man of him so he'll have a coloured cap,' old Maurus told my brother. 'You can even make something of a horse-thief, if you start at the right end,' he added. And what do you think happened? Karl Nõmme became a student. It cost a hell of a lot, but he did. Now he's been studying for six years, grumbling 'cause it costs even more money than with old Maurus. So it's a fine school. It's right here: out the door, first to your right, then right again and there you are. A stone building, but it's only like that at the front. At the back it's all wood, just wood. You could say: stone head, wooden tail. The tail's the main thing, the stone head is only a front and a recommendation, because it's written there: School of the Highest Standards. So there's none better in the whole wide world. Just like old Maurus himself, he's a first-rate teacher and a trained preacher. You get me? He might step up to the altar in the middle of the night or climb up onto the pulpit. Not like us two: one behind the counter, the other in front of it, nothing else. But the high-ups wouldn't give him a job. A few parishes wanted to get him, but the high-ups were against it everywhere. So old Maurus set up his own school of the highest standards and a source of wisdom. You can go there with peace of mind, because it's a pure Estonian school, previously teaching in German and now in Russian. But that doesn't matter: all Estonian schools are either German- or Russian-speaking, and there haven't been any other kinds of Estonian schools to this day, whatever an Estonian school might be…"

Step by step, Indrek had already been inching his way toward the door, but that didn't reduce the red-beard's torrent of words one bit. Luckily for him, a couple of men came in, and Indrek had the courage to make his escape. When the buffet-keeper saw that, he called after him. "Just keep going right, right only, and when you come back, keep left, always keep left!"

The muggy autumn day had meanwhile gone completely dark. Seen from afar, the burning lanterns in the steamy air looked like a halo. What looked like a swarm of countless tiny midges around them fled outwards as soon as Indrek approached them, as if they were afraid of him. "Keep left, always keep left" rang in his ears and he followed those words without thinking about it. But soon he noticed that he was approaching the edge of the town, and then it occurred to him that he was supposed to keep left on his way back. So he turned around and went back where he'd started, and began again, keeping to the right. He soon found the white stone building he'd been seeking, and someone was slipping in through the front door leaving a chink of light near Indrek on the road where here and there thin blades of grass crept up among the cobblestones. For some reason Indrek noticed this clearly, and it somehow struck him as comforting and welcoming, because it reminded him of a long single bent blade of grass which had once grown on the north side of the thatched eaves of the Vargamäe farmhouse.

He had barely concluded that thought process when the door was opened from inside and a young man wearing a uniform cap stepped out. Indrek pulled off his own cap and asked in his clerical assistant's Russian whether this was Mr Maurus's first-class educational establishment. That was what he said: "first-class educational establishment", because he was afraid that otherwise he might offend the dignity of the great white stone building. He got a most friendly answer, and in Estonian too: "Yes, this is Maurus's school; please step inside."

But when he saw Indrek's perplexity, he pulled the bell and waited for someone to come and open the door. Then he said in Russian: "Someone here to see Mr Maurus." Having said this, he vanished into the darkness.

Chapter 2

Indrek stepped inside. He was led through the hall under the feeble light of a ceiling lamp. There were two doors leading to unknown possibilities. Loud chatting and laughter could be heard from behind one of them. The other door was half-open, and in that room he could see a big table covered with black oilcloth on which a lamp with a white shade burned. Bigger and smaller boys were squeezed around the table. Someone opened the door fully and looked at Indrek, but he paid no attention to him, for his eyes were fixed on a swan with extended neck and arched wings which was hanging from the ceiling, as if hovering in flight. "Just like the angel of peace," thought Indrek as he eyed the swan. But he couldn't dwell on that thought, for the same boy who had opened the door was still standing in front of him sideways on, and asked in a pleading, almost guilty tone, "May I have your name?"

Once Indrek had replied the boy asked him to take a seat, and rushed upstairs somewhere, judging by the sound echoing on the stair. Indrek tried to collect his thoughts, but they were so dispersed that he couldn't catch a single one of them. Moreover the boy came back too quickly and said to Indrek: "Mr Maurus asks you to come upstairs." And when he had led Indrek back through the door he had just come through, he added, "Up the stairs, the door on the left."

Cap in hand, the grey long woollen coat knitted by his mother on his back, its hem hampering his steps like the tail of a skirt, Indrek climbed the narrow wooden staircase. All this was quite different from what he had imagined when he'd stood outside. Too ordinary, too everyday! There was only one thing that interested him, so much so that he even stopped halfway up. And he might have stood there even longer if he hadn't heard a door opening upstairs and slippers shuffling across the floor. Yes, if it hadn't been for that, he might have stood there for quite a while, sniffing the air continuously because the staircase smelt so sweet. Only once in his life had Indrek felt anything like this – so very fleetingly. Then he had been standing in a church by the end of a pew, and three women had passed him, all veiled and wearing black; one of them was old, and the other two were young and were comforting her. The three of them went up to the altar and knelt on the big flagstones in front of the whole congregation. "That teacher is mourning her only son," someone whispered in Indrek's ear. Even now he remembered how strangely those words had affected him at the time. Is that what a woman teacher in mourning smells like? he wondered to himself. He had seen so many tears, so much weeping, yet he had never smelled that scent before – never. Only the tears of a teacher could smell like that, when she was mourning in front of a whole congregation for her only son. The teacher's tears and the wooden staircase of Maurus's first-class educational establishment – those two things in the world.

At the top of the stairs a grey-bearded and bushy-browed old man in slippers awaited and extended his right hand to greet Indrek, while he held the sides of his dun-coloured dressing-gown together at the waist with his left hand.

"Hello, hello," he said in a mellow, reassuring voice, while his limp handshake drew the boy over the threshold into a little room. As the old gentleman went to close the door with his left hand, while his right hand still held onto Indrek's, his dressing-gown opened and his underwear became visible underneath.

"What was your name?" asked the old gentleman, adding, "I did hear it, but my old head can't retain it." And when Indrek replied, he said, "Beautiful name, very beautiful name. But in the book we'll write Heinrich, that's even more beautiful than Indrek. Sit down," he said then, opening a big book. Taking his seat he once more forgot about his dressing-gown and it opened completely to reveal what was underneath. His shirt was open too, and hairy skin was visible.

"Where did you go to school?" asked the old man, and when Indrek had revealed his education, he added the question: "*Deutsch sprechen Sie?*" to which Indrek wanted to reply "*Nein,*" but his tongue pronounced "neun". That was the end of their German conversation. Indrek was expecting the old gentleman to try his Russian too, but he didn't. Finally he felt it useful to say: "I know more Russian; I've studied that longer."

But this didn't seem to interest the old gentleman at all. He asked, "Your father has a farm?"

"Yes," replied Indrek.

"A big farm?" inquired the gentleman.

"Big, yes, but a bad one – it doesn't bring anything in," explained Indrek, remembering the cabman's words: "Keep a hold of your wallet," and with these words he finally understood that he was in the presence of Mr Maurus himself.

"Yes yes, well, of course, doesn't bring anything in," the headmaster seemed to agree.

"How much money did your father give you to bring?" he asked.

"Twenty roubles, I didn't get any more."

"That's not much, since you're almost a full-grown man already."

"My godfather gave me some too, and I have a bit of my own," explained Indrek.

"How much?"

"Fifty."

"Fifty of your own, twenty from your father and how much from your godfather?"

"No, no – fifty altogether," Indrek corrected him.

Without saying a word, the headmaster extended his hand and Indrek was unable to do anything but fish his wallet out of his pocket with its "little copper coins".

The headmaster recounted the money he had received and said: "Correct, fifty. So you have no more? Father didn't give you more?"

"No, no more."

"Nothing at all?"

"No," Indrek assured him, although it was a lie, as he had put quite a few roubles aside so as not to be caught short.

"I'm asking this for your own benefit, because it's not good for a young man to be carrying money around in town. You've been in the town before? No? Thank God for that, because then you don't know what can happen with your money in town – you'll have no temptations. That's the main thing – that there's no temptation. But anyway... Well! Now come here" – he pulled Indrek with his left hand: "and look with your own eyes at what I'm writing. You see: Bed and board, as well as school fee, fifty roubles: Paid In."

The headmaster did not desist until Indrek had read those words aloud from the book. Then he scribbled something extra in German, which Indrek didn't have the skill to understand. At the end the headmaster added the date. Now he took the money from the desk and went to put it in a drawer. But there he suddenly stopped to think. Finally he took a paper rouble and put it in Indrek's palm.

"Put that in your pocket. A big chap like you should always have a little money on him. How old are you? Turned eighteen? A lovely time, a good year, it brings luck. I'm over sixty myself."

Indrek hesitated to put the money in his pocket, because he felt terribly embarrassed that he had lied at first.

"I do have a little for myself," he said.

"What?" cried the headmaster. "You still have money? How much? Where?"

"Still in the box," replied Indrek.

"What! You have money in a box? And a box? At the hotel? Are you mad in the head? Money at the hotel in a box!

14

Is that your money, that's in the box? No, it isn't your money, it belongs to the first person to get their hands on it."

"It's only a couple of roubles," pleaded Indrek.

"Even a couple of kopecks!" cried the headmaster. "Keep in mind what Mr Maurus tells you, and he knows what he's talking about, because his hair's gone grey because of money – money and other things. He says: Don't ever put money in a box, not here, nor in a hotel, but bring it to Mr Maurus. Those who don't know how to handle their own money should bring it to me. Come even in the middle of the night, come and knock at my door, you see, like this: knock, knock, knock! – but not with your fist, so that the whole house wakes up – understand? For Mr Maurus is never asleep when someone's bringing him money. He puts the money in the book – then it's safe. A person will die, a book will not. We'll wake up on the Judgement Day, but what would be the point of money on such a day? There will the other things when Judgement Day comes. Do you believe in Judgement Day? Alright, alright, no need to answer that. It's not important until Judgement Day. But money: that is important, very important. How much is there? Are there two roubles or a bit more? Are there perhaps three or four? Surely you wouldn't be mad enough to leave five or ten roubles in the box? Tell me the truth! For in Mr Maurus's house everyone must speak the truth, that's what this house is like. Of course your father gave you more, a lot more, than twenty – after all he has a big farm, doesn't he?"

"No sir, father gave me only twenty; this time he couldn't give any more. Maybe there'll be more later."

"Exactly, there'll be more later, because you can't get by with just fifty. But maybe you had something of your own? How much of your own did you really have? Don't remember? Right, you don't remember. But how did you leave that money in the box anyway? Maybe you have something of your own in your bag? Have you got some in your bag or not? Maybe just a little?"

He stretched out his hand as if asking for the money-bag.

Indrek did take it from his pocket, and opened all its compartments before the headmaster's eyes to show him its true emptiness.

"I believe you, I believe you," intoned the headmaster, examining the empty wallet. "You have such an honest face. As long as there's honesty in the countryside, there will always be a future. You know who Jakobson was – that's Carl Robert Jakobson? Have you heard of him? And what he said? He said, 'The fate of our nation depends on the peasant.' Do you understand? I'm talking of our nation here! The Estonian people! And why is this? It's because the peasant is honest, God-fearing and loyal to his tsar. If we could get all the people to live in the country, then…"

He never finished the sentence. Instead he took the paper rouble from between Indrek's fingers, folded it up and put it in the bag which the boy was still holding.

"This is for being honest, for being the child of an honest father and mother. Mr Maurus loves honest people who tell the truth and don't lie. *Warten Sie, warten Sie!*"[3]

And now, as if forgetting Indrek, he gathered up the fringes of his nightshirt and rushed out the door. At the threshold he turned around and invited Indrek to follow him, but when the boy was about to rise from his chair, the headmaster gave a dismissive wave of his right hand, as if wanting to force the boy to sit down again. "Sit, sit down a moment!" he said. And when Indrek continued to stand in perplexity, the headmaster shouted impatiently through the doorway: "Sit, why don't you!" – adding hastily as he rushed out the door, "*Ein Augenblick!*"[4] But as soon as Indrek was on his own in the room, he let his gaze roam around it and came to rest at the sight of a bed with its bedclothes pulled back, as if the headmaster had only just woken up. Then the door suddenly opened once again and the headmaster's head poked in. "You'd better come with me after all," he told Indrek.

---

3   *Warten sie, …*: "Wait, …"
4   *Ein Augenblick*: "Just a moment."

So the two of them went down the narrow wooden stairs, the headmaster in front in his silent slippers, the tail of his dressing-gown flapping, and Indrek behind him in his stiff boots which were squeaking dreadfully. Down in the hall the headmaster knocked on the door from which the chatting and laughter had been heard earlier, and shouted "Herr Koovi!" When no reply came, he tried to open the door, but it was locked. Emptiness and silence now reigned everywhere. The lamp was still burning on the table in the big room, and a little to the side of it in the great room the white swan spread its wings under the ceiling like a dusty angel of peace. One corner of the room was separated from the rest by a dark red floral cretonne curtain, and as the headmaster anxiously paced up and down the room, as if he didn't know what to do, the tail of his dressing-gown took flight and set the floral cretonne flapping, which made it possible for Indrek to see behind it some bunk beds pushed together beyond the pillars. Next to a large cupboard, to which a wire was attached in order to hold up the curtain, stood two plaster busts, side by side. They were the things that caught Indrek's attention. But he had no time to linger over them, because the headmaster's anxiety seemed to be growing. "Kopfschneider! Kopfschneider!" he cried repeatedly in an ever shriller voice. When there was no reply and the person called didn't appear, the headmaster again pulled Indrek by the hand and opened the third door of the big room, which led to a small dark space. In the piercing light of the opened door Indrek saw more bunk beds.

"Come to heel!" the headmaster commanded, as Indrek had fallen a couple of steps behind him. "Otherwise you'll be knocking your eyes out of your head in the dark and Mr Maurus will have to pay. So keep close, always at my heels as Mr Maurus goes forward!"

The headmaster opened yet another door. Behind it, too, was an expanse of darkness and also warmth. And yet a little light was seeping in from somewhere. After a few moments it became clear that it came through a glass door, which the headmaster presently opened.

"Careful!" he commanded. "Otherwise you'll trip! A doorstep and then a stone floor. A young person must always be careful! Always careful! says Mr Maurus. He himself is old already, but even he is careful. An old man has to be careful too. Young and old!"

Suddenly he stopped.

"My shoe! I've lost my shoe!" he exclaimed.

Indrek bent down with the headmaster to look for the object in the pitch darkness. But the shoe couldn't be found.

"It came off my foot just now," explained the headmaster.

"It's not here," said Indrek.

"Lift your own feet, perhaps it's under your foot," said the headmaster.

Indrek did so, and indeed the headmaster's soft slipper was found under his right foot. It had occurred to him that he had stepped on something soft, but hadn't known what it was.

"You see now," said the headmaster, "how careful you have to be. Even when you're carefully looking for it, you trample on Mr Maurus' shoe. What would happen if you weren't being careful? What would be left of my poor old feet?"

In his fatherly way Mr Maurus thus taught his new charge, while he carried on through the dim corridor to some brighter upper room, which was more like a shed or a barn. From here doors went off to the right, left and straight ahead. Yet Mr Maurus did not use any of them, but rushed to the wooden stairs leading to another floor. At the top of the stairs there were more doors, leading to the right and left and straight ahead. This endless series of doors made Indrek quite giddy. Neither the old nor the new municipal offices had had so many doors. At first sight, the great number of doors seemed quite absurd. The headmaster opened the one on the right and it creaked and squeaked like an unlubricated wooden cart. Only later did Indrek find out the reason for the noisy doors; they were kept closed by a stone hanging on the end of a string, and since the wheel on which the string ran was unlubricated, it screeched. But the wheels would not be allowed to do this, Mr Maurus would assure Indrek later, as it was one of Indrek's duties to oil the wheel of the door with either grease or butter, it didn't matter which.

In the room they now stepped into, stood two long tables around which little children, youths and even grown men were sitting down to their supper.

"Hello!" said the headmaster in Russian, adding in German: "*Mahlzeit!*"[5] He lowered his chin to his chest and let his eyes run around the room over his spectacles. Suddenly he rushed at the lower edge of the first table and screamed in broken Russian (even Indrek realised that the headmaster's Russian was not at all fluent): "Kopfschneider! Schinder! Why is no one down in the hall? Why are you here? Mr Maurus has told you a thousand times: the downstairs room must never be empty. A person comes, wanting to bring money to Mr Maurus, because he wants to start studying, wants to go to university and become a student – but you aren't down there. No one's down there! The lower room is empty." The headmaster suddenly turned to Indrek and asked him, "Was the lower room empty?"

"Yes, it was," replied Indrek, as the eyes of everyone sitting at the table turned to him, and then laughter came from their mouths without Indrek realizing why.

"But I was downstairs when he came," a boy told the headmaster, indicating Indrek.

"You were, but you aren't any more. So what if someone comes right now and rings the bell? Will you hear it up here? He comes and rings the bell – once, twice, three times, ten times. Well, you tell me how long a person is supposed to ring the bell if he wants to bring money to Mr Maurus and nobody opens? He rings until he goes away and Mr Maurus is without his money. For anyone who brings money will not come back

---

5   *Mahlzeit*: "Enjoy your meal [German]

19

a second time. You there," the headmaster shouted at Indrek, "come closer, come here!"

This was one of the most embarrassing moments of Indrek's life, when he, in his hard and heavy boots – so terribly heavy and hard, and they clumped so loudly as he stepped across the room in full view of the others' scornful looks.

"Tell this Latvian – because this one is Latvian – tell him whether you would have come back to Mr Maurus bringing money if you hadn't been let in. Tell him in Russian, because the poor chap doesn't know Estonian. Two years he's been here, but he still can't speak it. Tell him whether you would have come or not."

"I suppose I would've come," said Indrek.

"What!" shouted the headmaster heatedly, and all the faces widened with a grin. When Mr Maurus noticed this, he declared in German: "*So ein Landscher, ein Tere-tere!*"[6] Then he turned to Indrek again and said in Estonian, "You say you would have come if you'd rung once and no one opened the door, a second time and no one opened the door, a third time and no one opened the door, a tenth time and no one opened the door? So why would you have come again if it was never opened? Just tell me, would you have come if it was never opened?"

"Then I wouldn't," Indrek now agreed.

"Well, then tell that Latvian in Russian so that he knows: Mr Maurus is right. It would be sacrilegious for Mr Maurus is wrong and not the Latvian. Tell him clearly: 'No, I wouldn't have come a second time, or brought the money,'" insisted the headmaster. And when Indrek had done that, Mr Maurus said to Kopfschneider: "You see, Mr Maurus is always right; that's why the room downstairs should never be empty. While the others are eating, you're downstairs; if someone else comes downstairs, you go and eat. Always take your turn. You have to take your turn. Understand?"

---

6   *So ein Landscher, ein Tere-Tere*: "Such a rustic scholar."

But the boy made a face as if he didn't understand a word of the headmaster's abysmal Russian. So the headmaster held the sides of his dressing-gown together with his left hand, while with the fingers of his right he made a clutching movement, waving them back and forward before his bulgy eyes, which was evidently meant to indicate that the Latvian was not right in the head, while he intoned derisively, "No, the Latvian doesn't understand. The Latvian never understands. The Latvian always understands things differently from us. That's the way the Latvian is and this is the way we are."

But when Kopfschneider wanted to leave his meal and go downstairs, the headmaster pushed him back into his place and said, "Sit down, sit down! Don't disobey Mr Maurus's commands! Did Mr Maurus say: Get up and go downstairs? No, Mr Maurus did not. Well, go on eating then, and don't get up! Don't disobey orders!"

And he added in Estonian: "The Latvian wants to eat too. The Latvian wants to eat more than we do, because he's used to better."

Suddenly the headmaster broke off and rushed past Indrek to the door, shouting: "Herr Koovi, Herr Koovi, *hören Sie!*"[7] But Mr Koovi had already got up from the table and vanished out of the door, so Mr Maurus went rushing after him and Indrek was left standing there, perplexed and unsure about what he should do. Eventually he found the courage to go off in search of the headmaster and ended up downstairs in the hall.

"Where are your things?" asked the headmaster as soon as he saw him. Indrek had barely answered the question when the headmaster rushed off once more towards the dining room and shouted through the doorway, "One moment!" He then reappeared a moment later with Kopfschneider, who had to leave his meal after all.

"What things have you brought with you?" the headmaster

---

7   *Herr Koovi, hören Sie:* "Mister Koovi, Listen to me."

asked Indrek. "A box? Big? Can the two of you carry it? Can you? Very good! So there'll be change from the cabman. Kopfschneider, put your cap on and go and help him bring that box back. At the double! Mr Maurus doesn't have time, because he's old. Old people never have time, as death is standing at their door. So hurry!"

He shouted those last words as the boys were leaving. But hardly had they stepped out onto the street when the outer doorbell rang, followed by the headmaster's voice.

"Kopfschneider! Kopfschneider!" he screamed.

The boys went back, the Latvian in front, the Estonian behind.

"But do you have money to pay there?" asked the headmaster. "Why don't you ask Mr Maurus for money when you go to the hotel? Always ask; you've got to ask, do you understand? Here's a silver rouble, don't pay any more than that. Tell them Mr Maurus ordered you not to pay more. Even that's too much; bring back the change. Haggle! A man must always haggle: what sort of person would fail to haggle. You are bigger and cleverer, and you're an Estonian – see to it that the Latvian doesn't pay too much," said the headmaster, turning to Indrek, at the same time putting the money in the Latvian's hands. "If you run short, there's also that paper rouble that I gave you upstairs. Now quickly! Run! You can run, can't you? Let's see who can get there first: the Latvian or the Estonian. Make a race of it as Mr Koovi and Timusk are waiting."

So the boys set off at a run, and they hardly heard the headmaster's last words in the darkness of the autumn evening, in which the street lamps were flickering as if they were encircled by tiny glistening swarms of midges.

Once the boys had returned with the box, the headmaster sent Indrek to the room from which he had previously heard people talking and laughing. Maurus threw in a few words of German uttered in the doorway without stepping into the room, as if he were banned from it.

Sitting at the table in the room were two gentlemen, the same ones the headmaster had been talking to at dinner. One of them was well-built and had a machine-shaven head and a clean-shaven, pockmarked and misshapen face; he had a timid or secretive look. The other man had yellowish whiskers, red lips, mild grey eyes and slightly curly hair combed over his head. The first wore grey clothes and the second wore black. They sat on either side of a table that was no grander than the office table at which Indrek had been writing. The chairs in this room were even more tatty than the office ones. The simple wooden bed by a wall had a striped woollen cover on it. The only thing that struck Indrek as civilised was the packed bookcase, reaching up to the ceiling and taking up nearly a whole wall. That was what drew Indrek's gaze, if anything did. But he had little time for that, for they were testing his knowledge from the very start. It must have taken about half an hour, and then the man in grey said in Estonian: "In Russian and arithmetic you get into fourth grade, but in history and Latin in particular, you will have to do some catching up. If you do a lot of work, even in the Christmas holidays, you may perhaps be able to catch up with the others next term. You're a full-grown man – get on with it. Get up early in the morning, in the evenings they make you go to bed. Have you got money for lessons? No? Well then, try on your own, ask the others – even me sometimes. Not constantly, because I haven't got time, but now and then."

Suddenly it seemed to Indrek that this man's eyes were as mellow as the other's, and he experienced a new kind of pleasure as he left the room. Soon the headmaster appeared, and when he had stepped for a moment into the examiners' room, he came up to Indrek and said, "Mr Koovi and Timusk put you in the fourth grade, but actually you should go into second or third. You're a big man – try to catch up with the smaller ones. Otherwise you'll end up after Christmas in second – and there's an even bigger and older one there.

You'll be going downwards. At Mr Maurus's, anyone who doesn't study or lags behind goes downwards. For what can Mr Maurus do with someone who doesn't study? If however someone comes to Mr Maurus, then he should study once, study twice, study three times, study with enthusiasm, study in a frenzy! How does work get done on the land? How is the hay reaped? How is the rye worked? Sweat comes pouring down in streams! That's how you have got to work. When someone comes to Mr Maurus and is already big and tall, that is what he has to do. Do you understand?"

"I understand," replied Indrek in a strange state of excitement; for some reason he was seized by a supreme feeling of happiness.

"'I understand, Mr Maurus, Sir' is what you're supposed to say," instructed the headmaster. "A young man must always be polite and respectful. So, always say: *Herr Direktor*, Herr Maurus, *Herr Lehrer*.[8] But carry on, carry on! Where are we going to put you to sleep? Where will we find space for you? Yes, polite and respectful. The Latin language and politeness rule in Mr Maurus's house. Latin! The Romans loved space, they loved plenty of space. Mr Maurus teaches Latin, but he doesn't have as much space as the Romans did. Mr Ollino, Mr Ollino! Where will we find space for this Roman? Where can he put his box?"

Once the headmaster had shouted, the previously locked door opened and from it emerged a pale, thickset man of average height. He had a round head and his large, slightly bulging eyes were almost white, which could have reminded Indrek of a wall-eyed horse, had they not been suffused by a crazed indifference or perhaps a weary iciness.

"There's still space upstairs," said Mr Ollino with no expression in his eyes.

"Call Jürka!" the headmaster commanded the Latvian.

---

8 *Herr Direkor ... Herr Lehrer*: "Mr Headmaster ... Mister Teacher" [German]

And when he appeared, he was given Indrek's box to carry on his back, and so began the journey through the dining room and up the stairs.

"There's nowhere else but Siberia," said Jürka as he passed, climbing the stairs with the box, "because the better places are already taken. The best places are for the ones who pay better. But there's always space in Siberia; it's never full up. Your teeth will chatter with the winter cold," asserted Jürka as he climbed the last steep step, with Indrek pushing from behind. So they finally got it through the trapdoor in the ceiling to the high attic room, where the weather conditions didn't differ from those outside.

"Have you slept in a loft in the country?" Mr Ollino asked Indrek, as he came up into Siberia. And when Indrek replied affirmatively, Ollino said quite indifferently, "Well then, it'll be like coming home. Clean fresh air and quiet, no noise or commotion, because no one comes through here; you can't get any higher."

"The chimney-sweep climbs higher," said Jürka.

"The chimney-sweep doesn't come up to sleep," replied Ollino. "A bit chilly in winter perhaps, but easier to wake up in the morning and a clearer head to start work with. In my time I've slept outside in the country on a pile of potatoes and it did me no harm, just a bit of pain in one side. Nobody's ever caught their death from a chill up here."

Chapter 3

The next morning Indrek woke to the sound of a bell. It was an ordinary sleigh bell, the kind he had heard from wedding guests or on Christmas Eve celebrations when people chased each other home in their rush to see hay and straw spread across the floor and the rooms so packed with delicious food that its smell wafted out into the yard. Today too, in his sleepiness Indrek felt something quite homely and familiar, a moment later the bell seemed to be clanging in his ear and it was so painful that all his sweet drowsiness vanished. He sat bolt upright: a grimy ceiling lamp was burning and the Latvian, who had helped him carry his box yesterday, was standing beside his bed, bell in hand. Apart from Indrek, no one was stirring. But when Kopfschneider didn't stop ringing it, voices were heard from several places: "That's enough! Go to hell, you great oaf! Get out of here!"

For some of them the ringing was a joke. They cried, "Come closer! I can't hear it properly! Bring two of them tomorrow!"

When the Latvian saw that the Estonians and Russians – there were no other nationalities in "Siberia" – were starting to move, he took the clapper of the bell and groped his way down the hatchway. Then someone shouted from his bed and put out the light, and everyone went back to sleep again – dawn sleep, as they called it. Indrek also snuggled under the covers, but sleep no longer came, although all around him he could hear the sleepers' deep breathing and even snoring. This didn't last long, for a new fumbling was heard from the stairs, and through a crack in the hatchway a ray of light flashed. "Light, boys!" cried someone who was awake.

26

The next moment the hatch opened and the white head of Mr Ollino came into view. The flickering candlelight threw a feeble glow onto the beds and the spaces between them.

"So what's this supposed to mean?" asked Ollino. "Didn't you hear the bell?"

"We didn't hear a thing," came the response from several quarters at once.

"That means a louder tinkle tomorrow," declared Ollino.

"Louder and longer," responded someone.

"Exactly," Ollino assured them. "But now get up, get up!" he repeated in a commanding tone and started to pull the covers off the sleepers.

"Mr Ollino, one moment longer," begged one little boy, holding his blanket under his chin. "I'm just stretching a little."

"There's no time," replied Ollino. "Up and get washed!"

"It's cold! I can't! I'm shivering even under the blanket," countered the boy.

"There's cold water downstairs – that'll warm you up nicely!" Ollino assured him, not leaving them in peace until the last boy had got out of bed. One by one they vanished through the hatch to go to the lower floor where the wash-room was. The whole building seemed to tremble under the trudge of sleepy, careless feet.

"Quiet there!" Mr Ollino called down through the opening. "You couldn't make more noise, even if you were wearing horseshoes!"

But the flood of footsteps flowed ever lower and filled the whole building with disruptive energy.

"We could wash upstairs, then we wouldn't need to tramp around like this," said Indrek to the boy in front of him.

"It's hard to carry water, and besides you'd freeze to death in Siberia," he replied.

"Oh, so cold!" exclaimed Indrek.

"Cold!" replied the other. "Jack Frost himself."

"So how can you sleep here?" asked Indrek uneasily.

"If you survive, you'll find out," came the calm reply. "You'll get used to it like the rest of us."

Indrek didn't appreciate those words now, but after a few weeks their meaning was clear to him; by then he was scrapping with the others to get his body warm, while squeezed into a cold place. Every evening this was their unique gymnastic exercise, in which many a boy's shirt or trousers got torn. There were also those who became so "enthusiastic" that they threw off their shirts, so that their bare hands and arms glowed. This "outpouring of the spirit" was known to the supervisors too, and was mostly overlooked, because participation in such outpourings came from the lower ranks, and as a consequence the noise could become unbearable. Then even the chairs, tables and beds could become embroiled in the vortex, in fact anything that stood in their way, and so some of those had to lose a leg or some other part. They would do headstands on chairs, balance on the ends of beds, jump in lines over tables and practise wrestling; they romped without any order or system. Indrek had never been much of a romper, but here he learned it with the others. The general mood spread to him and he entered into the spirit of it.

There was another means of getting warm: they pinched some wood from below and took it up to Siberia, or somehow persuaded Jürka to carry up the logs and hide them somewhere, for example a couple of logs behind each headboard. When everything had gone quiet in the evening, they would climb out of their places and set the big iron stove alight in the middle of the loft. Sometimes they lit it so that it glowed, and then they pushed the beds end to end nearer to the source of warmth. By morning, of course, the stove had cooled, and Siberia was as cold as ever. That is why some of them preferred "spirit" to the warmth of an iron stove.

"The stove inflames the spirit of bedbugs," they said in their worldly-wise way. "But it isn't good for a person to sleep when the bugs are inflamed."

"No, it's not good for people when the bugs are inflamed," the others confirmed.

"Better for people's own spirit to be inflamed," they would explain, and so, every evening, sometimes in the morning too, a hellish noise arose, the result of which was a cloud of dust like you'd get when burn-beating or threshing.

After washing, the tramp of feet streamed back upstairs and then back down again – to study in class. Indrek went with the others, actually with little Lible, who was also supposed to be in fourth class. From Lible he got his initiation into studying and the order of things. In his hand he saw for the first time a sort of coverless book composed of individual pages (books were 'cabbages' in Lible's language), from which he read *amo, amas, amat* and *mensa, mensarum*. For some reason this last declension of that unknown word stuck in his mind.

"Mensarum," Indrek repeated to Lible. "Mensarum," he asserted again.

"You want me to sell you this cabbage?" said Lible.

And without Indrek's even reasoning whether he needed that old 'cabbage', he searched for money in his pocket and paid the sum demanded. As it later turned out, this was almost the price of a new book. But that didn't matter. Indrek never took offence at Lible, because he was inexpressibly pleased that he had bought the first tangible book that bore the words *mensa, mensarum*.

Indrek bought another 'cabbage' from Lible – the one that frequently repeated the rare word that for years had enchanted his mind. In the meantime the word and the whole book had lost their charm, but Indrek bought it anyway, so dependent was he on those past memories.

Lible put even more 'cabbages' on the market; he would have put all his 'cabbages' on sale if Indrek had only bought them. But no, Indrek bought only those two.

"Why do you sell off your own books?" asked Indrek.

"To buy food," replied Lible.

"Do they give you so little to eat here?" inquired Indrek.

"I get enough to eat, but it isn't food," explained Lible,

without Indrek really understanding. Only at the dinner table did he begin to know what those words meant, because Lible appeared at it with his own bread – coarse brown bread, butter and sliced *Teerwurst*,[9] while the "old man" and his aunt only gave him rye bread, with butter already on it, and never coarse brown bread, only a little white bread in the mornings. Lible set upon his food with a great movement of the hands and a triumphant expression on his face, as if he had suddenly and unexpectedly, in a way that nobody understood, ascended to a higher state, allowing him to sit at the upper end of the table, occupied by Messieurs Koovi, Timusk and Ollino, and the most distinguished and wealthy of the students.

"I don't know what that little idiot is gobbling – his own cabbages or his body heat?" somebody asked across the table.

"Cabbages, just cabbages," replied another.

"So he must have found an even bigger idiot to buy them off him," opined the first.

"The big one sits next to the little one," said a third.

A smirk of envy spread among them.

From this Indrek surmised that little Lible was called Little Idiot and so he must be the Big one, since he had bought Lible's cabbages for a lot of money and thus enabled him to eat better morsels in front of the others. The new name soon stuck to Indrek, especially because in class and in the canteen he sat next to Little Idiot. Since the latter bore his name with calm indifference, Indrek followed his example and let himself be called Big Idiot even when he was one of the best in class for knowledge. There were times when no one could answer the teacher's question: that was when Lible cried in his high-pitched voice, "Teacher, Sir, Big Idiot knows!" and the teacher would reply with a laugh, "Ah, Little Idiot knows that Big Idiot knows? Well, please answer then," and Indrek would stand up and answer, as if his name of Big Idiot were already written in the church register.

---

9 *Teerwurst*: a smoked German sausage usually made of pork.

These were the strange consequences of Indrek buying two old books from Lible. But he later came to regret the second purchase of the item named after the "pope". This word had at times caused him strange dreams. In them the religious instructor bore his nickname, and changed into the very opposite of Indrek's childhood dreams and yearnings as a person. The man was plump, with a face that was big and somehow square, and he had a thick red neck, a strong jaw broad in the beam; his teeth were always clenched together so that he couldn't articulate his voice clearly, and his thick red lips were slightly twisted to the left in a superior or scornful smile; his forehead was a little narrower on top and wider below at his eye-sockets, while his hair bristled forming a ridge and his eyes were always a narrow slit in which something almost painful sparkled and twinkled. But one thing he had to grant Mr Vihalepp: his name "angry-alder" was well-suited. He was a stern believer, and God's word was in his eyes an eternal and unchanging treasure, which should not be allowed to crumble or disintegrate by the slightest crumb. Like a statue, his eyes little slits, he sat up in his office, his pencil upright in his hand, as he set about recounting a Bible story or rattling off Biblical hymns. After every little while he had to tap with his pencil on the rostrum, and in a small, unnaturally delicate feminine voice, would say: "Stop! Once more! You left out an 'and' here and there."

And the student would start over again. But soon this would be followed by a tap of the pencil and the delicate voice would say: "In this book it stops at this point: 'And it came to pass that...' So one more time from that point."

The student had to correct the mistake, and then he would encounter more distress, as the pope would say to him in a gentle voice: "Dear child, why are you mixing it up and faking it again? It says here 'and so', not just 'and'. One more time."

It was especially hard to find the right tone in answering. Often Indrek experienced this vicariously.

"A Bible story and the catechism are not a fairy story or

some old Estonian folk tale, which is an abomination before the Lord, but the holy Word of God," Mr Vihalepp instructed. "And the holy word is so holy that we sinful humans should not take it into our putrid mouths, but since we do so anyway because of our precious redemption, we must do it with crossed hands and in a voice as quiet and gentle as possible, as people who are aware of our own guilt, and ask forgiveness for it. Therefore, not like that but like this…"

And Mr Vihalepp showed us how a person should take the Holy Word of God into his putrid mouth.

Indrek got a slightly different impression of the Holy Word of God at morning prayers, for which they all gathered before lessons in the canteen, where the tables and benches were put in a corner for the duration, to make room. Prayers were read by Mr Maurus himself, and moreover from such an old and venerable German book that Lible called it the "prayer cabbage". As he read it, Mr Maurus placed his spectacles right at the end of his nose.

On the second day Indrek realised why the headmaster put his glasses in such an unnatural place when reading prayers. Indrek made this discovery because Mr Maurus suddenly stopped reading, pushed the book onto the windowsill and shouted like an angry bull at the boys, as he collared Lible, who was crouching down with another boy and doing some business deal. Mr Maurus pulled the boys over to the window and boxed them both on the ears with both hands.

"Schinder is like that," he told Lible, "he's corrupting all my boys, he's driving my whole school to ruin, and the boy's hair is so short that you can't get hold of it. Well, what's Mr Maurus supposed to do with a bald head like that? Why is your hair so short that Mr Maurus can't catch hold of it? Answer!"

"Mr Headmaster, sir, you yourself told me to get my hair cut short!" replied the boy with a whimper.

"Not that short, I didn't," replied the headmaster. "I always have to be able to grab it – otherwise what can I do with you?

Next time remember: not so short. Now stand here beside me, so you can't corrupt my boys anymore."

Mr Maurus took up the prayerbook again and started reading, but his eyes were rarely on the holy text; mostly he was spying on the boys over his glasses. Indrek doubted whether the headmaster was reading at all what was in the book – or had he learned it by heart over the years?

As he handed out the Russian lesson, he said: "Mr Maurus says: During prayers you mustn't play, you mustn't romp around, but what are Lible and that other boy doing? They're counting money under the table. Understand? They're counting money like Pharisees. Mr Maurus reads prayers, and they count money. Where's your money, Schinder?" he said, turning to Lible, who was supposed to stand beside him but had got away. "Where's Lible?" cried the headmaster. "Lible – come here!" and when the boy appeared from behind the others, Mr Maurus thundered: "Schinder, where are you? Where's your money?"

The boy handed over a few copper coins.

"You see now," the headmaster addressed the group. "He's been dealing in money during prayers. That's what Schinder is like!" and again he went to box the boy's ears, but he said: "Ah, your hair's so short! You deliberately had it cut short so that Mr Maurus couldn't punish you! But where did you get that money from?"

"Big Idiot gave it to him!" said a roguish voice.

"Who's that?" asked the headmaster. "Who is Big Idiot? You're the little one, but who's the big one?"

"Paas,[10] the tall one, who went to Siberia a couple of days ago," explained Mr Ollino.

"Paas! Paas!" called the headmaster. "Where are you?"

"Here," replied Indrek, who was standing behind the others against the wall, because of his height.

And when Indrek got through the crowd of boys in front

---

10 The protagonist's name is Indrek Paas.

of the headmaster, the latter said: "What does Mr Maurus say? He says: Nobody is allowed to give money to anyone else except Mr Maurus himself. But why did you give it to this short boy, when you're tall yourself? Answer! Quickly! Mr Maurus doesn't have time. Why?"

"I bought a book from him," replied Indrek.

"You dog, how dare you buy books from my boys? Did I give you a rouble coin so that you could buy books from my boys, because you're tall? What book was it?"

"A Latin textbook."

"Lible, why did you sell that book?" asked the headmaster.

"It was a lousy old thing, I didn't need it anymore," replied Lible.

"How so, you didn't need it? You, Schinder, tell lies to Mr Maurus during prayers. You've been in the same class for three years now – and you don't need a Latin textbook anymore! Mr Maurus is ashamed to take money from your honest father, because the boy didn't study last year, didn't study the year before, and this year he's selling his books to others. And you, the tall one, what's the use of your height if you go buying books from this short one? What's the use of your father feeding you your honest family's bread and bringing you up? You carry on acting as if you had a victualler's or a provender's bread-store in your bag. Now look, all of you, at this tall boy, look at his long face, this is the one who…"

God knows how long the headmaster would have carried on lecturing, and where it would have finally led, but Mr Ollino stepped up to him and whispered a few German words in his ear. He stopped in mid-word, only adding: "Later! Later! Mr Ollino will remind me later!"

He made a gesture with his left hand, and the boys started to file out noisily. Now something new had evidently occurred to the headmaster and he wanted to start lecturing again, but no one was listening anymore, so the prayer session remained unfinished.

"How is this going to turn out?" Indrek asked Lible in class.

34

"What are you talking about?" replied Lible, as if not comprehending.

"The books," said Indrek.

"Don't be silly!" cried Lible. "What I do with my old books has got nothing to do with the old man."

But actually it did have something to do with the old man, for after lunch he ordered Indrek to come with the books he had bought. "What did you pay for these?" he asked when he saw the books, and when Indrek had named the price, the headmaster said: "There you are: long in your bones and short in your understanding. Little Lible is like an old fox. I'll deal with him! Why did you buy these old things?" said the headmaster, indicating the Latin textbook.

"I liked it," replied Indrek lightly.

"You liked it!" exclaimed the headmaster, looking the boy in the face, as if he doubted his sanity. Then he turned around, looked out of the window and Indrek heard him mutter to himself: "*So ein grosser Narr!*"[11]

---

11 So ein grosser Narr: "Such a complete fool."

Chapter 4

The farce about the books suddenly made Indrek famous among his wider circle, and put him in the limelight. People started to chat with him and got to know him. In this way he soon became his own man.

One of those who approached him was Tigapuu, one of the amphibians who was neither pupil nor teacher, or was both together. Men like that would sit during the day with the others mostly in class, but after lunch they went walking with the younger ones or supervised their studies.

Tigapuu was about the same age as Indrek, but had been part of the institution's family for many years. At the moment he was in fifth grade, one grade higher than Indrek. Of average height, with a somewhat angular body, he had a reputation for fearing no one, not even the old man, and no one could beat him in a fight. Meeting a man like that seemed an honourable thing to Indrek.

"If you keep company with that pipsqueak, of course you're going to get caught," he told him with reference to Lible. "If only you'd come to me, I would have bought them cheaper for you, and we would both of us come out with a bargain. We'd have bought the books for practically nothing, if it had been a fair transaction."

And when Indrek came down from the headmaster's office with the books, Tigapuu asked: "Did the old man ask how much money you still had?"

"No," replied Indrek.

"You're lying," laughed Tigapuu haughtily, as if to say: whose leg are you pulling? "Did he count your assets with his own hands? Why be afraid of me? You're hiding something.

You've no reason to be afraid of me, although some people are. If you want, I'll take you to Nõmmann and Peeterson's after lunch; they have stacks of old books, and you can take your pick. And all dirt cheap. Specially when I'm there, because I have friends everywhere. You can sell them there too, if you want. But they don't buy stuff like Lible's old cabbages, not like those. They have to be better, much better. I'll show you later what they have to be like if you want to sell to Nõmmann or Peeterson. Let's go after lunch. We'll have a look around and get to know the town. That's something you really need to do. So that's agreed then! Your hand on it!"

"I suppose I could," said Indrek doubtfully.

"Not like that," instructed Tigapuu. "We don't talk like that. That's not how men do it. Not the comrades' way. You have to be sure when you answer. Yes or no."

"Alright, yes then," agreed Indrek.

"A man of his word," confirmed Tigapuu, as if there were something significant had occurred. "So then, when the others go for a walk, we'll set off to town. Generally those walks are simply awful. You have to jog along with all sorts of idiots as if you were having fun. That's the old man's grip on you: just a cattle-market, to catch people's eyes, so they'll stop to look and say: 'Look, there go Maurus's boys.' But they all just laugh. You don't know it yet, but you'll see that I'm right and he isn't. But we'll go on our own, the others will have nothing to do with us, it'll be quite different for the two of us."

"Alright," agreed Indrek.

"And keep in mind," continued Tigapuu, "you've given your word, and you have to keep it, whatever the cost – the word of a gentleman. *Tovarishch!*[12] It costs nothing to try our luck. For what would be the point of me getting permission from the old man, if you suddenly say 'No, I'm not coming today'? What would I do with the old man's permission then?

---

12 *Tovarishch*: "comrade" (Russian)

Where would I put it? Or do you think the old man likes doing business? You saw that farce about the books. And what was it about? One person had tricked another, that's all. But for the old man it was like starting a fire. You go and try to get permission from him to go out, and then it's: 'Where? For how long? Why? Alone? Who else?' And then: 'Have you got money? How much? Where did you get it? Who gave it to you? Why? When? What for?' And so on and so forth, till you get tired and say: 'Thanks very much, Mr Headmaster, sir, but I've had second thoughts, I won't go out after all, I'm not interested, I don't want to.' Because where will you go now, if half the time's been spent on questions? That's why the clever ones won't breathe a word, they just go out the back door, and when the caretaker locks up, you go to Jürka or you leap over the wall. Of course you don't have to think about it yet; that's why I'm going to the trouble of getting the old man's permission. But if you want to, you can ask permission yourself; I'm not against it, and it might even be better if…"

"No, no, it would be better if you asked, Tigapuu," replied Indrek.

"That would be most sensible," observed Tigapuu. "But you can stop calling me Tigapuu, we should be on first name terms if I have to ask the old man's permission to go to town. Only a comrade, a *tovarishch*, does that. Not even a friend does it, only a comrade, one that you drink a tankard of beer with, or something else. Actually with some twerp from first or second grade, I might be on surname terms with them, of course. Mr Tigapuu! *Gospodin klassnyi nastavnik!*[13] But the difference between us is only one class. That Latin, by the way, let's see how you get on with it – it's broken many a man."

After lunch Tigapuu instructed his stand-in: "Paas and I have to go into town; the old man ordered us to."

And they turned their backs on him and left, but through

---

13 *Gospodin klassnyi nastavnik*: "Mr Class Tutor" (Russian).

the main gate, because Tigapuu thought it was simpler that way, as it was less obtrusive and didn't arouse envy.

"Let's go here first of all," said Tigapuu, leading Indrek somewhere off the main road in town.

"We walked here yesterday," said Indrek, who somehow didn't realise why Tigapuu chose this road.

"Why are you talking about yesterday?" responded Tigapuu. "Yesterday we were with the others, now we're alone. Today is a time to look and find out how broad this river really is. And if you only knew how many people drown here in summer! Like flies! It's simply terrible! Nearly every day they're hauling people out. They try to swim across, and they just go to the bottom, because no one can swim over it. You get halfway and you're tired, you swim more than halfway and you get a cramp, and if you actually get to the bank, you have a stroke, but if you die on the spot, it makes it easier for others to pull you out. Even I pulled one man who'd had a stroke onto dry land, and then I went to the police. And if you don't get a cramp or a stroke, you get an oar in the head or you go under a steamboat. For there's one thing you ought to know: there are rowers here in good weather, like ants at the seaside. Yes, you'd see all this if it were summertime now. When the warm weather comes, it's always the students – students everywhere – Russians, Germans and Poles – all in their shirtsleeves, baskets of beer in the boats, boozing, singing. But now there's nothing, so we'll turn off to the right here, because you can look at the water for ages, water is the same at any time…"

As he talked, Tigapuu led his companion along a short side-street to a longer and broader one, where they turned right again, so that now Indrek thought they were going in the same direction from which they had just come. As they went, they made a couple of small detours, and thus they ended up by the river again, where the ferry crossed.

"Have you seen a contraption like that before?" asked Tigapuu somewhat triumphantly. "I wanted to show it to

39

you. You've probably gone over the bridge – now try the ferry for once. You don't have to pay – I will. I brought you here, I have to take you across, because otherwise you'll think: why didn't we go by the bridge, which doesn't cost a kopeck? So you're going at my expense."

When the ferry had started moving, Tigapuu asked Indrek in a businesslike way: "Oh yes! How much money do you have with you? Feel free to go to the shop and choose the books; you'll soon run out of money, but there's no shame! Because you must always remember this: in town it's shameful to have no money, so whether you have it or not, always act as if you have it. For in town there's nothing for it but to pay. Have you been in town before? … Just in Tallinn once? Well, then you don't know the half of it, because there are no university students there. They aren't anywhere else, just here. People hurrying back and forth along Rüütli street with crates of beer in their two-horse carriages, just to get others to drink, like throwing boiling water on stones in a sauna. And I tell you this: when I pass my university-entrance exams one day, they'd better watch out! I'll show them what a real university student is like. Actually I could have passed those exams already, if I'd wanted to. But I didn't want to, I just did not care. Because if you look at it dispassionately, you have to ask yourself: in what way is a university student smarter than we are? To tell the truth – not at all. We're taught by the same professors; it's just that they have different books. Our old man is devilish cunning. He says: 'I got a professor for you, otherwise you'll be off like a shot.' After he says that, he laughs. And that's how it goes – a professor here, a professor there – but still there's that name: university student! And the clothes? The uniform! Which would you like better – *Farbendeckel*14 or colleague? I'll take *Farbendeckel*! *Farbendeckel* and *Kaisermantel*!15 You go along, half the street

14 *Farbendeckel*: coloured cap worn by the university fraternities.
15 *Kaisermantel*: "imperial coat".

40

is full of people like you. You know, that big long coat with the wide hem. The tail whips up the dust or sweeps the mud like a woman's skirt. If you wanted to go in this door here with something like that" – they had reached a big stone house, below which was a little row of cellar-shops – "you simply wouldn't be able to, even if you took your coat on your arm. That's the kind of thing a *Kaisermantel* is, and that's what they do with it. Have you ever seen the like of it?"

"I don't suppose I have," answered Indrek.

"Of course you haven't," agreed Tigapuu. "You'd never had the chance to see it. There's no such thing in Tallinn, and only rarely do you see it here."

They were standing in front of a small food shop, the signboard depicted a steaming bowl of soup, a piece of sausage, half a ham, and loaves of black and white bread. A bearded man seated at an odd little table almost out of sight was shovelling soup into his gaping mouth. "Let's step in here for a bit. An acquaintance of mine, actually a good friend, comes here often to eat. Maybe we'll catch him, and I need to see him," explained Tigapuu.

And without waiting for Indrek's agreement, he descended the narrow staircase to the cellar room, so that Indrek had to go after him, like it or not. "You see how nice it is, and no sign of those imperial overcoats. What's more, you can get in from any door," said Tigapuu over his shoulder to Indrek. After going downstairs, he shouted, "Hello, Mrs Kroosu!"

"Good God – it's Mr Tigapuu! I haven't seen you for ages," replied the lady.

"Work, work, I haven't had time. I came looking for my friend Eller."

"What's he like? Tall or short?"

"More tall than short, always liked pork with sauerkraut. Don't you remember him?"

"Of course I do. But I haven't seen him for a long time."

"What a shame," sighed Tigapuu.

"Well, but how are you, young man?" she asked. "How

about a few slices of roasted piglet, but not overly so? And perhaps some cabbage as well? Or maybe some veal? Fattened on sweetmeal so it melts in your mouth – a deal for a friend."

"Not to my taste," replied Tigapuu.

"So the pork then? Two?"

"One is enough."

Having said that, Tigapuu turned to Indrek and complained. "There you are – you step in looking for a friend, but instead you have to start eating. I feel sorry for the poor old thing, with a flock of children to feed. She stands in this stuffy little room behind her counter all day, anxiously waiting for someone she can offer her pork or veal to, otherwise it would all go to waste, which would be such a shame! Because she really knows how to cook pork and sauerkraut, like no one else in the whole town. And at her place it costs next to nothing. She gives it dirt cheap to people she knows. If you give her fifteen or twenty kopecks, you can fill your stomach until it bursts. But what's fifteen or twenty kopecks for a bellyful of food like this? It's downright embarrassing to drive a bargain with her when she asks what you want. You've got no choice but to sit at the table and start eating, because you know that you're putting bread on this poor old woman's table so that she can feed her children. For it's the woman, not the old man, who feeds the children; he's always crawling around the pubs. That's the kind of lousy old man this woman has for the father of her children…"

At that moment the bread and the pork and cabbage arrived. "I didn't know what to order for you," explained Tigapuu to Indrek, starting immediately to shovel the pork and sauerkraut into his mouth. "If you want, get them to bring something for you too, maybe a glass of tea and a sugary bun. I don't think they have Napoleon cake here, otherwise you could have that; that's the best. Once you've put away three of those, your stomach will feel as tight as a drum. That way you get a little bit of food, otherwise it's always our slops. Your guts get their juices working, you'll see. Sometimes the others cry out in the middle of the night for a Napoleon or pork and sauerkraut. And take some of those, a portion or a half, a whole one for twenty, a half for twelve. I always take a whole one. You could try a half. Only twelve kopecks, including the bread. It's embarrassing for me to eat alone, while someone else is looking on and their mouth is watering."

Indrek's mouth really was starting to water when he saw the appetite with which Tigapuu was eating. But he replied: "No, I don't want anything."

"A glass of tea at least; how else can you sit at the table? It's the law of the tavern table, you know. Once you've sat down, you order; it's a different thing if you're standing up. This isn't like the countryside, the woodlands or the sticks; here you have to pay for sitting – that's the law of the town."

And without waiting for Indrek's opinion and with his mouth still full of bread, meat and cabbage, Tigapuu called over his shoulder to the lady of the house: "One tea!" Once the young waitress had put the glass of tea on the table, he said to Indrek in her hearing, "Did you notice how nice she is? In the countryside you wouldn't find one like that in the whole parish. Look at how she walks – as if she had springs under her. Legs like poles. For there's nothing like a skirt but you have to learn how to watch them."

When he had stuffed his mouth with food once more, he continued, "Well, nothing wrong with that lass, but have you seen our princess?"

"Who's that?" asked Indrek.

"What? You still don't know who our princess is? Then you still know nothing about the world. Our princess is the old man's daughter. At home for the first time this year. She's sitting and waiting for a husband. But she only interested in a doctor or a lawyer. Or maybe a priest. She speaks only German plus a bit of French but only with the Carousel – that's her aunt; she talks a bit of broken Estonian, because can't stand the Carousel's German. 'Liebe Tante, liebe Tante, I can't listen, I really can't!' she cries, when her aunt starts

43

talking German. You can talk Russian to her when you get the chance, and you will, for she loves to talk. With me she always talks German, you must know that, for she knows me and likes my German too. So, we can go now – drink up your tea to the bottom of the glass, for why would you leave it? You still have to pay for it. Twenty-five altogether – ridiculously little, when you think about it. That is, only twenty-five for two people's meals, for now you have to pay for me. I paid that cut-throat of a ferryman for your passage. So now we're square. The small difference that's left I'll pay you later, like a gentleman. Anyway, you were supposed to give me a treat; we can leave the difference to make up for the treat. Of course, pork and sauerkraut is not really a treat, but it's alright between friends. Anyway, if I pay you back the twenty, then there should be proper treats, and they aren't as cheap as pork and sauerkraut. So it would be entirely to your benefit if I never pay back the debt. Simple as that, don't you think? And thank God I brought you to the sort of place where you don't have to give a tip, otherwise it would've cost at least ten more. So I've helped you to save easily ten kopecks, so the debt is only ten, because you drank the tea yourself."

He raised his cap and said, through lips still glistening with pork-fat, "Good day to you, ma'am! When he comes, tell him I was asking for him."

And without waiting for a reply he stepped confidently up the narrow steps to where the withered autumn day was drawing towards evening. Tigapuu stopped there, and adopting a serious and thoughtful expression, he said, "I was thinking of where to go, into town or to Toome. But it's better to go to Toome anyway, because you'll soon see more than enough of the town. Actually Toome, it's a thing in itself, and you can't always get there… I mean, this way… You can see the covered market here and the statues, like a living forest. And also you'll know where to get the best things, if you want to go shopping. You'll always need to shop, if not today, then tomorrow."

When they got to the square, where somebody's bust stood on a big plinth, Tigapuu explained: "This is Parkalai. This is the square where the students come rushing up from Rüütli Street with their crates of beer. Always some bottle gets shaken loose and then they could come crashing down on your skull, which is now dripping with its contents! And then come the Russian rowing crews, called 'eights', so you have to burst into *'Deutschland, Deutschland, über alles!'* You get the idea? It's such a riot! One time it was going a bit lamely, but at just the right moment some sly fox started up with 'God! The Kaiser!' The rowers couldn't help but join in with their heels together and a hand to their ear, for how can they resist the Kaiser's anthem? And the students put one over them again. That's the true student life. And when I become a university student one day, I'll do the same. Just you wait!"

Toome Hill and the gardens on its slopes stood leafless. Yellowed leaves rustled underfoot on the path. Here and there a light was burning in the town. "Now there's nothing here," Tigapuu said of Toome, "but wait until spring – you'll hear it and see it. Blossoms, lots of blossoms, and nightingales! Many nightingales! The old man doesn't let us out at night, but in spring he says: 'Go and listen! Sit on a bench and listen, listen carefully, and you'll become another person.'"

Indrek tried to imagine what it might be like here in spring with its blossoms and nightingales, but somehow he didn't believe that it could match being high up on Vargamäe where the mating calls of the grouse can be heard, a crane cries in the distance, the snipes lament, and a thousand other birds and animals fill the land, water and air with their chatter. There is nowhere on earth more beautiful than Vargamäe, where the woodlands take on a bluish hue that extends as far as the horizon.

Suddenly Indrek noticed that in the darkness, between the trees, stood something dim, blurred and horribly imposing, facing towards him from that space. He took fright involuntarily and asked Tigapuu: "But what's that over there?"

"Oh, that! That's an old church, a monastery. It's not worth going there, stuff might fall on your neck and that's no joke. You'll see it later."

But Indrek would have liked to stop and look, because the silhouette appeared to increase in size and lack of definition when viewed from a distance.

When they finally got back to town, Tigapuu said, "Today we're too late for the shop, we'll go some other time. To tell the truth, there's little point in going to the shop, so let's step inside another friend's place. Känd is his name, and let's see if he still has the books he wanted to sell. We're sure to get them much more cheaply from him than from any shop, and you won't lose your money. The main thing is to keep it to yourself for dear life, and not tell a soul that you have money; you have to learn this – I say that as a friend. At first I didn't know how to go around with money either, but my uncle, a rich bachelor, taught me. He always says, 'Listen to me, young fellow, learn how to deal with money, because you must love both your fatherland and money. If someone doesn't love his fatherland,' he says, 'it doesn't matter whether you pour out a full or empty beer bottle on his head.' He's got a shrewd head on his shoulders, but he's terribly stingy. Look, here's the other end of Rüütli street; this is where the students with their crates of beer have to turn around. Now we'll go over the wooden bridge, so you can see that."

"I've seen it," replied Indrek, whose head was beginning to spin.

"It won't do any harm," answered Tigapuu. "Look again because, as the Romans used to say, *repetitio mater studiorum est*. You don't understand Latin yet, but keep those words in mind – you'll need them in life. 'Repetition is the mother of all learning.' Anyway, who knows how long this bridge will be here? Maybe next spring the ice-floes will carry it away; so you should take your chance to watch how it's done properly. A very interesting bridge! Last summer someone jumped off it, trying to drown himself, but a cabman jumped in and saved him. Full of emotion, he called to him: 'You could see I was jumping! What do you want from me? I jumped in, which meant that I wanted to die. So let me die!' 'But why did you cry for help?' answered the other. 'That's no concern of yours,' replied the first. 'I can drown if that's what I want, whether or not I cry out. You're not a policeman, so don't interfere in my affairs. But you want a reward for having saved a man. So, here's your reward!' he cried, and splat! bang! a fist right in the other man's wet face. Of course he was picked up, caught by the other, and went to the cabman who had had to sit down after being hit. 'But I'll drown myself anyway!' he shouted at the cabman. 'I'll drown in the middle of the night, when no one can hear my cries!' And he did too, as soon as he got free. It's God's truth I'm telling you. So what do you have to say about a bridge like that?"

But Indrek had nothing to say about such a strange bridge. So after a little while, Tigapuu continued, "But you know what I say: if I ever have to go and drown myself, I'll simply take a revolver with me, so that if anyone comes to save me, I'll blow their brains out! And I give you the same advice: if you think of drowning yourself, take a revolver. Otherwise you'll be fighting with strangers. As if it were with our old man. Because he's in the habit of leaping in and meddling in your affairs, as if you had just jumped off the wooden bridge into the river. So he'll ask, 'Where did you go? How long? Why? Who gave you permission?' Well, what can you say to that? What sort of revolver could you shove under his nose? Of course you can't answer, so you're for the high jump! But you should keep in mind that he can't do anything to us; he can only scream. You do realise that? He's such a strange person: you go and ask him for something, he'll happily give you permission straightaway. But when you come home, he'll have forgotten that he did, and so he attacks you: screams at you, as if you wanted to go and drown yourself off the wooden bridge. He's always like that: he can't remember anything that isn't written down in a book. If he hasn't written it, we have to be prepared. I would say that the main thing is: Do what you want, don't be afraid. And whatever happens, rely on me: I'll get you out of any fix. If he asks, 'Where were you?', then answer, 'Buying books!' If he asks what books, then say, 'I couldn't buy them, they weren't in stock. Tomorrow I'll try again.' 'What shop?' 'By the bridge made of stone and wood; I don't remember the name. Tigapuu told me, but I can't remember.' But of course the main thing is me, you don't count. The old man and I know each other."

Chapter 5

With these detailed explanations they reached the courtyard gate, where they wanted to creep in unobserved. But Jürka was expecting them, and said that the old man was very angry and waiting.

"Let me through," pleaded Tigapuu. "Don't tell him we've come now."

"No, I can't – the old man's absolutely furious," Jürka replied flatly.

"I'll make it a couple of beers," promised Tigapuu.

"That won't help," retorted Jürka.

"A whole pint," cried Tigapuu in a hoarse voice.

"Still won't help," answered Jürka. "If you were alone or with someone else, then yes, but this new one will get it in the neck, and pull us down with him. Do you think a pint is going to get you out of this?"

"Let's talk it over," said Tigapuu.

"Won't help," Jürka assured him, as before.

"Go to hell then!" cried Tigapuu angrily. "I'm not afraid of you or the old man. Just you wait – I won't forgive you for leaving a friend in the lurch like this."

"What friend am I to you?" responded Jürka.

"You fool!" cried Tigapuu. "You're not my friend, but until now I thought I was yours. Until now, I say. And you're kicking your friend in the teeth!"

"How am I doing that? You went out without permission, so I'm hardly kicking you!"

"In what way are you not kicking me?" countered Tigapuu. "Well? What does it cost you to say: they haven't come, I haven't seen them – and we climb up nicely to Siberia, and come down only for supper. And if the old man asks, we were asleep. Or even better: I was teaching him Latin in Siberia, where no one would disturb us."

"Not even I would believe a lie like that, let alone the old man. He doesn't even believe the truth, and still less a lie. You'd better face the music."

"I'm going and I will," said Tigapuu. "But I'll put you in the soup. Keep in mind: I know your business very well. There'll come a time when I tell the old man everything. Because why should I be your friend all the time, if you don't want to be my friend even for a day?"

But Tigapuu's threat didn't achieve the desired result: Jürka stuck to his guns and repeated: "It won't help, it just won't help. We'd all come a cropper." So they had to go straight to the headmaster – down to the big room. In the dark corridor Tigapuu whispered to Indrek: "This is what I was afraid of: not written in a book, therefore he doesn't remember. But that Jürka is a corrupt soul. He's a betrayer. A sniveller! That's why the old man pays him a wage. And always picking a fight. I wouldn't have a man like that in my own house for a moment. He says 'without permission'. How can it be 'without permission', if the old man doesn't remember?"

When Indrek and Tigapuu stepped into the big room, the headmaster was coming out of the door of the next room and wanting to get somewhere quickly. Seeing them, he raised his hand in front of him, saying absently: "*Warten Sie, warten Sie!*" But then he stepped over to Indrek and asked "Where were you?"

"We were buying books," replied Tigapuu, behind Indrek's back.

"Mr Tigapuu, I'm not asking you, but this tall one here," said the headmaster, controlling his irritation. Tigapuu felt that the headmaster was treating him in that formal manner in order to keep control. He only did that to hide his anger.

"So then, answer me: where were you?" said the headmaster, turning again to Indrek.

50

"We were buying books, Mr Headmaster, sir," replied Indrek.

"Where are the books you bought?" the headmaster further inquired.

"They weren't in stock," interjected Tigapuu again from behind Indrek's back.

"Mr Tigapuu!" the headmaster suddenly shouted in a voice that seemed barely human. "I've already told you once that I don't want to talk to you, but to this one here."

"But I want to talk to you, Mr Maurus," replied Tigapuu.

"Wait – your turn hasn't come yet," said the headmaster menacingly. "I'll speak in a different language to you than to this one here." And now he continued the interrogation of Indrek, who gave the answers he had been taught. The headmaster suddenly turned to Tigapuu and shouted into his face, his eyes staring furiously at him over his glasses: "Schinder! You have taught him to lie to me!"

The headmaster's arms rose involuntarily and made to box Tigapuu behind the ears, but he pushed them brusquely aside and said in a voice that expressed the depth of his indignation: "Mr Maurus, I'm no longer a little boy whose hair you can pull. I am to blame, so hear me out and punish me as is right and proper."

"Right and proper!" screamed the headmaster, starting to run around the room, his coat-tail flapping wildly. "I should have left long ago, but I can't because this person is corrupting my boys, teaching them to go out without leave."

"Mr Maurus, I wanted to ask leave, but you weren't at home," said Tigapuu.

"Herr Ollino, Herr Ollino!" cried the headmaster, stopping at the door of the next room. "Was I at home today or not? Is Mr Maurus ever away from home?"

"You have been at home all day," replied Ollino's voice from behind the door.

"Do you hear that? Mr Maurus has been at home all day. Mr Maurus is always at home, because he is God's deputy in this house, and if God himself ever goes out, he leaves in his place the Redeemer, and in Mr Maurus' place, Mr Ollino, for he is his Redeemer. Do you hear? So, Mr Maurus is always at home, and if Mr Ollino isn't here either, there are Herr Koovi and Herr Timusk, and finally there is Herr Kopfschneider down here – you can ask him. For if God himself isn't here, nor his son or the Virgin Mary, then there is at least one holy figure to help people. That is how Mr Maurus' home is run."

"I'm not going to start asking permission from some Kopfschneider," said Tigapuu scornfully.

"You must ask this big table, those chairs, that cupboard, you must ask even Goethe and Schiller at the end of the cupboard, you must ask, say, that stuffed swan that hangs from the ceiling if Mr Maurus orders you to do so. You must ask everyone, if they are God's deputies. The ancient and wise Egyptians asked a bull and a beetle, so why can't our Tigapuu ask Goethe and Schiller? And you – why didn't you come back?" said the headmaster, suddenly turning to Indrek.

"Tigapuu said that he had asked on behalf of us both," replied Indrek.

"This shameless man is corrupting my whole school!" screamed the headmaster, enraged again. "How do you, you dog, dare to go out without leave and take this one with you? Why didn't you come and ask?"

"Mr Maurus, I already told you, you were asleep at the time when we left," explained Tigapuu calmly.

"Do you hear, do you hear!" cried the headmaster, as he ran around the room – his fury renewed. "First I wasn't at home and now I was asleep! Am I going mad, or is it this man who's going mad? Tell me, if you're still in command of your senses – which one of us is mad, him or me?" The headmaster stood in front of Indrek, staring at him over his glasses. "Tell me sincerely – if you still have any common sense."

But before Indrek could find an answer, Tigapuu said gravely and almost scornfully: "Mr Maurus, why are we arguing over such a trifling matter?"

Again the headmaster started running around the room, as if he'd been stung by a wasp, crying: "Do you hear! Over a trifling matter! People are going mad, and yet it's a trifling matter! No, no, he's the one who has gone mad, not me. Our Tigapuu has gone mad. Just a while ago he was sane, but now he's mad. Quite mad. Did you see what it was that drove him out of his mind?" the headmaster asked Indrek, and without waiting for an answer, he continued: "Of course you don't know, because in the countryside people don't go mad, only in the town! A few years in town and you'll start to go mad… But where was your sanity when you went to town with this one! Why didn't you come and ask, 'Mr Maurus, may I go to town with this boy?' And Mr Maurus would have replied, 'No, not with him, because he's gone mad, or soon will. Better go alone, not with this madman!"

"Mr Maurus," Tigapuu interjected, "do what you want with me, but leave my friend and companion in peace, because I take full responsibility for him. I came to ask permission, and I also take responsibility."

As if jabbed by the red horns of some wild beast – such was the impact of Tigapuu's words – the headmaster jumped around on his ageing feet, and with each leap he shrieked because he couldn't find the words to express his fury. Eventually he found the wherewithal to splutter, "Herr Ollino! Herr Ollino! Do you hear? He takes responsibility! He came to ask! This man is crazy! Completely off his head! Herr Ollino, do come and look, our dear Tigapuu has gone mad. He takes responsibility! He wants to turn our home into a madhouse and he takes responsibility!"

The headmaster's voice gradually grew louder, and he started closing the shutters so that he couldn't be heard in the street. But when he reached the other room in this activity, Tigapuu stepped up to the shutter that had just been closed, opened it again behind the headmaster's back and opened the window as well.

"Who opened that?" roared the headmaster in an enraged voice when he saw the open window.

"I did, Mr Maurus," replied Tigapuu calmly. "I wanted some fresh air," he added.

This drove Mr Maurus into a frenzy, as if he were about to take leave of his senses. Ollino seemed to fear this as well, as his white head and lifeless eyes appeared in the doorway. After a little delay he stepped over to Tigapuu and motioned to him to be off. When he seemed to demur, he commanded him in Russian: "Out!" Tigapuu did not need to be told this twice. Then Ollino turned to the headmaster and said quite indifferently: "Mr Maurus, may I have a few words in private?"

And he took the headmaster by the hand and led him to his own room. It seemed that had been forgotten, but inquisitive eyes and mouths appeared from behind the curtain and from other rooms, and they wanted to know everything. While Indrek felt quite giddy, they merely laughed. "Tigapuu won't leave you in the lurch, he'll get you out of this," they told him. Indrek, on the other hand, couldn't work out what it was that Tigapuu was supposed to get him out of. As he pondered on it, Ollino opened the door of his room and yelled his name: "Paas!" Indrek went in, and once the door had been closed behind him and the thick curtain drawn, he was suddenly conscious of an unexpected feeling of serenity. The headmaster, who was sitting at the table, made a movement as if he wanted to get up or say something, but Ollino put a hand on his shoulder and said: "Mr Maurus, allow me," and turning to Indrek, he started presenting him with questions. When Indrek hesitated at first with his answers, he said, in a counselling tone, "Better tell the truth, because a lie won't get you far. Besides, what's the point in lying when it's such a trifling matter?"

That was what Indrek had felt and thought all along, and therefore he told everything step by step, word by word, bit by bit.

His tale apparently won the headmaster's confidence, for his face became ever kinder and friendlier, until he told

Ollino in German, "A true country scholar, never a truer one!"

To Indrek he said, "Call Tigapuu back!" But as he was about to go, Maurus added: "Perhaps it's better if Kopfschneider goes."

So the Latvian left and Indrek stayed put.

Tigapuu stepped in with a very grave and businesslike expression, and before anyone could open his mouth, he said in an almost demanding tone: "Mr Headmaster, sir, I would ask you to be quick, because I don't have time; I'm supposed to be keeping order in class. Lible and some others are disrupting our studies."

"What!" cried the headmaster at this. "Lible and some others are not letting you study! Who are those others? Their names?"

"First let's conclude the matters in hand," declared Ollino calmly. His calm affected the headmaster, who now said, "Well, Paas has explained everything beautifully. Very good! You are honest people, the children of honest parents. But everyone has to pay for his own pork and sauerkraut."

"Mr Maurus, that is a matter between friends and comrades," said Tigapuu. "I paid on the ferry, he did at the cafeteria, so it's all in order."

"All in order, we appreciate that," smiled Ollino.

"So, everyone has to pay for himself," continued the headmaster wearily. "But you always have to ask for permission. If not Mr Maurus himself, then Herr Ollino or Koovi, or in extremis Kopfschneider the Latvian. Every now and then an Estonian does have to ask a Latvian. So you can go now," the headmaster motioned sluggishly.

Such an ending had a deeper effect on Indrek than the whole affair. He hardly even believed it had happened. Everything seemed fanciful, illusory, even ominous.

The impression was shattered by the headmaster's voice, shouting: "Mr Tigapuu, Mr Tigapuu! Tell Lible and the others there that if they don't obey, Mr Maurus will come at the double!"

"I'll make short work of them!" replied Tigapuu confidently, but then added quietly to Indrek: "Fools! You don't know our old man. You always have to throw a spoke in his wheel, because he never actually gets around to anything. Or if he finally does, he's tired and irritable and strikes out with his hands. But you shouldn't have told him about the pork and sauerkraut. It doesn't matter that the old man heard about it, but in the case of Ollino it's disgusting. You saw how he smirked. Still, who cares! The main thing is that I was right when I told you: don't be afraid! I don't leave my comrades and friends in the lurch, like that Jürka does. Once I take on a responsibility, I take it seriously. But let's go up to Siberia – I've got something to show you. You mustn't breathe a single word about this – there are ears and eyes everywhere. Come on, we won't be there for long."

Indrek hauled himself up to Siberia, albeit reluctantly. There Tigapuu led him by the hand to sit on a bed, and put something soft on his knees.

"See if you can guess what that is," he said. "Isn't it soft? See if you can – feel it! Like silk! And how heavy! So, it's soft and heavy. Weighs over three pounds. A pure plucked feather, a clear mist, a gift from my rich uncle. Worth at least a couple of roubles. And the blanket about one and a half, but you wouldn't even get that in the Jewish market. If these went on the market, even a Tartar would pay three and a half for them. Three at least, no question. But I'm not thinking of selling them for that price. For what would my uncle say if he got to hear that I've sold his expensive gift to some Jew or Tartar. Actually there's the pawnshop, which is quite another thing. You can pawn for as little as you like, because you always get your things back from them. Here in town, these things are fixed up very nicely when it comes to that department in town: if you need something, you buy it, and if you don't need it any more, you make your way to the pawnshop and you get cash for it. It's that simple! And the money's quite different to what you get at the Jewish market, because there, remember, they don't pay anything. Your Jew simply doesn't have the wherewithal, that's your Jew at the market. But the pawnshop has, and it pays out. So why shouldn't they pay for things like what I have here? This cushion was ordered by my uncle specially for himself, or rather for his bride, when he was thinking of getting married. That's why it's so soft and light. Light, of course, for its size, and yet very heavy – try it! Well then, specially ordered for his bride, so anyone who puts his head on this pillow, it's as if he were in the arms of my uncle's bride. But since nothing came of my uncle's marriage, he couldn't get any peace unless he gave away his bride's things. That's how I got this lovely cushion, with the words: Take this as a reminder and a lesson that you can't trust women. So you see what this is: a family's dear memory. That's the reason why I wouldn't want to take it to the pawnshop, but I'd rather give it for safekeeping to some good friend, such as you. Besides, you're really going to need it in the winter, because, remember, it's cold in Siberia. The wind whooshes in and creates snowdrifts on the floor, which makes the boys' blankets frosty boys in the morning, and gnaws and sticks like chaff on frozen horse-droppings. You just can't get your feet warm, and your toes are always cracking under the covers. The only solution is to have one cushion under your head and another at your feet, for there's nothing warmer than a soft cushion like this one here. Here you see that I was thinking of you when I brought this blanket and cushion here, and you know how much I want for the lot? Only two! You understand, man, just two lousy roubles, and for things that would cost at least five. But if you regard yourself as my friend, as I do you, then find one and a half and the things are yours. Just bear in mind: not for good, because I can't sell them for good, I'm only pawning them, so to speak. In a week at the latest you can have your money back, in silver or paper, as you wish, with interest or without. Completely as you wish. You'll take your money and I'll take my things. Well, shall we say one and a half?"

"I don't have that much," said Indrek.

"Don't tell useless lies," replied Tigapuu. "There shouldn't be lies between friends and comrades. If we're actually quarrelling, then there are. But why quarrel? You'll get your money and I'll take my things. Besides, there's nothing greater than friendship, because friendship is eternal. Friends may quarrel, but they still remain friends. That's my principle. Fight, if you have to, but don't be a pig, and don't forget that you're a friend. So then – one twenty-five! Nothing more to say about it, or be afraid of."

"But I need that money for other things," countered Indrek.

"You'll get it back in a few days, and then do what you want with it. For you can only guess how long I can live without a cushion and a blanket. Besides, what kind of friendship is it if I'm always helping you, but you never help me? Real friendship is mutual, that's how I understand proper friendship. But to hell with it: give me a rouble and we're done. Go to the devil! I'll strike a match so you can see the things, and the money – otherwise you'll think I want to cheat you. But there mustn't be any cheating between friends."

Tigapuu did indeed strike a match, but Indrek never got his wallet out of his pocket. The actual reason was that Indrek didn't want to show Tigapuu how much money he really had. So a few more matches had to be struck until the expected item became visible. But before that he had already opened it in his pocket and arranged the bigger coins so that only one silver rouble and a few copper coins remained in his wallet.

Seeing how little cash Indrek had in his wallet, Tigapuu said accusingly, "How did you dare to leave home with so little money? Or has the old man cleaned you out? How much did he squeeze out of you?"

"Fifty," replied Indrek.

"Fifty!" cried Tigapuu. "Are you out of your mind? Fifty, straight to the old man! That's simply a swindle. A friend wants a rouble from you, but you toss fifty straight into the wolf's jaws! It's a downright shame that I give my friendship to someone with only lousy kopecks in his pocket. So, tell me: what will I get for this rouble? Where will I go with it? Whom do I dare to show it to? Pfui!" He spat heartily. "I couldn't let on that I only have one rouble in my pocket? God's truth – if you weren't my friend, I would give you a good thrashing for this swindle."

With those words he got up from the edge of the bed and groped his way to the hatchway, for he already had the rouble in his pocket. "You could break your neck in the dark!" he cursed as he went. "And for what? One lousy rouble! It makes me sick to think of the cheating that's going on here." Tigapuu's steps were heard on the stairs. Indrek was still sitting on the edge of the bed, the blanket and the cushion on his knees. He would have happily thrown them down through the hatch after Tigapuu. And to hell with that rouble, for he had a strong suspicion that he wouldn't see his rouble again.

He was still lost in this thought when Tigapuu's voice resounded again from down below. "Come down quickly, Mr Maurus is calling for you!" he shouted. "But don't break your neck in the dark; otherwise I'll be blamed again."

When Indrek got down safely, Tigapuu quietly rebuked him, "Now be a man, not a wimp. Of course the old man wants to make peace with us, so look offended and behave as if you're in a huff. Remember this and we'll get more out of him."

Down in the big room, Kopfschneider said to them: "Mr Maurus ordered you to come up."

With a somewhat pained expression of dignified importance, Tigapuu said to Indrek: "I suppose we have to go, if we're ordered."

Upstairs the headmaster greeted them with a chuckle. Seeing Tigapuu's offended expression, he said apologetically: "Let's make amends. I don't mean it badly, but I do have a right to ask where you've been. Doesn't Mr Maurus have that right?" he inquired of Indrek.

"Yes," he said, forgetting Tigapuu's instructions.

"But you, Tigapuu, what do you think, shouldn't Mr Maurus have that right?"

"He should," replied Tigapuu somewhat evasively. "But I should have that right too, for otherwise how shall I keep control of the boys? If I don't have any rights, they won't respect me."

"Yes, you should have that right too," agreed the headmaster in a conciliatory tone. "You should have the right, since you're my deputy. Subordination – that's what it should be. And that's what we're agreeing now." For some time now some silver coins had been jingling in the headmaster's pocket; now he took out a handful.

"Here are thirty kopecks for each of you," he said. "Go to the 'House of Temperance', Tigapuu knows it, and have a few Napoleon cakes and drink some tea. You can be absent from supper if you wish. I'm giving you this cash, Paas; you're the tallest, so you should pay the bill. Share it nicely and honestly, always honestly. We are poor, we're a poor nation, so we have to be honest. Honesty and justice are the shield of the poor. Well, off you go nicely, and you, Tigapuu, teach your friend. But come back soon, don't stay long. And don't play billiards or go anywhere else, because young men always want to go elsewhere. You, Paas, remind your friend of that when he gets the urge to go. Well now, off you go!"

The boys made to leave, but at the threshold the headmaster again took some jingling silver from his pocket, selected two twenty-kopeck pieces and put them in Tigapuu's palm.

"So you'll both have something," he said with a sly smile; "otherwise the other one might get very proud of his height. With a rouble you're two big men."

The boys went down the stairs with a roar, while the headmaster remained in the open doorway looking after them, his hands in his trouser pockets, and his dressing gown flapping around.

"The devil take him!" swore Tigapuu in Russian, when he

had got down ahead of Indrek through the big room, where a flock of boys was gathered around the long table.

"What's up?" they all asked inquisitively.

"Nothing to do with you," replied Tigapuu. "The old man has gone mad."

He whispered to Indrek, when they were alone: "Quick! Coat on, and out the main gate!"

As soon as they were both on the street, Tigapuu said, "You understood, you noticed what the old man wants: to make us quarrel. Make us quarrel! For example, the way I stepped out of there ahead of you, and that's what he's after. And how cunningly! He gives you money because you're taller. You see – taller! It would have been right to give me the money, because I'm already a bit of a teacher – you heard that – and I know how to handle money in town. And now, just think about this: the old man gives money to a schoolboy, and he's supposed to pay for a schoolteacher. Only our old man can get away with tricks like that. You know what trick I wanted to play on him? I wanted to simply say: No, Mr Maurus, I can't eat Napoleon cakes today, because I have a stomach-ache. And why, do you suppose, did I not do that? I didn't do that because I was only thinking of what's best for you, and for no other reason. Firstly, you've no idea of where to go and what to do with that money, and secondly, he would take that money back from you – that was beyond doubt. So I thought to myself: alright then, I'll pay the old man back some other time, but I won't leave my friend in the lurch. Let him get it, even if I don't."

"We're going halves on this, no other way," said Indrek.

"Going halves, of course, no question," replied Tigapuu. "But tell me: is it really fair to go halves? A schoolboy and a schoolmaster going halves? I don't believe the old man meant that. He only said that because he wanted to make us quarrel, whatever the cost. What kind of a world would we live in if schoolboys and schoolmasters went halves? Our classes have less trouble than our paid schoolmasters have, but the old man isn't paying us a single kopeck. And do the schoolmasters pass on a little bit of their wages to us? What would it cost them to say: 'Here, boys – a little something for you too, because we've all been striving and suffering together, so we should share out our rewards a little.' What do you think – would some boys start grumbling if they got a bit less than the schoolmasters? There's no one so foolish in the entire school. Naturally a schoolmaster should get more than a schoolboy. That's right, isn't it?"

"Of course you're right," agreed Indrek.

"It would be crazy if I weren't right about this," declared Tigapuu in a heartfelt way. "After all, the whole world hasn't gone mad, so that a schoolboy and a schoolmaster would get the same. Of course, with us it's a slightly different story; I'm not quite a schoolmaster yet, I haven't got my cap or my star yet. So you can't be left completely without. No, not at all! And even if the old man had meant it, I still would have secretly given you a little on the side. But only on condition that you keep your mouth shut. But what do you think now – how much are you going to give me of yours?"

"I think that if thirty..." began Indrek.

"How come, thirty!" interjected Tigapuu. "That's half, but didn't I just explain to you that a schoolboy and a schoolmaster can't go halves!"

"You got forty from the old man, and if you get thirty from me, then you'll have seventy altogether, but I'll have thirty in total," explained Indrek.

"Good God!" cried Tigapuu in great surprise. "You're suffering from apoplexy, or you're having a heart attack, or you've simply gone soft in the head! You're a complete muttonhead! Those forty? What are you talking about! They were given, obviously, only to me as a schoolmaster – do you understand? And what the old man gives to a schoolmaster, boys can't even get a sniff of! Never! That would be a fine joke, if schoolmasters started sharing their wages with boys! I mean, it can only be a question of sharing what's in your own hand. If the old man had wanted us to share all of it, why would he have given these forty into my hand? Why? Answer, unless you haven't completely gone off your head. Besides, he told me in clear words – you heard them yourself: 'There, this is for you!' But when he gave you money, what did he say then? Bring it to mind, remember it well. He said: 'Share it nicely'. But did he say anything to me about sharing? Did he use that word? Of course not, you know that as well as I do. But tell me: is it sharing nicely if you offer a schoolmaster as much as yourself? Thirty each: that's halving, that's not sharing. But the old man talked about sharing, not about halving. So tell me: did the old man order us to share nicely or to halve nicely?"

"To share," replied Indrek.

"Well, you see!" cried Tigapuu triumphantly. "So why do you want to halve, if the old man clearly told us to share? Better say it straight out: how much are you really thinking of giving me, so I know whom I'm dealing with," demanded Tigapuu, leading Indrek somewhere into the stairwell of the stone building. "Before we go inside, things have to be clear. You see what sort of a big and grand house this is, and what a fine staircase, with handrails and everything, and still you're bargaining over a few lousy kopecks. we're going to go up this grand staircase, and then to a left, not a right, remember that. Let's hurry, otherwise someone will come and see us here and think God knows what. In town it isn't decent to linger in the stairwell of a grand house with a wide staircase. And if you still have an ounce of a sense of fairness and decency in you, you'll give me two-thirds nicely and leave one good third for yourself. For there's one thing you should know: I'm almost a townsman already, and where a country boy can get by on twenty kopecks or so, a townsman has to have roubles in his pocket. So when I say a third, that's actually more than I'm getting myself. For what are those forty that you're intending and promising to give to me, a schoolmaster and almost a townsman? They're like nothing. But since I'm

63

your friend, I'm giving you five in good faith, so I've only got thirty-five left."

By this stage Indrek was exasperated, and took the money out of his pocket to give Tigapuu thirty-five, but unfortunately he only had twenty-kopeck pieces.

"Well, the money is such that I get two-thirds, you one-third," said Tigapuu. But don't be afraid: I'm a man of my word! I'll give you back the five kopecks some other time."

When Tigapuu had got his forty kopecks, he instructed Indrek: "Now go nicely up these stairs and go boldly in the door on the left. Never mind the grand stairs and the great big door, just go in. And look, you've got twenty. A Napoleon costs three, so that's almost seven Napoleons. Just keep one thing in mind: don't move until I get back, because we came out the door together, and we're going back in together; that's the way friends behave, because otherwise the old man will think God knows what. So, straight up the stairs, then turn left and straight in through the big door, because there isn't a smaller one in this building, everything's gigantic. And wait until I come. You won't get bored in there: you can read the papers or watch those billiard-balls clicking. Now up you go!"

Tigapuu accompanied Indrek inside, as if he didn't quite trust him, found a place at the table for him and ordered a glass of tea and three Napoleons. Then he said, "Can you feel how lovely and warm it is in here? And so bright! There's nothing wrong with sitting here and looking at other people having fun, is there? Take another glass of tea and a Napoleon later, and then you'll be full up. I can't take you with me, because you don't have the money. Where I'm going, you can't get anything for twenty. Anyway, you're not used to it, you're definitely better off in here. Just don't move till I come back."

And Tigapuu left.

Chapter 6

Indrek ate and drank and read the papers, but Tigapuu didn't come. Indrek ate and drank again, and still Tigapuu didn't come. Then Indrek went to watch a game of billiards, but even then Tigapuu didn't come, as if some accident had happened to him. Indrek got worried, and finally he felt sick in the stomach. Perhaps Tigapuu had just led him on: put him there to wait, with no intention of coming back, gone home long ago and was laughing about it.

By half-past ten Indrek's patience had run out; he put his coat on and left, his heart burning within him. What would happen if Tigapuu did come back and didn't find him there? Was that comradely? Hadn't he promised to wait? Down in the stairwell, where they had squabbled so long over money, he stopped, in case Tigapuu should come after all. But no, Tigapuu still didn't come. There was nothing for it: he had to go home alone. And when he set off like that, he suddenly had the feeling that today he was walking for the first time on this city street. Only when he saw the lamp on the street corner, its light shining like a halo, did it occur to him that he had seen that haloed light before. When? Oh yes! It was when that strange girl had smiled at him from an open doorway. Even now Indrek felt the warmth of that smile – such a smile it had been.

The main gate was closed. The front door was opened with a jangle by Kopfschneider.

"No Tigapuu?" he asked.

"No," replied Indrek. "Hasn't he come home?"

The Latvian shook his head and said: "You've been ordered to go up."

"Me alone?" asked Indrek.

"Both of you, Tigapuu too."

"But he isn't here yet," objected Indrek, to avoid the bothersome climb upstairs.

"So go alone, there's nothing else to do," said the Latvian. "You have to go straightaway."

So Indrek went up without even taking off his coat. But today the stairs didn't smell, as if who knows how long an interval had passed. It was a perfectly ordinary wooden staircase with iron fittings, which made a noise as you climbed, nothing more. "So it doesn't always smell," thought Indrek. Why Mr Maurus's stairs sometimes smelt like a teacher's wife mourning for her only son was something he would find out later.

The headmaster was in bed, behind a curtain.

"Is that you, Paas and Tigapuu?" he asked, as Indrek stepped inside, and hearing that he was alone, he said, "Come here, come closer."

Indrek stepped from behind the curtain which shielded him from the headmaster's eyes.

"Closer still," the headmaster ordered, and when Indrek hesitated, preferring to regard the space defined by the curtain as a sacred place onto which his feet could not step, Mr Maurus raised himself into a half-sitting position, patted the cover with his hand as if Indrek were to sit there, and compelled him: "Nearer, come nearer! How am I supposed to talk to you if you stand so far away, and you're so tall yourself that my old eyes can't look up to make you out?"

Indrek came further into the room, intending to stop at the foot of the bed. But even that wasn't enough for the headmaster. He invited Indrek even closer. And finally what the boy had feared happened: the headmaster made him sit on the edge of the bed, and since it made him bashful, he declared: "Bolder! Braver! Turn your eyes this way. There, like that!" The headmaster moved the boy's head with his hand. "And now, breathe towards me," he ordered. And when Indrek had done this repeatedly, the headmaster said with a smile: "Pure, perfectly pure, as if from a young girl's mouth. Only young girls breathe so purely, virgins I mean, not the others."

These words from the headmaster's mouth were so strange that Indrek had to avert his eyes. The headmaster laughed at this, and said: "You too are like a young virgin, innocent and pure. I saw that straightaway, but Mr Maurus always has to try, always has to test, when someone goes off with that Tigapuu. For Tigapuu, he's no longer a virgin, he no longer breathes the same breath as you do. Not like that at all. Oh, I know his breath! Even his clothes give off a different smell. You still have the scent of the earth and the forest; you definitely have it," said the headmaster, putting a hand on Indrek's knee, as he tried to stroke his hand. Then Indrek got up.

"Ah yes, *warten Sie, warten Sie!*" said the headmaster. "What did I want to ask you?" He put his hands before his eyes, as if he were deep in thought, but Indrek thought he was spying on him between his fingers. After a little while he said: "Right! But where's Tigapuu? Why don't you tell me anything about him? I sent the two of you off together. Where is he?"

"He's not here," replied Indrek.

"How come, not here? So where is he?" inquired the headmaster. "Weren't you together?"

"No," answered Indrek. "He went away."

"Where? Where did he go?"

"He didn't say where."

"But the money? I gave money to you."

"I had twenty left, he got forty," Indrek told him.

"You complete idiot!" cried the headmaster, but in his voice there was no hint of anger or reproach, only amusement and laughter. "That's why I gave the money to you – so it wouldn't go anywhere," said Mr Maurus. "With the forty that I gave him he wouldn't have done anything. So therefore he got himself eighty. Yes, eighty," repeated the headmaster, and then added:

"But that isn't much for going out anywhere. He must have got some from somewhere else. Didn't he ask you or borrow from you? You still had a little left, I suppose. Mr Maurus did say to give it all to him, so he can enter it in the books, but a young man doesn't believe old Maurus – the young believe the young, not the old. So then, one young man comes up and asks, a second one comes and asks, a third one comes, and so our young man's money runs out. What did he give you in pawn?" the headmaster suddenly asked. "He's always pawning something – anything, whether it belongs to him or someone else. For he's a complete madman. But you didn't give him much? When you do give, don't ever give it all, don't ever give much. But best of all: if you want to give Tigapuu money, come quietly to Mr Maurus and tell him privately – just between us, you see – that Mr Tigapuu wants to pawn his books, his blankets or his cushions: how much should I give for them? Because those books, blankets and cushions might not be his own, but borrowed from someone, as his own cushions and blankets might already be at the pawnshop."

The result of this long speech was that Indrek talked openly about both the borrowing of money and the visit to the 'Temperance'.

"I said straightaway that Tigapuu would take the money!" cried the headmaster triumphantly. "Mr Maurus knows his Tigapuu! But that you would lend him a whole rouble at a time – that's something I would never have believed. The Lord has given you height – if only it had come with a little common sense. But never mind! The gumption is sure to come with time! It didn't take you long to know what Tigapuu was up to, and what a con-man he is! But otherwise he's honest and loyal, not like some of the others here. At least Tigapuu doesn't steal, whereas some of the others do. There you see how hard it is for an old man like me to be the headmaster here – among such boys. Somebody like Tigapuu comes along, and he wants to turn all the boys into Tigapuus. But the fathers and mothers, uncles and aunts want Mr

Maurus to turn them into students, who don't pawn their books. He pawns them himself and he teaches others to do it. Alright if they're his own, but what about other people's? Why not other people's, if they give a rouble for them."

The headmaster laughed heartily. Indrek tried to laugh along with him, because he was trying against his will to convince himself that a bad joke was being played on him.

"Now you can go," the headmaster finally said. "But keep what we've talked about to yourself. Mr Maurus trusts you, that's why he's telling you this. You're already big and tall, and you have common sense. There are still honest people in the countryside. You know about the honesty of our ancestors, don't you? They chose their own kings and sent them to the lords of the castle, where they were all killed. That's how honest our ancestors were, and so we were left without our kings, and we still are to this day. But then we came to be ruled by the Russian Tsar, as did my school. Just as well, because otherwise the Germans would have closed down Mr Maurus's school long ago. So then, good night, good night! Go to bed, go straight to bed!"

When Tigapuu returned Indrek didn't know, because he was asleep up in Siberia, and Tigapuu was downstairs. But the next morning he grabbed Indrek, pulled him by the shirt-front into an empty classroom and said: "Why didn't you wait for me?"

"I did wait for you, but you didn't come," replied Indrek.

"You call that waiting – only until half past ten. Yet you want to be a friend. I run to the House of Temperance – you're not there! I run outside, in case you're out there walking in the fresh air, but no, you're not! I go in, I look around, I peep into rooms, but you're just not there. Believe it or not, this is the first time in my life I've come across a friend like you. And for that I get an ear-bashing from the old man now. Maybe we could leave it at that, but no, I'll definitely get some more of it today, I can feel it. Of course he was denigrating me last night, wasn't he?"

"No," replied Indrek tersely.

"What are you babbling about?" cried Tigapuu. "Of course he asked about the money?"

"He did ask," Indrek confirmed.

"You said we divided it nicely in half?"

"No, I said how things really were," Indrek declared.

"Man, you're really crazy!" screamed Tigapuu. "You can't be trusted one little bit! For God's sake – you rotten swine!"

"How come?" asked Indrek, suddenly serious and almost angry.

"He even asks!" shrieked Tigapuu. "Are you perhaps even worse than a swine? A swine who blabbers about other people! A snooper! Now I finally understand why the old man gave the money to you first. You're in cahoots with Lible and Kopfschneider."

These last words Tigapuu said to Indrek right up to his face and was preventing him from leaving the classroom. But before he could try that, Tigapuu grasped him by the arm and said: "Where are you running to? If you're an honest man, you must stay here and settle this!"

"I don't have anything to settle, leave me alone!" Indrek shouted back over his shoulder, wanting to leave.

Now Tigapuu grasped him even harder by the arm, but then something happened that must have been most unexpected to both parties. When Indrek tried to recall later, he couldn't decide whether it was deliberate or accidental. At the moment when Tigapuu seized him more firmly by the arm, he responded with an impatient or angry movement so that his palm slapped Tigapuu across the face.

"You bastard!" squealed Tigapuu. "What's that supposed to mean? You want to fight about it? Fight with me? You hit me in the face – me, Tigapuu? I'm going to give you what for, right now." Tigapuu was by the door, blocking his way.

"And I'll give you what for, if you don't leave me alone," countered Indrek furiously. But the next moment he got a fist under his chin, and he would have crashed backwards against the wall, if his hand hadn't involuntarily sought support from the table, which had an open leaf of the kind found in many classrooms. When he grasped it, it came away and, together with this loose wooden flap, he hurtled back into the wall. His vision was blurred from concussion and rage, and when Tigapuu approached him again, he lunged straight at him with the piece of wood still in his hand and without understanding his own actions. Tigapuu collapsed on the floor and lay there, as blood appeared in his hair and then streamed onto his face. Indrek stood and stared dumbstruck at his weapon, which he was still holding. Suddenly he rushed out of the classroom, not knowing where to go or what to do. He wanted to run away. He would probably have rushed to the headmaster's door upstairs, if Mr Ollino hadn't appeared, stopped him and asked him calmly: "What's wrong? What's happened?

"I knocked Tigapuu down," replied Indrek and burst into tears. He didn't know why.

"What? Where? When was this?" inquired Ollino.

"Now… there… in the classroom," replied Indrek.

They went to the scene of the incident. The terrible news spread like wildfire through the rooms and curious faces were teeming all around them. Fortunately the bell rang at that same moment and Ollino commanded the boys: "Dinner-time! At the double! Not a single face do I want to see hanging around here!"

So they were soon left alone, and they went to the classroom where the injured Tigapuu was supposed to be lying. But he was already sitting on a bench, just where he had been struck down, and wiping blood off his face.

"Keep the door closed, so that no one can get in!" Ollino told Indrek,

"Bloody bastard, he hit me on the head with a table-top, this broken bit," Tigapuu cursed. "I've told the old man that the desks should be repaired, otherwise there could be an accident – and now we have one. This swine doesn't know how to fight properly, he uses a table-top. And edgeways, too, for otherwise my head wouldn't…"

On hearing Tigapuu talking like this, Indrek no longer felt his recent mix of terror and pity, and it was replaced by a desire to hit Tigapuu over the head with whatever came to hand, should the occasion arise in the future. But at the same moment the memory of a green potato-field far away suddenly came to mind, and there, in the fresh soil on the ground, an old woman was crying out; before her stood a sulking boy – big and strong, bigger and stronger than Indrek.

"Go and wash your face in cold water in the washroom," said Ollino, giving Indrek his own handkerchief. Thus the distant vision was dispersed and actual life resumed. "Quickly!" cried Ollino after him, adding: "And not a word to anyone, understand?"

"I understand," replied Indrek, rushing down the corridor to the washroom. But he was confronted there by Lible and a couple of others, all of them burning with curiosity.

"What's going on?" they inquired. "Who's involved? Why the handkerchief?"

"Button your lips," replied Indrek and hurried back.

"What an idiot!" the boys cried after him.

In the classroom Ollino was examining Tigapuu's head.

"Well, how is it?" Tigapuu asked.

"It really did hit you edgeways, I suppose," opined Ollino. "A long red gash."

"That's what I thought, it knocked me right over," said Tigapuu. Seeing Indrek, he shouted, "You blockhead, it went straight in edgeways. Not into the bloody skull anyway. You just can't take a joke at all."

Mr Ollino remained absolutely calm, as if this were a perfectly ordinary matter. The only thing Indrek observed as he looked into his whitish, stony eyes, was a slight shimmer. And that shimmer did not seem in any way bad to Indrek. He thought of saying something, but at the same moment the

72

door burst open and the headmaster entered. Evidently the news had already reached him.

"What's going on here?" he asked Ollino.

"Nothing," he replied calmly. "Paas and Tigapuu were fooling around and Tigapuu fell against the edge of the desk and drew blood, nothing more. It's nothing, a little scratch."

But the headmaster wasn't satisfied with this explanation, and demanded more information. Tigapuu provided this so precisely and plausibly that the headmaster had to pretend that he believed him. But when classes had already begun, Indrek was called out of the classroom to go to the headmaster.

"You're the only honest person who tells me the truth," Mr Maurus began. "The others are all liars. Even Mr Ollino tells lies, even he does, but he does it for good reasons. So tell me now: what went on with you and Tigapuu this morning? How did Tigapuu get his head bloody?"

Indrek's heart started trembling. It wasn't that he was afraid of confessing his own action and, if necessary, getting punished for it, but something quite different occupied his mind. If Ollino and Tigapuu really were colluding and keeping the truth about the incident from the old man, and if he spilled the beans now, what could this be called? Wasn't this telling tales, almost snooping, as Lible or Kopfschneider might do, hiding in the washroom, behind closed doors, spying through keyholes, and then galloping off to tell the headmaster? The only thing, it seemed to Indrek, was that it affected him personally and therefore he could act as he pleased. Others could hide things if they wanted to, but he wouldn't. So he decided to tell the headmaster everything, and get the whole farce over and done with.

"I immediately thought," declared the headmaster when Indrek had finished, "what is this 'fooling around', since Tigapuu doesn't fool around? He goes straight in and fights. But I still don't understand how you got into such a scrap. You have such nice eyes."

"He swore at me," said Indrek, wanting to keep silent about the swear-words.

"I believe that," said the headmaster. "He swears like a trooper. And what did he call you? A gossiper, an informer, a snooper or a cheat?"

"He called me the whole lot," said Indrek against his will.

"Ah, the whole lot!" exclaimed the headmaster, surprised and curious. "You didn't tell him that we'd been talking to each other, did you? You really are silly! Remember: silence, silence, silence – otherwise everyone will start cursing you, just as Tigapuu did. Now you tell me: what can Mr Maurus do if the whole school starts cursing like that? Next time, be more careful: you mustn't hit people with a table-top, especially edgeways, because that way you can knock them down and end up in Siberia. Not our Siberia upstairs, but the other one, far away. Luckily this time it was Tigapuu's head, which is as hard as rock – lucky for you. It was God's will that it was Tigapuu's head. Not everyone has a head like Tigapuu's, so you must always be careful, always be careful! But never mind that he cursed you, because if anyone's so honest as to tell the truth, they'll always get cursed and teased. Nobody loves the truth. Only old Mr Maurus loves it, so he does. Because he knows the world stands on the truth, and it keeps Mr Maurus' school going. Anyone who doesn't love the truth will have to perish, but we two won't perish, not us, because we love the truth, even if we become the object of other people's curses."

The headmaster laughed weirdly as he stepped over to Indrek and put a few silver coins in his hand. Never before had Indrek held this kind of money in his hand: they felt slippery, slimy, cold, even though they were actually warm and dry. So strange was the money that the headmaster put in his palm.

"This is for you, for being an honest person and the child of honest parents," he said, intending to say more, but suddenly he changed his tone and started quite unexpectedly reprimanding Indrek.

"You dog!" he exclaimed; "you come here from the country and behave as if this were some sort of pub or tavern!"

And at the same time, as there was a knock at the door and Lible's inquisitive face appeared at it, the headmaster gave Indrek a punch in the chest with both hands.

"Shut the door!" cried the headmaster to Lible, who was of course listening behind the door with several others. And turning to Indrek, the headmaster continued: "You madman! In the end my school will be closed because of you, tall one! But where are my boys supposed to go then, and what will become of the Estonian people when Mr Maurus' school closes its doors? Am I supposed to go into the classroom and tell everyone: Beware of Paas, because he's long in the body and short on understanding? Or should I send you straight to the madhouse? What else are you fit for then? But go to your class now; I'll look at what to do with you afterwards."

With these last words he placed a few more coins in Indrek's palm, but they were even more loathsome than the previous ones. When Indrek was opening the door, the headmaster cried after him: "Do you understand now that Mr Maurus is right?"

"I do," replied Indrek through his teeth, and it was harder for him to utter those words than all other words that had passed through his mouth up to now. Suddenly he felt so completely surrounded by lies, deceit and hypocrisy that his body actually ached. In a place where people are usually alone, he wrapped the money he had received in paper and intended to throw it down through the hole. But suddenly he changed his mind and stuffed the money in his pocket.

In the classroom Lible was buzzing round Indrek like a bee, constantly questioning him about had happened between him and Tigapuu.

"Others can prattle on about that, but why should I?" said Indrek.

"The others know nothing about it," replied Lible simply.

"And I don't remember," smirked Indrek.

75

After lessons Indrek went to see Tigapuu, who was lying in bed, a cloth around his head.

"You're quite a pirate!" Tigapuu cried out to him almost heartily. "Right in there with a piece of table-top. But you were smart enough not to hit me in the face. So I feel that you're still a friend. Right now a couple of beers would be in order – that would be nice. I was a complete idiot yesterday. If you can find it in yourself, let's make up and forget it all."

Without saying a word, Indrek took the money he had received from the headmaster and put it in Tigapuu's palm.

"There's no more," he said; "be content with that."

"Well, so you're a proper man after all!" cried Tigapuu, seeing the money. "We may fight, but friendship doesn't die! Call Jürka for a moment."

When he had come and taken the money to buy beer, rolls and smoked sausage – specifically smoked sausage – Indrek and Tigapuu were left alone.

"The old man's been grilling you," said Tigapuu. "You didn't give us away?"

"No," replied Indrek, "but obviously he doesn't believe our explanations."

"Of course he doesn't," said Tigapuu. "He doesn't believe anything, whatever you say. He's been trained to be a teacher, that's why. Teachers don't believe anything, because they're supposed to study the Bible and the Bible isn't true. Have you ever heard that before – that the Bible isn't true?"

No, Indrek hadn't heard that.

"Well, you're hearing it for the first time from me," said Tigapuu. "Timusk explained it to me. So, as a friend, you should know it too: the Bible is phoney and a lie, and when a teacher studies it hard, soon he doesn't believe anything anymore. He loses his belief in the truth, because he thinks that the truth cannot exist if the Bible isn't true."

"How does he get to be a teacher if he doesn't believe?" asked Indrek curiously, because he still wanted to ask even though Tigapuu's explanations seemed to him to be the ravings of a sick mind.

"He becomes one anyway, having lost his belief but gained the gift of the gab. Whether you believe or not, the main thing is to be able to express yourself nicely. That's the most important thing in life, you should know that. When I graduate – and I definitely will – I'll become a teacher, because I know how…"

Jürka arrived with the shopping, and so Tigapuu didn't have time to finish his sentence. Instead he hit the first bottle Jürka put on the table a couple of times at the base which removed the cork. He raised the bottle to his mouth and drank deeply. Then he looked at it against the light, handed it to Jürka and said, "That's for you – for bringing it here! And a few tasty morsels too," he added, passing a roll and some sausage to Jürka. "That's for keeping quiet. And see that the old man doesn't come in unexpectedly. Understand?"

"Will do," replied Jürka, when he had emptied the bottle and stuffed the food in his pocket.

Tigapuu ate with great gusto. Eating and drinking raised his mood more and more. And the talk was in full flow, as if the beer had gone to his head.

"One thing you ought to know," he went on, "you were only saved by that broken table; otherwise I'd have beaten you senseless. Because force alone doesn't help; you have to know how to fight. Fighting is a great art! And you should know that if I'd been on top form today, that table-top wouldn't have done anything to me. God's truth – nothing! Nothing hurts a sozzled head. Throw the whole table at me. Even Ollino doesn't dare touch me when I'm fighting fit. By the way, hold onto your jaw, because if you start shouting at him, he'll make short work of you. And you know, when he's finished with you, you wouldn't want to take on anyone else, that's what he's like. But otherwise he's a friendly chap, like you. You bring me rolls and sausage, so I can eat my sick head back to health and wash it down with a drink of beer.

For you can see which way the wind is blowing: anyone who has the right must eat, and today I have the right, because you're not supposed to land your friends in trouble, that's for sure. That's betrayal, when someone promises to wait and then doesn't. You must wait, and you have to know where your friend is. Did you know where I was? No? But the old man does, he snoops and finds out. He stuck his nose in, and shouted: 'Schinder, you're coming back from the girls' place?' He knows that scent, oh, the old man knows it! You want me to take you with me next time? You don't? Alright then, I won't insist, because you need money there. But just wait till my uncle dies, then you'll get your rouble back. That'll happen soon, because my uncle's diabetic. You know what that is? It's when everything turns to sugar, everything, my whole uncle, and then death comes. For how can you go on living when you're sugar from top to bottom – you die as sugar. So then – just as soon as my uncle turns completely into sugar – I'll pay my debts. Till then, keep the cushion and the blanket, don't take them to the pawnshop or sell them to anyone else. For a start, you don't need them yet, as it's not cold enough. That may not happen before Christmas, so you'll just have to hang on to them. They'll be more of a hindrance than a help. So until then you could give them to me to sleep on, just for the sake of friendship. Not that I want them back from you, not at all, because the blanket and the cushion will stay yours, it's just that I'd sleep with them. If it should get cold, then that's a different thing. By then my head may have healed, I could maybe put it on a block of wood, but now it's a bit embarrassing in front of the others – a sick head and no pillow. Besides, I've been meaning to tell you for some time but keep forgetting: I have a strange head where memories just won't stay in place. That's how it is. It has cause me terrible suffering! Simply terrible! But what can I do? I can't unscrew my head and replace it with another one. Now all this has happened, and it only occurred to me afterwards, when nothing can be done about it. I wanted to tell you this yesterday, but I forgot then too, so I'm telling you today. In itself it's just a trifling thing, especially if I get to sleep with them, as if I hadn't pawned them. It's like this, you see: the blanket and the cushion don't actually belong to me, and I got them from someone else to sleep with, after I'd pawned my own ones. That's what happened, and tomorrow or the day after I'll get them back from the pawnbroker's and then I'll be able to return these ones I borrowed to their owner. So if you don't want to pawn other people's belongings, try to remember things, that's the most important thing. There's an art to keeping things in mind – mnemonics! If you ever see that word anywhere, you'll now know what it means. It strengthens your memory! Mine is terribly weak! The proof is to be found in the blanket and the cushion up in your place in Siberia. Would you want to go and get them immediately? Of course you do. Yes, mnemonics, mnemonics, keep that in mind!" Tigapuu shouted after Indrek as he went to fetch the blanket and cushion, because he suddenly felt that the sooner he got rid of them, the better.

Chapter 7

All the fuss and bother with Tigapuu and the headmaster affected Indrek in two ways – in himself personally and in his relations with others. He was increasingly aware that he would have to behave differently if he was to avoid getting involved in trivial arguments and squandering his last precious kopecks. He had to learn to live differently than he had at home or at the office, where he'd only had to deal with old Maie or a couple of the shop-boys who wanted to be his friends.

He soon noticed that he tended to be alone. This was partly due to himself, partly to others. He avoided the ones Tigapuu had branded as blabbermouths and traitors, even though he didn't fully understand what lay behind those words. Many of them seemed to be convinced that he was part of Lible's clique, because every time they were plotting to pull someone's leg, they all went quiet or scattered when Indrek approached. Consequently he withdrew into himself and sought solace in his studies. He was still unaware of how much there was to learn. So the days passed. By the time people had come to the conclusion that there was no need to hide anything from him and even desired his company, he had already found better companions in the form of books.

The greatest assistance in this task probably came from Mr Koovi, whom he turned to after considerable hesitation, as he needed help with his Latin. Indrek's heart was trembling as he knocked on the door.

"Who's there?" came a sleepy and irritable voice from within, and when Indrek had said his name and explained his wish, came the reply: "I was just sleeping."

"Then I'm sorry, I'll come some other time," said Indrek. "Why another time?" said the irritable voice. "You've spoilt my lunchtime nap anyway. Come in, and why stand there shouting at the door? It isn't locked."

As Indrek stepped inside, Koovi was lying in his old wooden bed, with its striped bedspread, and the bed creaked loudly every time he moved. His feet, complete with boots, were resting on the footboard.

For about half an hour Indrek sat in that little room overwhelmed by the exclusive presence of books stacked to the ceiling on shelves, by the window, on chairs and the floor – everywhere! And when he got up to go, Koovi said: "You must do more work! We old ones aren't going anywhere. Do what the headmaster says: study with enthusiasm, study like mad, he's right about that. And when you get bored with cramming, then here you are – take this and read it. You know enough Russian to understand it, I'm sure." He handed Indrek some sort of fat book. "And put some paper around the book, otherwise you'll smudge it, because you must always look after a book," he instructed, and as Indrek opened the door to go, he repeated: "Read, read, and leave the buffoonery to the likes of Tigapuu and the old man. Him too."

"I already have," said Indrek.

"All the better," Koovi replied.

There were others who occasionally visited Koovi for help or advice about this or that. From them he heard more about the man. Son of a cottar, he had attended the parish school and later become a local teacher. He somehow managed to move to town, where he worked in more congenial conditions until he had done his university-entrance exams. Now he was a university student over the age of forty. On top of that, he was giving lessons here, presenting scientific papers to societies, attending various meetings, as well as being engaged in some kind of business, the latter perhaps with no great enthusiasm, but he was doing it nonetheless. Of course he was also doing things unpaid, such as supervising Indrek and a few others. He was doing it because he had got caught up in circumstances where others were manipulating him and he couldn't resist. Sometimes he swore about all sorts of trivialities that impeded his more essential and impending tasks, but he was swept along relentlessly as though this were his inescapable fate. He toiled away from early morning until late evening, hardly earning enough to provide him with shelter, shabby clothing and the occasional book, something that he loved more than anything in the world. His most frequent companion was Timusk, with whom he would sit in the canteen at the pupils' table, eating the same slops as they did. Timusk was also at university and swept along by the same wind of fate as Koovi was, but his demon was more concealed – in the underground. Timusk was a very taciturn man by nature, and therefore he wanted to drive others to rebel, come what may. To rebel at any price and in any field at all. In Timusk's opinion there was no area of life where one couldn't rebel or one shouldn't rebel.

When Indrek turned to him, on Koovi's recommendation, about the German language – he had to go by way of dark stairs, almost up to the roof, into the realm of Siberia – he found his room to be just as simple and poor as Koovi's. He too had books lying everywhere. But in his room there were two desks, one larger, one smaller. The first of them was piled up with dried plants. Timusk was collecting their Estonian names, and therefore he would gather information about them from every visitor. He presented a few plants to Indrek too, asking: "Do you know this one? This one? And this? What name do you give it? Have you heard of it?"

Usually Timusk had to answer his own questions, giving the Russian, German and Latin names as well, as if repeating them as an aid to memory.

"In science, the name is the main thing," explained Timusk. "In the beginning was the word, that's the idea of science. It's just a shame that our language is still living – a living language is never as exact as a dead one. In general, you know, what is precise is only what is dead. You remember the legend about death and the Fall of Man? That if there had been no Fall, there would be no death and no dead people. Simple and clear, isn't it? But what would have become of human science if there had been no dead people? You could say that there would be little point of studying if we were immortal? Did the gods and the angels ever study? No, only humans study, because they're afraid of death. But have you heard how it is with God and his existence? Learn German properly, and I'll give you a book to read. It's banned, but I'll give it to you anyway. But until then, take this one," and he gave Indrek something in Estonian. "If you don't want to read anything else, at least read this one: *Our Planet's Past*. There's a bit in it about the creation of the world, death and the Fall, if you know how to read between the lines. You have to learn to read between the lines, because that's the most important thing with us, not what's in the educated world, where everything can be written in the lines."

And now Timusk began to teach Indrek the high art of reading between the lines, starting with the earth and the moon, the sun and the stars, the blissfulness of souls, immortality and redemption, science, freedom and revolution. As he spoke, the German language was forgotten completely, for in Timusk's opinion that was a trifling detail compared with the multitude of such cosmic questions.

When Indrek finally came away from Timusk's room, he was dizzy in the true sense of the word, so immense and significant were the things he'd been hearing about. He had never felt so foolish as he did that day. He was also astounded that a person who talked of such grand things could live in such a small, shabby room. How could he dress like that? Indrek had noticed long before that Timusk's student coat which now lay on his bed was threadbare, as were his other clothes, but only now did he think about it. His boots were worn and patched and then torn again beside the patch. The heels were extremely worn down and lopsided. How could

83

you have so many ideas like that and yet be surrounded by such privations?

But the next time he went to visit Timusk, suddenly everything seemed to make sense. Even on the stairs he could hear sounds – more beautiful than anything he'd heard before. He stopped and paused for a while. When he finally dared to go on and reached Timusk's door, he found that the sounds were coming from his room. He didn't presume to knock until the playing stopped. And finding Timusk alone in his room, he understood that he was the one who had been playing. This realisation was like discovering what is meaningful in life. Why wouldn't you discuss such momentous issues in your shabby boots, if you could play like that? How and why those momentous issues and that playing belonged together he couldn't explain to himself; he only felt that somehow they did belong together. Without question of doubt! Oh, he would want to live like that too, if only he could play like that!

"Did you hear me playing?" asked Timusk.

"It simply took my breath away," replied Indrek with a blush.

"I've had this ever since we had our own orchestra here," explained Timusk.

These words took Indrek aback. That meant that there had been better times in the past here too. Just as at Vargamäe! There among the swaying birches which you could shimmy up and let a cool wind blow through your heart, and hear the extraordinary sounds that enveloped your soul and made your heart thump. This world is strange: you always seem to be too late! For years and years Indrek had felt that and been saddened by it so many times, but today this meditation was interrupted by Timusk, who continued: "It's the greatest delusion in the world – music, I mean. Do you think that anything like it really exists? Foolishness! Then even horses would like Beethoven and Bach, because they have ears too. But only humans like it, just a few humans. I mean, if it could think, a horse might believe in our music, but not like it or feel it. Just like humans and God. You can only believe in it; you can't feel it. Do you believe in God?"

"I suppose I do," replied Indrek hesitantly.

"Why do you suppose?" asked Timusk. "How can you suppose you believe in God?"

"I think that I believe," Indrek corrected himself.

"So how do you think that you believe?" asked Timusk again.

Now Indrek could say nothing more.

"Of course," said Timusk haughtily, "you wouldn't understand that yet. You see, if you believe, you don't think, and if you think, you don't believe. Let's say you have some piece of wood in your pocket, because you think it's a god who created the heavens and the earth and mankind as well. Believing that is a pretty paltry thing, because people believe stupider things than that. There isn't an idiocy in the world that people haven't believed. But if you want to think, to presume with your reason, that you are carrying the creator of heaven and earth in your pocket, do you think that can be done?"

"I think that I believe," said Indrek.

"The same thing again!" cried Timusk. "You either think or believe, but you can't have both together."

"I think," said Indrek.

"So you think God exists," continued Timusk. "But what can you base your opinion on? For opinions always have to be justified."

But Indrek couldn't bring himself to base his opinion on anything.

"If you can't justify it, then don't think, but believe," instructed Timusk. "Belief doesn't have to be justified. Speaking logically, you should say: I believe that I believe. You understand?"

"I understand," replied Indrek and was quite pleased when he could finally leave, because this first lesson about belief and opinion almost terrified him. On the way downstairs he reasoned: "Alright! Let's say God doesn't exist and it's all a fairy tale, the creation of the world and everything, but what will happen if God suddenly does exist, without our knowledge or belief, he sees and hears everything, even what we say about him? What do we do then?"

So, as well as German, Indrek was studying belief and opinion.

These were happy days, full of mental exercises and anxieties. But they couldn't last long without interruption, because the headmaster soon called Indrek into his office and asked: "Why do you go disturbing Herr Timusk? Why don't you let him study?"

"I went because of German," replied Indrek.

"There are others who know German, not just Herr Timusk, who wants to study," explained the headmaster. "And why do you talk about God when you're studying German? What do you and that Timusk have to do with God? Mr Maurus knows everything, Mr Maurus hears everything, because he is the god of this house. And just as Mr Maurus sees and hears in this house, so God sees and hears over the whole world. What are you and that Timusk plotting against him?"

"We're not plotting anything," said Indrek.

"But that student Timusk talked to you about God," insisted the headmaster.

"He didn't say anything bad. And if he did, it wasn't about God, but about the creation of the world."

"So, even about the creation of the world! What did he say about the creation of the world?"

"He said that in the beginning God created the heaven and the earth…"

"Didn't he say that God did not create the world?" inquired the headmaster.

"No, he didn't say that," Indrek countered.

"But he did ask if you believed in God."

"He did," agreed Indrek, when he saw that the old man had surmised it.

"Well, you see now," said the headmaster. "What business does a person in his full senses have asking another whether he believes in God or not? Has anyone asked you that before? Has Mr Maurus asked you that?"

"No."

"Perhaps he has asked others?"

"He hasn't."

"But why doesn't he ask what you think?"

And when Indrek didn't answer straightaway, the headmaster himself said: "Because Mr Maurus is in his full senses. Nobody asks that if they're in their full senses. But when someone does ask, what kind of sense is he talking?"

Indrek was silent.

"Ah!" cried the headmaster. "You don't answer! For once Mr Maurus asks you something clearly and simply, but you don't answer! That means you agree with the man upstairs. You tend toward God's side, in my honest house you tend toward God's side! But tell me now, how did you answer when you were asked if you believe in God."

"I answered that I do."

"Did you really answer: I do? Not in some other way? Mightn't you have said: I suppose I do?" inquired the headmaster.

"Exactly," Indrek confirmed, astonished that the headmaster was so well informed.

"Did you hear that, did you?" screamed the headmaster. "This tall person supposes he believes! Which of you has ever seen or heard someone say such a thing?" he appealed to those standing around him, for whose instruction and admonition all this speech was intended. "Mr Maurus is old and he has a grey beard, but this is the first time he has heard someone say such a thing. What is your father's name?" he inquired of Indrek.

"Andres," replied Indrek without guessing what this was for.

"And the name of your father's farm?" continued the headmaster.

"Vargamäe."

"So, Vargamäe, eh?" repeated the headmaster, and turning with a smirk to the others he added: "Nice name, that Vargamäe, isn't it?"[16] But when the boys started laughing at it, he said, "No laughing while Mr Maurus is talking with this tall one about God, because otherwise God might think we're laughing at him." And turning again to Indrek, he asked, "So tell me now, does your father Andres at Vargamäe suppose he believes in God, or does he firmly believe?"

"He firmly believes," replied Indrek, suddenly feeling that he too now firmly believed.

"And your mother there at Vargamäe – does she believe?"

"Firmly as well," said Indrek.

"And your siblings – you do have brothers and sisters – how do they believe?"

"The same."

"And your relatives, neighbours and friends, do they also suppose they believe?"

"No, they also firmly believe."

"So you're the only one to suppose you believe, and all the others firmly believe," concluded the headmaster triumphantly. "But at Vargamäe, you did firmly believe, didn't you?"

"I did."

"Did you hear that!" cried the headmaster. "At Vargamäe he believed, but as soon as he comes to Mr Maurus's honest house, he no longer believes! In town he doesn't believe, because his father gave him a little money and sent him to Mr Maurus to study Latin!" And he came right up to Indrek's nose his unfocused eyes gazing at him over his spectacles, shook his grey head and said: "Aren't you ashamed in front

16 *Vargamäe* means "Thieves' Hill", as is explained in Volume One.

of your honest parents, your siblings and your whole family for not believing, when they all believe firmly?"

And Indrek did feel that he was being overcome by something like shame.

"And tell me now, can this young man be in possession of all his senses if he's enticing you away from the faith of your parents and siblings and from God and thereby making you an orphan? Can he or can't he?"

"He cannot," replied Indrek solely to get out of his current predicament.

"At last!" cried the headmaster, relieved. "Therefore keep away from people who are unable to reason. That gentleman upstairs has been studying for ages, but he will get nowhere, because he has no common sense. He prattles on about the creation of the world and God, as if he wanted to start creating a new world himself or as if he could reach God by acting like a doctor or a lawyer. But God has no need of a lawyer like that, he handles his own cases by himself, or through those who definitely believe."

Timusk also had to receive his due, because when Indrek went, on the headmaster's orders, to return the book he had taken to read, pleading lack of time, Timusk admonished him: "I thought you were old enough to realise – these are secret things. You understand? These are things that need to be heard between the words and read between the lines. Still, it's not your fault," he concluded.

Nonetheless Indrek felt guilty in front of Timusk, and it was embarrassing and shameful to look into his calm eyes. Luckily Timusk was leaving afterwards for the Christmas holidays – for St. Petersburg, they said – and thus Indrek was released from his guilt and shame. With that, he put aside the problems of the world and God for the time being. Years were to pass before they rekindled themselves.

"That's right," said the headmaster, and the door closed behind Timusk. "If someone wants to corrupt others, why does he have to do it in Mr Maurus's honest establishment?

Let him go and do it somewhere else. Let him corrupt the Russians if he wants, but I and my school have every intention of serving Jehovah."

Chapter 8

Soon after Timusk had left, two new members of staff members were taken on; one was Russian and the other Polish. They too moved into the schoolhouse and had to eat at the same table as the pupils. The Russian, Slopashev, was big and strong and spoke in a drone as if from the end of a tunnel. His legs were short and delicate compared with his plump body and he pattered along when he walked, as if he couldn't endure longer steps. Mr Slopashev always wore his hat a little askew and pulled down over his eyes, or else tilted back but never straight. Mr Slopashev, you see, did not like the golden mean in hat-wearing or in anything else – not even eating and drinking. And these were his predilections.

But his companion and later inseparable friend, Voitinski, loved rectitude, at least when it came to headgear. Every time he put on his velvet-trimmed teacher's cap, he would somehow measure it from his forehead with his palm, so that the cap was correctly placed on his head in the prescribed way. No excesses to the right or left, to the front or back. His steps, too, were short, but not on account of a heavy body, for Voitinski's body was like a knitting needle. It was down to his weak legs, which were always positioned with the knees together, as if tending to shiver in his wide trousers. His face was wrinkled and thin like a goat's hoof-print, his mouth was pale and slack like an old man's, and sad dull eyes looked out from behind his spectacles. In order to make an impression, he initially wore a teacher's coat with a velvet collar, adorned with a university emblem, but this was soon replaced by a heavy brown jacket, because Mr Voitinski was terribly afraid of the cold. Of average build, but looking taller because of his thinness, he strongly resembled a magpie when he stooped forward and that became his nickname for as long as he was there. His tremulous and chirruping voice was also more reminiscent of a bird than a man.

Mr Slopashev was given several names, but none suited him better than Bruin, the old nickname for a bear. That was what he had become. He himself was Bruin, and his room was the Bear's Den. He got Ollino's room, and Ollino moved into Koovi's, who moved up to Timusk's room. Voitinski's place was supposed to be down in the big room, from where one pupil was shifted up to Siberia, to free up the bed for the new teacher.

Placing two foreigners as teachers directly among the pupils was, the headmaster supposed, educationally important. It was an order from above that the pupils should speak Russian among themselves, and as Mr Maurus himself said, what kind of a first-class educational establishment would it be if the pupils were to speak in their mother-tongue to each other? One could also speak German, though not professionally of course, but otherwise it was acceptable because the headmaster spoke German whenever possible.

But, as became clear later, the newcomers were not at all concerned about which language their pupils spoke in. They had their own particular interests: they loved going for walks together, one with his stomach out in front, the other with his stooped back sticking out behind him. And they always came home in a better mood, which got even better after they'd been chatting in Slopashev's room for a while.

One day, when Mr Voitinski was coming away from Slopashev, his mood was so exalted that he was bursting into song. "Lalallallaa!" he sang every now and then as he walked across the big room, as if tuning up with some invisible choir. Soon he started chatting to the boys about himself and the Poles, assuring them that even Slopashev had Polish blood coursing in his veins, and that half the Russians were not Russians but Poles.

"They are the defectors and informers, because we are a conquered people, an enslaved people," he explained, desperately smacking his lips together and looking fearfully around him. "One mustn't talk about it," he said. "You Estonians mustn't talk about it either, about being enslaved. But it's easier for you than for us Poles, as there's no real problem given that you don't have a language or a culture. But think of our language and culture! The first in Europe, the first in the world!" He smacked his lips again, as if getting a taste of the primacy of that culture. "You didn't have anything, but now you're getting something, because the Russian language and culture do amount to something. As for your own language, that isn't a language! I listen to you and, believe it or not, it's just like being in a Jewish synagogue. A few decades ago I was taken to one by a young lady who was more beautiful than all the women in the world. Now there are no girls like that to be found – anywhere! But there were then, and so I went into the synagogue, for why else would I have gone there? She was above me, and I was below. And when she looked down on me from above, I repeated her name – Lea, Lea, Lea…"

"Mr Voitinski, are you a bachelor?" asked von Elbe, a German from Riga, who had small white hands and such long fingers that people had started calling him Pickpocket, which was insulting both to him and to Mr Maurus' establishment, which gave shelter to all sorts of layabouts, but never a pickpocket.

"How so?" cried Voitinski, as if offended. "Who told you I'm a bachelor?"

"Well, why did you go with that Jewish girl to the synagogue?" asked von Elbe.

"That's just it, that's just it," repeated Voitinski, smacking his lips as if there were a bad taste. "It started with Lea, only with her. After that the woman left me. She was in love, and that's why she left. Do you know who I am? Pan! Pa-an!" He stretched out that word and put a sort of sharp edge on the "n". "Pan! Panna! How does that sound? But you don't understand that, because you don't have any culture."

"Are you saying that I don't have one either?" asked von Elbe, putting his little white hand onto the table in front of the older man, as if it were proof of his culture.

"You're a German, aren't you?" asked Voitinski. "Of course you have! I've been to Vienna. Strauss and Offenbach! Oh, he came in person, Strauss I mean, violin in hand like this, you see?"

Mr Voitinski rose from his chair, raised his bony yellowed hands and moved his feeble legs, trying to show how Strauss had appeared on stage and how he had played. His weak voice sang some sort of waltz. The boys stood around him in a semicircle, watching, listening and laughing.

"You're laughing," said Voitinski and sat down again. "But if you'd heard it yourselves, you wouldn't have laughed. You would have only danced, because everybody danced. Of course I make you laugh, because a man who's in love is easy to ridicule. Do you understand, dear children? And you really are dear to me, and I don't have children of my own. But that's not my fault – my wife didn't want them, because she was young and loved to dance. How can you dance when you've got a child coming? So then, dear children, remember my words: love whoever you love, but don't love a Jew, because a Jew has hot blood. They have the blood of Jehovah and his prophets, do you hear? Would I be here if Lea didn't have Jehovah's blood? Ah, I remember so clearly that last summer in the Caucasus. Do you know where the Caucasus is? Mountains, mountains right up to the sky, and eternal snow in the sky, that's what the Caucasus is like. Elbruz and Kazbek! And there a person was like a tiny little grasshopper lost in the valley or on a mountain slope or riverbank. The river forever foaming, gurgling, rumbling! There my wife and I spent our last summer together. By a lake, quite alone, just the two of us, husband and wife. And she took her clothes off, you understand – she was naked, my wife I mean. She was naked and wanted to go for a swim. The sun was warm, but the water was cold, ice-cold like the snow up in the mountain. My wife loved that cold when the sun was warm. I didn't, I sat and watched. It strengthens you, said my wife, and it cools you down. She put one foot in, she put in just her big toe, and shrieked. She put in another toe and shrieked again. Have you children ever heard a young woman screaming like that as the sun warms her? And far away the mountains, the mountains! Somewhere a bird called back to her. 'Did you hear? A bird is answering, but you're silent!' said my wife reproachfully. Yet she hadn't anything to reproach me for, because I was just sitting and thinking. But it was my thinking she reproached me for, because no man is allowed to think when a woman is naked – no woman can forgive a man for that. She won't! And my wife didn't either, because from that moment on, she started wearing make-up and putting on fine clothes up until she left, and even today. The last time I saw her, she asked me: 'Are you happy now? Can you now think and snuffle to your heart's desire?' But I wasn't snuffling at that time; that came later. Of course, I could have taken her to the police, to court, but taking my wife to the police would be like catching a fox with fetters – it would bite your leg, your own leg, for God's sake! That's the story of my wife, dear children."

"But what about Lea? What happened to her?" asked von Elbe.

"What Lea?" exclaimed Voitinski, uncomprehending.

"You were talking about her just now."

"Ih, ih, ih, ih, ih," Voitinski giggled until he started choking. "You're still so green! Lea was my wife. Or did you think she was someone else? That I, a man of forty, had a wife of twenty? But you're still children – what would you know about women and love? Women, you know…" Voitinski smacked his toothless gums, so that the few grey hairs on his chin twitched – "love, you'll appreciate, you'll know women only when they're no longer around. Only then! Otherwise a man cannot appreciate them. When he no longer has them – that's when and only then! But I tell you, children, believe whoever you want, yes, it doesn't matter who…"

Voitinski stopped and smacked his lips, as if tasting something unpleasant. "But it's better if I don't tell you anything, for what would I say to you anyway?"

"Say it, Mr Voitinski, tell us!" begged the boys.

"No, no, children shouldn't be made wise before their time," replied Voitinski; "wisdom has never made anyone any happier. I was smart, I was the best mathematician, with a gold medal at high school, another one at university, offered professorships, invited for trips abroad. Commendations, stipends, ribbons – from counts, princes and grand dukes. With one of them I travelled to Berlin, Paris and Vienna. And now? Where am I now? Where did it get me? To a country without a language or a culture! Like a Jewish synagogue!"

That was the story of Mr Voitinski's life in his own words, when he was in "the right mood".

All this Indrek had to hear and see countless times, because he had been moved down from Siberia to the big room because of the changes, and ended up in the same place as Mr Voitinski. The change was due to the fact that fees had only been paid up till Christmas, and there was no chance of getting any more money. Instead of the promised larger sum, Maie the clerk sent only five roubles, and even that with "a bleeding heart", as she described it, because if her husband got to hear of it – as he surely would – he would beat her black and blue.

So one fine day, the headmaster invited Indrek to his office and said: "The new term is well advanced now, but you haven't brought me any money. Where's the money?"

"I don't have any," said Indrek.

"When will you get it?"

"Someone promised to send it, but now they're not going to," explained Indrek.

"If they'd given, and you'd taken it straightaway and

96

brought it to Mr Maurus, he would have entered it in the book. Money always straightaway, anything else can take time. Is this someone a relative or an acquaintance, a man or a woman?"

"A woman," answered Indrek.

"What?" cried the headmaster. "A woman promised you money, and on that promise you come to Mr Maurus' school? Now tell me, what is Mr Maurus to do with a woman's promise? Since when has a woman's promise to pay been reliable? From a woman you must always take everything straightaway, otherwise you're left with nothing, because women are always changing their minds. A woman always promises for that occasion, because next time she'll want to promise something else. And you end up with no money at all?"

"She sent five roubles," said Indrek at length, though he had been planning to keep that a secret.

"What? You have five roubles in your pocket, and you say you don't have money!" cried the headmaster, and Indrek could not understand whether he was being serious or joking. And when Indrek handed him his five-rouble note, he crumpled it in his hand and put his hand in his trouser pocket. Then he turned toward the window, peered out over his glasses and said as if to himself: "*Warten Sie.* Yes, women can't be trusted. You have to take from them immediately, otherwise you go without... Is this woman old or young?" The headmaster turned suddenly to Indrek, who told him Maie's age.

"So she is old then!" cried the headmaster. "And we're a couple of fools who believed an old woman! Never believe an old woman – never. If she were a few years older, she wouldn't even have sent us these five roubles. At least we have that. And to make sure, we'll enter it in the ledger right away. A ledger isn't a woman; it doesn't lie. Put the truth in it, and treat it like gold later. And what is this woman's name? Maie? Well, we'll enter that in the ledger too. Five roubles received from Maie, and that's the whole truth."

The headmaster talked as he wrote. And when he had shown Indrek that Maie's five roubles really were entered, he continued: "Now then, let's think whether Mr Maurus should close his school, or whether you'll be leaving it, because Mr Maurus should close his school if every pupil only brings him five roubles. Maurus doesn't have money, he doesn't have anything. Even this building is not his own, it's bequeathed from mother to daughter. And Mr Maurus isn't her guardian, either. You understand? He isn't even the guardian of his own child. See! That's female economics for you. The daughter is rich, but the father is poor, and paying rent to her. So he's in debt! Of course, the daughter wouldn't leave her own father and the boys in the lurch, because she's young with a young heart, but her aunt is old. That's why we have to put up with women: Mr Maurus with his, you with yours. But why doesn't your father pay the fees?" the headmaster suddenly inquired.

"Father doesn't have any money," replied Indrek.

"How come he doesn't?" countered the headmaster. "In the book it says: Father has large farm."

"But it doesn't bring anything in," explained Indrek.

"What's this – a large farm that doesn't bring anything in?"

"Poor harvests," lamented Indrek. "And my older sisters got married..."

"Those women again," interjected the headmaster. "They're everywhere."

"My elder brother had to do his military service, I came here, and at home there are only my old father and mother while my brothers and sisters are still small children," continued Indrek.

"That's a different matter," agreed the headmaster as he reopened the ledger and muttered, "*Warten Sie, warten Sie.*" And he noted in the book: "Daughters married, son on military service, siblings young."

"How many sisters got married?" he asked.

"Two," replied Indrek.

"Of course, if two daughters got married. Well, of course,"

agreed the headmaster. "The daughters are taken away from the farm, the sons are taken in; for who would want a wife if they didn't get something with it? In payment, that is. So there's no hope from home?"

"Not at the moment," said Indrek, "but if I could somehow get through till summer, then I would get myself a job." His heart was trembling, as if his whole life were in the balance.

"How would you earn it?" asked the headmaster.

"I'd go back to working as a clerk; the boss has invited me back."

"Yes, yes, to the clerk's office," intoned the headmaster, as if this news was no consolation at all. "Summer is still far away, and there will be plenty of expenses before then – many expenses. But how would it be if you helped me a little, like Kopfschneider or one of the others? What if you took Kopfschneider's place for a bit? But then you'll have to have light feet and be a light sleeper, because otherwise you won't hear the bell ring at night. There aren't so many keys to Mr Maurus' house that all the boys and masters can get in by themselves when they come at night. Where would I put all those keys and how many would get lost? The whole town would soon be full of keys to Mr Maurus' house. You don't have slippers? Of course not, what would you do with them in the country! All the better: leave your socks on at night, then it's a bit warmer when you go to open the door, as it's really cold in the hall; they bring the snow inside on their feet. And when you've turned the lock in the door, then always check that it's properly bolted. Always check afterwards! And then, back to your place and straight off to sleep, otherwise you won't get enough rest before the next one turns up. You'll always have to get up immediately as soon as the bell rings again. So then we won't need that Latvian, that Kopfschneider, anymore; we can get rid of him. He's been here for three years already, but he's not making any progress; it's best that he goes somewhere more suitable. And let's manage on our own without the Latvian; that's so much better. On our own! There'll still be plenty of others left here anyway, so we'll let Kopfschneider go."

"Would I still get classes?" asked Indrek.

"But of course, plenty of classes; what would you do without classes?" replied the headmaster. "Only sometimes, when there's a real emergency, when something's badly needed, you might have some errand and then you might not attend them. And sometimes you'll have to be down in the big room, when there's no one else, because that room can't be left empty, as someone could turn up at any time. They might ask for Mr Maurus, and if I'm not there, you'll be in my place, so you receive them and talk to them. But if the one-eyed one comes, or the pock-marked one, then Mr Maurus is never at home, do you understand? Simply isn't at home, and that's that. And the pock-marked one – he's fat, slant-eyed and always wheezing with his thick nose, so you'll recognize him as soon as you see him – he only wants my money. They're both crazy fellows who just want some of Mr Maurus's money. So now you know what to do with those two – I'm not at home, and that's that. If they want to wait, give them a chair downstairs and let me know on the quiet. But if, at the same time as one of them is waiting, someone else comes with the intention of paying Mr Maurus – you can always see straightaway if someone's bringing money – yes, if they come with money – it rarely happens, of course, but still it might happen and that's why I'm telling you this – well in that case of someone who's got money on them, send them straight up. Otherwise the one-eyed one will see – and remember, it makes no odds that he has one eye, for he can see better with one than some people can with two – so, if he's watching, ask the money-bringer to wait: please sit down! And again, get a message to me that there could be someone willing to cough up, and then Mr Maurus will know what to do. But actually you could also send them up and you tell the one-eyed one that they've gone to see Mrs Malmberg. Or that they had business with the young lady: hats, dresses and stuff like that.

You could say that. Now you know: those two are the most dangerous ones. If you need to, ask Mr Ollino, but always ask so that the one-eyed one hears it. Ask like this: 'Is Mr Maurus at home?' and then Ollino will know how to answer, if he sees the pock-marked one or the one-eyed one. So that's it, you're coming downstairs to take Kopfschneider's place, and Mr Maurus will have to send him packing."

"If Kopfschneider has to go for my sake, it's better that I go," said Indrek.

"No, no, not you!" exclaimed the headmaster. "The Latvian has to go, because he doesn't know how to talk to those two. We have to know how to deal with them. You, on the other hand, have such an honest face and honest eyes; they'll believe you, they'll believe you on several occasions and that way we'll soon be rid of them. They'll go away when you say that Mr Maurus isn't here. But they don't believe the Latvian, not any longer; the Latvian has turned himself into a liar. This is what you'll do when you have to say that Mr Maurus isn't at home, when he actually is, then explain that Mrs Malmberg said that he isn't. Or still better, that the young lady said this. That way you're free of guilt and they'll still believe you, they'll believe you and go, because a man always goes when he believes: he takes up his bed and walks. Sometimes when things go completely mad and they both come together and sit, you could run to the bridge and wait there, because Mr Maurus always comes over the bridge. But don't look over the edge, or you'll be dicing with death and thinking maybe that you want to throw yourself in. Of course, you can do it a couple of times, because every ordinary honest person is allowed to look into the water a couple of times. Nobody can forbid that. And when Mr Maurus comes, you must tell him immediately and not let him go past. And then he'll know which door to go through. So that's all clear. *Warten Sie, warten Sie!* Yes, the Latvian has to go now. Why keep him here, when he doesn't pay any money? Mr Maurus isn't running a Latvian school but a pure Estonian school. That's why the Germans and Russians won't put up with Mr Maurus. They can't stand an Estonian, they don't like him. Nobody likes an Estonian, not even an Estonian does. Russians like Russians, Germans like Germans, but Estonians don't like Estonians, they like Russians and Germans – that's Estonians for you. But Estonians should like Estonians, as Mr Maurus does. A foreigner will bring in money, but Mr Maurus won't like him, not at all. Foreigners are here for money. Either they're lazy or they've been thrown out of another school, so where do they go? They come to Mr Maurus and bring money from far away. But they're cheats and liars, teaching our boys to cheat Mr Maurus and lie to him, because an Estonian loves to study. Yes, an Estonian really does study! So the Latvian leaves, and Estonians take over. And since we two Estonian men are taking over, the Latvian has to go. But for today, you'll go upstairs to sleep – just for today."

Chapter 9

Indrek finally was able to get away, after being called back several times from the doorway and even from halfway down the stairs, as the headmaster kept thinking of things which he had to say immediately.

Instead of being a full-time pupil, Indrek became something ill-defined: a pupil but occasionally also a servant, errand-boy, assistant cook and doorkeeper. He came down from Siberia to the big room along with his trunk, which he placed behind the curtain against the wall. Kopfschneider had to give up the space to him and leave for good. Whether he blamed Indrek for this he never did find out, but just as Kopfschneider had once helped him to carry in his box, he now helped to escort Kopfschneider to the coach. As Kopfschneider clambered in, it seemed to Indrek that he did it with a very heavy heart, almost with tears in his eyes. His mouth was moving but no voice could be heard, which was something Indrek had never seen before.

Indrek's bed was right opposite Mr Voitinski's, both on the ground floor between the columns. Vainukägu and Sikk also had their beds there. Vainukägu was a pleasant boy who was tall, pale and fresh-faced, with a parting over his left eye. This was forbidden as it was considered vain and affected, because a "decent and honest" schoolboy was supposed to have either a completely shaven head or his hair cut so short that it stands up. His shirt was of bluish-black homespun cloth with matching trousers, which he went to iron in the washroom at night to get a sharp crease. But the crease had a strange quirk, it never stayed in its place on the front of the trousers but shifted to the side-seam, as if the latter were inherently more important. Therefore Vainukägu always had to keep his hands in his trouser pockets, to keep things aligned between the crease and the seam. These were the oddities of Vainukägu's trousers. Generally this worked quite well, but things got more complicated on more formal and ceremonial occasions, for how can you stand with your hands in your pockets if you want to read aloud from the New Testament or sing from the songbook! And Vainukägu did want to do that, especially on Saturday evenings, because his most ardent wish, shared by his parents, was to become a pastor or at least a parish clerk. That's what had brought him here. At home his father had read Mr Maurus's advertisement in the newspaper, which claimed that his first-class institution provided training for every vocation, which would obviously include that of a parish clerk, and so he had brought the boy here to sing and play music to a congregation. Vainukägu would practise his singing on Saturday evenings.

Sikk, whose bunk was above Mr Voitinski's, was a man of a slightly different breed. He had soft white hair and exceptionally delicate voice for his plump build, so they started calling him Rose. He placed more emphasis on his boots than his trousers. He carefully polished the heels of his boots until they were shiny; even between lessons he would go downstairs behind the curtain to brush them. People would say, "Rose is polishing his trotters", and went to great lengths to smear them, so there would be another polishing session to laugh at. But smudging Sikk's "trotters" could cost them dear, because what Rose prized even above shiny heels was strength, and you can't argue with a strong man. In gymnastics he was mainly interested in weightlifting with hands and feet, standing, crouching and lying. He was always exercising his muscles – in class, in the bedroom, in the corridor and outdoors: he would lift chairs, tables and people, do physical exercises on the floor, on chairs, on desks, on beds, on rungs, in fact anything you could lift, hang from or balance. You could often see him going past a room with one arm bent and hitting his muscles with the fist of his other arm. Or he would rip his own shirt open and pummel his chest muscles with both fists, in the hope of making them stronger and more resilient. "Sikk is hammering himself again," people would comment. He was always putting two chairs or other objects together at a distance, and then doing press-ups with his hands on one and his feet on the other. Sikk was always "straining himself", as people used to joke, even when Vainukägu was reading loudly from the New Testament or singing from the songbook.

These were Indrek's close neighbours. In the neighbouring rooms there were the most successful and distinguished pupils – the pride and joy of the whole establishment. There was the ethnic German from Bessarabia called Müller, who was small, skinny and pale with brown eyes, blond hair and a grey shirt. There was nothing special about him, but he could whinny like a horse, and so loudly that the whole house was amazed at his skill and power. Such a skinny body and such a loud and natural voice!

Sleeping below Müller was the Estonian Vutt, a mischievous scoundrel, fifteen or sixteen years old, already a veteran of several schools. No one would have paid any special attention to him, since there were plenty of layabouts like him at the school, were it not for his strange and unique habit of positioning himself standing or sitting next to some bigger or stronger boy, carefully taking his left hand, reaching for the little finger of the left hand – specifically the left – and picking at its nail, while at the same time putting the tip of his tongue between his lower lip and his teeth, and moving it around slowly.

Also sleeping in the same room was Laane, a strong country boy with a bull's head and a low forehead, with a short, thick neck, almost disappearing into his high shoulders. Anyone could prod him without him reacting, because he would always say to the other person, "What are you hitting me for" and let them go unpunished. He would only wave his long arms about, as if they had been taken from some gorilla and put on his own broad hunched shoulders. Equally alien, were his shortish legs, with crooked knees, the toes facing inward. He scuttled about on tiptoe, and with each step, one foot seemed to trample the other foot's toes. His almost flaxen-blue slanted eyes peered from under bushy eyebrows, always cast to the ground as he walked, and his broad, angular, square-jawed and big-mouthed face was constantly in a state of profound concentration. Only rarely did he cast his gaze elsewhere, and then always furtively, shamefully or secretively. Usually Laane had some book in his hand, one whose content he hadn't yet mastered. And since he was only in third grade, he especially loved the set of algebra exercises, because that subject only began in fourth grade. He was enchanted by everything that was incomprehensible, because the incomprehensible had its secrets, which instilled awe and almost terror. Of languages, he was most in awe of Latin. At the very first opportunity he asked Indrek: "Do you know what the Latin for 'thief' is?"

"Why?" replied Indrek, uncomprehending.

"You mean you don't know yet," smiled Laane with sly diffidence. "But I know," he added proudly, and was about to add something more, but he was interrupted by Vutt, who asked quite innocently: "And what's the word for 'louse' in Latin?"

"What do you mean?" exclaimed Laane in a distressed voice, and broke off the conversation.

"You mean you don't know," said Vutt. "But you should know that, because the old Gorilla teaches that to his boys in all languages, directly."

"Don't curse," said Laane.

"How am I cursing?" complained Vutt; "a stuffed gorilla, that's what you are. It would be a different matter if I'd said Spiritualist – that's your nickname."

"Listen, you're looking for a punch in the face," Laane threatened.

"I wouldn't do that; it'll get others involved," replied Vutt, who explained to Indrek after Laane had gone: "Take note: if you come across a grey louse, you'll know it's from him. You mustn't kill them, because they're like cockroaches: as soon as you start to kill them or burn them, they climb onto you even more savagely. A swarm of them! Just put them nicely and delicately back on their host, then they won't come back and they won't climb up your body."

Indrek would later learn from his own body – and no matter what you do, they keep on crawling and they weren't only coming from Gorilla; Magpie was also breeding them. On some people they were bigger and darker and on others smaller and paler, more or less the colour of flax stalks.

"Due to his filthiness," they said about the first one.

"Due to his struggles," they thought about the second.

Above Laane slept the Russian Tatar Bashkirtsev from Kazan – a small man with yellow skin and hair like soot. A great smoker who inhaled deeply, which was why his chest was wheezier than old Voitinski's. He took morphine, and talked whenever he could about the night haunts of his home town, an inexhaustible source of obscene tales, so much so that it seemed he made up new ones every day. He would stand or sit somewhere in a dark corner, a greasy lustre in his eyes, with the boys swarming around him – for Bashkirtsev was never short of an audience.

In the next spacious room lived Von Elbe from Riga, Count Mannheim from St. Petersburg, Prince Bebutov from Tbilisi, Pan Chodkiewicz from Warsaw and the Englishman, King, the son of a factory-owner in Moscow. They were all important men, so important that they slept only on the *bel étage*. For how could you put a count above a prince, or a prince above a count? Even a Polish pan couldn't be put above or below someone else. Perhaps the most tolerant might have been the Englishman, because he was always so polite and modest that he could be expected to put up with anything. Similarly the count might have put up with most things, because he was living in a first-rate educational establishment like some bird in a totally alien environment. How much and what he had studied before, no one could ascertain, but at the school the only thing that seemed to interest him was his balalaika. He was constantly strumming it and bent over it with one leg on the other knee. "He plays like the devil," the boys would say, as they gathered around him; even Bashkirtsev would come away from his lurid stories to listen to the balalaika. Somehow Indrek was always overcome with sadness when he heard the count playing or saw his brown eyes, which were so beautiful to look at. For a long time he'd believed that everyone came to listen to the count because he had such beautiful eyes and played the balalaika so well, but all this wouldn't have preserved the count's name and memory after his departure (for he didn't stay here long) if he hadn't taught them one particular song in which the solo voice in the first half was intended to be sad and dreamy and the chorus in the second part downright mournful. The words went like this:

A priest once had a little dog
That he dearly loved.
When doggie chewed a piece of fat,
The priest put him to sleep.
Chorus: He buried him below the ground,
On the tomb it read,
A priest once had a little dog [and so forth]

This song caught on with everyone from the start, regardless of nationality. Even Mr Slopashev could be occasionally heard growling it. But Voitinski smacked his yellowed chops on hearing it and repeated to himself, "Oh the fools! Oh the scatterbrains! Oh the silly fools!"

That was what he used to say, so they wouldn't allow him to sing along. But he could laugh as he heard them sing, and that he did. Laugh and curse! Yet no one paid the slightest attention to his cursing, because the endless little song was still being sung when Voitinski's ears were irreversibly deafened and his mouth filled with earth. Possibly the song outlived even the count who brought it, because art endures while life's a fleeting moment. But we cannot say, for no more was known of the count after he left than had been known before he came.

Next to Voitinski was the Englishman King, who never sang about the priest's beloved dog. But that was hardly strange, because he never sang at all. Mother Nature had provided him with a slender, supple and almost girlish body and such a delicate and mellifluous voice that his every word sounded like music. So why would he sing, when his speech could fill the day with music all by itself? But the count's balalaika did appeal to the Englishman. He was so happy when it was played that he put something colourful on his head, wrapped himself in something loose and billowy, and started to dance.

"The beautiful Helena is dancing," Von Elbe would say, but then Pan Chodkiewicz would press his white chin into his chest and say something in his monotonous voice that was supposed to diminish the import of Von Elbe's words. That was the way with him. No matter what anyone said in words of praise, he always had an expression that seemed to say: Not bad, but come to us in Warsaw, then you'll really see something! He always walked around with his hands in his trouser pockets, not even taking them out as he sat at his desk in class. The whole servant class was in his terms "the people", while others were "gentlefolk". He had classed Indrek as one of "the plebs" on his second or third day, when he wanted him to fetch him something from the shop. But when Indrek didn't react to his command, he repeated it right to his face, so that there could be no doubt which particular "pleb" he was referring to.

"Who are you calling a pleb?" asked Indrek in a voice trembling with anger.

"What are you then?" the Pole replied haughtily. "You're the same as that Latvian: an errand-boy, a messenger, a servant."

Actually he hadn't completed that last word when Indrek

punched him on the chin which wasn't on his chest at the time. This was followed by a fist-fight which ended indecisively, for the others broke them up before that. The Pole wanted to complain to the headmaster, but he wasn't allowed to.

"It's a comradely thing – comrades themselves will sort it out," said Prince Bebutov.

"He's not my comrade," said Chodkiewicz, referring to Indrek.

"Why isn't he?" responded the prince. "If you have a fist-fight with him, he then becomes your comrade."

"That's right," said the count, "if you accepted his challenge, then he's a comrade; otherwise you should have gone straight to the headmaster, as is right and proper."

It took quite a while before the pan accepted the logic of this and offered Indrek his hand.

"If you want, I'll go and fetch what you need now," said Indrek.

"Don't be so silly!" interjected Sikk in Estonian, flexing the muscles on his arm.

Indrek was silly anyway, and he did go. The only thing that troubled him was that he didn't have his brother Andres' strength and fists. He'd already had a couple of scraps that needed his fists and muscles, but until that day he hadn't given it a thought.

The headmaster found out about this fight immediately, and he told Indrek: "It's good that you gave him what for. Don't forget that you're my deputy here. We have a pure Estonian school here, so what right does a Pole have to say what he wants? However you shouldn't start hitting everyone like that, or you'll end up emptying the school. Word will get around that Mr Maurus has a tall, strong bloke downstairs who does nothing but fight. He fought with Tigapuu, he fought with Chodkiewicz and now we don't know whose turn it will be next. But what could you have against a Pole? A German – well, that's a different matter – we've been at loggerheads with them for the last seven hundred years. So tell me, what do you have against the Pole?"

"He called me a name," said Indrek.

"Let the Pole say whatever he wants; why would you want to punch him for that? The Russians will beat him up, of course. The Germans beat us up and the Russians beat up the Poles, but if we start bashing each other up, what are the German and Russian supposed to do?"

Such was the headmaster's opinion, and such were the people in whose proximity Indrek now had to live. They were mostly privileged people, if not formally, then at least in practice, and therefore they caused a fuss, day and night.

During the first couple of weeks in his new post, Indrek went almost entirely without sleep, because he was frightened that he wouldn't hear the bell if he fell asleep. Or if he did sleep, he might hear the doorbell when in fact it was all quiet outside except for the sounds of the cold cracking the ice and footsteps crunching in the snow.

Sleep was also prevented by the fun being had by Slopashev and Voitinski, which was always lively. Their chummy chatter and laughter often turned to song: Slopashev would growl like a bear and Voitinski would chirrup like a little bird. On the other side of the door, the boys were caterwauling while the count was playing his balalaika, Vainukägu was singing "Take now the Lord", Chodkiewicz was pressing his chin into his chest and grunting, and Sikk was beating out a drum roll with a broom handle on the chalked floor. Müller was whinnying and others roaring along in chorus. This was all possible because the headmaster was hardly ever at home in the evenings and even Ollino was often absent. Once, when Slopashev was annoyed about the noise, he came to silence the boys. But before the door was opened they all fled, with only Indrek and Elbe remaining at the table.

"Who was shouting here? What's all the noise for?" demanded Slopashev.

"Where? When?" responded Elbe, surprised.

"Right here, outside the door of my room of course!" said Slopashev.

"We were here all the time, reading, but we haven't heard anything," said Elbe. "Maybe you're hearing things, Mr Teacher, sir."

"Ivan Vassilievich, Ivan Vassilievich!" Slopashev called to his companion, and when he appeared at the door, he told him, "You'll never believe what they're saying. They say that no one was shouting here. But you heard it quite clearly, didn't you?"

"Quite clearly, very clearly, Lord bless us!" creaked Voitinski. "You're lying, gentlemen, you're lying, for God's sake!" he added decorously, for alcohol always made him polite.

"You're lying, for God's sake," Slopashev concurred.

"For God's sake, we're not!" countered Von Elbe. "If you like, I'll cross my heart that we're not. I may be a Lutheran, but if you gentlemen refuse to believe me, then I can still cross myself." And he started to cross himself.

"Alright, we believe you, we believe you!" Voitinski and Slopashev cried out together, "Just leave the holy cross out of it."

The teachers went back to their room and the boys crept to the door to listen.

"Have you ever heard something when there was nothing to hear?" Slopashev asked Voitinski.

"Not so far," he replied.

"But it has happened to me, I swear to God it has. And today too," declared Slopashev.

"Don't believe them, they're lying, Aleksander Matveyich," Voitinski consoled him.

"Do you really think so?" Slopashev hesitated.

"Of course they're lying!" Voitinski assured him.

"Well, then go and get some more," commanded Slopashev. "Is half a pint of vodka enough?"

The boys fled away from the door, and when Voitinski came out, fastening his jacket, raising his collar and taking his cap from the peg, Elbe asked him in the most courteous manner: "Where are you going so late in the evening, Mr Teacher, sir?"

"For a little walk, a stroll in the fresh air, my head's a little groggy after having been indoors all day," replied Voitinski with a serious, almost saintly expression, and he left once Elbe had politely escorted him through the hall.

"I checked: the bottle is in his left-hand pocket," said Elbe when he got back to the room. And he quickly got a bottle of the same kind and filled it with water. Then he stayed and waited for Voitinski, having gone to meet him at the front door, where the two had a long talk about the stroll that had taken place, the weather, the cold, the stars in the sky and sundry other matters. The chat was so absorbing that the two men lingered in the cold ill-lit entrance hall. It was, of course, one of those situations where if one of them stopped, so did the other, and when one wanted to go inside, so did his companion. Inevitably they tended to bump into each other on the way. It's simply ridiculous that people sometimes want to do things together at exactly the same time! Even in the middle of the night, which is quite laughable, and it even made Mr Voitinski laugh, who was at first so serious and almost saintly. But now at last they got inside and Voitinski went to Slopashev's room.

"He's here, just you wait," said Elbe. "He went into the room with a bottle of water! Wait! Listen!"

It didn't take long until something flew with a bang against the door and Mr Slopashev started furiously spluttering.

"The Lord bless us!" cried Voitinski. "What can be the matter, Aleksander Matveyich?"

"This is neat water!" roared Slopashev at the top of his voice. "You've played a rotten trick on me!"

"How come?" squeaked Voitinski. "What joke? Would I joke with you, Aleksander Matveyich?"

"Taste it for yourself!" cried Slopashev.

"Water, it's definitely water," Voitinski confirmed a moment later. "For God's sake, it's water! What's this supposed to mean, Holy Mother of God? They cheated us at the tavern!"

"Did you actually get to the tavern?" asked Slopashev mockingly.

"Where else, Lord bless us!" replied Voitinski. "I saw some friends too, we said hello."

"So what's going on here?" said Slopashev thoughtfully. "First we heard a great commotion, and they said that they knew nothing about it; now you buy vodka at the tavern but when we taste it, it's water."

"Lord, I can't explain it either. I swear to God I that I can't imagine how this happened," said Voitinski as he picked up the bottle to take it back to the tavern. He rattled and clattered as he went through the big room, and Elbe did everything in his power to ease the older man's condition, even accompanying him some of the way along the street, because there was terribly deep snow. And when he got back to the room, he had his old bottle of water with him again.

Soon Voitinski was back, but his laughter could not conceal a degree of anxiety.

"What now? What's supposed to have happened?" exclaimed Elbe, rushing toward him. "You look as if you've seen a ghost, Mr Voitinski! For God's sake, tell me!"

"Miracles have happened before your eyes!" Voitinski replied.

"What!" cried Elbe. "What miracles?"

"It's like the wedding feast at Cana. Christ is reborn. The Antichrist!"

"God bless us," Elbe showed his dismay. "You're telling wicked lies tonight, Mr Voitinski."

The boys came from the other rooms and all pressed around Mr Voitinski.

"I swear to God that it's true," he asserted. "Vodka turned to water and water to vodka."

"Where? When? How?" exclaimed the boys.

"In my pocket, in a bottle, in Aleksander Matveyich's hand," Voitinski became increasingly shrill.

"Holy Mother of God, what a tale, what a night!" exclaimed the boys. "But then you're the Antichrist yourself, Mr Voitinski. How do we live with you under the same roof? We'll definitely have to inform Mr Maurus. We'll have to say: Sorry, Mr Maurus, but it turns out that Mr Voitinski is the Antichrist."

"What! what!" shrieked the old man. "I, the Antichrist?" And then he laughed

"Ivan Vassilievich!" called Slopashev from his room.

"He's calling," said Voitinski anxiously. "Let me through, gentlemen. Let me through."

This time the old man got in with the right bottle, because Elbe's long fingers were not quick enough to swap them.

"You're a fool, Ivan Vassilievich, I tell you that out of sincere friendship," shouted Slopashev to his friend as soon as he opened the door. "It's they who are Antichrists, not us! This whole school is an Antichrist, you'll see, Ivan Vassilievich."

The fact is that as soon as Voitinski drank alcohol, he understood very little of what was being said to him or what was happening around him. That was why the most extraordinary things could happen to him.

There were evenings when people came from more distant rooms, even down from Siberia, to make fun of Slopashev and Voitinski when they were trying to hold one of their jolly meetings late into the night. On one occasion, the fire in the big room went out, so the boys went to bed. But someone crept to Slopashev's door in the darkness and knocked.

"Come in!" Slopashev growled.

No one came in, but a little later another knock could be heard.

"Come in, I said!" Slopashev yelled.

No one appeared.

"Maybe the door is locked, Aleksander Matveyich," Voitinski squealed.

"Try it," instructed Slopashev.

With a great effort Voitinski heaved himself up and

approached the door slowly, groping as he went. But by the time he got to the door, whoever had knocked was long gone.

"There's no one there," said Voitinski, smacking his lips to express his disbelief. "The room's dark, and they're all asleep."

"But there was a knock," countered Slopashev. "You heard it yourself."

"I think I did, yes," tinkled Voitinski. "I swear to God, I thought I heard it."

The gentlemen sat down at the table again and raised their glasses to each other's health. The boys continued their game until Slopashev's patience ran out and he opened the door himself, stepping into the room to look for the ghosts. But at that moment a heavy ball flew out of the darkness and hit his legs, and he fled in terror back into his room.

"Heavens above!" squealed Voitinski from the table. "What is it?"

"Something jumped at my feet," replied Slopashev.

"Just like ghosts," Voitinski was unable to restrain his nervous laughter.

Slopashev took the lamp from the table and went to look in the big room, but he found nothing, because in the meantime the football had been taken away. He went up to the beds, raised the curtain, but everyone was sleeping soundly. Since Slopashev's encounter with the ball, his impatience with all the tricks being played on him and his best friend had turned into rage. He rushed up to the first bed and with a single blow threw whoever was sleeping in it onto the floor. At the same time the swan, which had been spreading its wings under the ceiling like an angel of peace, came down with him in a cloud of dust, for the boy quite naturally sought to grab hold of something, and it happened to be its long neck.

"Son of a bitch!" roared Slopashev, "you've hit your own teacher in the legs with a ball! You've knocked on his door while he's spending a quiet hour chatting with a close friend!"

The second boy he yanked was Sikk, who really was asleep, for he never took part in those pranks. And since his sleepy

116

head couldn't comprehend what was happening to him, he thought the other boys were up to their tricks, and grabbed the first person standing in front of him as hard as he could around the waist. A scuffle broke out. Slopashev was wearing a long wide dressing-gown, while Sikk was in just a shirt, hardly reaching to his knees, for he thought that anyone who slept in their underwear would never grow up to be a real man.

The wrestlers' feet slipped on something soft and they stumbled against the half-open door of Slopashev's room, which slammed shut. Pitch-darkness suddenly prevailed, and all hell was let loose because everyone was shouting at once.

"Pull, Rose!" cried the Estonians in their own language. "Be a man, give it to the Russian! Squeeze him hard! But not so hard that he bursts. If a Russian were to burst, there would be a flood and we would all drown!"

"Light, more light!" Slopashev cried, as if he were trying to joke, and then added: "Ivan Vassilievich, open the door!"

But Voitinski couldn't open the door, because someone on the other side was keeping it shut.

"Lord in heaven above!" squealed Voitinski; "the door won't open! What's wrong, Aleksander Matveyich?"

"A struggle! A struggle not for life, but to the death," wheezed Slopashev.

But before he could finish saying these words a chain reaction was set off, because once again the wrestlers had stumbled into something, fallen against the table and overturned a couple of chairs. From there they headed with a new burst of energy towards a double row of beds and the big wardrobe on which the plaster busts of Goethe and Schiller stood proudly side by side. As their base started to sway, they lost their balance and crashed down from the top of the wardrobe, one straight to the floor, the other onto Slopashev's head, knocking him over. This was followed by a deathly silence. Nobody dared to utter a sound, such was the terrible crash in the darkness. The prince ran out of his room with a lamp, his companions at his heels. Voitinski finally managed to open his door.

A sorry sight confronted the onlookers: Goethe and Schiller were shattered into a thousand pieces and among them lay Slopashev's stout and heavy form. The whole room was full of the feathers and the noble dust of the poor swan. The swan, having been trampled by the wrestlers' feet, was now headless and with broken wings. It was a distressing spectacle to see it lying motionless under the table.

"Oh my Lord!" squealed Voitinski, on seeing Slopashev on the floor and a trouserless Sikk panting in front of him.

The pan and the count rushed up to help Slopashev, and even Sikk helped out. Thus they got the unfortunate man to his feet. Once he had got his breath back, he wanted to rush off to see the headmaster, but Indrek in his shirtsleeves stood in his way and tried to explain that the headmaster wasn't at home, and upstairs he would only disturb the peace of Miss Maurus and Mrs Malmberg. Ollino was also absent, and if he hadn't been, Slopashev wouldn't even have got past him. Only Tigapuu seemed to be in charge, although these rooms weren't under his jurisdiction. He got Jürka to come with a broom, a dustpan and a bucket, and soon all that remained of Goethe and Schiller was a little dust. He also cleared the swan out from under the table and tried to gather up its feathers which had scattered far and wide.

"*Sic transit gloria mundi,*"[17] declared worldly-wise Slopashev as he surveyed this scene and his anger subsided once he could compare his own fate with that of Goethe, Schiller and the swan. But Voitinski continued to vociferate, "I swear to God, this makes no sense at all: I tried to open the door, but the door stayed shut. Then there's a blood-curdling scream and a terrible crash, and when the door finally opens you, Aleksander Matveyich, are lying on the floor motionless.

---

17 *Sic transit gloria mundi*: "Thus passes glory in this world" or per-
    haps "This is how worldly glory ends up" [Latin].

And the whole place full of sawdust and feathers! I swear to God, I cannot understand what's going on."

"It was all the fault of Goethe and Schiller, damn them," explained Slopashev in his room, "otherwise I would have pulverised that boy." And when he had cleared the class-room, he added jokingly, "Just as well it was either Goethe or Schiller, because I would be dead by now if it had been Pushkin or Tolstoy."

"By God," agreed Voitinski, "if it were Pushkin, you'd definitely be dead."

Soon the friends were in a better mood than they had been up till now. This gave no peace to the pupils, because they wanted, come what may, to spoil the teachers' mood. But the old tricks would no longer do, because the teachers no longer reacted to the caterwauling or the knocking. Then it occurred to someone to start trying out who could jump further up the wall of the teachers' room. But when the teachers wouldn't let themselves be drawn out even by this, they started jumping against the door which was made of panels, bang, bang, bang! This activity was so exciting, so utterly gripping, that everyone ended up joining in, even the von, the prince and the pan. Only the count didn't take part in this physical exercise, but sat at the corner of the long table playing his balalaika, as if he wanted to set the beat to which the other would do their jumping. Eventually even Tigapuu forgot that he was the one in charge and started jumping against the door, because he wanted to show the others the proper way to do the jumping. Time after time with ever greater momentum he rushed at the door, until he flew, together with some of the panels, through the door into Slopashev's room. This happened so unexpectedly for everyone that they just looked on in open-mouthed disbelief. The first to give voice to this was Voitinski, "Good God! What's going on now? The door wasn't locked."

"That's right, the door was unlocked," added Slopashev.

At those words, the startled Tigapuu perked up and saw

the way out of his predicament.

"But the door was definitely locked," he said, bounding over to the door, as if wanting to find confirmation of his words there. However, he actually turned the lock before trying to open what remained of the door. "You see, it was locked!" he cried, pretending to outraged.

The boys' mocking faces could be seen through the broken door. The count was still sitting at the end of the table, playing his balalaika.

"What's this?" asked Voitinski in despair. "You didn't lock the door, did you, Aleksander Matveyevich?"

"You came in last, Ivan Vassilievich, so how could I have?" replied Slopashev.

"I don't know who turned the lock, but you see with your own eyes that it's locked," declared Tigapuu.

"But so what if it's locked?" it finally occurred to Slopashev to say. "Can a door be broken for that?"

But Tigapuu answered gravely and assuredly: "Gentlemen, I'm in charge today, because Mr Maurus and Ollino are away from home. The pupils were complaining to me that they can't sleep here, because of the singing and laughter in your room. When I came here…"

"Out of here, you impudent…" roared Slopashev.

"Alright," said Tigapuu menacingly, "but the whole building is under my supervision, and I have to take responsibility. These people are witnesses to what has just happened – the busts, the swan, and the other things. But now I call for peace, otherwise I'll have to take more effective measures."

With those words Tigapuu made to leave the room, without knowing what to do next. Matters took the desired turn at the last moment when Voitinski said, smacking his lips: "Gentlemen, why quarrel? Goethe and Schiller have turned to dust, and so has the door, what else is there to fight about, Mr Tigapuu?"

"I don't like quarrelling," replied Tigapuu, stopping, "but if you gentlemen…"

"Let it go," Slopashev interjected. "Ivan Vassilievich is absolutely right – why quarrel, if everything's in pieces anyway? We'd better discuss what to do with the door."

"That's a minor thing," replied Tigapuu. "I'll repair the door."

And straight away, helped by the others, he put the door back in place, positioning the surviving panels on the outside and securing them with small nails.

"Amazing!" cried the teachers. "Such brilliance. May I ..." said Slopashev, upending the bottles only to find that none of them contained a single drop. "Huh! Empty!" he yelled. "I wanted to offer you a drink, but as you can see, there's none left. Some other time, if you'll allow me, definitely some other time."

So on that occasion Tigapuu's mouth and throat remained unwetted.

"Goethe and Schiller, I'll attend to those myself," Slopashev told Tigapuu. "Tell the others, please, that if Mr Maurus asks, let them answer that I'll do it, no one else, understand? Of course I'll tell Mr Maurus myself what happened. The main thing is: don't talk too much, I'll do the explaining," Slopashev assured him.

"What about the swan?" asked Tigapuu.

"Lord bless us – the swan!" squealed Voitinski, trying to laugh.

"The swan goes together with Goethe and Schiller," replied Slopashev, after a little thought.

"The swan, Goethe and Schiller – you understand?" said Voitinski, licking his lips, as if some ground-breaking idea had just been put before the assembly. But no one found anything particular in it, and therefore they continued with their agenda: Tigapuu sent the boys to bed and Slopashev led the near-demented Voitinski to his room.

That day it seemed that the devil himself had taken hold of everyone and was borne along by four fire-breathing demons. For as soon as Voitinski had gone off to sleep, Vutt woke him to say, "Mr Slopashev is calling you."

"Right away, right away," replied the sleepy old man, as soon as he realized what was going on. And he dragged his brown coat on, drew his boots onto his bare feet and went to the door to knock. But he had to knock hard and long before his sleeping friend heard him.

"Who's there?" roared Slopashev at length.

"It's me, Ivan Vassilievich," squealed Voitinski at the door.

"Ah, it's you!" cried Slopashev. "One moment, one moment! For you the doors of my chamber are always open; for you I'm always awake."

And he let Voitinski in, sat him down at the table, lit the lamp, chatted, finally led him to bed and tucked him warmly in. Then he remarked: "Sleep like a dog in his kennel, Vassilievich, for even a colleague who provides good counsel is a dog in God's presence."

"A dog in God's presence, Aleksander Matveyich," Voitinski echoed his friend.

"So, good night, God's puppy," said Slopashev. "Sleep well!"

"And you too," replied Voitinski, choking with emotion.

"What a couple of old rogues we are," said Slopashev sadly.

"True, true, Aleksander Matveyich," affirmed Voitinski.

"True as true can be," Slopashev reaffirmed. "And I love truth more than anything. I love truth terribly much. I say this for the sake of truth, because it would be sad to live in a world bereft of truth, would it not?"

"It would, I swear to God it would," Voitinski confirmed.

"And if all people loved the truth, God would believe in people just as people believe in God. Would the Devil and hell be of any use to him then? There would be no need for angels either."

"I swear to God there wouldn't!" Voitinski assured him.

"A man would walk arm in arm with God like man and wife, and fig-trees could grow without leaves. For what would a fig-tree do with leaves, if a man was eternal and walked arm in arm with God?" continued Slopashev.

"A man, yes, but not his wife," countered Voitinski.

"Why not," inquired Slopashev, "if a man and his wife are eternal? Think about it: e-ter-nal!"

"That's not enough, it doesn't help," declared Voitinski. "Where there is Woman, there is also the Devil, for woman herself is the Devil."

"If a woman is the devil, then you can't get by without the devil," said Slopashev. "But if she's the devil, why would a man have this eternal life then? No, no, if she's the devil, there's no eternal life, no eternal man. For God hasn't gone so mad that he would fertilize, bear and raise a person only to make him suffer eternally. Does he bless him just to give him into the hands of an eternal devil? No, no! Either a man is eternal, and therefore there's no devil or suffering, or he's mortal and then dies, in which case it isn't possible to suffer eternally. One or the other, but the devil loses out."

But even after this wise counsel there was no peace, for the boys continued their tricks, as if the old devil himself were spurring them on. Peace arrived only when Ollino came home and began his usual rounds. Going through the big room, he heard Voitinski's tinkling voice, pulled the curtain aside and asked: "Not sleeping yet, Mr Voitinski?"

"No, Mr Ollino," he replied.

"Why not?"

"I'm thinking over matters of God's kingdom."

"Not worth the trouble;" declared Ollino, "death will come just the same."

"It will come anyway, by God," agreed Voitinski.

So ended their conversation and Ollino continued into the back room.

Chapter 10

Strangely enough, that night Ollino didn't notice the absence of the swan or its companions, Goethe and Schiller, as if those objects had never been of great importance. The disappearance of the last two he might not have noticed immediately in the morning, but the empty hook in the ceiling did catch his eye, and he asked himself: why was nothing hanging from that hook? And only then did the question occur to him: what's become of the swan? First of all he wanted to find out from Vutt, who just pulled a face and slyly replied with a question of his own: "Only the swan, Mr Ollino?"

Ollino let his eyes travel around the room, and then asked, "Where have Goethe and Schiller gone? What can this mean?"

Vutt had no idea. He simply couldn't understand it. Sikk and Indrek didn't know either. Only from Tigapuu did Ollino find out that he had got Jürka to take them to the rubbish-bin, and it was all Slopashev's work.

"Alright," said Ollino at length, and left things at that. He went upstairs to the headmaster's office. Now the boys had a chance to prepare for more eavesdropping and discussion. They involved Voitinski, the prince, the count and the Pan in the conspiracy – in short anyone who might be asked anything. But all this preparation seemed to be pointless, for Mr Maurus did not act as expected. When he came down, he feigned almost complete indifference to the whole thing. Firstly he called only Tigapuu upstairs and praised him for his actions. And as if shielding himself from the others, while yet in their hearing, he said: "Mr Maurus gave an order long ago to get rid of them, but you know what Mr Ollino is like.

You never get anywhere with him. Yesterday evening, for instance: as soon as Mr Maurus goes out, he isn't at home either. But how can that man go out when Mr Maurus is out? Would you go out if Mr Maurus is out?"

"I was at home keeping order," said Tigapuu gravely and self-importantly.

"You see – you were at home keeping order. Any honest person is at home keeping order when Mr Maurus is out. But Mr Ollino doesn't keep order, and now Goethe and Schiller are in the rubbish-bin. Of course, Goethe and Schiller gathered dust, even when they were alive they did. Just as well it wasn't Heine – he would have gathered even more. Heine was a Jew – that's why the Germans don't like him. He may've been a Jew, but he sang so never mind the dust. A Jew knows how to sing, oh yes, he can! That's why nobody loves him. But we love the Russians, because the Russian Tsar is our Tsar too. God save the Tsar! That's what they sang yesterday with great enthusiasm. Mr Maurus loves Russian enthusiasm, and that's why he goes to the Russian club. But where does Mr Ollino have to go? Is he promoting the Estonian cause? No, but Mr Maurus is promoting the Estonian cause at the Russian club. That's why he doesn't have time to check whether the Germans have been taken off the top of the wardrobe or whether they're still there…"

The headmaster's talk was interrupted by Slopashev, who appeared at the door of his own room – his face unwashed, his hair in disarray, his trousers hanging off his hips, braces hanging almost to the floor, his jacket over his undershirt, his collar up, revealing a bare neck and hairy chest.

"Mr Maurus, forgive me," he said in a quavering voice. "I'm appearing *déshabillé*, because I heard your voice and I wanted a couple of words in private, to avoid certain misunderstandings."

"Mr Slopashev," replied the headmaster coldly and formally, "I have no secrets if you have none. I'm conducting my business openly. Please conduct yours here, if you wish."

"Alright then," replied Slopashev. "Of course you know what I want to talk about – those busts that are no longer on top of the wardrobe."

The headmaster merely bowed respectfully.

"It was my work," said Slopashev, "and I want to take the full blame for it."

"I haven't even given it any thought," replied the headmaster, "for I myself gave an order long ago for them to be removed and replaced by something more contemporary. Only because of the failure to obey my orders did they stay in place. But apparently they didn't do anyone any harm, because we were so used to them that no one even noticed them any longer. Even their loss wasn't noticed, as if those two Germans had never lived."

"But as a Russian I found them jarring, up there on top of the wardrobe," declared Slopashev, in an injured tone. "They offended my pure Russian soul, and do you understand, Mr Maurus, what it means when someone's pure patriotic soul is offended every day? Especially in an institution where, in my opinion, there should have been quite a different atmosphere prevailing for a long time now."

"It does prevail, Mr Slopashev, and it prevailed long before you, and it will still prevail even when you may no longer be here," interjected the headmaster, while Mr Slopashev carried on regardless: "But why then are there these outward signs of an alien spirit, which lead every honest Russian to start off on the wrong path? Why these various Germans, these Castors and Polluxes. Alright, there is a reason for their fame, but what I'm asking is does it have anything to do with us Russians? What do we have to do with some 'Song of the Bell' or *Faust*? What do they say to the pure Russian soul and heart? Do they mention the Volga or the steppes? Is there any mention of reality, as in *Dead Souls* or *The Bronze Horseman*? We demand realism, true Russian realism, because that is our reality, which warms our hearts and makes our souls tremble. Pushkin and Gogol say much more to us than Goethe and Schiller. Am I telling the truth, Mr Maurus?"

"The pure truth, Mr Slopashev, that's precisely my opinion. You heard: orders had already been given to remove those busts from that prominent position, but because of our neglect you encountered them, and you did a praiseworthy job. Of course it could have been done without dust and without any fuss or bother. If you notice something like that another time, something that offends your eyes, please tell me or Mr Ollino; we'll arrange it all without the dust and fuss. But what do you think, Mr Slopashev – what shall we put in place of those mournful Germans? It would be so nice if something could take their place."

"You know what, Mr Maurus," said Slopashev, "I got rid of the Germans, so allow me to sort out their replacements."

"I'm very grateful to you," replied the headmaster with a bow, "but I'd ask you to inform me in time what you've decided and how much it will cost."

"Very good," agreed Slopashev. "I'll definitely notify you and listen to your opinion, because after all it's your room and your establishment."

"But don't forget, Mr Slopashev, that though it's my establishment, it's under the protection of the benevolent Russian eagle," said the headmaster.

"Quite right!" affirmed Slopashev. "That's very handsome of you, Mr Maurus."

"The Estonian people and I know how indebted we are," explained the headmaster, "which is to the honour of Russia in all its strength and greatness, and to the benefit of the small Estonian nation. That's my watchword, my goal in life."

"You'll triumph under that banner," said Slopashev solemnly, as if the headmaster's words had moved him and as if, in speaking, he had completely forgotten the origin of the whole affair. Thus the great uproar and the considerable collision of world-views ended in a conciliatory spirit and complete harmony.

But those who knew the whole story were not satisfied with Slopashev's stance in closing the issue for the time being. The first to express his view was the prince.

"Comrades," he said, "how do you like that drunken patriotism of Slopashev's?"

"Only Russians act like that," opined the Pan, as if he had had that opinion in reserve for ages.

"And did you hear what he said about Goethe and Schiller?" remarked Elbe.

"Yes, comparing them with Gogol and Pushkin," noted the Pan, "rather than talking of Mickiewicz and Sienkiewicz."

The count didn't say anything, but merely took up his balalaika and played to himself, starting on the song "A priest once had a dog". Soon the others were joining in. But Mr Ollino wasn't going to sing, and as he walked back and forth across the room, his hands in his trouser pockets and a burned-out fag-end in his mouth, he muttered through his teeth: "What a bastard!"

But Mr Maurus didn't curse, not initially at least, because in his own crazy suspicions and impossible assumptions he really did believe that Slopashev, in his drunken patriotism, had pulverized Goethe and Schiller. Mr Maurus cursed later when the others were laughing, because here in this first-rate establishment everyone laughed when Mr Maurus got angry. It was that sort of establishment. However, Mr Maurus now announced triumphantly, "Oh, I know my friends! Mr Maurus knows his good friends, because he's old and cunning. Let him go and talk, let him complain, if he wants, that Pushkin hasn't been put on display. My hands are clean of the dust of Goethe and Schiller."

The next evening Mr Voitinski smacked his lips for a long time as he treated his headache in his friend's company, before saying with a laugh: "Dirty tricks! By God, the swine!"

"What do you mean, dear Ivan Vassilievich?" asked Slopashev.

"About Goethe and Schiller of course," tinkled Voitinski in reply. "The eternal Man, and then those Germans, then Gogol and Pushkin and the true Russian soul. It's all a dirty trick, isn't it? You as an honest man will understand that."

"I do, dear friend," agreed Slopashev, "even when I'm drunk, I understand it. But man is a swine, whether he believes in God or not."

"By God, an eternal swine," squeaked Voitinski, starting to choke with laughter.

"Man is always a swine, when he goes out of himself and helps others in distress," mused Slopashev. "For you only become a swine if you want to help someone. But you know, dear friend, I'm going to play another swinish trick, a trick against the Russian spirit, and it's just the same as a trick against the Holy Spirit. Take note: I'm not thinking of Gogol or Pushkin. I'm not going to get some Gogol or Pushkin. What do we need them for? And why should I be the one to do it?"

"But you promised, Aleksander Matveyich," said Voitinski.

"Doesn't matter what I promised."

"So what's to be put in place of Goethe and Schiller – Shakespeare or Cervantes?"

"What? Bloody Cervantes?" roared Slopashev. "Let them display one of their own. Who cares if nobody knows them? They'll know their own!" he affirmed. "Knee-high midgets, but they'll know them. It's not like with us. We die, and still we don't know our own; they know their own right from birth, as if they had a dog's nose and a cat's eye."

"That's what always happens in places with no culture," asserted Voitinski. "Barbarians have strong animal instincts."

"Very strong!" Slopashev assured him. "Look with the eye of a cultured person, with your glasses on, and you can't really see whether it's a dog or a wolf, but a dog recognizes a dog straight away. Well, tell me yourself, Ivan Vassilievich, because you're an educated man, a university graduate, you've taught young people and received awards for that noble activity; tell me now, if some uncouth bastard asks you: could a dog suddenly forget that he's a dog, even though he's an educated one, one that's graduated from university?"

"So how could a dog graduate from university?" responded Voitinski, puzzled.

"Well, let's say from a dogs' university," replied Slopashev, staring across the table at his friend.

Voitinski started laughing, coughing with laughter, and it took a little while before he could gasp, "Aleksander Matveyich, you're my only true friend and an educated man, but still you're a pig and a misanthrope – don't take offence – a great misanthrope," he spluttered, as if it were a joke.

"How come, a misanthrope!" cried Slopashev in amazement. "I love humanity. Listen first, and then decide. Alright, there's no dogs' university, not for now there isn't. But if an educated dog hid away from another dog because he was better educated? No, or rather: what if an educated sheepdog turned into a sporting dog, a beagle or a greyhound because it was educated? Hold that thought! Hold it! Don't answer, because my question isn't finished yet. Now, really, you must listen: would an educated dog start bleating or crowing like a cock, instead of barking? Have you ever heard a dog that moos or neighs?"

"By God, I haven't!" Voitinski squealed with laughter.

"Well, you see!" cried Slopashev triumphantly. "But what does a human do when he's educated? I ask you: what does an educated man do? An educated person starts mooing, starts crowing like a cock, even starts doing that '*Sprechen Sie deutsch? Parlez-vous français?*' Is that a real human language? Does a true Russian man talk like that? 'Speak Russian' – that's what they understand on the Volga, and that's the language used by Pushkin and Gogol. But what have our so-called educated people done for centuries? Do they even know yet that Gogol and Pushkin are dead? They moo instead of talking! Does a real dog ever start mooing – does it forget how to bark? Tell me from your heart, because you're a Pole, you're a man of honour, Ivan Vassilievich."

"It doesn't forget, by God, it doesn't forget," said Voitinski.

"You see what it means when there isn't a university, when there's no education," declared Slopashev.

"You're a great enemy of education, Aleksander Matveyich."

"If there were no education or God," continued Slopashev without heeding his friend's words. "For dogs don't have a God, only humans have one. As soon as the Russian learned to know God, he immediately started mooing instead of barking – started betraying his fatherland. And you know what I think? Even the Englishman doesn't have a God: that's why he doesn't bleat or moo. The Englishman only believes in humanity, eternal humanity, he doesn't believe in God. The Englishman only believes in the Englishman, that's why. Everyone believes in the English, as do the Germans and the French, and of course so do we. And I think that if God were ever to start believing in people, he'd also only believe in the English – your Englishman is that kind of bastard. Do you understand."

"I understand alright, by God!" Voitinski affirmed.

"But nobody believes in us," complained Slopashev sadly. "We don't even believe in that ourselves."

"By God, we don't," agreed Voitinski.

"Or do you think that Mr Maurus believes? He doesn't, dear friend, he doesn't! He only makes out that he does, but actually he doesn't. He believes more in the German than the Russian, that's his faith in Russians. But he's the headmaster of the school himself! Do you understand? The headmaster of this school doesn't believe in the Russians! And yet any Russian inspector and director could shut his little enterprise down. Even I can, if I want, what with Goethe and Schiller in the rubbish bin. You want to bet that I can? Within a month, right away – what do you bet?"

"You can't," objected Voitinski. "Not with Goethe and Schiller, you can't."

"I can!" asserted Slopashev.

"You can't. And you know why?"

"Well?"

"You have too good a heart for it, dear friend. I know you," said Voitinski. "If I offered you, say, a million roubles today or tomorrow and said: here's some money, but you have to close the school – and if I said to the boys: 'Go and ask Mr Slopashev, because he's a good man, but he wants to close your school for a price of a million roubles – and then if all those boys came – I say: boys! – all of those, young and old, who now have nowhere else to go, if they all came here to your door, as we sit here, our glasses full and a few tasty sweetmeats before us, and they said, 'Mr Slopashev, we heard that you want to close our school, because Goethe and Schiller fell off the cupboard and broke into pieces, but why are you doing that, being a Russian and a good man? Can a good man be such a swine as to close the school?' Tell me now, wouldn't you feel sorry for them, big and small, swarming around the threshold of your door? Put your hand on your heart and tell me straight out and openly, Aleksander Matveyich."

But Slopashev didn't answer directly. He looked aside with a somewhat shamefaced expression and said: "That's just it. I'm a good man, but otherwise…"

"You see, a good man goes without the million," said Voitinski in triumph.

"Did you really think that for a million I would…?" asked Slopashev.

"I did, by God," replied Voitinski.

"I'd close the school for a million? Do you know what I'm telling you, Ivan Vassilievich? You're a bigger swine than I am; otherwise you wouldn't think that of your best friend. You're the biggest swine I've ever seen."

"The biggest you've ever seen, by God," said Voitinski, splitting his sides with laughter.

"The eternal swine!"

"Eternal!" squealed Voitinski.

Chapter 11

Thus the two good friends chatted as they nursed their heads, while Indrek was sitting downstairs at the table in the big room, doing his professional duties, having to receive visitors if they happened to come, and studying Latin, as Mr Maurus loved to say. But how could he study when in the next room they were debating such weighty questions, and almost every word could be heard?

Mr Maurus prowled around like either a roaring lion or a sly fox. Every so often he would stop to think something over with a sudden thoughtful or troubled expression. If something important suddenly occurred to him, he would rush off somewhere, stop again halfway and start muttering to himself.

"It must be hard for a person to live when he hesitates about everything," thought Indrek.

But soon he saw how hard it was for himself when Mr Maurus hesitated so much.

"How was it that you didn't hear that din?" he once asked Indrek as if in passing, emphasizing the words "that din" as if he knew what kind of din it was.

"I'd just fallen asleep, that's probably why," replied Indrek.

"So what use are you if you sleep so heavily that you don't even hear the bell?"

"No, I've always heard the bell," declared Indrek.

"You hear the bell, yet you don't hear Goethe and Schiller crashing to the floor?" exclaimed the headmaster.

"I'm not used to hearing that, that's why," replied Indrek.

"And of course you're not used to hearing it, because Goethe and Schiller were falling for the first time," agreed the headmaster with a grin.

But a couple of days later Mr Maurus asked again, "Haven't you noticed that something has happened to the door of Mr Slopashev's room?"

"I haven't noticed a thing," replied Indrek, though somehow he couldn't look the headmaster in the eye, but turned his gaze aside. He even blushed a little.

"Well, it might have been before you," the headmaster suggested on that occasion, but soon he was asking again: "Who threw a ball at Mr Slopashev's feet? Or were you asleep then?"

"No, I was at my post then, but I hadn't gone to sleep yet," replied Indrek.

"So you saw it then?" inquired the headmaster.

"I didn't, because the room was dark."

"But you did hear?"

"I did."

"Thank God!" sighed Mr Maurus from the bottom of his heart. "At least you're not completely deaf. Your eyesight has gone, but your ears can still hear a little." After those words he turned suddenly to Indrek, looked him steadily in the eye and asked: "Why do you lie to an old man like me? Did I keep you here without school fees for you to start lying to me? Those who do pay, or those whom I pay, of course they lie to me. But why do you lie? I don't pay you and you don't have anything to pay to me."

"I didn't lie before, I learned to do that here," replied Indrek plainly, because he really did want to get that off his chest.

"Who taught you to lie here? Who taught you? Tell me his name, hand him over to old Mr Maurus! Who is it?"

"You did that yourself, Mr Maurus," replied Indrek quietly, even taking himself by surprise.

"Shameless! Shameless!" cried the headmaster, starting to run back and forth across the large room. "Herr Ollino, Herr Ollino! Herr Ollino, are you deaf or what? Come here, come at once! Shameless person! This shameless person!"

But Mr Ollino didn't appear; the door of his room was locked. In his place there happened to come Vainukägu, Vutt and Laane. The headmaster then invited them to adjudicate between himself and Indrek.

"Listen, Vainukägu," said the headmaster, "you sing from the hymn book and read aloud from the Gospels; tell me from your pure and righteous heart whether Mr Maurus has taught you or anyone else to tell lies. Has he? Tell me! Has he taught you?"

"No," replied Vainukägu, adjusting the crease on his trousers, as if the truth were to be found there.

"Has he taught you?" the headmaster turned to Vutt.

"No, Mr Maurus," replied Vutt, clutching at Vainukägu's little finger and starting to fidget with its nail.

"And you, Laane?" – the headmaster turned to him, as he stood there, awkward and angular, with his long slender arms, his gaze seemingly turned inward, as he strained to call to mind the Latin word for "to lie".

"No," replied the boy, as if waking suddenly from a dream with a grunt.

"*Tres faciunt collegium*,"[18] said the headmaster solemnly. "And this shameless tall one here says that Mr Maurus has taught him to lie, that Mr Maurus runs a school of lying, with the approval of the Tsar of Russia. Has anyone heard that before?"

But none of them had ever heard it.

"So look at this tall one here," declared the headmaster, pointing to Indrek as if he were a sea monster. "Mr Maurus keeps him here without fees, by the grace of God, because he hopes this person will gain some sense, but he only says that Mr Maurus teaches him to tell lies. But Mr Maurus insists: truth, truth, nothing but the truth."

"Mr Maurus, I can go away if you think that…" said Indrek, thoroughly humiliated.

---

18 *Tres faciunt collegium*: "Three can make a *collegium* [the word that gives us 'college' and 'colleague', but in its loosest sense a group of people who come together for a common purpose".

"Don't interrupt when Mr Maurus is explaining," shouted the headmaster, and turning to his tribunal, said: "Did you hear that? He can go away. Oh he says he can: did you hear that? First he says that Mr Maurus tells lies, and then that he can go. He can! But how can a tall one like him gain sense if he goes away? Who will study here for him? Mr Maurus? No, Mr Maurus will not start studying in place of this tall one. The tall one has to study for himself."

And turning particularly to Vutt, he told him in German: "This tall country scholar is a real bumpkin, a proper one. He says: Mr Maurus's first-rate establishment teaches you to lie. That's what comes of the great learning and great Latin of the oversized rustic."

And he looked straight at Vutt over his spectacles, waving the splayed fingers of his right hand in front of his eyes and shaking his head, by which he meant that someone was mentally defective.

"Go now," said the headmaster suddenly in a different tone, as if something special had occurred to him. "And why are you here? Why aren't you studying in class? You don't have anything to do here now."

With those words the high commission of the "adjudicators" was ended. The headmaster indicated to Indrek with his hand that he was to follow him – up to his room.

"How can you say to Mr Maurus in front of others that you can go away?" began the headmaster. "Where will you go if you don't have money? Where will they teach you Latin if you don't have the wherewithal?"

"I'll have to go without studying Latin," replied Indrek.

"You're mad, you're really mad!" cried the headmaster. "You come here to study Latin, and when Mr Maurus lets you study without fees, you say that you'll go without studying. Don't you understand what that means? What do you actually want? Do you want Mr Maurus to have only blockheads, like those three down there, one with a face like this, another like this, the other like this?" The headmaster tried to imitate each face in turn. "Do you think they study Latin and algebra with faces like those? Why do you think there are students at Mr Maurus's who have enough money to pay? So that an Estonian who has little money can study. That's why! Why would an Estonian study Latin if he has money? Have you seen Russians, Germans, Poles, Armenians, Georgians, Turks, Chinese, and so on and so forth, studying when they have money? No! They only pay and bring in money so that some poor boy can study. So what is Mr Maurus supposed to do when even the poor boy says that he'll go without studying? Then Mr Maurus has to close his school, has to close it because of poor Estonian boys who no longer want to study Latin. Or should Mr Maurus become a Latvian, and start teaching Latin to Latvians? Because a poor Latvian studies; oh yes, a Latvian studies, and even a rich one does. You saw how poor Kopfschneider, the "head-cutter",[19] went on his way? He was crying when he left! But what can Mr Maurus do about that, being an Estonian and not a Latvian, and there are enough poor Estonian boys who want to study without fees? But suddenly those poor Estonian boys are saying to Mr Maurus that they don't want to. And why don't they want to? Why, I ask? Because, and only because, Mr Maurus makes a demand on one poor Estonian boy: he has to tell the truth, the plain truth. But that poor boy wants to lie, like the rich ones do. In that way Mr Maurus will never get at the truth. But the truth is the face of Jehovah, which Moses was only allowed to see with his back turned, before he went to the people with the tablet of commandments. Do you understand – to the people! And the people! The people couldn't even see the truth from behind, they only got the commandments. You are my Moses and I am your Jehovah and you must turn the face of truth towards me, so I can see it and command it. But you don't want to be my Moses, you

---

19 "head-cutter": this is an ironic translation of Kopfschneider's name.

don't want to turn the face of truth towards me, but how then can I let you study Latin without fees? Did Moses tell the truth to Jehovah, do you think?"

Indrek didn't answer, for he was thinking of something else.

"I asked you: did Moses tell the truth to Jehovah?" said the headmaster more loudly.

"I don't know," replied Indrek, because everything was getting confused in his head.

So Mr Maurus had to go on explaining.

Indrek didn't know how or why, but as he listened to the headmaster talking, not only about Moses and Jehovah and Israel, but also about the Estonian people and the Russian Tsar, the Kalevipoeg epic poem, about Gogol and Pushkin, Goethe and Schiller, he began to feel sorry for him. Maybe this was because of his grey beard, maybe because of his thinning grey hair, which tended to stand up on the top of his head and tremble as he spoke. That must have been why Indrek was beginning to pity him, because they reminded him of his own father, standing somewhere near a bog in windy weather after cold rain which had been pouring down for days during haymaking. To pass the time they had been uprooting willow-bushes, and weeding out dwarf birches on ground that had previously been burnt. And then, when at last the clouds parted and the sun showed its face, his father remained standing by that ravaged bog, removed his soaked cap from his head, wiped his brow with his hand and said: "Thank heavens, the sun's out for once!" The wind had torn at his hair, and only now as he looked at the headmaster did Indrek recall or realise that even then his father's hair was tinged with grey, very like Mr Maurus's. Appreciating that fact now, his heart was melted and his tongue was loosened, so that he told the headmaster everything as it had happened. The strangest thing of all was that, when he told him about the ball-throwing incident and referred to Slopashev's legs as "spokes", the headmaster didn't take the slightest offence, but merely laughed. In fact he laughed heartily, so amusing did he find Indrek's tale. But at the end Indrek spoiled the beautiful mood with a little mistake: he also related how Slopashev and Voitinski had been chatting in their cups about closing down the school. That wiped the smile right off the old man's face. "Now you see what that good Russian is like," he declared. "He drinks himself silly, goes and fights with an Estonian and smashes two great Germans. And so Mr Maurus isn't going to get to know the truth. He wants to close down the school, because of the Germans who are in the dog house. The Russian can't read, so why should an Estonian? So you can never trust a good person, because they will do bad things for the sake of absolute justice – so that everyone is equal. A good Russian wants to love everyone like himself, and that's why he would close Estonian schools. Your Russian is better than a god, better than the Redeemer, maybe only the Virgin Mary is as good as your Russian. That's a Russian for you. Oh, Mr Maurus knows the Russians well…"

The more the headmaster praised the good Russian, the more the clouds of anxiety seemed to come over his face. You could clearly see that he was saying one thing and thinking another – who knew what exactly? The main thing was that he doubted everything, even what Indrek was telling him. In his head, everything had its own twisted logic, and even the simplest of events could be inverted into something crazy.

"We have to stick together," he told Indrek on the threshold in a secretive whisper. "Estonians have to stick together, because there are so few of us. But Estonians don't stick to the Estonian side; they support either the Germans or the Russians, even if they're working people. They trust a German and a Russian more than an Estonian, and put their hopes in a German and a Russian, rather than an Estonian. Kreutzwald had hopes for the Estonians, but now he's dead. Jakobson had a few hopes too, but he's dead too. They're all dead, those who put their trust in Estonians. Men and women! Especially women! For a woman only has hopes for your German or your Russian. Only! But off you go now, nobody must know about this conversation – only the two of us. The fate of the people of Israel is in the hands of us two Estonian men, Jehovah and Moses," laughed the headmaster as Indrek went downstairs, as if their words were nothing more than a silly joke.

But this wasn't a joke for Indrek – not in the slightest. Day by day he felt an increasing sense of dread, as though he were being sucked into a sinkhole up to his head. He felt dizzy, his ears ringing and his limbs were getting heavier. He had no desire to move his arms or legs.

Chapter 12

Another quite novel factor came into play in this tense environment and it came like a flash of sunlight. It was the headmaster's daughter, who was always called Miss or Princess. When Indrek had to slice bread and lay the table, which was a duty he had to carry out every two or three days on top of everything else, Miss would occasionally appear in the dining room where she would sit on the windowsill or even the table, and swing her long delicate legs. Initially Indrek did not welcome her arrival, as it was embarrassing to carve the bread or drop a knife on the table with the ensuing clatter while someone followed his every movement with their eyes. It was a little easier when Mrs Malmberg, the young lady's aunt, was also in the dining room, because she would send the young lady away or scold her incessantly.

"Why are you sitting there?" Mrs Malmberg would usually cry. "That's where the others are supposed to eat! Have you no shame?"

"What's there to be ashamed about?" she responded. "My clothes are clean."

"Is that what you were taught at the German boarding school?"

"That's precisely what we learned. We were always sitting somewhere on a tabletop or somewhere high-up," she explained.

Once when her aunt wasn't within earshot, she asked Indrek: "Do you mind if I sit here?"

"I don't eat there, miss," replied Indrek.

"Where do you eat?"

"Wherever I am, but not there – that's where Mr Ollino eats."

"He didn't eat here before," she said jumping up from the table. "Ooh, what a fright you gave me! If he'd seen that, my father would have sent me a lengthy epistle. So who eats next to him, here on the left?"

"Mr Koovi."

"And on the right?"

"The prince."

"Where does the count eat, the one who plays so beautifully?"

"First on the other side of the table."

"Next to him?"

"Von Elbe and then Chodkiewicz."

"He's the one with his hands always in his pockets, isn't he?"

"That's the one. But how did you know that?"

"I know, I know everything. Where is Vutt's place?"

"Here," indicated Indrek.

"That's where I'll sit," she said. But before she could act upon her decision, her aunt came in with the news that her father was home, and she vanished immediately from the dining room, because her presence there was strictly forbidden.

Another time, as she was again sitting in the dining room swinging her legs, she said to Indrek, "Why aren't your slices of bread all of the same thickness? Look at that! Whose teeth could bite through that?"

"I'm saving that one for myself," replied Indrek lightly.

"So you have such long teeth?" she laughed.

"I can manage with an even thicker piece."

"You have a nice life!" she sighed at length.

"Really?" exclaimed Indrek.

"Well, don't you?" she asked.

"You very probably have a good life, miss," ventured Indrek.

"Me? I'm bored, terribly bored. I'm not allowed to do or say anything. I can't even go anywhere – my aunt or someone else is always on my tail."

"But I can't go anywhere – there's no time or opportunity," said Indrek.

"You have to be downstairs, don't you? You don't have money to pay father, do you?"

Indrek didn't answer, but just clattered the plates, knives and forks.

"Why are you here, really? To cut bread and set the table?" she asked.

"To study," replied Indrek.

"So when do you study, if you're always working – do you run off somewhere or do you sit down in the room? There's no peace even at night, when the bell rings – you can hear it upstairs. You open the door, don't you?"

"I do," replied Indrek.

"You see, I even know that. So when do you study?"

"There's enough time for that," responded Indrek, to make his situation seem at least a little brighter.

"What do you like most of all? *Lateinisch*,[20] as father calls it, do you? Father thinks that everyone's always studying *Lateinisch*. I don't like it, for what will I do with it, where will it get me? I like German, that's the most beautiful language. You can't speak German? What a pity! Then there would be no need for us to speak Russian. Why don't you learn it? Do you want me to teach you? I'll start by speaking only German to you, *nur deutsch!* Just German! Every educated person speaks German, because without German there's no education and no educated people. Everyone says that – father, auntie, everyone, everybody, *die ganze Welt. Und was können wir gegen die ganze Welt? Verstehen Sie?*"[21]

And she started the teaching straight away, taking a plate, a knife or a fork as an example and asking: *"Was ist das?"*[22] to which Indrek was supposed to answer in German.

---

20 Lateinisch: "Latin" [German]

21 "… the whole world. And we can't go against the whole world? Do you understand?" [German]

22 *Was ist das?*: "What is it?" [German]

"This way you don't lose any time: you work and you study German while you're at it. Like now: *was machen Sie jetzt?*"[23] she asked as Indrek cut the bread. "And I've found myself a task in life: I'll start teaching German to boys. I'm doing something useful, I'm working," she exclaimed. "First of all I'm going to teach you German properly. Because Estonian is impossible."

"Why is it?" asked Indrek.

"In Estonian all the beautiful and ugly words have an *s* in them, that's why. *Armas, kallis, sõrmus!*[24] But in German there isn't an *s: Ich liebe dich, ich bin verliebt! Ring! Brautring!*[25] *Bräutigam!* How beautiful it sounds! So first things first: learn German properly. And I'll teach. I'm happy to do it because of that terrible *s*."

"Why don't you like the *s*, miss?" asked Indrek.

"I can't tell you that," she replied with a slight blush. "I've told auntie and she just laughs. Auntie doesn't have fine feelings, sometimes she has no understanding of how I feel. Once I've got my independence, I'm going to go travelling – that's one thing that's certain – and I'll look for a language without an *s*, because there must be a language like that somewhere. There has to be at least one nation in the world with fine feelings like that. In the whole world, you see. And I won't ever speak Estonian again when I become independent, because I'll marry anyone, as long as he's not an Estonian. Not one of those people! I'll marry someone who doesn't even understand Estonian, who's never even heard of it!"

Once she asked Indrek, "How do you like my name – Ramilda? Isn't it pretty?"

"Very pretty!" exclaimed Indrek.

---

23 "What are you doing now?" [German]

24 "Lovely, darling, ring." [Estonian]

25 "I love you; I'm in love. Ring! Wedding ring!" [German]

"Do you know what it really is? It's Miralda. My real name is Miralda. But I don't like it. Ramilda is much prettier. And a finer, grander name. Once I've got my independence, I'm definitely going to change my name to Ramilda. If I can't, I'll petition the Tsar. From Miralda you can get many pretty names, but Ramilda is the prettiest. Listen: Miralda, Marilda, Rimalda, Ramilda, Ridalma, Radilma, Diralma, Darilma, Ramaldi, Maraldi, Ramidla, Maridla, Miradla – an endless number! But I wouldn't petition the Tsar about those others, only about Ramilda. I've got the petition ready, not on paper of course, but in my head. Every night before I go to sleep, I read it out in my head to the Tsar so it'll have a greater effect once I send it off. What do you think – will the Tsar give me permission to take Ramilda instead of Miralda?"

"I wouldn't know, miss," replied Indrek.

"But what do you think, I'm asking – just your opinion?"

"I think he would," said Indrek.

"Do you really?" ventured Ramilda.

"Truly, miss," the boy assured her.

"It couldn't be otherwise, could it?" said Ramilda joyfully. "How could the Tsar object to it? Your hand on it." She jumped down with both feet at once from the window-sill to the floor and extended her hand to Indrek, and when he had pressed it, she said: "Tigapuu has a bigger hand than you. He's shorter than you, but his hand is bigger and stronger. Once more! Squeeze harder, so that I feel it."

And Indrek had to squeeze her hand again, and she said: "Tigapuu's still stronger. Do you like him?"

"He's one class higher than me," replied Indrek.

"And he speaks German, speaks it very nicely, just like an educated person. He likes it here a lot. Do you like it?"

"I do," replied Indrek.

"It's fun, isn't it? Father is terribly worried about the boys, because they're very unruly. Are you wild yourself sometimes?"

"I don't think so," replied Indrek.

"Of course – you're big already, that's why. But Tigapuu is;

I know he is. What happened with Goethe and Schiller? Do tell me. I asked Tigapuu, but he said he didn't know. He won't tell me. But you can. You can tell me, and I won't tell anyone. I won't even tell auntie or father. So that just we two know it. I so much want to know what happened, because I like wild boys so, so much. Boys in general. Überhaupt!²⁶ Boys are so nice, so manly. Girls are jealous, terribly jealous. And mean! To me they're so jealous and mean. They say I'm silly. But I think there are plenty of girls sillier than me. What do you think – who are the silliest? Tell me straight from the heart."

"I don't know any girls," said Indrek.

"That's a good thing for you – that you don't know any girls, I mean; they're all so horribly touchy. I'm horribly touchy too. But am I as silly as the jealous ones say, what do you think? Just your opinion. You gave me your opinion about the petition to the Tsar, so why can't do the same about my silliness? Tell me now," pleaded Ramilda.

"I don't believe so," said Indrek at length, turning aside.

"You're so right!" cried Ramilda joyfully. "Would every girl have petitioned the Tsar, or would every girl have made Ramilda out of Miralda? They can't do anything. But I can. I'm so happy that you have the same opinion as I do. *Ich bin so glücklich, so glücklich!*²⁷ But you have to learn German, you have to! That's what Ramilda, Rimalda, Radilma, Darilma, Ramaldi, Maraldi, Ramilda, Rimadla wants!"

Twittering like a little bird she vanished out of the door full of happiness. But in his heart Indrek felt a sort of tender heaviness, and those first painful pangs.

Thus the days passed and the weeks vanished, but Indrek didn't notice them. He had an eye for only one thing: would she appear on a certain day in the dining room to teach him German or not? He was almost forgetting the other subjects, because he was swotting up so much on his German grammar.

---

26 "Absolutely." [German]

27 "I am so happy, so happy!" [German]

But when she didn't appear in the dining room, Indrek was surly and sad, especially when he heard that she had gone to have fun with someone else.

Like Indrek, many others – maybe everyone – knew where Ramilda had got her name from along with all those other names, which seemed so beautiful that they were quietly recited here and there. Every man would have his own pretty version of her name which she loved and made the object of her enthusiasm and admiration. But behind all those pretty names there was only one woman who chirruped her ten thousand names to various men, and an intoxicated swarm of men chirruped them after her. It was no wonder that Indrek started to chirrup as well, sometimes consciously, sometimes unconsciously, extrapolating the names to the last possibility and creating ever newer and newer ones. This game or pastime helped to while away the tedium. And it spread so swiftly and firmly that it competed with the Count's song, only with the difference that the song was sung aloud and in unison, while the names were repeated by each boy to himself.

Indrek came to understand this only when he came across Tigapuu as he was going through those names. "What are you on about?" Tigapuu asked Indrek angrily, as he was softly repeating: Rimadla, Ramidla, Maridla, Miradla.

"Nothing," replied Indrek.

"What do you mean 'nothing' – I could clearly hear you."

"What did you hear? The song of the swallow: Midli-Madli, Kidli-Kadli."

"No, I heard something else," retorted Tigapuu.

"For God's sake! What then?" cried Indrek, irritated by Tigapuu's tone of voice.

"I heard just what you said, and I forbid you to say it again, do you hear?" replied Tigapuu menacingly.

"What? You forbid me? Others have the power to do the forbidding in this place."

"You'll get this, if you don't obey," said Tigapuu, putting his fist under Indrek's nose.

"You'll get it in the head if you use that fist," said Indrek.

"There aren't any table-ends in here," smirked Tigapuu.

"There's always something to bash your head with," replied Indrek.

Those last words were heard by Mr Ollino, who asked jokingly: "Whom is this Paas going to bash on the head now?"

"Tigapuu as usual," replied Indrek, "because he stuck his fist under my nose when I sang the song of the swallow: Midli-Madli, Kidli-Kadli."

"Don't lie!" cried Tigapuu angrily.

"Why are you so nasty?" Ollino asked Tigapuu.

"Paas is lying!" cried Tigapuu.

"So what if he's lying?" suggested Ollino. "We all tell lies at times."

"There's a difference between lies and lies," declared Tigapuu.

"So what did Paas say?"

"That's my business to sort out," replied Tigapuu.

Ollino smirked.

"You can all laugh if you like, but in my opinion it's not nice at all to play around with a young lady's name as if it were some sort of plaything, quite apart from the fact that the young lady is the daughter of our own headmaster," Tigapuu now explained.

"But that young lady does play around with her own name just like that," objected Ollino.

"A person can do what they like with their own name and their own self, but that's no reason for others to do it. It's not right to be disrespectful to others. We've never been allowed to be in the company of the young lady, as she's the headmaster's daughter and it's not polite."

Ollino responded to this learned argument with a song to the tune of "Oh Tannenbaum":

"Oh Tigapuu, oh Tigapuu,
Du bist doch ganz verliebt."[28]

---

28 "You are completely in love." [German]

148

"I'll thank you not to joke about such a serious matter," said Tigapuu furiously.

"Since when have you been standing up for people's rights?" asked Ollino.

"If anyone steps over the line with someone, I'm always ready to step in and defend them," said Tigapuu.

"So!" exclaimed Ollino, and turned to Indrek with a question: "What do you think of this, Paas? Has Tigapuu stood up for you too?"

"I don't recall," Indrek replied and decided to take advantage of the opportunity, "but he won't pay back the money he borrowed from me."

"What has money got to do with people's rights?" yelled Tigapuu. "And when have I borrowed anything from you?"

"Long ago," replied Indrek. "In the autumn, just after I came here."

"I borrowed from you? I'm in debt to you?" exclaimed Tigapuu.

"At least that rouble for the blanket."

"But for that you slept with my blanket and cushion."

"Not a single night – you took them back."

"You gave them."

"You said yourself they were other people's."

"Which you believed, as I said it."

"So you were cheating me?"

"Why did you let yourself get cheated?"

"Ah, so that's your right?"

"It is my right, when someone else is so stupid."

These statements were exchanged rapidly, more or less straight back and forth into each other's faces. Ollino stood, his hands in his trouser pockets, looking at the boys. At Tigapuu's last words, he said with a grin as he turned towards Indrek: "Tigapuu's in love, that's for certain. For if a person can think he has the right to cheat another, he's definitely in love – bear that in mind." As he said this he walked across the room, as if the whole issue had been resolved. Indrek didn't know whether to take his words seriously or as a joke. Only many years later could he perceive how much truth there was in Ollino's words, but by that time he had forgotten those words.

The next day the young lady asked him in the dining room: "Is it true that you had a fight with Tigapuu about my name?"

"Not about your name," Indrek lied, even as he recalled Ollino's words: a person in love thinks he has the right to cheat.

"So what was it about then?" asked Ramilda, as if she was sorry to hear this.

"I was just singing Midli-Madli, Kidli-Kadli – the song of the swallow."

"Was it really like that?" inquired Ramilda, staring into Indrek's eyes as if in disappointment. "But weren't you thinking about my name as you sang?"

"I don't remember clearly, but I suppose I was."

"Bring it clearly to mind," insisted Ramilda. "Rimadla, Ramidla, Miradla, Maridla, Ridla, Radla, Ridli, Radli, Kidli-Kadli, Midli-Madli. It would definitely have been like that, wouldn't it?"

"I don't know, maybe."

"*Ganz bestimmt, so war es!*"[29] Ramilda asserted, adding as if to herself: "So then, Tigapuu was right! Tigapuu was right!"

With those words she went skipping out the door, as if hurrying to deliver some message of joy, and Indrek absently repeated after her: "Tigapuu was right, Tigapuu was right!" while in his heart he suddenly felt an inexplicable heaviness, which caused his whole body to feel strangely hot. But suddenly he saw himself somewhere by the corner of a cemetery, where dark spruce-trees were rustling, and someone else was standing in front of him who ran away. But he stayed on the spot. Today someone else was running away; there was always someone running away, and only he was left alone.

---

29 "So it definitely was." [German]

These thoughts were running through Indrek's mind as he sliced the bread, and Mrs Malmberg stepped in and asked, "Why are you slicing the bread so carelessly today?"

"The knife must be blunt," suggested Indrek.

"Sharpen the knife, otherwise you'll crumble more than you slice."

That day Indrek had trouble handling the plates and knives and forks; they kept dropping and clattering.

"What's wrong with you today? Are you tired or sick?" asked Mrs Malmberg.

"The bell rang a lot in the night," said Indrek. "I couldn't sleep."

"Poor boy!" sympathised the lady. "But there won't be much left of those poor plates and cups soon if you treat them so roughly. You can see for yourself, the plates are all chipped on the edges and the cups don't have any handles at all."

"It's more convenient without handles," suggested Indrek, "they fit into each other so much better."

"But what does a cup look like when it has no handles!" said Mrs Malmberg instructively. "What would people look like if they didn't have ears? They wouldn't have a face. It's the same with a cup: it's always in a person's hand and it should have a handle attached to it."

"Yes, of course, Mrs Malmberg," agreed Indrek.

"But why do you knock the ears off the cups, if you have ears of your own?"

"I don't knock them, they come off by themselves," replied Indrek. "If people's ears were as delicate as they are on cups, I expect that there would be a lot of people without ears."

"And that would be right and proper," Mrs Malmberg observed, "for why should people have ears, if cups don't have them?"

"But cups' ears can't hear," Indrek attempted to parry.

"Can all human ears hear?" asked Mrs Malmberg. "My father's ears couldn't hear a thing by the end, but did anyone pull them off because of that? A body goes to the grave with deaf ears and will rise again on Judgement Day."

"And cups won't rise again," Indrek still contended.

"Do all humans rise?" asked Mrs Malmberg. "Where is the one who will raise the Jews or pagans? Who will wake them? No one! So it's not important whether they have ears when they die or not. But they do have them, so why shouldn't a cup have them too?"

This was what Mrs Malmberg taught Indrek; she made it clear to him that cups should have ears on them, even though they are not mortal like humans – Christian, Jew and heathen. Mrs Malmberg elucidated such things for the benefit of Indrek and all the other young people who were however barred from producing any elucidations of their own. Yet the winners in these debates were always the youths, not Mrs Malmberg. She loved to debate with youngsters more than they did with her, because she wanted to teach them more than they wanted to learn.

The question of cups' ears and human ears was full of foreboding. This was understood best of all by Mrs Malmberg. Only a couple of days had passed when the prince was late for lunch, as had happened with him previously too. But today he was especially late, and since Mrs Malmberg loved order, she wouldn't let the prince eat any longer, assuring him that from that day onwards anyone who didn't appear at table at the right time would go without. The exceptions were only Ollino, who had plenty to do, and Paas, who was often on duty downstairs at the time when the others were at table.

Today, too, Indrek had only just started to eat when the prince stepped in, took a seat at the head of the table and said: "Please lay a place for me here."

Since the prince only spoke Russian, which Mrs Malmberg didn't understand, she asked Indrek what he wanted, and got him to tell the prince that he would no longer get lunch today. But the prince would hear nothing of this, and replied: "My stomach is empty and I want to eat."

"Then you'll have to look for it somewhere else, not here," Indrek had to interpret to the prince in reply.

"I'm not moving from here until I can eat," said the prince firmly.

"I'm afraid you'll have to wait a very long time," said Indrek.

In reply the prince struck his hand on the table and turned to Indrek: "Tell this old woman once more that she will give me food immediately, otherwise I won't be responsible for my actions."

When Indrek had politely passed on these words, he was told to answer: "Mrs Malmberg is responsible for her actions, since she isn't of the princely line. She is responsible, and won't give the prince a meal, whatever he does."

"Set the table this instant!" screamed the prince, slamming his fist on the table.

Now Indrek had to tell the prince that he needn't scream, because here he wasn't a prince but only a schoolboy who was late for lunch. Actually this was the last thing that Indrek had to interpret, because after that the German and Russian slanging match became so heated that it was no longer possible to interpret. The fierce gestures, the flashing eyes and the distorted faces spoke a language clearer than any mouth could. Finally the prince and Mrs Malmberg stood facing each other at the table, on which were piled clean cups and plates still wet from washing; they stood screaming at each other words whose meanings they had to guess at rather than understood.

"For the last time, are you going to give me a meal?" yelled Bebutov. "Yes or no?"

"Get out and don't scream in here!" cried Mrs Malmberg back, pointing to the door. But then something suddenly happened that none of them could have been prepared for, not even the prince. It was the consequence of some momentary confusion. The prince evidently wanted to do something else, for his black burning eyes ran around the big room in search of something, but they found nothing more appropriate than the piles of crockery. And so he grabbed the first pile of cups and sent it crashing to the floor, while he

153

screamed, staring Mrs Malmberg in the face: "Give me food!"

"You're mad!" shouted Mrs Malmberg at him, without moving from the spot.

Crockery again crashed to the floor, smashing into a thousand pieces which scattered across the whole room.

A girl rushed terrified to the door and screamed from there: "Madam, madam, let me bring something; otherwise he'll smash everything to pieces!"

"Be quiet, you!" shouted Mrs Malmberg in reply, herself withdrawing toward the door, retreating from the enraged man. And turning to Indrek, who had leapt up, she commanded: "Tell him firmly one more time that he's not getting any food, even if he breaks up the whole house."

"Ah, not getting any!" the prince screamed at Indrek, when he had passed on these words from Mrs Malmberg, and grabbing more crockery from the table with both hands he proceeded to smash it on the floor with a fearful crash. He would probably have destroyed every last one of them if Ramilda hadn't happened to come in. She paid no attention to the other frightened faces, seeing only the prince as he methodically went about the business of expressing his rage.

"Wonderful! Utterly superb!" she whooped for joy, as the prince smashed piles of crockery onto the floor. "I've never heard such a noise as that, even from fireworks!"

These words were said in German, and therefore the prince couldn't understand them, but he heard a new voice and looked around. And seeing Ramilda standing with a gleeful expression in the middle of the room looking at the destruction he'd wreaked on the dining hall, he came back to his senses and stopped.

"Do it again!" begged Ramilda in Russian. "It was so beautiful: crrrashh!" she shrieked and whooped. But the prince stood stupefied in the midst of all the shattered crockery, unable to move.

"Don't stick your nose into my business!" yelled Mrs Malmberg to her niece.

"No, dear aunt," replied Ramilda. "But why did he start smashing things?"

"He didn't get any food," replied Mrs Malmberg.

"Why not? Wasn't there any?"

"He was too late. He's always late, but there has to be order in my house," declared Mrs Malmberg.

"So, because he was hungry," stated Ramilda, "because of an empty stomach the poor chap started smashing things up." And approaching the prince, she said to him: "You know, if it's from hunger, this is not worth it – auntie won't give you food anyway. Believe me, I know her. When she says no, she means no."

Ramilda said this as simply and sincerely as if she were talking to a child. The prince didn't know what else to do but to bow, apologize and leave.

"That man is completely crazy!" said Mrs Malmberg. "Look at what he's done!"

"But if his stomach was really empty…" Ramilda tried to defend the prince. "I'd go mad too if I saw that there was food and I wasn't going to get any. It would be a different matter if there wasn't any – then I wouldn't get so mad."

"He was mad even before he came here," replied Mrs Malmberg. "But I've got a cure for him."

"Maybe he was starved at home too, that's why," suggested Ramilda. "Hunger brings out madness in people; otherwise they just keep it concealed within themselves. Where else does madness come from, if not from some hunger or other great trouble which must have already been within them?"

"Do stop your mindless chatter," Mrs Malmberg told her niece.

"It's not mindless, dear auntie," objected Ramilda. "People don't go crazy when they don't have serious problems. But as soon as they do have them, they all go crazy. As happened with the prince: did you see what his eyes were like? You should know, dear auntie, that if we were in serious trouble, we would have eyes like that."

"He's always had eyes like that, whether he gets food or not."

"Then it's better to give it to him, dear auntie," implored Ramilda. "For why would you starve him if he has eyes like that?"

"Leave me alone!" shouted Mrs Malmberg. "I know what I'm doing. Get out of here this instant!"

"I'm going, I'm going," replied Ramilda, but she still stopped at the door to say, "But it was wonderful seeing those plates being thrown up with both hands high over his head and then coming down suddenly – crrassh! And the cups! The poor old cups! They didn't even have handles on them. Or maybe some of them did?" Ramilda asked Indrek.

"Some still did," he replied.

"Poor ears! Just think how…"

"Listen, just get out of here!" Mrs Malmberg shouted to her niece. But when she opened the door, Mr Maurus and Ollino came through.

"Why are you here?" the headmaster asked his daughter. "This place is not the place for you."

"I just came to look," replied Ramilda. "The whole floor is full of …!"

"Just go," commanded the headmaster, proceeding into the dining room with Ollino. Once he had surveyed the destruction, he smiled with satisfaction and said to Ollino and Mrs Malmberg: "A shame that he didn't smash them all – and then we could have replaced them all."

"He could well have smashed them all, but Ramilda stopped him," Mrs Malmberg reported.

"She always comes where she's not needed," said the head-master in in a voice that seemed to imply a wider meaning. And then he turned to Indrek and said: "Call Jürka to clean up the floor."

"But I need crockery for the evening," exclaimed Mrs Malmberg.

"Of course we need crockery," agreed the headmaster.

"Write down what you need, I'll go with the prince and buy new replacements, since he has to pay. The prince has to pay."

But the prince didn't go with the headmaster to buy crockery; no, he most certainly did not. As for payment, he demanded that a bill be sent to the prince's father with a covering letter in the prince's own hand, which Mr Maurus carefully read through and then personally sent by registered post. He did this in the interests of the economy of labour: the prince had smashed up his old crockery and consequently he put the prince's letter in the post, so that no one would have cause to complain. Thus all the parties to the dispute were completely satisfied: the prince had shown that he was not to be trifled with, Ramilda had shown by her behaviour that she had a sympathetic heart but could also delight in unfortunate events, Mrs Malmberg's excessive zeal for order had demonstrated what a woman is capable of when she has a firm nature, and Mr Maurus had proved to himself and others that even the most insane acts can have beneficial consequences, for now his boys could eat from new plates and drink from cups with handles, and it didn't cost him a single penny.

That, of course, is how things seemed to begin with. Later there were distressing days for several of them. One of those who had to suffer without gaining anything was Indrek. He had to carry on eating and drinking from the old damaged crockery, because he was starting to lay them out on the table from the upper end, and before he got to the lower end he had run out of new ones and he had to put out the old ones for himself and some other lads. He still sipped coffee and tea from handleless cups, even though Mrs Malmberg had impressed upon him the importance of a handle to a cup. Still worse was the fact that he had to protect the cup handles as if they were his own life. Whereas until now he had been able to clatter the crockery for his own and others' amusement, now silence had to reign in the dining room, as if wooden or rubber plates were being spread out on the table. And to make sure that

157

her orders were being fully obeyed, Mrs Malmberg herself would stand on guard duty whenever the table was being laid or cleared, lest a plate's rim were chipped or a cup lost its handle. Or if she had to leave the dining room for a moment, she would ensure that all the doors leading to her own quarters were open, so as to monitor any sound that could give rise to the slightest apprehension. The situation in the dining room became quite unbearable, also because of Ramilda. Previously she could occasionally spend a while alone with the boys in the dining room, but this was no longer possible: she had to leave immediately or her aunt would listen in to her every word.

"I want to see whether or not the cups still have their handles," Mrs Malmberg reiterated as if she had to prove a point. But she wasn't intending to prove any point; she was of such a firm disposition that if she started doing something, she had to follow it through to the bitter end, even the end of her life – even if she had to suffer because of it. As was happening now! For was standing like a police officer on duty in the dining room really worth her while? Was she only driven by the memory of what the prince had done when he went without his meal? And the inspection of each cup handle had become an integral part of everyday life. It lasted from morning to evening, and was ultimately just annoying and stressful. The mood had changed! Everyone noticed that the new crockery was ruining Mrs Malmberg's state of mind. That was why Ramilda once whispered secretively to Indrek: "Auntie is gradually going crazy over the new cups."

"Why?" asked Indrek.

"Because they have handles."

"But they could break off," joked Indrek.

"Just what I was thinking," Ramilda smiled conspiratorially. And as if something had been agreed between them, she grasped a bright new cup from Indrek's hands, and before he could stop her, she had knocked the handle against the edge of the table, and off it came. Now the first brand-new cup had lost its brand-new handle, which Ramilda handed to

Indrek and said, "Put it in your pocket and throw it away later where no one will find it. Quick!" Indrek was rooted to the spot. "And…" she added, but instead of words she raised her index finger to her lips. This was the moment when Indrek noticed what delicate fingers Ramilda had. He also noticed that the tip of her finger rested on the end of her nose and left a fleeting little white spot there. And every time he saw in his mind's eye a broken cup-handle, that tiny white spot on the tip of Ramilda's nose came vividly to mind.

A little later, when Mrs Malmberg came into the dining room, Ramilda ran up to her at the threshold and cried: "Auntie, dear auntie, one of the cups has lost its ear! Come and look, come quick!"

And she ran and grabbed the cup from the table to show it to Mrs Malmberg, but before she could do that, she dropped the cup on the floor, where it shattered into pieces. Shocked and most disappointed, Ramilda stopped and then glanced first at her aunt and then at Indrek. Suddenly Indrek had a feeling that he ought to take the cup's handle out of his pocket and dash it on the floor among the other broken pottery. Only with difficulty did he refrain from doing this.

"How awful! What a bungler you are!" yelled Mrs Malmberg angrily. "Now you've smashed a new cup."

"But it didn't have a handle!" objected Ramilda. "The new cup didn't have an ear, dear auntie – that's what I wanted to show you."

"Of course it won't have a handle anymore!" said Mrs Malmberg.

"No, it had already lost its ear before it fell. It was complete, but didn't have an ear."

"I don't believe it, that simply isn't possible," countered Mrs Malmberg.

"It is possible," Ramilda assured her. "I saw it with my own two eyes, and so did Mr Paas."

"Then you must have broken the ear off yourself just now," said Mrs Malmberg, turning to Indrek.

"I didn't," replied Indrek.

"He didn't," confirmed Ramilda.

"How do you know that so well?" Mrs Malmberg asked her niece.

"I was here," said Ramilda. "I saw him just taking a cup and showing me the ear was off it. He asked me, dear auntie, to be a witness to you that he didn't do it, because Mr Paas knows how much you love our new cups to have their handles."

"I love order and you should too," Mrs Malmberg answered before turning to Indrek: "So who broke that ear off? Who could it be, if not you?"

"I have no idea," Indrek replied.

"Perhaps it was already faulty and just fell off by itself," ventured Ramilda.

"Nothing falls off by itself," said Mrs Malmberg in her worldly way, "there always has to be someone who takes it or knocks it off."

But since Mrs Malmberg couldn't presume to know who that someone was, she decided that the cup still had its handle when it smashed. So she started looking for the cup handle on the floor, and Ramilda and Indrek joined in. When she couldn't find it, she concluded, "So someone must really must have broken it off and concealed it."

"Someone definitely must have," affirmed Ramilda.

"But thank God it was you that dropped the cup; at least we've got that straight. Now we'll fetch a new one to replace it, and I want to check that all the cups have their handles on. In our home, not a single one of Grandmother's coffee cups had a missing handle, but here they don't last for more than a couple of days. You have to learn how to treat cups with the required delicacy! But people simply don't acquire the necessary skills. My husband tried to learn for ten years, but he went to his grave without ever knowing how to treat them. That's how men are. If they were responsible for bringing up children, then those children would probably be missing ears and other body parts – forget their cups. In my whole life

I've never knocked a handle off a cup, and my niece Miralda here…"

"Dear auntie, it's Ramilda please, not Miralda, otherwise both my ears will drop off," pleaded the young lady.

"Don't interrupt when I'm giving instructions to a young person," said Mrs Malmberg. "After all, someone has to teach the young people and bring them up in family life, because they'll need it in life. What's the use of Latin, if you don't know how to treat coffee cups and their handles break off? There's not much use in German either. Just think, what would be the good of all our young people being educated and speaking German, if everyone was breaking handles off cups?"

"Mr Paas can't speak German properly yet; he could still break a few cup handles, couldn't he, dear auntie?" said Ramilda.

"Everything's laughter and joking for you, and you don't understand what life's about," Mrs Malmberg sighed.

"I'll learn, dear auntie, believe me, I'll learn," Ramilda assured her. "But let's go and fetch that new cup, it's badly needed."

"There's time for that," replied Mrs Malmberg.

"No, no, let's go right away, dear auntie," insisted Ramilda, taking Mrs Malmberg by the hand, and she finally gave in and let herself be led out the door.

After a little while Ramilda ran back into the dining room, already wearing her coat, and whispered to Indrek: "You know what you've got to do now. Quick! It's your turn now, otherwise I won't teach you any more German. Cup-handle or German!" Then she vanished just as she had appeared: lightly, nimbly and unexpectedly.

After dinner it was found that one cup was again missing its ear.

"That was very nice of you!" Ramilda exclaimed to Indrek. "Now I'll trust you, only you. Papa trusts you too, I know. And do you know what auntie said? She said, 'Well, now it's all over, because if a handle has broken off, the other ones will soon be gone." So in a couple of days you'll need one more broken handle, and she'll be certain of her own words. The most important thing for her is belief. And hold onto those handles as a keepsake, won't you? I'm very sorry for auntie. Because of the way she keeps watch, she can't get any peace; even at night she dreams about cup handles. Poor auntie! So just one more, and auntie will be able to believe. She won't need any more."

And Ramilda was right: when another new cup was found to be missing its handle, Mrs Malmberg said in Indrek's presence, "Why do I bother to educate other people. Let them eat and drink like pigs at a trough. What else can you do?"

Chapter 13

Ramilda regained her ability to chat in the dining room, but nothing much came of her teaching Indrek German. This subject was regarded as terribly important, but nobody took effective charge of it. In class it was entrusted to an old German with a stoop, who from his very first day was christened Perpendicular, and the Estonians called him Plumbline, for Mr Schulz wore a long black coat, and his curved back and peculiar gait caused its tail to move oddly behind his back. Later both names fell into disuse and were replaced by Copula, which stuck with him to the end.

This name was based on the fact that Mr Schulz began his teaching of German in class with a definition of a copula or the word that connects the subject and the complement. He would search in a book for a sentence in Russian, translate it into German and then ask a pupil to write it out on the blackboard, so that the whole class could see what a Russian sentence was in German. Once the students were familiar with this exercise, he started looking for copulas in the sentence. At the end of the lesson the pupils wrote the sentence from the blackboard in their own exercise-books, and in the next lesson it would be parsed again. This process was repeated ad nauseam, and the boys felt that they were learning about copulas rather than German. "One moment, Mr Teacher of the German language, sir!" If they were asked anything, they would randomly answer, "Copula." From the beginning the old man thought this to be a joke, but when the whole class started singing, "Copula, copula", he lost patience and ordered Indrek to summon the headmaster.

"Don't go!" the others countermanded in Estonian, which

the teacher didn't understand at all, for he had only recently come to the Baltic lands from somewhere on the banks of the Volga. "He should go himself."

So Indrek didn't go.

"Then I'll go myself," said Mr Schulz threateningly, and left the classroom, and since Mr Maurus happened to be at home at the time, he soon came back in the latter's company.

"Who was the one who didn't come to fetch Mr Maurus?" asked the headmaster.

"This one," said the teacher, indicating Indrek.

"I ordered him to, but he wouldn't go – he said the class were against it."

"You shameless person!" shouted the headmaster in Estonian right under Indrek's nose, as if he wanted to pounce on him. "You big tall one! What do you do in a class of little short ones when the schoolteacher gives you an order? The schoolteacher here is Mr Maurus's deputy and his word should be obeyed by everyone. You have to obey me, don't you?"

"I do," answered Indrek.

"So why didn't you obey Mr Schulz's word, who is my deputy?"

"I didn't know that…" Indrek tried to say.

"What!" screamed the headmaster. "You didn't know that the schoolteacher is my deputy? You thought that Lible there is my deputy. You embarrass me in front of this German with your height and foolishness. So what can you tell him now?"

And he turned to the teacher and said in German, "This tall one is so short on brains that he didn't know… He thought that if the class is against it, he ought to obey the word of the class, because the class is many, but you are merely one. Well, what can I do with him, if he is so tall but short on common sense? He's also short of money. Next time, send somebody shorter, as he may well be longer on common sense. And now that other thing – what was it? I'm asking in Russian, so that everyone understands."

"Look, Mr Headmaster, Sir," began the teacher, "I've tried to make it clear to them what a copula is, because the copula a very important thing, not only in German but in every other language too, for instance: *Der Mann ist klein, das Kind ist gross.*"[30]

"How come?" exclaimed the headmaster. "What is this *Der Mann ist klein, das Kind ist gross…?*"

"I say that only as an example, so the content doesn't have to be true, Mr Headmaster, Sir," explained the teacher apologetically.

"It always has to be true, even if it's an example," said the headmaster. "In Mr Maurus' school even the teachers tell the truth, not only Mr Maurus and his pupils."

"Alright then, Mr Headmaster, Sir," agreed the teacher. "So let's say, '*Der Mann ist gross, das Kind ist klein.*' In both sentences the word *ist* is repeated, which connects the other words; that's why it's called a copula. You will perhaps agree, Mr Headmaster, with my explanation?"

"It is quite correct," Mr Maurus assured him.

"And clear?" the teacher asked.

"Quite clear," said Mr Maurus.

"I'm very pleased, Mr Headmaster, Sir, that you're of the same opinion as me," said the teacher, "but these boys seem to think that I'm teaching them something impossible or perhaps quite ludicrous. They make jokes about it all and answer all my questions with 'Copula', as if I'd taught them nothing else, or as if that was the whole of German grammar. Of course, I'm not denying that if you adopted a philosophical approach to the question, you could derive a whole system out of the single concept, indeed develop a whole world view, but I don't believe we could or should deal with that important issue so thoroughly in our present company, or that the pupils would be able to comprehend the philosophical

_____

30 *Der Mann ist klein, das Kind ist gross*: "The man is small, the child is big" [German]

significance of the copula in human speech, but I do think that they want to mock my repeated questions. I have come to this conclusion, Mr Headmaster."

"So have I," agreed Mr Maurus, as if this brought him a little pleasure. "But who answered your questions in that manner?"

"All of them."

"But who? Give me some examples. Give me the name of just one of the rascals."

"One moment, Mr Headmaster, Sir, I'll look up the book, I've got them marked down. They're all marked in my book. For example Lible." The teacher stressed the last syllable, so that Lible became Liblee.

"Ah, you, little Lible; you're the villain in the class!" cried the headmaster. "That's why you've gone to the bench at the back of the classroom. Come here now, come to the front row, stand here next to this tall one, while the teacher questions you."

At the headmaster's command, Lible came up beside Indrek, who was sitting in the front row of desks.

"Now question this little one," the headmaster ordered the teacher.

But his thoughts were evidently busy elsewhere, and so he didn't notice that he was posing the boy a question to which he had to answer, like it or not, with "Copula", and he didn't want to give a false answer. And hardly had that word fallen from Lible's lips than the headmaster seized him by the ears with both hands, as he screamed, "*Du kleiner Schinder!*"[31]

"Mr Headmaster, sir!" exclaimed the teacher, "he has answered correctly, it was I who gave him the wrong question."

Only now did Mr Maurus realise what he had done, and turning to the class, he told them in Estonian, peering over his glasses: "Now you can see the foolishness of this German. This is what we've had to put up with for the last seven hundred years."

---

31 *Du kleiner Schinder*: "You little rascal."

And as he was nearly finished, he splayed the fingers of his right hand in front of his eyes to signify that the teacher was out of his mind, but just at the right moment he pulled it back. He shook his grey head and said, "My good little boy had to get punished for no reason because of this German. Forever we've been beaten because of the Germans. It's a shame, but you've got to learn that lesson!"

And turning toward the teacher, he added in German: "Now you can continue, I've told them everything they need to know."

The headmaster left, but Mr Schulz didn't ask any grammatical questions of the class, fearing he would hear "Copula!" in reply. The next day when Indrek he didn't have lessons at the school, Mr Maurus gave him a letter after lunch, and asked him to take it to Mr Schulz. *

"Look after it," he said; "as it contains money. Give him the letter and come straight back. Don't stay and talk, don't listen to that old fool, because he loves to talk if anyone's listening."

The address on the letter led Indrek to the edge of town, where the cabmen with their horses and carts sometimes got stuck in the mud in spring. Mr Schulz lived in a little house looking out on a courtyard. Outside by the door on a stack of logs sat a frail old man in the March sunlight. Indrek inquired of him about Mr Schulz, but the old man didn't answer, as if lost in deep thought. The door was opened to Indrek by Mr Schulz himself.

"Ah, it's you!" he cried, as if he was very glad to see Indrek. "Please come in, come in, please. I have so few visitors that…"

"I just have this letter to give you," said Indrek.

"Do step inside," Mr Schulz implored, "just for a moment! Or am I really so awful that you can't even step into my home for a minute?"

Indrek stepped inside and handed over the letter.

"Who's it from?" asked Schulz. "From Mr Maurus? Why would Mr Maurus write to me? I was in his company only yesterday."

He opened the letter with nervous fingers and read it.

"Do you know what this letter is?" Mr Schulz asked Indrek. "Mr Maurus has calculated the number of my lessons, and here is my final salary. But do you know, Mr ... Mr ... sorry, what was your esteemed name? I don't have a gift for names, I never have had, all my life. Even my fiancée abandoned me, because after a three-month engagement I still couldn't remember her name. So if I may, I'll write down your honourable name in a book; a book never forgets. A book has a better memory than a human being. So Mr Paas, do you know the content of Mr Maurus's letter, which you've brought me?"

"You've already told me," replied Indrek.

"Ah, I've already told you! Very good, then you know. But do you also know what it means that Mr Maurus has been totting up my hours? No, you don't know at all, you're too young for that, Mr ... Mr ..." he looked into his book and said, "Mr Paas, you're too young for that. Those are almost my last lessons – almost, I say – you understand? But perhaps you saw that old gentleman out there by the door in the sunshine? That's my father, and he's quite deaf, it's not worth talking to him, he can't hear and he doesn't want to hear, he's that old. He's waiting for death and wants me to bury him in his home soil – by the Rhine, that's what he wants, for that's our home. But I can't take him to the banks of the Rhine if Mr Maurus has calculated my hours. Perhaps you don't know what a homeland is, because you don't have a proper homeland. You don't have the Rhine, you don't have a Frankfurt-am-Main that is really your own. Isn't that so? You live in a foreign land, you live in a Germany that is located in Russia; that's the kind of foreign land you live in. You talk a foreign language too, because you don't have a language of your own to speak. We two are talking a foreign language between ourselves, because we don't have a common language of our own. But you understand enough German to know what *die Heimat* means. *Die wahre Menschheit kann nur im Heimatland gedeihen!*"[32] And after that, he only spoke in German: "But where there is no homeland, where people live in a foreign land, humanity is absent too – true, real humanity. For what does Kant say: Act as if your actions could constitute a rule for living. Respect yourself by respecting others. For he who doesn't respect others doesn't respect himself. A person who doesn't have a proper language or homeland cannot respect himself, because a person first must be something, and only then can he begin to respect himself. The primary assets of a true human being are his language and homeland. Do you understand?"

"I do," Indrek assured him.

"Then I'll carry on speaking German, because a person should always speak his mother-tongue, always his mother-tongue, remember that. Love your mother-tongue, then you'll learn to love other languages, for how can you love a foreign one if you don't love your own? Your own and yourself, you must love; everything else comes as a matter of course. For what did Socrates say? 'Know thyself.' And how can you know anyone if you don't love them? And how can you love anyone if you don't even remember their name? But in class I didn't remember your names. That means that I, your teacher, didn't love you, didn't teach you love, so how could you love me? No, you couldn't. Only now do I understand that. But we need to love. So don't forget the name of the one you love, never forget it. – Yes, if you had a proper homeland to love, you would learn to love Russia too. You could even love German a little, as well as Germany and the German people, even a German like me. I'm not a landowner, for my father was a teacher, but if you could learn to love me, then you could also love the lords of the manor a little bit. You understand? Even your own landlord you could

---

32   *die Heimat … Die wahre Menschheit kann nur im Heimatland gedeihen*: "Homeland … True humanity can only thrive in the homeland." [German]

love and respect a little, if you had your own language and homeland. But you don't have one, there isn't one, you live in a foreign land and you talk a foreign language, so how could you respect and love me? I think you can't even respect and love yourself; that's my opinion. If I were richer, if I were a little younger and my farther wasn't awaiting death outside in the sunshine, I would invite you to the banks of the Rhine, I would invite you and show you what a real homeland is like. It was only on the banks of the Volga that I properly understood what it means for a person to have a homeland. Notice that: only on the banks of the Volga! That's where I appreciated it! And if you went to the banks of the Rhine, you would appreciate it too; you most definitely would, my dear young man. You must believe an old man like me. Only in a homeland does a human being truly come into existence ..."

Long before this, Indrek had stood up and walked backwards towards the door until he reached back to open it. Mr Schulz followed him and talked, while he was retreating through a dark, narrow hall. The last words he shouted to him from the front door into the spring sunshine, in whose rays the frail old man continued to sit, waiting for death.

Back home, Mr Maurus asked him, "Did he say anything?"

"No, he just took the letter at the door," Indrek replied.

"That old fool must be learning to see sense," Mr Maurus commented.

Left alone, Indrek repeated to himself, "Never forget the name of the one you love," followed shortly by the question: "But who do I love? Do I love anyone?" No, he didn't love anyone, no one at all. It seemed to him that he didn't even love his father and mother, or his sisters and brothers. He was not sure that he even loved Vargamäe. Now it seemed that he didn't even love that, so it wasn't worth remembering its name. Everything suddenly seemed distant and indifferent. Yet he still kept all these names in his mind, as if he loved them all.

At the same time he put his hand in his pocket and found two cup handles there, took them out and examined them in his hand. Two new cup handles! Actually there should have been three of them, but one, the last, he had thrown away. He didn't like it. Anyway, why would he have three when two were sufficient?

"Which one did I break and which did she?" he wondered. No answer came to mind. Two nameless cup handles! "Never forget the name of the one you love!" he repeated again. What if there are several names, countless ones? What if it's Ramilda, Rimalda, Marilda, Miralda? If there are countless ones, is it possible to remember them all, when you're in love? No, it isn't possible. Love it may be, but still you couldn't do it. Countless names amount to nothing; it's like having no name at all. Ridalma, Radilma, Diralma, Darilma, Ramaldi, Maraldi! And Vargamäe! Was there something about that name worth remembering? Did it mean anything worth loving? Madilra, Dimalra, Midalra, Damilra... Indrek began to wrap the cup handles in a single piece of paper, and they produced a slight rasping sound as they had done in his pocket. "Cup handles shouldn't be put in the same paper, never," he said to himself. "Why not?" he then asked, as he suddenly realized that it was a silly thing to say. It occurred to him that the cup handles were naked, like two people side by side and actually touching each other. He felt ashamed for the naked cup handles, and he quickly wrapped them separately, and then together in the same paper. "This is just for now," he said then; "later I'll buy you some softer and silkier paper. Cup handles should be in silky paper when they're together." Damirla, Madirla, Dimarla, Midarla... Only in silk does humanity truly come into existence, and only on a human being does silk truly come into existence. If there were no human being, there would be no silk, and if there were no silk, there would be no... Madness! Maldari, Dalmari, Raldami, amavi... Amatur! Amo, amas, amat... Only in love does humanity truly come into existence. Humanity is love. "Is" is a copula... Love is a copula; a copula is love. "Love" has an s in Estonian – *armastus*. All

171

ugly words have an *s*. *Armastus* is an ugly word. Estonian can only be used in the bedroom. *Deutsche Sprache* can be used in the bedroom – it has two S's in it. The phrase "in the bedroom" in Estonian – *magamistoas* – is ugly. The word for "word" – *sõna* – there are S's everywhere. And yet – "homeland", "beauty" and "beloved" don't have any. *Die wahre Liebe gedeiht in Heimatland, in Brautring.*[33] Not an Estonian *sõrmus*! *Sõrmus* is ugly! *Ich liebe, bin geliebt, verliebt.*[34] Midli-Madli, Kidli-Kadli…

The cup handles were hidden in the bottom of the box – no one could find them there. No one! He alone knew where those two were together.

---

33 "True love flourishes in the homeland, in the wedding ring." [German]
34 "I love, I am loved, in love." [German]

Chapter 14

Indrek's musing were interrupted by the doorbell. When it rang, someone was supposed to be coming or going by the front door. That person might as well have had a bell tied around their neck. But that only applied to the front door. No bell rang for those leaving by the back door. People simply went, and there was nothing else to it; they went out and turned left or right just as they wished, but they had to turn because they couldn't do otherwise. That was the way of it in town: if you wanted to get somewhere, you would have to turn and you would have had to turn at the right time and place, otherwise you would have definitely come across something that barred your way. In the countryside, things are done quite differently. There you simply step out of the front door and start walking straight ahead, perhaps veering off wherever your fancy takes you. If you come to some ditches, they either have planks across them or you jump across. Rivers have bridges, and streams always have dams which come and go according to the smallholder's requirements, which means that people can continue in a straight line. Fields have embankments to guide you, and you can even walk between potato and rye furrows. There are also embankments in the bogs and between the pools so people can find their way through if they want to, and it is entirely their own affair whether they decide to go by night or by day. However at night, it's certainly a good idea to go by moonlight. Try that in the town! It is not like the countryside: there you're always turning corners, always left or right, if you want to get anywhere.

So it is with the people who leave from Mr Maurus'

establishment by the back door. But those who choose the front door go down through the big room, where Indrek sits at a long table, or tinkers with something in his box behind the curtain, as he is today. But some of them, maybe the count, the prince, the pan, the von, or our good friend Tigapuu, make some sort of secret signal to Indrek, and then he gets up and goes with them to the front door, and then for some strange reason the door doesn't ring at all. Consequently Mr Maurus knows nothing about those people who manage to leave without making a sound, even if he's looking for them or asking about them. Nor does Indrek know anything, because in such cases he becomes suddenly blind and deaf. The person has vanished into thin air. It's quite a different matter if they trigger the doorbell. Then they are heard by everyone – and everyone knows who has left and when. That is the difference between going out with or without the doorbell.

The same thing happens in reverse when someone comes in. When the doorbell rings, half the house can hear you, and Indrek of Vargamäe or occasionally someone else rushes to meet you. Ask why, what and with whom? And you have to answer. But if the door is arranged so that you can get in without ringing, then you could stand, move or look around in the big room for quite a while before anyone questions you or offers you a chair. You can examine that large cupboard, on the top of which the stone busts of Goethe and Schiller once sat. Now they are no longer there, and nothing has come to take their place, and the silent witness would know nothing of their existence, nor would it ever occur to you that statues had once sat on top of such an imposing cupboard. Things would have been so much better when you could have seen those two sitting up there, or the angel of peace hanging from the ceiling. You would ask and find out everything – the who, the what, the why and the what for – and would leave this first-rate establishment with much greater knowledge and a wider view of the world. If you were a curious silent new arrival there were one or two things that you could have still done in the old way: you could have raised the floral curtain, because it billowed at the slightest gust of air, as if this sudden movement could have whisked you away. Behind the curtain you would have found bunk beds, and quite possibly old Voitinski who loved to lie down in one of the lower beds. He would have pulled his worn, greasy brown jacket around himself, as he rested peacefully and occasionally panted like a little dog.

One day the bell rang twice, and as he heard the shoes brushing on the doormat, Indrek concluded that this arrival was no stranger but an old acquaintance he had invited for four or five o'clock but had completely forgotten. But Mr Mäeberg doesn't forget when he is "ordered". He always remembers, as he comes even when he hasn't been "ordered", so he would definitely come when he has been. He comes and he wipes his thigh boots, as he does today. There is a particular sound to how Mr Mäeberg brushes his boots on the mat, and Indrek can distinguish it from all the other boots that come to the doorbell of Mr Maurus's establishment. Perhaps it is because their owner has only one eye, whereas people generally have two of them. Indrek has only now fully realised that if a person has two eyes, you can lie to them and look them straight in the face, because it's possible to shift your gaze back and forth. But if a one-eyed person comes, such as Mr Mäeberg, and stands on his stout legs, his stomach protruding, with his double chin, the eyelid drooping over his single eye and a wrinkled brow above the lid, and looks straight at you quizzically, there is nowhere for you to avert your gaze, you can't move it, for that would sow the mustard seed of suspicion in his soul. So looking straight and unflinchingly into a person's single eye and then lying to him was something Indrek simply could not do. He didn't even try, because he knew he would start to stammer and blush, and that would be the end of it. He therefore chose in his dealings with Mäeberg not to lie as required by the house rules, but to talk about matters that had no basis in reality. In this way he had no trouble in staring directly into Mr Mäeberg's solitary eye and fulfilling his professional obligations.

"I don't know what business you have with me today, Mr Mäeberg," said Indrek who was adjusting his chair which gave him something to do and allowed him to avoid the single eye of his visitor who was still wheezing from his exertions.

"Nothing, again?" Mr Mäeberg panted.

"It's worse than that," replied Indrek, "there's not much hope for the near future either."

"What's this?" cried the visitor. "But you guaranteed payment by this time. Because I value your word, I've kept away for two weeks; otherwise I would have come much earlier. Listen, young man, don't start lying to me like that Latvian who was here before you. He used to lie like a Russian. If it's a Jew or a Tatar, you know already that they're going to lie, but as for a Russian, you just don't know. You think that you're dealing with a Christian, and then they go and lie worse than a Jew or a Tatar. Take you, for instance: I trust you and put my affairs in your hands so to speak, and you…"

"You're quite right," agreed Indrek, "I can't defend myself at all, and I am to blame. You have to keep on coming…"

"Coming doesn't mean anything," interjected Mäeberg, "I'm happy to come, as long as it isn't about some deception. I don't like deception and lies; I've never liked them all my life. Why would you cheat and lie if you're a true Christian and your Tsar's subject…?"

"Alright, alright," Indrek affirmed, "I'm very embarrassed, but I simply couldn't have guessed what was going to happen. Believe it or not, but there have been literally thousands of creditors."

"Who then? Who are you talking about?" asked Mäeberg.

"If you let me speak, I'll tell you in a few words, so that you can see the true circumstances."

"Alright," Mäeberg panted agreement. "Anyway I need to catch my breath."

"As you know," began Indrek, "Mr Maurus is always in financial difficulties. But I knew that one of these days he was going to receive a largish sum of money – I heard that quite by accident – a few boys were supposed to repay their old debts. Well, I thought that this would be the ideal time for you to collect your share; you've had so many wasted journeys."

"That's true," exclaimed Mr Mäeberg. "Between ourselves, I've been living like a stray dog."

"Of course, that's why I thought this the best way to resolve that. The money did come, because my information was correct, but I was wrong about the time. And I was wrong about a couple of other things too. I thought that only I knew about the money coming in, but as it turned out, others knew about it too – many others. By the end of that week, it was raining creditors – schoolteachers, shopkeepers, butchers, tailors, cobblers, washerwomen, seamstresses, they all came swarming in. And Mr Maurus started forking out the money again and again until there was very little left, and Mr Ollino told him that at this rate, we'll end up hungry ourselves. So the paying had to stop. But then a fisherwoman came in the morning from the riverside, and she swore like a trooper as she demanded her money. She'd sold us fresh live fish, taken in a net straight from the bargeman, and now she was demanding payment. It would have been a different matter if Mr Maurus had been given fish that weren't fresh – she could have put up with that, but not when they were fresh. Both Mr Maurus and Mr Ollino tried to explain that they no longer had money – let her come another time – but then the Russian woman started swearing, cursing and threatening! Then Mr Ollino's patience snapped, he took the old woman by the hand and threw her out the door into the street. All hell broke loose: the old hag stood in the middle of the street in front of our house, sticking out her stomach, her legs akimbo, hands on hips, shouting for all she was worth. Ollino laughed, but Mr Maurus took fright, because it was a Russian shouting, not an Estonian or a German, and before anyone could stop him, he opened the front door, invited the fishwife back inside and paid her off – to the last kopeck, whether or not the fish was fresh. So that was the last of the money. There wasn't even enough, as Mr Ollino had lent a bit extra, just to get rid of the screaming fisherwoman. That was the main thing that I couldn't have foreseen. If I'd been able to, I would have told you not to come today."

"So, you wipe your mouth clean for the sake of a Russian," said Mr Mäeberg portentously. "So when am I supposed to come then?"

"I don't dare to promise anything anymore, I'd only be lying," replied Indrek. "If you knew how hard my position is!"

"I appreciate that, young man," said Mr Mäeberg, supporting himself with his stick as he got out of his chair. "But there's one thing I'm glad about anyway: I became wiser today, and we get wiser with every passing day until our dying hour. You have to follow the example of the Russians if you want to get your money. Start screaming, make a scene in the middle of the street, and you'll get paid soon enough, because it's shameful to let a person scream in front of your house in broad daylight. I understand Mr Maurus very well; I have a house of my own. Out of shame a person will do anything – even give away his last kopeck for his soul."

"Of course," agreed Indrek, "but if ten fishwives screamed in front of his house now, Mr Maurus might die of shame, but he wouldn't pay them, because he simply doesn't have it."

"Quite right," Mr Mäeberg assured him, "if someone doesn't have it, he simply can't pay, however much people may scream in front of the house. I'm not, of course, going to scream in front of Mr Maurus's house, since things are not as bad as that just yet. I'm not a Russian. Money is money, but a brother is still a brother. And Mr Maurus and I are brothers. We were together in the Society of Letters. That's where we became acquaintances and later friends. I was the man who put the idea of this school in Mr Maurus's head. I was the one, young man, and standing before you, you have

178

the spiritual father of Mr Maurus's first-rate school. It was at one of those heated meetings that I said to Maurus, who was seated next to me, that we had too few men of letters in the Society of Letters, and that was why we had such fierce arguments. 'We're supposed to be a Society of Letters, but the ones who do all the arguing are priests and politicians. Where are the real men of letters going to come from? Where else but from a school, and the bigger the school, the greater the men of letters.' So I said to Maurus, 'Set up a school, set up an Estonian school, so we can have Estonian men of letters. It doesn't matter,' I said, 'if they aren't quite as great and famous as some Russian or German ones, for how would an Estonian literary person suddenly be as famous as a Russian or German? It'll be enough if he's a real Estonian literary person like Jannsen or Koidula, who are already dead, for all the real Estonian literary figures are dead.' 'But I don't have any money,' Maurus replied to me at that meeting of the Society of Letters. 'Educating men of letters takes a lot of money,' he said. I patted him on the shoulder, right there in front of others, and said the money was sure to turn up, as long as there was one man, a son of his fatherland, who was willing to establish a proper school of letters and bring an end to those eternal squabbles at the Society of Letters. So then, old Maurus – he was still a young man then, and so was I – took up my idea and got his school going with my money. All these years I've been waiting for my money back, and sooner or later I want to have it back. For that's the way of the world, including Estonia: you either go bankrupt like Linda,[35] and then you don't pay your debts, or you keep going like that house that I bought after the Linda bankruptcy, and then it pays off its debts, because there isn't a single kopeck of debt left on my house. Well, Maurus's school has kept going, and so I'd like to get my debt paid, now wouldn't I?"

---

35 Linda was an Estonian feminist literary magazine which was published from 1887 to 1905.

"Naturally," Indrek assured him.

"But of course," Mr Mäeberg went on, "this has to be dealt with properly, not like at the Society of Letters: everyone with their own agenda. At the time I said, 'Let's elect a president and put the matter in his hands, let's hand it over to one man, a leader, so to speak, and then all we have to do is obey his instructions.' I'd like to see what sort of squabbles there would be at the Society of Letters if all the literary types had to obey orders. But you're still too young to understand such things. If you took the trouble to visit me, I would explain the Estonian cause to you – you're going to need it in life. I know the men of the people, as I've been dealing with them quite enough. I was a man of the people myself and still am a little bit, but I'm old now and have worries at home to contend with. You'd be very welcome, and we could talk a bit about Estonia and the Estonian cause. Young people aren't interested in the Estonian cause, because they don't have any ideals. Yet people should have ideals, as we had in our day. You should come and make an old man happy."

"I'll definitely come," said Indrek, though inwardly he was thinking the opposite. Yet he did what he said, not what he thought. Why? He didn't know. Mr Mäeberg had to have his say. And what's more, his first visit would not to be his last.

Mostly Mr Mäeberg was alone, but on a couple of occasions Indrek also met visitors there –only stout, solid men. Mäeberg didn't care for women anymore. Once he'd had ideals, as he said himself, and since that time he'd kept some pictures of a few women, which he loved to show people with a triumphant and meaningful smile. Now he warned everyone, especially the younger generation, against women, although he did keep a plump and florid servant girl, because he loved to see youth around him, as he would explain to acquaintances. A homely atmosphere prevailed in the house, so you could easily get the impression that Mr Mäeberg was living with his grown-up daughter or a strikingly young wife. To avoid misunderstandings, Mr Mäeberg would lose no time in introducing her jocularly, "This is my housekeeper – by the name of Liisi."

When this housekeeper was introduced to Indrek, Mäeberg twitched the corners of his mouth as though he were about to smile.

"She spoils me," explained Mäeberg with a certain delicacy; "she eats with me at the same table because otherwise an old man gets lonely. But it's all entirely decent: she has no boyfriends, she doesn't go to dances and doesn't wear corsets, which I don't approve of. A girl like that is suitable for a good man. Sometimes I joke with her: Get married and I'll give you a good dowry, but bury me first – and then you'll have an even better dowry. I doubt that a husband would be a better arrangement. She lives here with me as a person in her own right. I'm truly a man of the people, and it doesn't matter that I have a big house. I've had to put up with a lot in life to be a man of the people, because men of the people always have to suffer. Don't take offence, my dear young man, but I think Christ was a man of the people too, that's why he came to such a miserable end. Christ was a man of the Jews. Men of the people always die before their time. It's the same with us. Take Jannsen, Veske, Kunder, Jakobson for example. That's why I'm so worried for my own health, that I won't live for the time God has allotted me – but I'll have to die like a man of the people. I comfort myself with these words: Don't worry, Tõnis Mäeberg! The candle of your life might go out, but your life's work will remain. Your name won't die in your fatherland's history, because you've been a force for promoting the Estonian way of life. You've blown a tuba in three bands, and all those brass bands have won prizes, merits or other plaudits, so my name will remain in the annals of musical achievements. I've still got my tuba. If you want, I'll blow on my tuba for a bit, so you can hear what proper brass sounds like. Be so kind as to step onto that chair, put those old newspapers aside on the top of the cupboard, you'll see what comes out from under them. It's to keep the dust off…"

And Indrek had to step up onto a chair, shift the dusty pile of newspapers aside and take down the famous tuba, which had won prizes for three brass bands, and merited so many plaudits. Mr Mäeberg put the tuba to his lips and blew. Liisi quietly opened the door of the next room and grinned meaningfully at Indrek. The cat jumped off the sofa, where it had been sleeping curled up, and onto the floor where stretched itself to its full extent. Mr Mäeberg blew to warm up the instrument, and eventually played a little of "The People of Kungla", ending with "Now We Bury the Dear Departed". He played only a little of each, just enough to give us an idea.

"This isn't a simple shepherd's horn," he explained as he gasped for breath, "and you don't blow it on your own, but always in groups. And when everyone is blasting away, that's a proper brass sound, and it's beautiful. Well, what do you think of that, young man?"

"Even on its own it's very beautiful," declared Indrek.

"Well now!" cried his host. "Tõnis Mäeberg plays, and then it isn't beautiful! I would have kept playing right up to today, but other patriotic things came along – bankruptcies and deaths, and then I bought this house, and I started lending people money at a reasonable interest rate and then collecting antiquities for Dr. Hurt, so that when Dr. Hurt becomes famous for his ancient relics, the name of Tõnis Mäeberg won't be hidden under a bushel either. I'm a man of letters too – although a bit on the plump side. I hope that death is not in a hurry, because my heart would be at peace if I could find some young person to take on the burden of this cause beforehand. These days young people don't have any real love or understanding for patriotic causes. You see, I'm my own biographer and the biographer of all the other important men that I've come across and with whom I have talked of patriotic matters. The title will be *The Works and Achievements of Tõnis Mäeberg*. I think that it has an agreeable sound to it. What do you think?"

"Definitely," Indrek ventured his opinion.

Mr Mäeberg wanted no more or less than that Indrek would become the custodian of his literary inheritance. Once Indrek had given the impression of agreeing to this, the old man soon came upon the second worry of his life, which he went on to explain to his young Estonian friend: "There is one other thing to be settled before I die, because when a decent man dies he should leave everything in order. This isn't just my affair, but the person it concerns also concerns me a little, so her affairs are also my affairs. She was just a quiet and pious girl from the countryside when I took her in; you could say that I did it out of pity and fatherly concern, so that she would grow into a well-rounded and competent person. And that is what I've made of her, and she has become my own housekeeper, who knows that all that's shines isn't silver and all that glitters isn't gold. But what is to become of her after my death? She can't settle for just any bumpkin, can she? She has a little education, but she doesn't understand German – well, maybe a word or two that she's heard from me. Of course this house is going to her, you must know that. But a house alone isn't much for a young woman; she needs support too, proper support. And now I thought of this: if the young man who publishes *The Works and Achievements of Tõnis Mäeberg* were the heir to Tõnis Mäeberg, as far as this house is concerned, … Do you follow me? But of course, he would have to be a real support to her. A genuine one with the rings and the bride's cap and all that sort of thing. For it doesn't matter that Liisi is perhaps older than that young Estonian man and dear kinsman. It is not a problem for Liisi either, I can assure you of that. She has a particular nature. It doesn't matter, not when you think of the house and everything associated with it, along with the reliable tenants. Not every young man is good enough for that, for Liisi won't have dealings with just anyone. Tõnis Mäeberg can only bequeath his house and housekeeper to a suitable Estonian young man. But my money, my cash and my bonds, for I have those too, will go to him along with the money as, so to speak, a monument to my soul and to my spirit in this world, so that the name of Tõnis Mäeberg shall be eternal, as will the memory of his flesh and body, which once played the tuba, brewed beer and made vodka, for I was a trained distiller and brewer by trade. Yes, my name with its cash and my body with what can also be turned into cash – by which I mean the house with the maid. So what do you say to that, young man? Isn't that a good idea? Eh?"

"Very good!" Indrek affirmed.

That was the supreme moment for Mäeberg's plans. But when people are within grasping distance of something truly amazing, there is still time for their downfall, for there's little time for daydreaming in this world. That's a mortal's lot.

Hardly had Indrek given his affirmative answer than the smiling Liisi appeared in the doorway of the dining room, announcing that coffee was on the table, and at once the avalanche began to shift and destruction could not be far off.

Mäeberg noticed that when Liisi notified them of the coffee, she addressed the invitation to the guest rather than himself. In any event, the smile was not directed at him as master of the house, but to the visitor, as she had never smiled at her master in that way. Liisi was smiling at the guest as if he were her new master and her former one was already dead and a new chapter in her life had begun. Or so it appeared to Mr Mäeberg as the beaming Liisi, his housekeeper stood in the doorway of the dining room, which a sweet smell of coffee emanated from. It suddenly occurred to Mr Mäeberg that this was how it had always been – since the young man had first visited – yet he, Tõnis Mäeberg, had never noticed it before, possibly because he only had one eye. But now he was going to watch his housekeeper and his guest very carefully, as carefully as someone with two eyes. So it took Mr Mäeberg no more than half an hour to give up all his plans, and he made a new and irrevocable decision: this young man would never step over his threshold again, for he was too tall and too thin for that.

Liisi had also noticed Indrek's tallness and thinness, it now seemed to Mr Mäeberg, and she had even asked, quite innocently of course, whether it would be possible to feed up such a lad, flesh out those bones and make him a bit plumper. Indeed, that was definitely what Liisi had talked about on Indrek's first visit, and then her employer carelessly went so far as to suggest that someone should try. Yes, that was what must have happened. Liisi did try. She even went so far as to put sweetmeats in Indrek's pocket, though concealing this from Mr Mäeberg and Indrek himself, for Liisi loved her secrets. She did that on that day, along with a slip of paper, on which she scribbled, "Friday between five and seven o'clock when old man is in Sauna". This was the culmination of Liisi's plans, but Mr Mäeberg had already made his fatal decision.

If Mr Mäeberg had announced his decision to Indrek right there and then, and asked his opinion, as he did with other things, he would definitely have got an affirmative answer, especially if he had asked Indrek's opinion after the latter had read Liisi's secret message by the light of a street lamp. For as soon as he had done that, he ripped the slip of paper into a thousand pieces and threw it onto the pavement, but he carried the little packet he'd found in his pocket along the street bustling with the cabmen and incomers from the countryside. He set off for the school as though people were chasing him.

When he got there, Indrek first had to check whether the cup handles were still at the bottom of the box, because they had come to mind while he was reading Liisi's secret message. There they were! The cup handles were there! Both of them! Just where Indrek had last put them in their silken wrapping. And at that moment he felt that now he could lie to Mr Mäeberg about whatever and whenever, without a flicker of fear as he stared into his single eye.

However, the affairs of this world turned out to be stranger than Indrek could ever have guessed. Though ready to demonstrate how easy it would be to lie to the old man, there didn't seem to be any need, because Mr Mäeberg didn't show his face again throughout the spring. The other creditor still came, but there were no difficulties with him as he never believed a single word he heard in that house. He could have told the truth just as easily.

"The one-eyed one is nowhere to be seen," Mr Maurus once observed. "I hope that he's not sick. God preserve him, otherwise his heirs will be chasing me."

"I saw him in the street recently," Indrek said to reassure him.

"Strange;" said the headmaster, "he used to be the one that came most often."

"Yes, now it's the other one," said Indrek, pleased to agree with the headmaster.

Chapter 15

The spring came without Indrek noticing. Only when he happened to be out with others in the sunshine and the warm wind and saw the slanted fields in the distance did he suddenly become aware that spring was there.

"Now the river will soon flow through the marsh birches," he said to himself as he thought of home. "Yes, shortly you'll be able to see it from the field on the hill – as the sun gets warmer and keeps getting warmer, while this same wind is blowing."

And as if for the first time in his life he really appreciated how the river had glittered in spring as it ran through to Vargamäe alongside and the marsh birches when they were still in bud and even later when their bright greenery reached its fullness. There would be a glow and sparkle that played on the substance of the water. Even many versts further on, your eyes were blinded by the sight of it. It was as if the sun itself had come down and walked on the Vargamäe river, winding its way between marshes and bogs, meadows and forests, flowing ever onward through them all, maybe to the ends of the earth. But not even in spring can the Vargamäe river reach the sea. As it approaches the sea, it stops and can flow no further.

Yes, only in spring do the heavens so graciously send the sun to walk along the Vargamäe river, allowing the people of Vargamäe to see it and sense it, and thus not to feel that it has orphaned them. Only now did Indrek start to understand this. Those around him had also sensed something of this, and hence they were walking out of the darkness like wise men who have discovered some new truth.

Indrek had come to the town with such high hopes and intentions, but how differently it had turned out! He had wanted to discover something momentous, something beautiful, and yet the year was passing as if he had been chasing a directionless wind. His lofty expectations and naive preconceptions and his exalted expectations had been reduced to an absurd maze of petty everyday affairs, and quite grotesquely the only thing with any real meaning seemed to be that for half the year he had been slicing bread and laying plates, knives and forks and handleless cups on the table. And now he had two cup handles at the bottom of his box.

Then it happened that some things had gone missing, and Maurus made the boys open their boxes for a search. Indrek was the first to have his box turned inside out, and Ollino found the cup handles and handed them to Maurus.

"Where are these from and what are they for?" the headmaster asked Indrek, and the grins on the boys' faces grew wider and wider, especially when Indrek wouldn't answer. Vutt was in such a good mood that he fiddled with Sikk's little finger.

"Ah, so it's you who've been breaking the cup handles!" screamed the headmaster. "You, the tall one! You, who incited old Mr Schulz to come to me! You..."

"Those are not the handles of your cups," declared Indrek.

"What? Not mine? But whose then? Where did you take them from?" asked the headmaster.

"That I will tell only you alone, Mr Headmaster," replied Indrek.

"Mr Maurus has no secrets," said the headmaster. "My house is like a glass dome; everyone can look in, anyone who wants to, for truth and justice prevail here."

But apparently Indrek didn't love truth and justice, so he went silent. Finally there was no way out for the headmaster but to go into another room with the boy, where he explained: "Before I came away from home, I broke the handles off two cups, and my mother told me that they were lucky handles, she wrapped them in paper and put them in my box for me. For my mother's sake I didn't want to say it in front of others, Mr Headmaster."

"Well, alright then, if they're your mother's lucky handles," said the headmaster now, "but make sure they don't bring you bad luck." These last words sounded like a joke. And Mr Maurus turned back to the others, saying to Ollino: "Give Paas back his things."

Ollino was just then looking at the cup handles as if there were something special about them or as if he had a sense of their real significance. And as Indrek was starting to wrap them in paper again, Ollino said: "A kind of talisman, eh?"

The word *talisman* appealed to the boys so much that from that moment on, they started calling Indrek "Tall-is-man",[36] not with one "l" but with two.

And so Indrek and his cup handles came to be on everyone's lips. The only possible competitor with him in terms of fame was Laane, but he didn't get much benefit from his fame, as he had to leave the school. A pocketbook was found on him, containing, amongst other things, a section called "Thefts".

This was a collection of reports taken from Estonian, Russian and German newspapers all about thefts. Details were also found about criminal jargon which were followed by a note in red ink, "Very important", underlined three times and followed by three exclamation marks. There was a fragment of an essay dealing with theft as a social phenomenon – "Theft and Other Crimes". Followed by "A Meditation", which had then been crossed out and replaced with, "Thoughts about theft". The essay then proceeded:

---

36 The original pun in Estonian is that *tall* in Estonian means "stable" and *tallis* means "in the stable", and is therefore is a joke about Indrek's rural origins. Coincidentally we can generate an English pun with the double "l" in the variant which can be broken down into "Tall is man," given that Maurus always calls him "the tall one".

189

"Theft is a social activity, since a single person cannot steal, because no one can steal from themselves. The ancient Romans were not allowed to steal, but the Greeks were, as long as it wasn't discovered, because exposure was strictly forbidden. *Strogo vospreshcheno!*[37] You can't steal in Russia either, so theft is a dangerous activity. A thief is bold, a bandit is not, for why else would he kill his victims because of his fear that the theft will be exposed. The thief is not afraid of being discovered and therefore doesn't kill. God was the first thief because he stole Adam's rib and made Eve out of it, so that woman is created from theft and is herself a thief. My mother is a thief too; she steals from father, but father doesn't steal from mother, but he does steal battens, poles and switches from the landowner's forest, because spruce and juniper switches are better than willow and birch; they don't rot so fast. I have also stolen spruce and juniper wood…"

This outburst robbed Mr Maurus of his senses. With great effort Ollino managed to calm him down, so he could continue his reading.

One of the papers continued: *Whawer wawer stewer? Iwer wanter stealer.* To this was added an explanation: "What do you want? I want to steal." On the next two pages were large headlines: *Oyu stum least*, and then: *Oyu veha losten*. Both pages were full of writing in this lingo. With a bit of effort you could make out that the first must have meant "You must steal", and underneath were listed all the things you could steal, together with an indication of their number, and the second: "You have stolen", accompanied by a list of things stolen, together with an indication of whether they were intact or broken, and where they were hidden.

On the basis of the information in the book, they started to look for the things in their hiding places, and it turned out that these accounts were perfectly accurate, which made everyone laugh, even Mr Maurus himself. For you couldn't

---

37 "Strictly forbidden!" [Russian]

wish for anything more satisfying than a book that instructed you on exactly where to find and recover a particular object such as a fork, knife or spoon hidden in a cavity in Siberia.

The only mystery was why were there so many old and broken things among the stolen items? Mr Maurus was so interested in this question that he got Laane under his roof for one night just to grill him and wheedle out his secrets. But it was to no avail, and the next day the boy left without Mr Maurus having satisfied his curiosity.

Since Laane didn't have a single kopeck in his pocket, Maurus himself had to give him some travelling money, because otherwise he wouldn't have been able to get rid of him. But his spirit would stalk the rooms of the institution for a while afterward, mainly because of Mr Maurus's repeated assertions that Laane had not interpreted the scriptures correctly when he said that God was the first thief.

"Thieves should not seek justification for their actions in God's," said the headmaster during prayers the very next morning, "for the acts of God are God's, human acts are human. When God put Adam to sleep in Eden and took his rib and made a woman of it, it was not a theft, as he was merely taking what was his. So it says in Scripture: God took. For Adam belonged to God. Now if someone takes something that is his own, is he stealing? No, he most certainly isn't! When a master takes from his slave, is he stealing? The slave himself and all his possessions belong to the master. Adam and all of us who descend from him belong to God – and also to our Tsar; therefore if God or the Tsar takes anything from us, including our own lives, they are not stealing. But if one human mortal takes from another human mortal, that is theft; for a human has never made another human out of the soil nor breathed life into his nose, although humans do beget other humans through sinful lust. So therefore a woman is not stolen from anything, nor is she something stolen…"

This recurring topic of conversation, apart from the search for the original thief, was the age-old "palace of commas", as Mr Koovi called it. This subject never disappeared from ·

the suppertime teaching about decency and manners, and it always seemed fresh in the mouth of Mr Maurus, so fresh that once at supper Koovi said in the full hearing of all the pupils: "Mr Maurus, you speak so clearly that I feel as if I were sitting in a palace of commas and not a dining room."

"It little matters that you, Mr Koovi, feel that way," replied the headmaster straightaway, "but my boys should feel that way, for it's not the schoolteachers but they who must put down the commas, and they won't do that until they have the same feelings as you."

Not even Mr Koovi objected to this, as it was so clearly correct, and therefore Mr Maurus was emboldened to continue: "Do you not know Jehovah's command to the people of Israel, that every man should go behind his tent and should take a peg and make a hole in the ground with it and drive the earth down with it? Did Jehovah say 'with a finger'? No, Jehovah said 'with a peg'. Estonian men do not need to make a hole, thank God, because the hole was there already, but Estonian men may have to insert commas not with their fingers but with a pencil or a pen, which are both peglike – that is Jehovah's command. But if anyone is so poor that he doesn't have God's paper, then let him come to Mr Maurus, let him come in secret if he is ashamed of his poverty, let him come and say: 'Mr Maurus, I and my parents, we are all so poor that we cannot afford the paper that must stand for the peg of the man of Israel. And Mr Maurus will then give him the paper for today and tomorrow, for this week and next week, for he does not want to be ashamed of his boys. And if there is one among you who says that he has no paper, then that person is lying to Mr Maurus, as he who said that God is a thief was also lying. He received his wage and that one will not go without. Therefore beware that you do not start stealing paper for the sake of commas, for that would be as the ancient Romans said: *summum jus, summa injuria.*[38] And you should be

---

38 "Extreme application of the law leads to maximum injustice." [Latin]

ashamed to study Pushkin and Goethe if you know that you're not putting commas in the right places. You would blush to sing
Über *allen Gipfeln*
Ist Ruh',
In allen Wipfeln
Spürest du
Kaum einen Hauch...[39]
if you knew that you didn't have any paper on which to place the Israeli men's peg. On his Italian journey Goethe did come across some palaces, but he didn't put commas in, so he could be a useful example not only of singing but of everyday life too."

In this and other ways Mr Maurus instructed his pupils and teachers at the supper table, but he could never instil in them the essence of Mr Koovi's observation on his dining-hall lectures. Thus he kept trying to teach this to them by speaking in ever clearer and stronger language.

39 It's calm above the peaks, on all mountaintops you hardly feel the wind's breath." [German]

Chapter 16

One evening Mr Maurus concluded his edifying speech in Estonian: "Mr Maurus would normally be speaking to you about the palace of commas, but today it is my duty to tell you that, Professor Köler[40] is dying in St. Petersburg. You need to understand the gravity of this! None other than Professor Köler! Our last great man and a true friend of the Estonian people! And Dr. Hurt as well."

There were few sitting at the table who had heard the name of Professor Köler, even fewer who would have known what he had done. Therefore we yad no prior notice of this announcement, although the term "professor" did register with some because it commanded respect. But the next morning the headmaster recalled that name again at prayers, and now there were a few who sensed some recognition in the words, when he addressed himself only to the Estonians in their language: "So what is to become of us? What fate awaits our nation, if all those who love it are dying? Are we to perish with them? No, not perish, for the sun will still rise, and as the bard once sung:

Should the sound of the Estonian language disappear, You as well will have no reason to rise up and live.

"But when indeed those who love the Estonian nation do die, then we must take their places so that they don't remain empty. We must all – young and old, big and small – love our

---

40   Johann Köler (1826-1899) was a painter and a leading figure in the Estonian National Awakening. He came from a peasant family and rose up to the rank of professor in the Imperial Academy of Arts.

Estonian nation, as did those great men who have already died or are yet to die. Yes, even the small ones must love it, as if they were bigger, for love is what makes the small grow bigger. And tell me now, does our nation have anything to fear if we love it with all our heart? No, such a nation has nothing to fear, it must live, for love is life. So, boys, love your nation, love yourselves, as the English and the Germans love themselves. Love the Estonian nation, but be loyal to your Tsar, for in his hands are the keys to your life and the shackles of your death."

When the news of the death arrived, the headmaster announced that he had decreed a special memorial service, and that everyone of Estonian blood was going to it. But evidently there were few among the Estonians who had Estonian blood, for only a handful of people turned up in church. Of Mr Maurus's pupils it was mainly those who lived in the boarding house who came, as they were ordered to go directly to the church. It was not easy to escape that slavery, for the boys were lined up in front of the schoolhouse in two rows, the smaller ones in front and the bigger ones behind. The line moved off in pairs with Mr Maurus ahead and Mr Ollino bringing up the rear to make sure that no one slipped away behind Mr Maurus's back. So they proceeded through the town, so that everyone could see how Mr Maurus was taking his pupils to commemorate Professor Köler.

Present in the church was the old grey-haired pastor, who stood with his hands together and alone at the altar when Mr Maurus entered leading his flock. The pastor lingered by the altarpiece and said, "Dear children, the man who created this painting is now dead. Or rather his flesh has died, but his spirit lives on in the Redeemer at this altar. Let us bow before his living spirit and pray for the body of the deceased." At this the pastor turned his back and sank to his knees; Mr Maurus, a few steps lower from the altar, did the same and his example was followed by his pupils.

Who knows how this happened? When Indrek saw those

two men, both of them old and kneeling in front of the altar, and when he heard the strange tone of the pastor's voice falling sharply at the end of a sentence, as if he were heading into the depths of hell, and when he noticed that the other one who always loved to talk was now kneeling in silence, he could hardly keep back his tears. It was the silence of his headmaster that most affected him, and he was suddenly overcome by inexplicable sorrow. He only held back his tears because he would have been ashamed in front of the others – his fellow pupils and Ramilda, who had appeared in the choir with her aunt. But when they finally rose and Indrek saw that both the preacher and Mr Maurus were wiping their eyes, it was with regret that he realised he could have done the same. On leaving the church he felt that he'd spoilt the most beautiful moment of his life, and went home sadder than when he came.

He was tormented by one inescapable thought: everything that was great or beautiful in this world belonged to the past. The great and the beautiful were dead. The great and beautiful were times gone. He had come too late to the town, just as he had come too late to Vargamäe. And again the question arose: is there nothing great and beautiful left? Once there had been Koidula, Kreutzwald, Jakobson and Köler, and now they were no more. Once there had been Goethe, Schiller and Pushkin, and now nothing remained. There was still Tolstoy, but they weren't allowed to read him, or if they did, it had to be in secret. That all the works of these were great and beautiful had to be kept secret; only when they died could the truth be revealed. Now it was the same for Köler: Indrek had never heard of him before, but as soon as he died, everybody was talking about him – the whole world was, so that you wouldn't be able to forget him in the future. Now Indrek would never forget his name! As if a true living soul only entered some people at death! All this was so strange that he might also have wanted to be one of the living dead. It wouldn't matter what he had done or how he had lived, as long as he had got that true living spirit at death. Such a silly and senseless desire was sprouting in Indrek as he left the church where he had repelled those unwept tears that rose in his throat.

"Did you cry in church too?" Ramilda, whom he hadn't seen for a long time, asked him the next day.

"No," replied Indrek.

"But Papa cried and the preacher was also wiping his eyes," declared Ramilda. "Köler was their friend. I wanted to cry terribly too, but it wouldn't come. And do you know why? I've seen Köler a few times, ever since childhood, but if you've seen someone so often, it isn't easy to cry over them. You just get to the point where you feel, here come the tears, but then something suddenly comes to mind and it drives the thought away. I remembered Köler's scanty beard and that immediately quelled my desire to cry. How could I cry over him when he had such a scanty beard? Silly, isn't it? After that I forgot about his beard, because I simply pulled myself together and forgot, but then I recalled how he once stayed overnight with us, just a couple of years ago. His mouth was open and his expression was one of profound indifference. As soon as that came to mind – something else came to mind too, but I won't tell you that now, I can't – but when what I can't tell you came to mind, it suddenly dawned on me that the Redeemer in his painting had his very own face and that if that Redeemer came to stay, even by accident, then his mouth would stay open and his expression would have been of indifference like Köler's and he would have nothing to do with anyone in the whole wide world. Now tell me, could you cry if something like that occurred to you?"

"Of course I couldn't, if it were something like that."

"I couldn't either, for I thought straightaway, how could I cry for a person who made the Redeemer in his own image, so that if the Redeemer happened to fall asleep, he would have had the same indifferent expression, not like the one in the picture. It's all very silly, because the Redeemer didn't ever

197

just happen to fall asleep, but that's what his apostles did in the garden of Gethsemane, but you can look at it in different ways. Have you ever thought about something in church in two different ways?"

"I haven't," replied Indrek.

"So what were you thinking, if you weren't thinking in two different ways? I can never think for a long time in just one way. No matter how widely and deeply I think, somehow my thoughts get tied up in knots, and even without my knowing it, they come back to where they started, like someone lost in the woods. It goes on and on, and still it's in the same place. Our thought is circular, and so everything is circular. And it's that circularity I'm afraid of. I don't ever like going back to where I was, and that's why I think two different ways, so that the thought won't come back round. But a circular thought is like an eternal life. When the teacher started explaining this in class, I got shivers up my spine. In my mind, eternal life was always terribly circular, as the pastor explained, the same one who was in church. That's the main reason why I couldn't cry, no matter how much I wanted to. Not because of Köler. Anyway there's always a nice easy feeling after crying. And you know why? Auntie always says, when I laugh a lot: mind yourself, after laughter come tears. But if tears come after laughter, doesn't laughter come after tears, as no one can cry forever. That's why I try to have a good old cry, and then I think, 'So, I've no tears left, and there's nothing to fear for a while. So I went into church mainly so that I could cry my fill, because that's a polite place and a polite occasion too – as Köler is dead. But it all came to nothing. Because as soon as I saw the pastor's grey head, I thought: there he is, kneeling and thinking about his eternal life, but he's arranged his grey hair so that his bald head won't show. But why is he so worried about the crown of his head if he believes in eternal life? Tell me why? Don't you know? I do. It's because the pastor's eternal life is circular and he knows that himself, but to us children he didn't say that. He was shielding the truth from us. He was always repeating to us: eternal life, eternal life, but what he wanted to say was: circular eternal life, circular eternal. As soon as I had that thought, the tears were knocked out of me. Father and the pastor were crying in their circular eternity, but I couldn't. You see now what silly things you can think in church. But what were you thinking there, when everyone was kneeling? Were you thinking of anything at all?"

"I was thinking that the best or greatest times in the world are in the past," said Indrek.

"I've never thought of that before, never," declared Ramilda. "But why did you think that?" she asked in amazement.

"Everything great and beautiful belongs to the past. Goethe is dead, Schiller is dead, Pushkin and Köler, all of them."

"But it's good that Goethe is dead," said Ramilda.

"Why?" it was Indrek's turn to be amazed.

"He was very old before he died, and if he'd lived until today, he would be even older. Don Juan should never grow old, because an old Don Juan is ridiculous, and Goethe was a great Don Juan. You know, he was already over seventy when he proposed to an eighteen-year-old? Can you imagine? Seventy and eighteen! If he were still alive today, I wouldn't have any peace, day or night, for I'd be always afraid that he might propose to me, if he happened to see me. Now tell me, what would I be supposed to do, if horribly ancient Goethe proposed to me?"

Ramilda was silent for a moment, as if thinking of something, or as if something new had occurred to her. Then she smiled and said, as if embarrassed: "You want me to tell you a secret, a big, big secret?"

"Better not tell me, Miss," begged Indrek; "I'm afraid I might accidentally blurt it out."

"You have to learn to keep secrets," said Ramilda knowingly. "Secrets are a great asset, and why would you want to live without such assets? You don't want to go on slicing bread and clattering plates forever! Listen, auntie and father want

199

to send me to Germany, but I don't want to go. And do you know why? Guess."

For some reason Indrek's heart started trembling, and the trembling spread over his whole body.

"Well, can't you guess?"

"I don't know," Indrek could hardly reply, because the trembling that spread from his heart had got to his tongue.

"You great big dummy," said Ramilda, suddenly tenderly, as if she too were taking part in Indrek's trembling. "You Tallisman! We were just talking about it. What were we talking about?"

"A great secret," replied Indrek in low voice.

"And the great secret was Goethe," said Ramilda with a laugh. "The thing is turned around, you see: I don't want to go to Germany, because Goethe is dead. Nobody but you knows the reason. But if Goethe were still alive, if there were one thousandth of a chance that he was, then I'd go right away, this very evening, and I'd come back safely. For just to think that you might go somewhere where Goethe might be, who loved a young girl at a great age, that you might even see him from far away, that it's even possible, though it would never happen – you know, it would be a healthier option than any spa, for an old Goethe is even better than Brummfeldt's refreshing spa. But now I won't go, I don't want to. Besides, there's something else that involves you. Not you personally, but you boys generally. At Christmas, when Dr. Brummfeldt was recommending me a change of climate, father said it isn't possible now, for where would he leave his boys – meaning the princes, counts and Tigapuus. You too, of course. Can you imagine? The doctor says I have to go, because young ladies need a change of climate, and father answers, "The boys". Because of the boys, brought together from all over the world, my trip was postponed. Now tell me, is that all I'm worth, when my spa waters, my German "health resort" and my meeting with Goethe depend on the boys' pleasure and their humdrum requirements? What am I living for, if the boys' soup is more important than my journey? Father and auntie both tell me I can't, for who will cook the boys' soup? A thousand times I've wished that you were in my place and I in yours, just for one moment, then I'd see what you'd do if you had to travel somewhere soon, but can't because father and auntie keep repeating: wait, wait until spring, then Ramilda won't want soup any more, then we'll go. Tell me, what would you do?"

"I don't know what I'd do then," replied Indrek, "but one thing I do know..."

"What do you know?" asked Ramilda.

"I know that if you'd said that to me earlier, I would have been ready to leave the school on any pretext, so that auntie wouldn't have to cook soup anymore, and you could have gone straightaway."

"But the others? They would have still wanted their soup."

"If the others had known too that it's all for the sake of our soup, they'd have left with me," said Indrek firmly. "We'd do anything for you, miss."

Ramilda stared solemnly at Indrek, and her strangely large mouth made some indefinite movements, as if preparing to laugh or cry. But that lasted only a brief moment and then she said, "But what about father? What would become of him, if you all run off for my sake? Oh, God! It's so terrible it doesn't bear thinking about, so let's forget all about it. I think that if one fine day the Redeemer Himself went up to father and said to him, 'I'll give you eternal life; I shall confer on you true and just eternal life – not of the circular variety that your good old friend talks about – but only if you immediately and without any hesitation give up your boys and Mr Ollino and come with me,' then Papa would answer him without hesitation, 'No, dear Redeemer, I would gladly come with you for eternal life, but only on one condition – that I can take my boys and Mr Ollino with me. Otherwise I'm not coming, otherwise I'll settle for my old friend's eternal life, the circular one.' Believe it or not, but that's how father would reply to the

Redeemer, without question of doubt. And what do you think the Redeemer would reply, if he were the real Redeemer, not a circular one that could fall asleep with his mouth open to express his indifference? He would unquestionably tell father, 'Then no matter: if you can't come without the boys, then come with them.' And so Papa would go with the boys and a cauldron of soup. Auntie would also get into Paradise, for who would cook soup for the boys if she didn't? You would go too, to slice bread and lay the table, only I would be left alone, walking past the empty rooms. No one would admit me to eternal life, for I'm an egotist, an awful egotist. Auntie is angry, but I'm an egotist. Sometimes auntie is terribly angry because she has to cook soup for the boys, but then her anger passes and she carries on cooking, because in the end even she loves the boys. She has learnt that from father. She's fed up with them, but she still loves them. She loves all those lazybones and good-for-nothings – that's what she calls them when she's making soup, and the kitchen's full of steam and fumes. But I don't love anyone, I don't even love you and the prince and Tigapuu, perhaps Mr Ollino because of his ugly eyes. That's why I'll be left alone. It's better that way, for you too, because if the prince smashes up old cups again, you won't need to break the handles off the new ones anymore. Will you? But where are they, the ones we broke that time? Still in the bottom of your box? I know what you told father, when he asked you about them. That was a great lie! So much better than what I said. As a memory, it isn't nearly as good as self-defence and great, great joy. Joy, let it be so huge that it drives you crazy, let it not be better than that! Joy and love!"

Mrs Malmberg's heavy steps were heard at the door and Ramilda broke off, continuing in a new tone, "Again the slices of bread are first thick, then thin. You seem incapable of learning anything."

"Don't trouble yourself about that," auntie scolded Ramilda. "Leave it to me; I'm used to it."

"I'm going, I'm going, I just came in for a moment," replied

Ramilda, heading for the door, where she stopped to ask: "Dear auntie, what do you think – will Köler go to heaven? I asked Mr Paas, but he doesn't know, because nobody had asked him about it. But what do you think, dear auntie?"

"What silly questions you worry your head about!" sighed auntie. "What's to become of you?"

"Is it such a silly question, dear auntie?" asked Ramilda, somewhat ruefully.

"For us people it's a pretty silly question," declared Mrs Malmberg. "It's a matter for God – who goes to hell and who to heaven. We can do nothing but check that the soup's salty and rich, that the bread's sliced and the table laid, because the boys will be coming in soon, as hungry as horses. The good Lord doesn't worry about them, so why should we worry about heaven and hell?"

"That's just Mr Paas's opinion!" exclaimed Ramilda, and continued, "But I often think about heaven and hell. I think Köler will definitely get to heaven, because he's painted such beautiful pictures of Jesus, so the Redeemer won't let him go to hell. And you know what else I think, dear auntie? Köler lived in St. Petersburg, the Tsar lives in St. Petersburg too, and if he goes to heaven, then maybe Köler will too. And I don't think the good Lord would let the Tsar of Russia go to hell. Why would he be a Tsar if he was going to the Devil in hell anyway?"

"Leave off your wisecracks and go," said Mrs Malmberg. "Don't utter the name of the Tsar, for father will say that's politics, and you shouldn't talk about politics."

"For father everything's politics and you can't talk about anything," replied Ramilda. "He thinks even heaven and hell are politics, and so I can never ask him whether Köler will go to heaven or to hell."

"No, dear child, if Köler is going to hell, it doesn't matter, let him go, but if the Tsar is going to hell, that's politics," explained Mrs Malmberg.

"But if the Tsar goes to heaven, is that politics?" asked Ramilda.

"No, that's not politics, because as you said yourself, dear child, the Tsar of Russia can't go anywhere but to heaven."

"So if the good Lord suddenly took the Tsar and put him in hell, that would be nothing more than pure politics," said Ramilda.

"Oh, good Lord!" cried Mrs Malmberg impatiently. "You can exasperate people! Always politics, politics! Look, get this – if it's hell, then it's politics."

"But is Goethe in hell or heaven, what do you think?" asked Ramilda.

"No one can know that apart from the good Lord," Mrs Malmberg insisted.

"You know what I'll do when I die, auntie? I'll ask God himself, a few angels, or Jesus Christ, where Goethe is, and I'll go there too, to see him with my own eyes, even after death."

"Dear child, what are you talking about!" cried Mrs Malmberg. "Your own eyes! There are no 'own eyes' in heaven; everyone has special eyes."

"But are there 'own eyes' in hell?"

"Listen, don't drive me mad, just get out of here!" said Mrs Malmberg.

"I'm going, but if there are 'own eyes' in hell, then definitely I'm going there," she said and left.

"That child will be the death of me, and herself too, as she was the death of her mother when she was born," Mrs Malmberg complained to Indrek. "Why does she want to know everything? In that way she takes after her mother. My departed sister was like that too: just kept on asking. And even the questions are pretty much the same. Can you guess what she asked me today: Can you die of love, just die of pure love? Those were her words. And her mother's last question as she died was – for she died in my care, I was older, she was younger, so she asked me directly, 'Has this death been caused by love? Am I dying of love? Does my husband now believe that I love him? Do the others believe it?' My sister was much younger than her husband, you see, and that's why nobody believed, even Mr Maurus didn't really believe, that Miralda loved him. On her deathbed I assured my sister that now everyone would believe her love, everyone, for what can you tell a dying person – but God knows those people. Sometimes it seems that people don't know what love is. Not even women know, let alone men. They look after their wives and are terribly affectionate, but what love is they don't really know. That isn't love. Love would almost be like cruelty. I saw that in my sister, for she truly loved her husband. But as soon as her husband didn't fulfil her slightest whim, she would get terribly angry, in a real temper, promising to burn her husband at the stake, grind him up and take him out with the ashes to the rubbish bin. 'That is the place for an old man who doesn't love her,' she used to say. 'Young people don't love, of course, because they expect to be loved,' she would say. 'I married the old man just so he would love me.' 'He does love you,' I consoled her, 'but he can't fulfil everything that you ask.' 'What kind of love is that if he can't do it all,' my sister answered me. 'Real love can do everything. Real love can lie and steal, rob and murder, real love can even bark like a dog.' That's what she said, and started laughing, for she was really imagining how it would be if love suddenly barked like a dog, all furry and wagging its tail. That was how my sister was about love, and her daughter's the same about heaven and hell."

The bell rang, signalling the end of lessons, and the whole house hummed like a beehive. Some rushed home, others into the dining room, where they were greeted by plates and steaming food.

Chapter 17

The impressions left by Köler's death might perhaps have lasted longer if Pushkin's birthday had not come along. This day had first occurred a hundred years before, but at that time no one in the world would have known that the day would be especially celebrated. In the meantime Pushkin had long since died and had had time to die 2.702702 times if he had lived his allotted span each time. This was worked out by both Jaan Vainukägu and Adalbert Sikk, but only approximately, as they said, since there was little need for such precision, once the man had died. They even told Mr Slopashev the result of their calculations when he recalled Pushkin's birthday, but Slopashev answered them quite indifferently: "Pushkin might die a thousand times, but he lives on anyway, for at the same time as he died a thousand times, he is born ten thousand times."

All over the town or at least at the first-class institution of learning, everyone – whatever their rank – was making every effort to look anxious and concerned, as though Pushkin really could be reborn if the proper steps were taken. For a couple of weeks Mr Slopashev, whose face now appeared particularly bloated, had been going about engaged in what he called a "colloquium" with his friend Voitinski. This usually took place in his own room but then was shifted to a quiet corner outside when the boys' pranks grew a little too lively. And Slopashev's flights of fancy rose to the heights of exaltation, ultimately comparing Pushkin to Christ. He argued that if God intended to redeem mankind with the blood of His own son once more, then he would surely be born in Russia, because Pushkin had shown the way, and in any case He no longer needed to redeem the Jews.

"Mr Slopashev, Pushkin cannot be compared with Christ," said the headmaster.

"Now you've shown yourself up," cried Slopashev triumphantly, "you have no idea who Pushkin is! What's the difference between those two? Were they not both poets, great poets, except that Pushkin wrote his own verses, while Christ let others write them, possibly because he lacked that skill? You of course think that Christ is greater than Pushkin as a poet, but let's wait until the two-thousandth anniversary of Pushkin's birth and we'll discuss it then. I say that when Pushkin has been ten thousand years in the earth, he will be worth more than Christ, who has sat at the right hand of God for two thousand years."

Mr Maurus was not amused by such ravings, and he alluded to the imbibing of spirits which Slopashev knowingly replied to, "It is a matter of no great consequence when a teacher indulges in the odd drink, as it is only the pupil who has to be sober. Learning is harder than teaching. You can even teach when you don't understand, whilst you definitely have to understand if you're learning, ..."

Such were the fanciful expectations of the centenary of Pushkin's birth in Slopashev's excited soul. His excitement appeared to be infecting the pupils in more than one class. Eager preparations were veiled by secrecy. Lible, Vutt and Vainukägu were particularly busy. When the anticipated day and hour finally arrived, the atmosphere was positively electric.

Slopashev appeared in the classroom in a state of great excitement, his expression full of animated expectation. "Today, children, I'm going to tell you about Pushkin, the world's greatest and most brilliant writer. I want to tell you about Pushkin as a man, dear children." Thus began Slopashev's lecture once he had taken his seat at the lectern. But he could not remain seated for long, for he was so inspired by his own words that he had to stand up straight at first, then on tiptoe and finally, at the moment of greatest ecstasy, he stood alongside the lectern and spread his arms wide, as if he wanted to take flight and hover over the pupils' heads, having been taken over by Pushkin's spirit. His face was bloated and his eyes as red as a pool of blood.

That was the moment when something tiny and fragile appeared from behind a beam and as it descended from the ceiling in front of Slopashev's watery eyes, it waved its limbs a little and then vanished as abruptly as it had appeared. Slopashev had stretched out his left hand towards his pupils, and in that moment it froze, while his right hand continued to make some ill-defined movements, and then he covered his eyes, as if he wanted to grab something there. Now his left hand also reached his eyes, and after he had rubbed them for a while, he opened them, blinking, and asked in alarm: "Did you see something flying about?"

"No," yelled the boys in chorus, and loudest of all was Lible with his shrill voice from the back row.

"It appeared before me like a ghost," said the teacher.

"That was Pushkin's soul," they replied.

"Don't desecrate a noble memory with your silly jokes," declared Slopashev, resuming his lecture. However, it wasn't long before his own speech was driving him to tears. But then the flimsy little image appeared again from behind the beam, waving its pale limbs before Slopashev's watery eyes, which he immediately rubbed with both hands.

"It's starting again," he said.

"What's starting again?" asked the pupils.

"You won't understand it, children, you haven't lived that long," said Slopashev in a sad voice, and continued with his lecture.

"We'll understand everything if you explain," answered the boys.

"No, no, children," contested Slopashev, "first Pushkin, then this."

But ecstasy and high spirits were now beyond his reach. He only squawked twice like an over-excited cockerel, as he was in the habit of doing at the peak of his enthusiasm. Even those attempts at this vocal signal were seized upon by the ghostlike being hiding behind the beam, which showed its daring by leaping again in front of Slopashev's eyes. And suddenly Slopashev had it in his palm and interrupted his speech mid-word to roar like a lion, "Ah! What's this?" And before anyone could utter a word of explanation, this little white cardboard ghost, whose limbs were controlled by threads that led back to Lible's hands, was crushed to a pulp and thrown at the class. Only one grinning face remained and that person still held the threads. Slopashev cried triumphantly: "I know! You devil! Your hands are under the desk!"

With those words he heaved his heavy body from the lectern to go and catch his persecutor. That was the moment when the drama of Pushkin's birthday became altogether more extreme. All the rows of desks and the spaces between them were planted with paper percussion caps. There was no shortage of them even under the desks – in that classroom and the others, so the pupils' feet could set them off at an agreed moment. So now, when Mr Slopashev, full of righteous anger, leapt down from his lectern to grab the presumed culprit, a series of bangs and crackles was set off by his feet. Following the teacher's example, the pupils started to stamp on theirs, multiplying the same effect across the classroom, and then echoed in the adjacent classrooms, until the entire third storey of the house was a mass of pops and crackles. Only the two highest classrooms remained silent. And the pops and crackles were accompanied by the boys' shouts and whistles, as if the whole of Mr Maurus's first-rate establishment had suddenly gone mad. Actually they only screamed when the teacher turned his gaze away from the class; otherwise they were all quiet, with the popping only coming from under the table, whenever the teacher's feet set the percussion caps off. Because he couldn't make up his mind whether to face the class or turn his back on them, the room was by turns silent or full of a hellish din. Listening from the sidelines, one would have thought that Mr Maurus had bought himself some kind of strange toy, for which the off-and-on mechanism was currently being tested; in short, it was turning his educational establishment into a zoo..

For a while the whole building was engulfed by this intermittent racket, and the teachers, utterly unprepared, lost their heads and ran off. They wanted to appeal to Mr Maurus, but he wasn't there. Ollino was no help, as he couldn't control his own class. While these desperate teachers discussed the situation in the big room downstairs and in the other classrooms percussion caps exploded and boys screamed, things took an unexpected turn in Slopashev's class where it had gone completely silent.

Slopashev had tried to grab hold of Lible and threatened to beat him to such a pulp that not even a wet puddle would be left behind, but when the boy darted under the table to avoid being caught, the teacher gave up and went slowly back to his lectern. He had sat down, covered his eyes with his hands, and no longer paid any attention to the banging and screaming. And when he finally took his hands away from his eyes to look at the now silent class, all the boys – including Lible who had come back out from under his desk – saw that Mr Slopashev was crying. His face was wet with tears streaming down his face, and he seemed to be talking to himself about Pushkin, the greatest poet in the world. Nobody had been prepared for this and everyone was equally affected. For the boys, Slopashev's tears were a revelation. Now the other classes could bang and scream as much as they liked, but from Slopashev's class you couldn't hear a squeak. In the silence, Slopashev eventually asked in a quiet voice, "Children, why did you do this to me?"

But nobody replied.

"Have I been bad to you?" Slopashev pursued his query. "Paas, you're already grown up – you tell me whether I've been bad."

"No," answered Indrek.

"So why do you do this to me?"

"You're often drunk, Mr Teacher, sir," Indrek now replied. But apparently this was the answer Slopashev was least expecting. His large eyes froze and continued to stare at Indrek, and only after a little while did he shift his gaze around to the other faces. When finally his gaze rested again on Indrek, Slopashev said with a sigh of resignation, "That's true, and I'm drunk today as well. While drunk I've been talking to you about the world's greatest poet – a noble man. So you've seen how much of a pig a man can be. Only a man! And I'm not ashamed to say it, because it's the truth. I don't set you a good example, because not every teacher is a worthy model. Even Pushkin isn't a good example in every respect, still less am I. You see, dear children, that's just it, a proper education is an example in itself, never mind that there are so few good examples for you here. But tell me now, what sort of example am I setting you if I talk while drunk about the world's greatest poet? What is to become of you, dear children, if you have a teacher like me? But would you put up with me, if I promise – and swear on the holy name of the immortal poet Pushkin – that from this day forth I want to improve myself. Should I lose my way again, then remind me of my sacred oath, as I want to act according to your wishes. You will see, dear children, that even in old age I can achieve something, if you start to educate me. For it's not parents who should bring up their children, or teachers their pupils, but the other way around, because parents and teachers are more depraved than children and pupils. That is what Christ was thinking when he said, 'Suffer little children, and forbid them not, to come unto me: for of such is the kingdom of heaven.' Did he say, 'Suffer parents?' No: 'Suffer little children.' So you, dear children, should educate your teachers, you must be an example to them, and then things will soon improve. You young people are the world and its future, and if you don't want it to be ruined, if you don't want old people to drive it to ruin, to corrupt you thoroughly with our bad example, you should take tight hold of the reins. You are sitting in the lap of Christ, not of us old people, and if…"

Slopashev couldn't finish, because Mr Maurus stepped into the classroom. But evidently he was very surprised that complete peace reigned there, because from the other classrooms isolated bangs and shrieks could still be heard. From what he knew, things should have been quite otherwise. So he didn't have time to stop here before peace was restored all over the house. Only then did he come back again, and announce slyly, "Mr Slopashev, something strange, very strange, has happened today."

"What was that?" asked Slopashev as if he were curious.

"When I was coming over the bridge with the cabman, I suddenly heard a terrible banging and shouting. So I said to the cabman, 'Mr Cabman, do you have good hearing?' And the cabman drew his horses to a halt and said, 'Why does the gentleman ask that?' 'Mr Cabman, do you have good hearing or not?' Now the cabman said, 'It's not great – one ear is always blocked and the other one has a ringing sound.' So I asked, 'Mr Cabman, can you hear anything?' And he replied: 'What is there to hear?' 'What can you hear, Mr Cabman?' I inquired. 'Over the river there seems to be a zoo, like last year,' this half-deaf cabman told me. And do you know what I did? I got out of the cab, paid him off and gave him an extra twenty for not driving me all the way, and said, 'Thanks, Mr Cabman, but unfortunately I won't be needing you, for you're not completely deaf. I can only ride up to my house with a completely deaf cabman – otherwise I would be ashamed.' So I came on foot. And at home, when I started to ask, they all said, 'Mr Slopashev knows.' And now I want to know what you know."

"Mr Maurus," Slopashev said, "you put my class in an embarrassing situation, because I don't know anything of what you're talking about. Only when talking about Pushkin did I perhaps rise to a greater enthusiasm than is proper for a teacher, and I dragged my pupils into it. Just now I was explaining to them that every excess comes from a weakness of character, and that a person must have a strong character. Every individual should have it, as well as the whole nation. We Russians don't have a strong character, and therefore it would be good, Mr Maurus, if you asked the class, in Estonian, which I don't understand, so that their answers needn't embarrass me. Or perhaps you'd like me to leave for a moment?"

"No, no," replied the headmaster, "my boys always dare to tell the truth."

But this praiseworthy boldness must have been quite a dubious thing, because the headmaster turned to Lible in Estonian, as Slopashev had recommended.

"You great oaf," he said, "tell me without dissembling what happened here, and don't lie, for Mr Maurus has eyes and ears that reach out over the river and through the walls. Tell me, or else…"

"Mr Maurus, nothing happened here," said Lible without batting an eyelid.

"You didn't scream?" inquired the headmaster.

"No," replied the boy.

"Not at all?"

"Only a little, like sometimes before."

"So why did you scream?"

"It was so ridiculous, what Mr Slopashev was telling us about Pushkin."

Mr Maurus turned to a few of the boys, but the answers were much the same. Finally he came to stand in front of Indrek and said to him, "But you, tall old serious man of Israel, who has no guile in him, what do you say?"

"Nothing but what the others said, except that…"

Indrek stopped, because he regretted that he'd been about to say more than the others.

"Well, tell me what, then," insisted the headmaster.

"Except that Mr Slopashev was moved to tears by Pushkin and we laughed," concluded Indrek.

"Why weren't you ashamed!" cried Mr Maurus.

"I was, for us," said Indrek, by way of an excuse.

"Lible, were you also?" asked the headmaster.

"I was," replied the boy, as if telling the truth.

"Well, then that's alright," said the headmaster, and turning to Slopashev, continued in Russian: "They're ashamed and they regret that they laughed at the celebration of Pushkin's birth. But forgive them, because the young don't know that birth is as difficult and important as death. We old people know that and we are moved by it, but it just makes them laugh."

At this the headmaster left the classroom.

"I thank you, children," said Slopashev, and wanted to add something more, but somehow the words stuck in his throat, and so he simply raised his right hand, made a sort of gesture with it and followed Mr Maurus, as the bell had rung long before.

Only after class did the headmaster ask Indrek in private: "Is it true that you told Mr Slopashev in front of the class that he was drunk?"

"No," answered Indrek, "I said he was often drunk and we don't like it."

"That's very good," declared Mr Maurus. "He doesn't listen to me, but maybe he'll listen to you. "An old person is always shamed more by the young than by his own kind. Otherwise he's a good man, a clever man. What's more, he's a Russian, with connections One brother in Riga and another in St. Petersburg, where their word carries weight. People like that are what Mr Maurus needs, you see. For how else are we going to manage if we don't have men whose words count?"

*

Pushkin's birthday was the last event that gathered the whole establishment together; after that the decline set in. It seemed that everyone had lost interest in learning and teaching; they thought and talked only about travelling, and waited for the day when they could take their bundle and go. Indrek wondered whether to go to the clerk's office for the summer or stay here with Ollino as caretaker, as Mr Maurus wished.

"I wouldn't want you to stay here," said Ramilda when they talked about it.

"Why not, miss?" asked Indrek.

"I'm going away, that's why," Ramilda replied. "You know where I'm going? To Germany. Are you surprised? But I'm not as whimsical as I sound. Goethe is dead, and there's little I can do about that, but I can go to a sanatorium. Today I looked at myself in the mirror, and can you guess what I found? I found some little wrinkles on my face. Tiny little ones, but there they were! Do you understand the gravity of it? I haven't started living, but I already have wrinkles on my face! But then I thought, 'The wrinkles are there because I haven't started living, but if I go to Germany, I can start my life there and those wrinkles will surely go away.' And if there's no life there, then... Do you know what'll happen then?" She stepped closer to Indrek, looked him straight in the eyes and said, "Then death will come. How it will come, I don't know yet, but it will most certainly come. Are you afraid of death? Tell me truthfully, because we'll be apart for a long time. Does it frighten you?"

"No," Indrek answered. "I don't even think about it."

"But I do," declared Ramilda. "Death is something I some-times think about. I once had a friend – she was my only one – and she died. I went to look at her corpse and I kissed her on the brow. I said the Lord's Prayer and then kissed her. Whenever I want to think about death, I always think of that kiss. I do this so I can think about myself when I'm dead: I stand in front of the mirror with a frozen expression and stare at myself; then I close my eyes, purse my lips – that was how I kissed my friend – and I kiss myself in the mirror. The cool glass gives me the shivers, which is both horrible and pleas-ant, and I think: that coldness was my own forehead, because

215

a corpse has a cold forehead. It means that I am deathly cold – that I am dead. I don't dare to open my eyes again, because I'm scared of seeing myself dead in the mirror. I turn aside in horror, I clamber onto the sofa, I bury my head in the pillow and only then can I open my eyes again. If you knew what a pleasure that is: to be alone and feel that you're still alive, that you've just been dead, but you've risen from the dead, whole. Auntie doesn't understand this at all. Do you?"

"I do," replied Indrek.

"What do you understand about it?" asked Ramilda.

"I can't say it, but I feel that I've understood something," explained Indrek.

"That's just it!" affirmed Ramilda. "It's as if it were somewhere at the back of your throat or on your back, so you can't put it into words. For instance, I have no idea whether I'll ever get married or who I'll marry if I do, and yet sometimes I think: what would it be like if the prince was my husband? What would I do if my husband started smashing the crockery? And you know what I'd do? I'd hand him the crockery myself, I'd say, 'Go on, take it, smash it, dear husband, if you can't do anything else. I'd open the cupboard doors and empty them all onto the table, so my husband could break them up. Go ahead, smash them, because you're my lord and master, you're the head of the household. Do you believe I'd ever do anything like that?"

"I don't know, I really don't know," replied Indrek quietly, as if it were too much for him.

"You never know," Ramilda chimed in heatedly. "But I do! I know that there's nobody's husband who would start gleefully smashing up crockery; only my auntie does that, when she's having a terrible quarrel with father. Then she smashes everything she can get hold of, and she cries afterwards, when she thinks about what it will all cost. A husband comes straight onto the attack – that's a real husband. If the prince had attacked auntie that time, then he would have been in the right. He could have attacked me too, for what right did

216

I have to talk to him? But he didn't do that either. I was just thinking, he's going to attack me, but no! He just smashed things, smashed up old crockery! Now you know what I think of men like the prince. But I shouldn't be talking to you like this, because you'll lure me into doing something silly, says auntie."

"Miss, I won't do that, I won't say a word," Indrek defended himself.

"That's just how you lure me: you don't talk yourself, you let me, and that's how it happens."

"I can't talk as beautifully as you do," said Indrek.

"Can't talk as beautifully…" repeated Ramilda, as if wanting to mock him, but suddenly she asked brightly: "Do I really talk beautifully?"

"I think you do."

"Honestly?"

"Honestly," Indrek assured her.

"That's so beautiful, that you told me that," said Ramilda, now in a sort of ecstasy. "Finally one person who sees something in me! But I won't tell it to a soul. Not even in Germany. And you won't tell anyone either, will you?"

"I won't," Indrek promised, suddenly feeling a sort of shame.

After that they never exchanged another word. It made an impression when Indrek travelled home and felt a yearning. For a long time he was pursued by the thought that the last thing they'd spoken of was death, as though this was particularly significant. Only later did Indrek realise that it might have signified something after all. Late at night, as he started to walk home from the railway station, his bundle on his back, he thought of their last conversation, as he walked through the forest or by the rye field. It was so strange to walk like that by night. At first he hurried, but then he felt that there was no point in rushing on a bright spring night, as the cuckoo called almost until morning, when it started up with new force, and the crow cawed and a thousand marsh birds took up the tired cuckoo's call. He walked as if half-asleep, his whole body filled with a sweet stupor, from which he was jolted when an unsettled hare hopped across the road or a stranger's dog barked from beyond a gate.

Chapter 18

At home Indrek was greeted by a dog with a fierce bark. With great effort and a stout cane, he managed to get past the gate by the barn and close it again after him, while the dog remained behind it barking and sniffing. It was an unpleasant surprise to find this strange dog at the gate to his home, and once he had lain down in the hayloft, he waited in vain for sleep to come. Everything in this world is so changeable! He did eventually fall asleep, and didn't wake until his father came in mid-morning to fetch hay for the horses.

"Ah, so you were the one having such a quarrel with the dog in the night," said his father. He spread out his arms and bundled the hay together, so he could throw it down a hatch to the horses. Indrek, who was already sitting up, noticed how bent his father's back was, and how gnarled his splayed fingers. It was the latter which particularly caught his attention. As his father approached the ladder to go back down, Indrek walked over to him at the edge of the loft and held out his hand in greeting.

"Yes, of course," said his father, "we haven't shaken hands yet; when you're working hard you forget about that." And again Indrek noticed his father's gnarled fingers. While he went down the ladder, he reflected on this momentous truth he'd just discovered: "They're crooked, there can be no doubt about it."

That wasn't the only unexpected change Indrek had to confront on arriving at his home. So much joy shone in his mother's eyes on greeting him, and yet she turned her gaze shyly away, as if the mournful mass of wrinkles that played around her mouth pained her when she attempted to smile.

He'd never seen her like this before. Indrek had watched that mouth so many times, but he saw it now as if it were for the first time. For some reason it seemed to him that someone with a mouth like that shouldn't say anything, or if they did, it would have to be sad and serious. So all he could say to his mother was banal and pointless. His mother also seemed to be struggling to say something. Only when they were alone did Indrek say, "Father's hands are gnarled and twisted."

Mother's whole body seemed startled, she turned around, looked at her son and asked: "What makes you think that?" There was such a bright glow in her eyes, and the mournful wrinkle around her mouth seemed to have diminished a little.

"I saw how he was scooping the hay together in the loft and then we went down the ladder. His fingers couldn't bend around its sides, and he could only hold the rungs," said Indrek.

His mother turned her face away and remained hunched and tense with stooped shoulders standing before her son. And suddenly Indrek recalled some long-past event, for then too his mother had stood likewise with stooped shoulders. But that time it was in the middle of the yard where she had gathered up half a bundle of firewood.

After a little while his mother asked: "So you only noticed that now?"

"Just this morning for the first time," replied Indrek.

"But it's been like that for ages," declared mother. "Clearly school in town has opened your eyes."

"You really think so – school has done that?" queried Indrek.

"Where else then?" replied his mother, looking straight at her son. "At school, nowhere else. School and in service to the Crown are the only things that open people's eyes. Did Andres see his father's old age or how he slaved away when he was at home? Of course he didn't, but now he does. Now he can see it when he's a thousand versts away, and he wrote a letter. When father read that, he wiped his eyes several times. He blamed his glasses, saying that they were too

220

strong, but it wasn't the strength of the glasses – it was young Andres's letter. A few days later, father said: 'Andres might yet make something of himself, you know. Being in service to the Crown makes a man of you.' So you see, father hopes he'll come back to Vargamäe, once he's done his service. Has he written to you?"

"No," answered Indrek.

"Old Sauna-Madis thinks so too: let him stick it out for a year or two with the Crown, then he'll be glad to come back to Vargamäe to take over from the bent and worn-out old man."

"He won't come," said Ants, who had heard Indrek and his mother's last words. "I don't believe he'll come back."

"You go on believing that," replied mother. "That's all you've got to say: 'He won't come, he won't come.' Of course he won't come if everyone keeps repeating, 'He won't come, he won't come.'"

And turning to Indrek, mother complained: "Ants seems to have lost his mind, always insisting that Andres won't come back. As if he were sorry for Andres or jealous of him in the event of him coming home."

"Mother, leave it off with your sorries and jealousies," Ants retorted. "I'm completely unbothered about Andres's return, because when I go off for military service, I won't ever come back to Vargamäe, that's for sure. I wouldn't even come if father offered me Vargamäe."

"Listen now," said Mother, her lips trembling and her eyes going watery. "That's what he always says when we talk about Andres. He even told his father that once, so father had to hit him."

"So where do you want to go, or what are you planning to do?" Indrek asked his brother, who had grown into a man over the winter.

"I don't know at the moment," replied Ants, "but there must be something in the world for me to do. I don't care where I go or what I do."

"You'd rather be someone else's servant than master of Vargamäe?" Indrek challenged him.

"Why someone else's servant?" asked Ants, glaring at him. "Aren't you a servant somewhere?"

"Of course I'm a servant, what did you think?" Indrek replied to his brother.

"Yeah!" Ants didn't suppress his incredulity. "So now I've got to be a servant! I know your serving kind, even though you're playing the lord! But of course, I couldn't become the lord of the manor, and that's why you and mother think I have to stay at Vargamäe. I'm the best one for that."

"Listen, Ants, where do you get that idea?" asked Indrek, who was sad and surprised. It seemed to him that his brother's mouth was taking on a similar shape to his mother's. "I don't think of it like you do. When I say I'm in service, then I really am. I'm even the servant of a servant. Do you know what it's like going to school without money? I and a few others like me do things you'd find humiliating, because you'd say: 'That's women's work.' But I do it so that I can study."

What Ants would now say was so terrible and astonishing to Indrek that he was left speechless and would regret every word of what he had just said, because Ants answered, "I'd work as a night-soil man, if that allowed me to do some studying."

His eyes turned aside, he stood with his stocky body facing his brother's, glowering as if he was about to attack him. But nothing happened; he merely left slamming the door behind him, perhaps in shame or embarrassment.

Indrek felt a complete stranger at home amongst his own people, and an object of derision. "That's why the dog was so keen to attack me last night," he thought. Even the landscape he'd walked through and taken pleasure in at night, now seemed utterly alien. If he'd wanted to talk about it here, he would have been as little understood as the cup handles he was carrying in his pocket wrapped in silk paper. The cuckoo might call all night, the marsh birds might scream like banshees, the swallows might twitter from early morning till late evening and the sun might feed the rosy-white clouds in the sky, but people had nothing to do with all that; they had their own affairs and their own worries.

At mid-morning Indrek went by the cattle path down to the meadow. Seeing the boundary ditch which ran in a straight line through to the Jõessaare river, he felt an urge to walk along it. But the ditch seemed to have caved in, and the spring floods had hollowed it out. Everything had become different in the meantime. Or did his memory deceive him? Perhaps he himself had changed more and faster than this ditch, with its muddy banks?

Silently he walked as far as the river. But here in the bright greenness and by the dazzling brilliant surface of the water, where the tireless swallows made their zig-zag way, he felt the wish to make a noise, to join the birds in song. He shouted once, he shouted twice, as if hoping for a response from somewhere. But there was no one to respond by the riverbank among the grey barns which stood in a straggly row on both sides of the river everywhere the eye could reach, ultimately vanishing into the sunshine and the gusts of air.

Finally an answer came to Indrek not from the riverbank but from the forest. And without reasoning to himself who might be answering from there, he started making his way in a straight line through the thicket to the source of the voice. But when he got to the spot, he stopped, looked this way and that, and said to himself: "Tiiu and Kadri of course."

"We thought someone was lost, couldn't get out of the bushes," declared Tiiu in response to his greeting.

"Do you know about Polla?" asked Kadri, as if it were the biggest news and most important event in all the time since her brother had left for the town. "Polla has died! Vanished last winter and was never found again. We thought a wolf did it, and we went looking for its tracks, but there was nothing. We went as far as the spring, and then suddenly there was Polla, between a pile of sticks and a snowdrift, her nose backwards, as if she'd tried to squeeze in there. Daddy said Polla had gone there to die. She was older than me, that's why. Dogs don't live as long as we do, mummy says. Is that true – that we grow older than dogs?"

"It is," replied Indrek.

"And horses? Do they die before we do?" persisted Kadri.

"They do too," Indrek confirmed.

"And pigs?"

"Pigs as well," said Indrek.

"So we live the longest," concluded Kadri and then asked conspiratorially, "And ghosts? How long do they live?"

"Ghosts?" repeated Indrek, surprised.

"Yeah," his sister affirmed, scratching her bare brown thigh. "Mother's always saying: when Indrek comes, ask him, he'll know," said the girl, looking gravely at her brother with her brown eyes.

Now there was nothing Indrek could do but take his sister's hand, tanned by wind and sun, and pull her onto his lap.

"Have you heard that one fool can ask more than nine wise men can answer?" he asked his sister.

"Mummy says the same," laughed Tiiu, stepping closer.

"But what do they teach you there in town, if you don't know about ghosts?" asked Kadri.

"What did you study last winter yourself?" countered Indrek.

"The Russian letters," answered Kadri. "So they don't teach letters in town?"

"Did I learn letters?" Tiiu said now; "I was learning words."

"So they teach both letters and words in town!" exclaimed Kadri.

"Only letters and words," replied Indrek, quite sadly, to his little sister.

"And all in Russian?"

"German and Latin too."

"What other languages are there?"

"English and French," ventured Tiiu.

"What else?" Kadri inquired of her brother.

"Heaps and heaps of others," he replied.

"Tell me one, name one that I've never heard of before."

"Dutch."

"I've heard of that!" cried Tiiu triumphantly.

"Herero," said Indrek.

"That doesn't exist," they both declared.

"But is there a language that neither you nor the schoolmaster have heard of?" asked Kadri.

"There must be," guessed Indrek.

"What would be the name of a language like that?" wondered Kadri. But neither Tiiu nor Indrek could answer that, so all three of them were equally ignorant. So Tiiu could also sit down on the sod beside her big brother, and could place her brown thighs next to his white ones in the sun.

"Look, Indrek, at your legs and ours," she said. "Like the devil's paw and God's hand."

"Like the devil's paw and God's hand," repeated Kadri, putting her legs next to her brother's. They then had quite a talk about legs. Firstly Kadri showed her brother the big carbuncle under her foot, over which she had cried so much and had sleepless nights, for nothing had helped – not tea-leaves, not golden saxifrage or burdock leaves, not pork-rind or soaked rye-bread pieces, which mother put on her. Even now she had to limp and hold her foot, which was so hard to do in a bog. They led Indrek to a bird's nest, which had a long, winding entrance through the grass and moss, and the bird itself was so bold that it flew right into Tiiu's hand as she quietly crept up to the nest and put her little brown hand in front of the mouth of the nest.

"But now she'll abandon her nest," said Indrek.

"That bird won't leave it," the children cried; "we've already caught her once before."

Then they showed Indrek a small mound, where they had seen two large snakes on several occasions. They asked their brother for advice on how to catch them: you could cut a ditch around the area to prevent them from leaving it, you could place crossed sticks on the hummock to prevent them from sleeping, as the man from the sauna taught them, or insert milk bottles so the snakes would crawl into them. You could even try burning straw after sunset, so the snakes would have to come straight out in the firelight, and then you could get the little rascals! Indrek thought a dog would be good; it would drive them away from the mound, or they could destroy the mound, but neither suggestion met with the girls' approval, because they didn't have a good dog, and how could they get rid of that mound with the birch-trees on it! In other things, too, Indrek was of no help to his sisters in advice or in action, and so they soon realized that Indrek's faraway school in town had to be very different from how mother imagined it. It seemed that they didn't teach anything there that would bring in extra money or be of some use in life. They didn't teach anything about the longevity of ghosts, the name of the language that no one has ever heard of or how to catch snakes in a mound. Only that a dog was a useful thing to have. Even Tiiu and Kadri knew that if there were such a dog, you would take it to the mound, it would scrabble around a little, sniff the air in the mound and listen! A snake would start hissing. Then you just had to wait with a stick. But they didn't have the right kind of dog, and neither did their neighbour or the people at Aaseme, Ämmasoo, Soovälja and Hundipalu. None had been heard of at Rava, at Kukesaare or on the other side of the great forest where the fields start. There was one at Kassiaru, but it went mad. It ripped at the snakes until it lost its senses, for God didn't want Kassiaru to lose all its snakes, because how then would their sins be forgiven? And if there are snakes, there's nothing for it but to go into the swamp and strike one down, and nine sins would be forgiven. If you manage to kill two or three, then eighteen or twenty-seven of your sins will be redeemed. But how many sins do people have to have in order to be sure that there are enough snakes to redeem people?

That was the case with the snakes, and Tiiu and Kadri were

well acquainted with these concepts. They also knew about the last snake-killing dog at Kassiaru, named Loki. And there would never be the like of him again, because it wasn't the old days anymore. That was why they sought their brother's help, as he'd come straight from the school in town. How else were they going to get help? But it turned out that he knew no more than they did. The sisters were disappointed, and Indrek's inexplicable melancholy returned. It was what had driven him down to the marsh and the river in the first place.

Having finally got back to the riverbank, Indrek started to walk around it. He stopped at the boundary garden to reflect on disputes over Vargamäe's boundaries which even went to court, and then he walked from the garden to the Valley land. He didn't even notice how softly and caressingly the young leaves were rustling in the alders and birches. Unconsciously he headed away from the edge of the field, back almost as far as the marsh to where the willows grew intermittently with their shiny arrow-shaped leaves, which Indrek instinctively had to touch and stroke. He was still carrying his boots in his left hand, and the fingers on his right hand became caught up in fresh, sap-filled and resinous leaves, which also stuck to his arm and were torn off the branches. For some reason it felt so good to tear from the trees and bushes those sap-filled leaves, and feel them infusing his very hand when he crushed the firm thick leaves into a delicate green ball in his palm, with which he could play, as if the air were full of green, slushy snow.

Walking in this haphazard manner, he returned to the path, and there he saw Pearu at a little distance, standing by a ditch. At first Indrek thought of jumping over the ditch and going straight on, as if he hadn't noticed his neighbour, but then he called, unexpectedly even to himself: "Hello, neighbour! Hello father!"

Pearu turned towards him and Indrek saw that there was a smile on his old and troubled face, something of a grateful mildness. That day, it's true, Indrek saw that even Pearu's face

227

was old and troubled, as he stood amongst the greenness of the vegetation. A man in his declining years surrounded by greenery. There was no sign of the spark he'd once had in his eyes, which were now quite blue. And he said, "Why, they've let our neighbour's boy, Indrek, out of the town."

"Nice weather drove me out," Indrek responded.

"Well now, in spring there's no point lingering in the town, where it starts to stink and get dusty. But look what I've got here, how thick and dense it is."

And he gestured with his hand to where Indrek had come from.

"I've been thinking," continued Pearu, "about how to dig it here, so that the water will run away properly, because this is forest land. Your father is digging away over there, and I want to start here, because this is the real forest land."

Indrek had no answer to this, and when Pearu had spent some time explaining his "forest land" without getting any reply, he changed the subject: "Given that you've been living in town for a while now and been close to all those newspapers and journals, have you heard whether there's going to be war or not?"

But Indrek hadn't heard anything in particular. "Hundipalu, he knows because he gets those papers and things but I haven't seen him for ages, so I don't know anything," Pearu carried on.

When their chat ended for the time being, Indrek wished him good day and continued on his way. Pearu stayed where he was to do his thinking, wearing leggings on his feet, with the tops folded down, a jacket on his back, the front open and the neck of his shirt unbuttoned, so the sun shone on his hairy chest.

That summer Indrek would meet Pearu one more time. It was at the clerk's office in the council building, where his neighbour had important business, and consequently could not avoid taking a sip or two from both the women's and the men's bottle in the clerk's living-room. This made him increasingly loquacious, and after he had got so loud that Indrek could hear him through two walls, Pearu decided to come over and share his loquaciousness with Indrek as well. "Hello, young whelp of a neighbour!" he shouted to Indrek extending his hand, which the latter shook and became painfully aware that Pearu's fingers were not as crooked as his father's. His neighbour held his hand for a long time, calling him a "whelp" a couple more times, who knows why? That was how he liked to converse.

"Last autumn I said in the tavern to your father, my neighbour Andres – that strong old man, very strong, because I'm strong myself, so how could my neighbour get past me if he wasn't even stronger – I said to him that the pirate who is his young Andres and your brother or more correctly half-brother, and went to do his military service – the one who in the spring broke my embankment when I was making a level area for hay over by Jõessaar, you know the story, that same pirate that old Andres sent off to the army ... well, I told him – I told him out of sheer stubbornness just to tease and pick on him – I said, 'Now you've sent one son off to sup at that trough in service of the Crown, and the other one to town at your behest to learn how to become a horse-thief, for that is what the school is supposed to make of you. And then I added that we've got a shortage of horse-thieves now, because not a single horse has been stolen from Vargamäe yet. And do you know what old Andres, that neighbour of mine and your dear father, told me in front of the whole tavern? He said that you'd gone into town not to learn to be a horse-thief, but to study truth and justice. So now in the spring, when you came past my land, I saw you coming – and don't think I didn't see – you came, boots in your hand and your pants hitched up, because you're like a landlord now, you came and you were pulling leaves in your other hand and tossing them into the ditch, that's what you did as you came past my land. And I said to myself there as I stood by the ditch, while I was thinking about serious matters, and the sun was shining so warmly, and the birds were singing and the bees flying, for no one else has got bees here, your father hasn't, that strong old man, nor has Aaseme, nor anyone at Sooväli, nor at Ämmasoo, only Hundipalu has them, but his bees won't fly far, because bees are not so foolish enough as come over the river here into the big marsh when they find plenty of honey closer to home, so that was definitely my bee flying by while I was thinking about serious matters. So there I was standing there looking at my bee flying around the willow-bush, and I thought, there he is now, my bee, that little one flying and flying and collecting honey from the side of the marsh-willow, and I was just looking and waiting for when that tiny chap will get his honeycomb full so I can just go and take it. But then you came out of my forest, you jumped over the ditch and you wanted to go onto your own land and act as if I wasn't there, neither me or my bee that was flying around the willow. Don't deny it, I know that's what you wanted to do, but you didn't, instead you said... But do you even know what you said to me, as I was watching my bee in the sunshine? 'Hello, neighbour! Hello, father!' you said. And I raised my voice to the Lord Jesus and I said to my bee: 'You see, my bee, that man by the bank of the ditch?' – because you're a grown man now, Indrek – 'you see him,' I said before my Redeemer, 'and you heard how he said to me, a poor old man who wants to feed himself on your handiwork, oh bee, how he said with a great big voice: 'Hello Father!' Do you know, my boy, son of my dear neighbour, what I was thinking then, when you greeted me like that by my own ditch, because it is my ditch, the soil of the ditch is on my land? I was thinking, 'Oh mighty Jehovah, that is the voice of the blessed Krõõt, it was none other than she who blessed that bright little voice, greeting me there with the soul of its heart. But we buried her long ago, and I myself made a road for her so she could travel in her coffin more smoothly, and leave her beloved dwelling-place at Vargamäe, where she had had enough of shaking and tossing. But old Andres, your father, took offence at me, because blessed Krõõt was his first wife and the mistress of Vargamäe and there will never be the like of her again. But I still haven't killed my first wife for her sins, nor have I buried her because she has hard bones and thick legs and nothing can have a go at her. She'll outlive all my mares and cows, and who can count all those ewes in her meadow! That's what I was thinking there by the side of the ditch in front of my bee, and I said to Jesus Christ: Oh Immanuel, there's the son of my dear neighbour greeting me now with a bright voice, and yet he isn't the son of the blessed Krõõt, because I was smoothing Krõõt's path even before this man was born – the one who's coming out of the forest and over the ditch. Why does he greet me saying 'Hello father?' And my mind took pity and I opened my mouth before that marsh willow and I raised my voice when I said: 'Wondrous are Thy ways, oh merciful Lord, for I called this young man who speaks in Krõõt's voice and is learning to be a horse-thief, but he calls me father. So am I the father of a horse-thief? And behold, Indrek, your father had the spirit of God upon him last autumn, when he said by the tavern bar: 'This young man should proclaim truth and justice.' And now you have proclaimed it to me there in the marsh by the ditch in front of the willow bush and in the hearing of the bee while I was chatting with him as if he were my redeemer, and you have called me your father, when I bore hatred toward your father, his sons and daughters and you yourself. For I said to my bee when I saw you in my forest, 'Look, my honey-bringer, there comes the horse-thief from the other family.' But just then you jumped over my ditch, as if you'd learned to do that in town, and you called in a bright voice: 'Hello, neighbour. Hello father!' Why did you do that, young man? Why did you bring shame on this poor old man, who feeds himself on his bee's handiwork? Tell me, dear young man, tell your old neighbour and tough foe of your strong father, why did you do that there in the sunshine by the side of the ditch?"

"Because I wasn't a horse-thief," Indrek replied jokingly.

"That's right!" cried Pearu. "You weren't a horse-thief. And you won't become one either. But if you come to Vargamäe sometimes, then know that all my land is open to you. And if you ever see me – a poor old man – even from far off, don't just go past me, but always greet me. Call out to me from far off: 'Hello, neighbour; hello father!' and I want to tell my sons and daughters that they too can call your father that. Because there's nothing to stop him accepting the greetings of my sons and daughters, just because they don't have such bright voices as my strong neighbour's sons and daughters. Because only the departed Krõõt had such a bright voice when she opened her mouth and…"

The clerk led Pearu away, for otherwise his chatter would never have ended.

*

After lunch Indrek went to Hundipalu, as his godfather had wanted to see him when he returned from town. Tiit was just stumbling among the woodpiles when Indrek got to Hundipalu, and so they sat down right there in the sunshine.

"An old man loves the sun," said Tiit, "because an old man's blood can't warm up any other way, it starts to curdle."

So, sitting there among the birches, they began their chat about "politics", a word he pronounced awkwardly, as though he'd learned it from a book.

"There isn't a single soul here who understands politics, no one reads the papers or anything else," Tiit began. "Your father always read the most, but now he's just lumbering around and working as though a man can only be blessed by working. You're now becoming a full-grown man and so you should learn something about politics. Don't they talk about politics at your school? Old Maurus himself was always a great one for politics."

"I thought that they spoke of little else," said Indrek.

"When Jakobson was still alive," Tiit continued, "politics was a big issue. Since Jakobson we haven't had much in the way of politicking. The Jews had their Moses, and we had our Jakobson. If he had lived, they wouldn't have closed the Society of Men of Letters. Jakobson wouldn't have let it happen; he would have gone to the Tsar himself in St. Petersburg. And right enough, Alexander would have received us then, not like now, and shares in 'Linda' would have still kept their price. But he died – the rulers killed him there in Vändra forest, and I'll believe that till my dying hour – and everything went backwards, there was no help any more from Sahaskoi or Mannasein.[41] So our political cause has been completely in the shit since he died. I can say that to you now, because you're a grown man; you're living in town, I hear, so you have to understand all about politics."

Unfortunately Indrek understood these "political" matters very dimly and vaguely, although he was getting on for twenty years old. Just one thing amazed him: Hundipalu Tiit talked about the same things and names that he had heard in town from his headmaster, some teachers and students, either when they were chatting amongst themselves or in speeches at some social event. Until then, Indrek had not thought of it as important; it had just gone in one ear and come out the other, but now that he heard of them from Tiit, he decided that this subject must be more important than he'd thought.

"In its day, the paper *Virulane* had the sort of articles that Jakobson's *Sakala* had, but they squandered that talent and he left," Tiit carried on explaining to his godson. "*Valgus* had good articles, as nobody else had had articles as long and good as those in *Valgus*, but its political coverage was crap. The landlords bought them off, and it went over to

---

41 Sahaskoi: mispronunciation of Shakhovskoy – Prince Sergey (1852-1894), Governor of Estonia 1885-1894 who implemented the Russification policy, while Nikolay Manassein was Minister of Justice of Russia under Tsar Alexander III, who in 1882 conducted an audit of the Baltic lands in the Empire and proposed the Russification policy.

the Russian side – it didn't love its own Estonian people anymore. It was really a shame that what started off so well went wrong. I used to read it for a bit, but then I stopped. If you, you young scamp, don't love the Estonian people, then I won't read your articles, I don't care if they're the best and longest in the world. Now I read *Postimees*. It's a paper for farmers and the temperance movement. I don't hold with the teetotallers, because I like to have a beer on my days off, and after communion I like to take a shot of spirits for my watery heart – I can't live without that. But I'm part of the Farmers' Association, and tomorrow morning I'm going to be working for that cause. Others go to church, but I go to the Farmers' Association. I've invited your father there too, but he says, 'What have I got to do with that society; the association won't come and lift my stones and dig my ditches. But maybe one day they'll come and, who knows, I'll go off to help them.' If nothing else, I may come across someone with whom I can discuss political matters; otherwise I'll live like a wolf here at Hundipalu.[42] Who will fight for us, now we don't have Jakobson anymore? We'll have to do it ourselves, as we can't just give up on the Estonian cause. And I tell you this too, dear godson, there's no use in learning anything in this world if you don't love the Estonian people and you don't know how to run its political cause. Of course you're learning everything in Russian…"

"The catechism and Bible reading are in Estonian, the sermon too," interjected Indrek.

"The catechism and Bible reading, of course," agreed Tiit, "because they haven't got around to translating those into Russian. But our masters will probably get around to that too, because that's the way they hope to divide us more quickly. They'll make Russians of us and when they've have finished with us, there'll be nothing left but to drag us off to Crimea,

---

42 *Hundipalu* [Estonian] is the name of Tiit's farm and means "Wolf's Heath".

Sukhumi or Samara, and bring the Germans in from Germany in our place. That's been their plan from the beginning. So for the moment there's just the catechism and Bible-reading, a breathing-space for our language. But the catechism and Bible-reading aren't science; you only learn science in Russian. What science is there in the catechism and Bible-reading? The catechism and Bible-reading are religious concerns, but we've taken on the Germans' faith, which makes us more German anyway. Always remember that, godson. If you learn a bit more of the Germans' faith, you'll soon become a German and start believing the German god. For a true Estonian there's never any profit to be had in religious matters, even if they're written in Estonian. That's why I always get irritated with *Postimees* when it lets religious people spread their wings. I just don't believe them! Sooner or later they'll have us on the side of our German overlords. Remember that. But science won't – science won't lead you anywhere, no matter in what language. That's why you have to have science and not religion, for science is a weapon in a man's hand, if he has a real Estonian mind. That's the difference between science and religion, and that's why I was always on Jakobson's side against Hurt. And I was right, because if Hurt was a real Estonian man and a leader of the people, the overlords would have killed him, but instead they killed Jakobson."

"This year Köler died too," Indrek thought it prudent to point out, so as to say something about political things. "We were taken to the church, shown his altar picture, even the old teacher was wiping his eyes."

"Well, that's how those people understand it," said Tiit derisively. "But I wouldn't ever believe it, even if they wipe their eyes a thousand times. And what's more, I think that if the teachers are wiping their eyes so much over someone, he can't be a real man of the Estonian people. Of course, you shouldn't say that about Köler, because he was a friend of Jakobson and…"

"The headmaster said he was our last great Estonian, and

now he's dead," Indrek interjected.

"Yes, the time of the great ones is past," Tiit concurred. "But you should know, godson, that there's no truth in saying that the great ones' time is gone, because it's the same story with great men of the people as it is with farms and stallions. Everyone has scraggy horses working at home, which can barely limp or wear a harness, but on Sundays there are so many neighing stallions around the churchyard that you can't hear the church organ. Lately I've been noticing that the strong stallions are getting fewer, but then the carthorses are getting sturdier. And what do you think – is it better for a person to have a bellowing stallion at church on Sundays or that he's got two or three good working animals at home that can even pull the cart to church as well? I think it's better without the stallions. Of course a few good stallions are a necessary and beautiful thing, because they show all the parishioners what sort of an animal a stallion should really be, so that a blind and stupid people get the right idea or ideal of a proper stallion, as *Postimees* calls it. It's the same way with a great statesman: he gives a blind and stupid people a proper idea of what a real son of the fatherland should be. The people get ideals, because an ideal is what's put before the people. A statesman like Jakobson creates an ideal for a men of the people ..."

Chapter 19

The sun was low in the sky by the time Indrek got home, where he found his mother, out in the garden, hanging up the washing to dry. As soon as she saw Indrek, she said, "I remembered just in time, I had a look in your knapsack for your shirts and trousers. I see they're pretty threadbare already, it gave me quite a shock! It wasn't so long ago that I made you new ones out of pure linen, and now they're worn through! It must be how they do the washing in town. Who does it for you?"

"A laundrywoman comes," said Indrek.

"So it's her fault then," said mother. "The way I look after them, shirts last a good few years. You should tell her they're pure linen, they don't need much cleaning, no need to scrub them so hard. But don't you start wearing dirty shirts mind; otherwise, bugs will breed, and we don't want that! I'll try to make you a new shirt or two for autumn, I've got a bit of fine linen left over. I'll leave these ones out overnight so they catch the dew, it'll do them good – they won't get that in town."

Liine had been standing within earshot, and now she joined in: "So you're going to use that fine linen you've got in the chest to make Indrek shirts? But you promised that to me!"

"I'll spin some new linen for you, don't you worry about that," said mother.

"But it won't be ready until next year," said Liine.

"So what," said mother, "it's not as if you're going for your confirmation this winter."

"When then?" Liine asked. "Everyone else my age is going this winter, why should I have to wait until I'm old."

"It won't do you any harm to wait a year; anyway, you're not going to get married right away!"

"But I want to go now, with everyone else," said Liine resolutely. "So you have to keep that linen for me."

"My dear child," mother began in a hectoring tone, "what silly talk is that? You can manage without for a while, but Indrek needs a new shirt right away, as he's going to town. You can't do without a nice new shirt in town, but here in the countryside we can get by without; we can make do with tow cloth if we have to."

"Of course," said Liine sarcastically, "the one who's going to town and has got nothing to do there gets a linen shirt right away, but everyone else can wait, there's no hurry for them."

And with those words Liine headed towards the barn, where Liisi and Maret used to like sitting in the spring and summer months, to talk about things which Indrek wouldn't understand, or if he did understand, wasn't allowed to hear. All he could do was sit behind the pile of wood, peaking in the direction of the barn, but he couldn't hear anything, apart from singing and laughter.

But Liine wasn't singing, maybe because she was alone, or maybe because she was still thinking about that linen cloth which she wanted mother to make her a confirmation shirt from. It's not easy to sing, when you're thinking of pure linen. Indrek realised that, and so he went to sit on the barn steps by the open door from where he could look at the blood-red glow of the setting sun. He sat there and watched his sister rummaging in her chest, the same chest which used to belong to Maret. Indrek sat there waiting, waiting and watching, just as he used to when he was little, and his sisters were already grown-up.

"Are you angry with me or something, Liine?" he asked, when it became clear that his sister wasn't going to acknowledge his presence.

"Why should I be angry?" she replied sulkily.

"Well, because of that shirt material," said Indrek.

"It's not as if it belongs to me," said Liine. "It's mother's material, and she can do what she wants with it."

"But if she promised it to you."

"Promised," Liine repeated mockingly. "She promises all sorts of things. If there's anything left over after you, then maybe. The rest of us are lucky to get your leftovers." Indrek was pained by Liine's words.

"I'm going to tell mother not to use that material for my shirt; then you won't have to miss your confirmation this winter."

And having said that he got up from the steps and started to leave, as if he had nothing more to say.

"Are you going already?" Liine asked. "I thought you might sit here for a while longer?"

Indrek sensed how grateful his sister was. He could have sat there talking to her for a while longer, until the last rays of the sunset had faded, but he didn't want to; while gazing at the blood-tinged glow he had remembered Kadri's story about the dog which had crawled between the woodpile and snowdrift to die. The thought of that dog took away any urge to talk. As far as Indrek could remember, no other dog had died like that at Vargamäe, or anywhere else that he knew of. And Indrek had the feeling that something else had died at Vargamäe, together with that dog.

Liine started to descend the barn steps, watching her brother walk off, as if he'd forgotten all about her. Then she went back inside the barn, sat down on the edge of her chest, and stayed there for a while. But either the edge of the chest was too hard, or her joy over the linen was too great, because Liine burst into tears, and now her face didn't show a trace of the headstrongness which she had demonstrated earlier. If Indrek were to see her now even from behind then, if he had any sense, he would have said without thinking: "What a child!" But it seemed that Indrek didn't have any sense, because he went straight to mother and said, "Let Liine have that material, so she can go to her confirmation this winter."

"Heaven help me, what will I use for your shirt then!" mother cried in exasperation.

"Whatever you want," Indrek said. "I'll do without, if I have to, but I don't want that material, I refuse to wear any shirt made from it."

And with those words, he left.

Now the tears started streaming down his mother's face, and she carried on crying as she milked the cows, as if she were sorry for Tõmmik and Päitsik, because their calves had had their milk taken away from them, and all got in exchange was a mixture of flour and water with a bit of sour milk mixed in to give it a milky taste, although it was really little more than a sweetish stench. Tõmmik's calf got less because he was older, Päitsik's got more because he was young and still feeble.

And so the whole family had fallen out, and no one had much time for anyone. That was the mood that prevailed that evening as they went to bed. The next morning, Indrek was wakened by the distant peel of church bells. He jumped out of bed, hurried down from the hayloft, and then, barefoot and wearing only his shirt, he went straight to the gate, as if he were expecting to see something there. He stood there a while, reliving the experience of the boy who many years earlier had sat and cried next to the barking dog. But this time Indrek didn't cry, he just stood there silently. And there was no dog standing barking next to him, instead he stood there completely alone, and every chime of the bell felt like a painful blow to his heart. It was only in Vargamäe that church bells rang like that, nowhere else in the great wide world were there church bells like the ones at Vargamäe. No other smith had ever smelted such magnificent bells, and this one had done so only once in his life. There may have been all manner of beautiful and expensive things in the world, but there weren't any Sunday mornings nor church bells like these ones, because nowhere else were there the same open marshes and bogs for the bells to ring out across. Indrek could tell the difference now, because he'd lived in town and heard the sound of the church bells there. And so he was sure that even if he acquired all the treasures of the world he would still be poor, because nowhere else were there Sunday mornings and church bells like the ones at Vargamäe.

Who knows how long Indrek would have stood there at the gate if his father hadn't come in from the meadow, and asked him, "What are you looking at so intently?"

"Nothing, I was just listening to the church bells," said Indrek.

His father stood still and listened, as if he wanted to hear for himself whether the ringing of the bells could really pain the heart, but a moment later he said, "They've already stopped ringing, I heard them when I was out."

It was true that the bells had stopped ringing a while back, but Indrek could still feel them ringing away deep inside him, somewhere in his head or his chest.

"So is life a bit easier for you there than it was here at home?" father asked after a while.

"It's hard to say," Indrek said.

"I just think that if you could find a way of earning your daily bread a little easier than us here, then there would be some sense to all the trouble and expense, otherwise…"

Father didn't finish his sentence.

"I will eventually," Indrek said.

"It's been hard enough for me," said father, "and I'm not likely to see brighter days until I'm lying with my arms folded across my chest, maybe then things will get be a bit easier. But I have to push on somehow; whatever is beyond my strength simply won't get done."

"You've done a great deal already," Indrek said, trying to comfort his father. Grateful for Indrek's efforts, his father answered in an emotional tone, as if he also had memories of standing by the gate under his rowan tree, listening to the most sonorous bells in the world.

"Believe me, my son, in this world you always have to struggle to do more, if you want to achieve anything at all.

And even then, it won't be enough, even then you will never get everything you want."

Most of the churchgoers had already passed the Eespere gate on their way home by the time Indrek had gathered up his knapsack and readied himself to leave.

Mother was fussing around her departing son with a worried look on her face, as if there was something she wanted to tell him, or she was waiting for him to tell her something. But her son was silent, and so mother didn't utter a single word either. Only when Indrek had passed through the gates, the latch had been put back in place, and Indek had turned his back, did his mother manage to call through the bars of the gate:

"Indrek, would you really refuse to wear those shirts if I made them for you?"

At that moment Liine appeared next to her mother, and spoke across the gate too. Now Indrek noticed that she was already as tall as mother, a little taller even, and her eyes were the same shade of brown.

"You know what we did," she said, as if she were about to reveal something miraculous. "We measured the material out so that each of us gets half, only I get a little bit more, just a tiny bit more. Both of us will get two shirts. Do you agree? It works out just fine! You don't believe me? Come and have a look, come to the barn!"

Before they knew it the gate was unlatched and wide open, and Liine had taken her brother by the arm to lead him back into the yard, and from there to the barn. Inside, vats of meat and salted herring stood against one wall, together with a large chopping block, and all sorts of supplies, hanging from the wall, while a large chest stood by the opposite wall, and then a smaller one with a studded lid, the one which had always creaked when it opened. Liine opened it so eagerly that it let out a sharp squeak, and she hurriedly started to measure out the cloth, right there and there in front of Indrek's eyes. Indrek wouldn't have stood there and watched, but a smell came from that chest like nothing he had smelled anywhere else, a smell which soothed his nerves and reconciled him in a moment. And so his mother and sister got their way.

When Liine next spoke it sounded as if she was calling Indrek through a fog, or across a waterlogged bog: "Check it yourself if you don't believe me, then you'll see that it works out, it works out just fine, you'll be able to go to school, and I'll go to my confirmation. And look, look at what I'm going to do: I'll cut off my share right now, right in front of your eyes, and I'll put it into my box, and we'll leave your share in this chest. That's fair isn't it? We'll cut it in half. Neither of us will be able to grumble then, will they?"

And Indrek didn't grumble. Not now that he was standing with his mother and sister next to this fine-smelling chest.

"So I can start making those two shirts then," mother said eventually.

"That's right, you make them, and I'll wear them thread-bare," said Indrek affectionately.

"Didn't I tell you that Indrek would agree!" Liine cried joyfully. And as soon as Indrek started to leave again, she said: "Let me carry your knapsack, I'll come to see you off."

And so brother and sister set off through Vargamäe, Liine carrying Indrek's knapsack on her back, the two of them smiling happily, as if some good fortune had befallen them. Mother was smiling too as she stood at the gate and watched her children go. And that evening, when she knelt down to milk Päitsik and Tõmmik, she was no longer in the slightest bit concerned that the warm milk from their swollen udders was splashing into the milk pail, and not into the calve's mouths. And Vargamäe Mari would have gone to bed with a smile on her face, as if she were no longer mistress of the house, but a young girl once again, the same young girl who used to sing her heart out at every opportunity. But then, just when the pail was almost full, a wobbling white froth spilling over the brim, Päitsik lifted a muddy hind leg and kicked the pail right over. Mari hadn't got round to greasing her split teats that morning.

"I would have preferred it if the pigs or calves had got the milk," Mari said, scolding Pätsik. Then she added in a world-weary tone: "It's full of fun and laughter, an old woman's life: milk spilt everywhere, and everyone has to go without. Endless fun and laughter!"

And so that Sunday evening Vargamäe Mari couldn't go to bed with a smile on her face.

Chapter 20

The teaching was already in full swing at Mr Maurus's establishment by the time Indrek arrived there in autumn. He had turned up a little late, just as in the previous year. It seemed that was to be his fate in this world.

When Indrek arrived Maurus was in the large downstairs room, where he was handling some matter relating to Tigapuu and the duke; they had become great friends after having spent the summer break there. Now they went everywhere together, making good use of the duke's funds and Tigapuu's local knowledge. But whenever they left the building they would make sure that the duke went out through the front door, while Tigapuu slipped out the back, or if the duke had reason to leave by the back door, then Tigapuu would use the front door. That was what they had agreed as part of their vow of friendship. But by the time they got home they were normally in such fine spirits that they completely forgot their vow of friendship, and both came in through the front door with a great clatter and jangling of bells, bringing with them smells of the alehouse and the florist. And it was those smells which Mr Maurus was investigating as Indrek entered, carrying his knapsack. Which meant that Mr Maurus now had two pressing matters in hand: to ascertain the source of those smells, and to ask Indrek whether he had brought any money. One of the matters could not be ignored, and the other couldn't be delayed, because smells can disperse quickly, and you can never be sure of money until you're holding it in your hand. But Maurus resolved the dilemma like this: he had Indrek and his knapsack wait in the front room, the same place he had waited the previous autumn, the only difference being that back then the Latvian Kopfschneider had given him a chair to sit on, whereas this year there was no one to treat him as one of their own. And so Indrek had to stand there with his knapsack without even removing his coat, because no one was allowed to go anywhere if Mr Maurus wanted to talk to him about money; Indrek had to stand there, watching and listening as Mr Maurus tried to resolve the matter of the smells.

"Who's been here? Who's passed through here?" he asked, sniffing at one bystander, then another, then a third, trying to track down the source of the smells. "Why are the windows open? Did someone open the windows?"

"It was Tigapuu," they answered in unison.

"Aha!" cried Mr Maurus, "Call Tigapuu here!"

And as soon as Tigapuu appeared, Maurus went up to him, sniffed his clothes, asked him to blow into his face, poked his chest, and then cried: "Du Schinder! Wo warst du?"[43]

When Tigapuu failed to answer, headmaster Maurus carried on yelling, "What are those sweet smells? Where did you pick up those smells?"

"I paid a visit to a student friend, he lives with his wife, maybe that's where they come from," Tigapuu explained.

"Who's this student friend who lives with his wife? What's his name?"

"I can't remember his name," Tigapuu said.

"What do you mean?" the headmaster yelled. "A student friend of yours, who lives with some woman, and you can't remember his name? Our Tigapuu can't remember the name of this student friend who lives with some wife!"

"He's a friend of the duke's, that's why," said Tigapuu.

Now the duke was summoned, and Maurus sniffed him up and down too. Strangely enough the duke from the Caucasus smelled exactly like Tigapuu, the only difference being that

---

43 *Du Schinder! Wo warst du?*: "You scoundrel! Where have you been?

he knew the name of the student in question, the one who lived with his sweet-scented wife, whereas Tigapuu did not.

"But this is my establishment, and in my establishment there is a strict rule, that none of the boys are allowed to go and visit any friends with sweet-scented wives, otherwise they'll bring the woman's scent into my establishment," said Mr Maurus, before adding in a threatening tone: "But I'd like to hear it from you, does your friend have such a sweet-scented wife; that's what I would like to know, then Mr Maurus will have another word to say on the matter. Herr Ollino, Herr Ollino!" yelled Mr Maurus, dashing into Ollino's room, "come and write the name of that student in the book, the one with the sweet-scented wife whose scent Mr Maurus's nose can still detect."

But Ollino wasn't there, and so the name of the student with the sweet-scented wife never got written down. In any case, Mr Maurus didn't have time to hang around, because Vargamäe Indrek was waiting with some money for him. And so he rushed through the front hall, beckoned to Indrek, and the two of them went up the stairs together, the same stairs which the previous autumn had smelled to Indrek like a mourning school mistress at church. But this year, Indrek could smell nothing at all. That was probably why his nerves were steeled, or at least they were better prepared than Maurus would have liked. Reaching his room, Maurus turned round and stood there in front of Indrek, peering at him over the top of his glasses, and addressing him with casual familiarity: "How much money have you got for me then?" he said, holding out his hand as if he were expecting Indrek to count out the money right into it. But Indrek didn't do so, because he wanted to talk to Mr Maurus first.

"Money first, then talking," said Maurus. "The old debt, with interest on top, that first, then we can talk."

Indrek wanted to forget all about the old debt, and any interest on top of it, he wanted to use the money he had bought with him to agree a new contract, to start his life at the school afresh. And that life would hopefully be a life in which Indrek didn't have to sleep in the downstairs room, and didn't have any doorbell duties, so that all he had to do was study and then go to class to show them what he had learned – that was the new life Indrek wanted at Mr Maurus's establishment in exchange for his money.

"So how much money have you got then?" asked Mr Maurus again. And then when Indrek named the sum, he said, "That's not enough, it won't do at all: you're going to be joining a more senior class, the teachers are more expensive."

Maurus had his hand held out to receive the money, as if they had already reached an agreement. Indrek gave him the sum he'd mentioned, Maurus hid it in his drawer, and asked, "But what about the interest? What are we going to do about that? Have you really got nothing more at all?"

Indrek told Maurus that he didn't.

"Very well then," said Mr Maurus, "I won't insist on the interest, but you will have to make sure to be a good student." And at that he looked at Indrek and chuckled, as if it were all just a silly joke.

And so Indrek was a fully-fledge student again, with the same rights and privileges as the others, so he had no reason to feel inferior to a German von-something-or-other, a Polish nobleman, or a count of any description. But none of them had come back to school anyway. In their place was a new crowd, who were none of Indrek's concern. The only one of the "bigwig" students to remain was the duke, although his splendour was fading by the day. Some Georgian or Armenian had turned up from Tbilisi and declared that the Caucasus was "packed with people just like the duke. Herds of them, five or six living together in one damp little room."

It turned out there was nothing special about the duke, if he lived like a bedbug, with a herd of other bedbugs, in a fusty old room.

Of course everyone was disappointed that the establishment had lost some of its former glory, old Mr Maurus more than anyone. In order to reduce the influence of the student from Tbilisi, he informed everyone that he wasn't in fact a Georgian or an Armenian, but a pure-blooded jew, and a tailor's son into the bargain.

Maurus was convinced that all Jews were nihilists, socialists, or revolutionaries – and had been since the time of Ahaseurus – so you had to be wary of them, because they were fond of killing dukes, kings and kaisers.

"But what business is that of ours," said Maurus. "We have no dukes, kings or kaisers. And that's why any person with an ounce of wit about him knows that we have no need of socialism or nihilism. Let the French, the English and the Germans build socialism if they want to: they've got kings and dukes of their own to kill – but our little Estonia has no business with any of that! If the Armenian loves uprisings and nihilism, then let him go back to his mountaintops and rise up all he wants; Mr Maurus will happily pay his fare. And he'd better not come bothering the dukes in our flatlands, here on the banks of the Emajõgi river, otherwise we'll give him a taste of nihilism. You know what the word means, don't you; you've had a whole year of Latin now. *Nihil* – nothing. Which means that if someone says: I'm a nihilist, he's really saying: I'm nothing. But Maurus says: *Nihil* – nothing of the sort! As far as regicide is concerned, then all of us Estonian men are nihilists – me, you, Tigapuu, Lible, Vainukägu, all of us, every last one. Frenchmen and Englishmen aren't nihilists, they kill their king or keiser straight off, as soon as they get their hands on him. The Russians are just the same, they won't be second best to anyone. Jakobson became a socialist in St. Petersburg, and then he met his death in Pärnu Forest. The old bear died in Vändra Forest, in Pärnu county. Because God said: *nihil* – nothing of the sort in Vändra Forest, in Pärnu County. And so there's nothing left of him other than a mound under a tree on Vändra River's green banks. That's all that's left of him, *nihil*, apart from that there's nothing at all! That's what becomes of socialists and troublemakers of their ilk. God has no love for them, because he's a bit of a nihilist himself, he says: *nihil* – I'll have nothing of the sort happening under my watch in Estonia! That's why his own son was born in Israel, because he was a bit of a socialist himself. Like all the Jews, because of course our Saviour was a Jew too, maybe not completely, because he had God's blood running in his veins too, but a Jew all the same. All Jews are socialists, their motto is 'whatever's yours is mine'. After all, Jesus and his disciples plucked those ears of corn, that's pure socialism for you. And the fig tree which he cursed, that was pure socialism too. What do you reckon, could a son like that bring joy to his father?" Mr Maurus asked, turning to Indrek.

"No, he couldn't" said Indrek.

"That's right," Maurus said. "Of course he couldn't. That was where God went wrong, sending his son to the land of the Jews, and that was why Jesus had to go back to heaven while he was still so young – why he had to die before his time. He died at the hand of an honest Roman, who was neither a Jew nor a socialist. It was in God's power to make sure his son died at the hand of a decent Roman, not some socialist. The honest virgin Mary gave birth to him, and a loyal Roman killed him."

And so Maurus taught Indrek and the others all about socialism, nihilism, revolution, and global salvation – all those big themes, which they knew so little about. The conversation would have finished there and then, with headmaster Maurus turning to leave, but before he had got through the door, he recalled something important, and so he turned round and asked Indrek, "But what do you reckon, what would have happened to Jesus Christ, if God had decided he should be born to an honest Estonian woman? In that case would he have also ended up a bit of a socialist, and gone off with the rest of his disciples to pick those ears of corn which belonged to someone else?"

"No, in that case he wouldn't," said Indrek.

"No of course, he wouldn't," the headmaster Maurus

confirmed, "because an honest and decent Estonian man would never pick someone else's ears of corn. But in that case would God have summoned him back to heaven so soon?"

"Probably not," Indrek replied.

"That's right, he wouldn't," said headmaster Maurus. "But what would have happened then? How long would Christ have lived? What do you think?"

Indrek didn't know what to think.

"In that case Christ could still be alive today, after all, what's a couple of thousand years for God. It could have been thus, if God had wanted. But God wanted his son to be a Jew, that was God's will. And so all we got from God was Jakobson…"

At that, Mr Maurus seemed to grow despondent. He stood there silently in front of Indrek for a while, as if he'd been unable to say the most important thing.

Chapter 21

While Mr Maurus indulged in lofty thoughts, the day-to-day work of his establishment continued. Vihalepp the theology teacher, who was still referred to as the pope, oversaw the students with increasing vigilance, making sure that not a word of God's holy scriptures went astray as the students recited them. His warning taps on the lectern grew more and more frequent, until eventually he had no choice but to stop the class and explain things clearly himself: "We're God's servants, Christ's soldiers, and soldiers have to fulfil the orders of their commander to a 't'. To a 't', you understand! And how can anyone fulfil the orders of the holy father to a 't', if he doesn't even know the orders. So please bear this in mind: word for word, letter for letter, because on judgement day we will have to account to our Lord Jesus Christ for every word, every single letter, which has passed through our lips."

But that was not enough for Vihalepp, he demanded more, for otherwise his pupils would never become true soldiers of Christ. As Christ's general, he wanted to be able to come into the classroom and say "one", and have all the students jump up; "two" – and they would all sit down. "three" – desks unlocked, "four" – hands on the desk, "five" – arms crossed, "six" – all eyes on Vihalepp, and "seven" – the head boy would stand up to report on the assignment for that day. And since Vihalepp was of the view that a soldier should react like lightening from the heavens above, he gradually sped up the exercise, until it became: one – up, two – down, three – locks, four – hands, five – crossed, six – eyes, seven – head boy.

One time Mr Maurus caught the class in the middle of the one of their tests of piety, and asked, "That's all well and

252

good, but what would God have to say about the boys rattling their desk locks like that?"

"It just takes a little getting used to, Mr Maurus," Vihalepp explained, "just a short while, and then it's not a problem."

"I suppose that God will take a little while to get used to it too," headmaster Maurus agreed. Then as soon as the bell rang to announce the end of class, he asked Vihalepp to leave, and stayed behind with the class.

"He's a clever man, a pious man, and a good man, but he doesn't have an ounce of sense about him," Mr Maurus explained. "Teaching has made him lose his mind. That often happens with clever men: they teach and they teach, they use up all their cleverness and truthfulness, until one fine day it turns out that that teacher hasn't a shred of sense left, the clever man has gone mad. And then you have to find a stupider one, one who still has some sense left in him."

At the next theology lesson, a small, spritely old man appeared before the class. He gave the impression that he was drowning in grey, because everything about him was grey: his beard, his whiskers, his eyes, his eyebrows, his hair and even his clothes. Even the New Testament under his arm looked grey as he paced backwards and forwards in front of the desks, his gaze fixed to the floor, mumbling to himself: "*kelk* – sledge, now is the verb *kelkama* or *kelgutama? Kelk, kelkama, kelgutama*". Eventually he stopped in his tracks, looked up at the students and smiled good-naturedly, as if he were with old friends.

"Hello, children. Where did we get to last time? This old head of mine can't retain anything anymore. Head boy, where did we finish?"

"Dear teacher, you're here for the very first time," said the head boy.

"What? The first time?" the old man said in amazement, before smiling coyly into his beard. "Oh, so it's the first time. Well then, we've done the catechism, we've done the bible stories. I know Mr Vihalepp, he's an upstanding, loyal servant of the Lord. Word-for-word, eh? There's no other way, my dear children, it has to be word-for-word, if it's God's word! But now let's make a start on Paul's journeys. What do you think, is this *reis* in the German sense, meaning travels, or *reis* in the Estonian sense, meaning thigh? German, you reckon. But it could very well be Estonian too. Because in that sense one would make a journey by moving one's thighs, meaning that one would travel. Is that not so? If one walks with ones feet, then one travels with ones thighs. But perhaps the verb from *reis* should therefore be *reietama*, "to thigh". Which would mean that we must talk of Paul's *reietused*, his 'thigh-neys'.[44] In any case, we'll leave that for now, lest we get too far down one path. But you all know the word *kelk*, don't you? What is a *kelk*? Is it a sledge? No it isn't. Is it a sleigh. No it isn't. Is it a *kresku*? Head boy!"

But the head boy didn't know.

"Who knows what a *kresku* is?"

Vargamäe Indrek knew what it was, and so it was his job to explain it to the head boy and the rest of the class.

"Very good," said the teacher, "now you all know what a *kresku* is, a toboggan. And you didn't need my help at all, did you. That's the first thing we've learned about Saint Paul's journeys and his 'thighneys'. But what's your name?" the teacher asked, turning to Indrek. When Indrek told him, the teacher said, "Very good. So it's Paas then. I'll write the name in my pocket book. The first name from Saint Paul's journeys. Now, very good… Paas… mmm… Paas – Pae or Paas – Paasi, which is right, how should one decline it, recline it?"

"Paas-Paasi," said Indrek.

---

44 "thighneys": this tortuous and unsuccessful play on words by a slightly deranged teacher is almost impossible to translate; it is a pun on *reis* which in Estonian means both "thigh" and "journey" and the teacher uses it to invent a new verb, "to thigh" in order to mean "to journey". "thighney" sounds ridiculous, but so does the original invention in Estonian – *reietused*.

"Very good," said the teacher. "Paas – Paasi… I'll make a note of that in my book too, so as to avoid any mistakes in the future… Paas – Paasi. Which means that if it's paas as in slate, then it's pae, but if it's a person, then it's Paas – Paasi. Let's keep the kingdom of man separate from the kingdom of minerals. But what do you think, is there really a big difference, a profound difference, between Paas and a paas – that's to say, between the human and mineral kingdoms? Is there a big difference or isn't there, what do you think? Head boy!"

The head boy thought that there was, since one was a living creature, while the other was dead.

"But a human could also be dead; what would we say then, Paas – Paasi or Paas – Pae? You're not dead yet, but your name places you so close to the mineral kingdom; what do you say to that? How would you like it if your name were declined Paas-Pae, as if you were stone or soil?"

"I don't care either way," said Indrek.

"But do you remember what the scriptures say – according to which you would have the right to be Paas-Pae, because man is never far from rock and earth?"

"From the soil you were taken and soil you shall become," said Indrek.

"That's right! From the soil you were taken and soil you shall become. We start off as soil and we end up as soil. Paas – pae is mightier than Paas – Paasi. Paas – pae stands close to eternity, that's why. Paas – pae is more closely linked to God. Paas – pae or Paas – Paasi. One with a capital P, the other lower case."

The teacher fell silent and appeared to be lost in thought. But before long he jerked back into life: "Right then – Saint Paul's journeys, his trips, his hikes, his travels, his thighneys, his walks, his sleighrides. That's right! Where did we get to? Paas explained to us what a *kresku* is. But we still didn't get to *kelk*. One thing we can say for sure is that a *kelk* is not a sleigh, it's not a toboggan. But what is a *kelk* then? What does the verb *kelkama* mean? Not *kelgutama*, to sleigh, but *kelkama*.

Can we say that Paulus didn't go travelling, but he went to *kelkama*, to slope about?"

It was only after considerable debate that the teacher felt able to conclude that Paul's journeys weren't anything to do with the verb *kelkama*. And once that truth had been affirmed, the class ended. The bell rang, the old man stood up from his chair, closed his Old Testament, put it under his arm, and said, "Next time we'll continue where we left off, with Saint Paul, he's got a lot to say, and he's worth listening to… So then, I know two of you already – the head boy, *priimus*, and Paas, both starting with a 'p', a hard 'p', not a soft 'b', because us Estonians are a tough lot."

And then he left, having earned himself the nickname *Kresku*. And that name stuck. But in the next lesson there was no longer any talk of *kreskus* or *kelks*, instead they talked of Jerusalem, the Mount of Olives, the Dead Sea, Egypt, the pyramids, the Apis bull, and the muds of the river Nile, the layers of which could be used to estimate the age of the planet Earth.

"And you know what, my children," he said, "it's really very strange, because those mud- measurers are sure that the mud of the Nile is older than the planet itself. Just think about that: the mud of the Nile is older than Earth. But that means that the Nile is also older than Earth. What do you say to that? How much time has passed since the Earth was created? Who knows? Head boy! Paas!"

Neither of them knew how many years had passed since the Earth had been created. No one in the class did.

"I don't know either," said the teacher despondently. "I can't remember, my old head can't retain it anymore. But a few thousand years or so must have passed, at least five thousand, or six, or even more. It's difficult to put a precise number on it, yes it's rather difficult, my dear children. I'm thinking of the time when the first human appeared, that Adam. Let's not call him old Adam, but simply Adam, the one who was father of Cain and Abel, the one who fathered the first murderer. The first man and the first woman; as soon as they met they copulated, and she gave birth to a murderer. They could have been a bit patient, but no, they had to go and create a murderer. Adam never killed anyone, but he had a son who did. The son was the killer! It's like that in our day too, father doesn't murder, he gets by just fine without killing anyone, but the son just can't help himself... Right then: it's easy to work out the age of the earth from the moment when man first appeared, because a human day is the same as an earth day, which means that when humankind counts the days he's been here, he's also counting the number of days the earth has been here. It makes no difference if someone has conceived a murderer, or if he is a murderer himself, everyone passes their days in much the same way, all the more so in the old days behind the gates of Eden, before they'd invented the gallows. So much for humans. But what are we going to do about all those days which came before humankind? Well you see, my children, those days are counted according to the layers of mud in the river Nile, and they've discovered that the mud is older than Earth itself, which means older than man, and so it fits well with the scriptures: first came the soil, then came man, otherwise it wouldn't have been possible for God to make man from the soil. First, the eternal mud, then eternal man. How long exactly that eternal mud has been around for, no one knows, my dear children. And although God must know, he won't ever tell us mortals. But does he know? Is it possible for an eternal being to know an eternity? What does eternal mean? Who knows? Head boy! Paas! You don't know? I don't know either. My old head can't retain it anymore, that's the trouble an old man has with his old head. Ah! But there, at the back, someone knows. What's your name? Lible? What a nice name! Let the boy with the nice name tell us what eternal means."

"Eternal means something which was, is, and always will be," said Lible.

"Right," said the teacher. "That's right! Nicely put. But

257

there's one problem with that: we don't know what was, what is, and what will be; we know hardly anything about what is. But maybe you, Lible, with your nice name, maybe you know something which was, which is, which will be? What is it? What might it be? The moon, the sun, the stars in the sky? But they weren't there in the beginning, the scripture confirms that. There was a time when they didn't exist, and a time will come again, when they won't exist. What do you say? God? Yes, him of course, because he existed before everything. But unfortunately we know next to nothing about God. In fact, we know little enough about mortal man. You see it's like this, my children, it's the same story with God as it is with the history of the world: it's possible to work it out since the time when humans came into existence, but what happened before, or what will come after, we have no way of knowing that. At least there is one good thing as far as the Earth is concerned – there's the mud on the banks of the Nile, which we can use to work out its age. But what are we supposed to do with our God? How are we supposed to work out his age? We have nothing more at our disposal than man and his mortal days, and therefore it seems as if God was born on the same day as man. He was born, and he will die, as if he wasn't even eternal. That's the sad truth about our knowledge of God. That's why it doesn't do to utter God's name in vain… but who's clattering about over there? What? The end of the lesson? Ahh, so it's the end already. Very well, let's leave Saint Paul and God for now, we'll carry on where we left off next time. But as far as God is concerned, he is eternal for sure, only that we don't know that, because man's feeble mind can't grasp the eternal. He can't even grasp the mortal very well. That's why we'll come back to Saint Paul's journeys in the next lesson."

Gripping the Old Testament under his arm, his head bowed, the teacher left the classroom, looking as if he were a little saddened by the fact that man's feeble mind wasn't capable of grasping anything much. The next lesson turned out to be a repeat of the previous ones: no sooner had the teacher managed to open the Old Testament than he was distracted by some thought which caused him to forget all about Paul and his journeys. After all, what was the point of travelling with Saint Paul when you could fly with the storks, who nested somewhere in Lapland, and then traversed the whole of Europe in autumn, flying across the Mediterranean to the banks of the Nile, and from there further south, where there was such an abundance of bright, warm sunshine. Oh! Those endless flocks of birds, they make your heart skip a beat, they rouse an old man to flights of fancy. Or why not take a seat in a fishing boat and row to somewhere near Newfoundland to catch some fish, and then salt them! Why not climb onto an elephant's back and set off on a tiger hunt, or join a camel caravan and cross the sand dunes from one palm-fringed oasis to another, then stop to wonder at the Fata Morgana! Or you could plant some mulberries, pluck their lush leaves, and feed them to the silkworms. Or you could visit some catacombs, or the ruins of Herculaneum, because they were somewhere in the vicinity of Paul's journeys too. Or wonder at the waterfalls, the mountains, the cacti and the turtles, the sweet-smelling flowers, and the poisonous snakes, the bees, the ants and the termites too, because there is so much beauty and so much of interest in this world that it seems there is no end to it all. Half a year might pass, but there will still be no end of interesting things to see. A whole year might pass, but the grey old man, whose hair was almost white by now, would still be telling his fascinating stories. And he would always be sure to know some miniscule yet significant detail, with which to link the story to humankind and the whole of creation.

But one difficult thing waited for the old man at the end of every half year. When he complained about it to the class the first time, he sighed from the depths of his heart, which aroused everyone's interest in what might follow.

"What's the most difficult thing we have to face?" the

teacher asked the class. "Who knows? Who will answer? Head boy! Paas! Lible! What? No one knows, not even Lible. All he knows is that God is eternal… Assigning the numbers is the most difficult thing, my dear children. After all, we've still not done anything which we could assign numbers to. We wanted to go travelling with Paul, but we couldn't, as you saw for yourselves. Thus was God's will. But what should we do now then? What numbers shall we assign? Head boy, what number should I give you. You don't know? The head boy doesn't know! The head boy doesn't know that he always earns a five, top marks in theology, otherwise he wouldn't be the head boy. Paas, what about you? What? Zero? Paas has to settle with a zero. Right, that's right! Zero is a fine number. But given that God favours the meek, and you've already been confirmed, and you're a Christian, then you shall receive top marks too, otherwise what kind of confirmed Christian would you be? Do you know your 'Our Father'? You know the commandments off by heart? Scriptures all clear? The bible story as clear as drinking water? What else could one ask for? A serious Christian doesn't need for much. Which means – a five for you, Paas, top marks for your knowledge of the scriptures. Lible, I assume you have nothing against getting top marks as well? No? You agree with my decision? Excellent! But what's the point of all this talking, let's just give everyone top marks, then they'll be no cause for grumbling. Is anyone against? No? Ok then, top marks for everyone! But of course, it wouldn't do any harm to read a bit about Paul's journeys, you never know when someone might ask you about them. That's right! So, top marks for all of you then! Christians, all of you are good Christians, so why shouldn't you all have top marks…"

Chapter 22

Kurlov the mathematics teacher loved nothing more than ones and zeros. With those ones and zeros he graded the students' knowledge, and the solutions to his assignments were to be found in ones and zeros too. He liked to say to the students with a contented smile on his face, "You're making it needlessly difficult for yourselves, when in fact it's so easy: either a one or a zero. And that's all that you need, because between the two of them lies infinity. Do you understand?"

But the students understood nothing at all about the infinity which occupied the space between zero and one, and nor did they want to, because they had not the slightest need for infinity. And so they consulted amongst themselves, and then went to see Ollino with the request that he speak to Mr Maurus about finding a new mathematics teacher. As soon as Mr Maurus heard that, he came to speak to the class, "What do you want a new teacher for? Is that clever chap not good enough for you? I pay him good money, and you come and tell me to get rid of him. Where is Mr Maurus supposed to send him? In any case, that clever man has some important friends. So I tell you: Mr Kurlov stays. After all, who is the headmaster here? Mr Maurus is, and whatever the headmaster says, goes."

Of course things didn't turn out quite as the headmaster wanted. A few days later Tigapuu delivered the following monologue, "Boys, do you know what the right of patronage is? You don't? Then you've been living in the dark ages. Right of patronage means that the lord of the manor chooses a teacher for the parish school. But it doesn't have to be like that anymore, because we're no longer living in the dark ages. Education means enlightenment, and if the lord of the manor no longer has to choose a teacher, and the parish has to choose one for itself, why then should the headmaster choose the school masters? Are we inferior to a parish? We're all supposed to be educated people, we can speak Russian; does the parish speak Russian? So I say down with the right of patronage! Down with Mr Maurus' tyranny! All who are in agreement, raise your right hand, not your left one, because an educated man always raises his right hand. So, everyone agrees with me then. I thank you! Right: from now on we won't be attending those infinity classes, because we're going on strike. The right of patronage has to go, for ever! Am I right? So – that's agreed then! Infinity must end, together with all those zeros! And please bear in mind: I have your word. And whoever fails to keep his word will get a taste of this!"

Tigapuu reached across the lectern, brandishing his hefty fist in the direction of his classmates: that would be his sanction against anyone who dared to uphold the right of patronage.

The next day Mr Kurlov found himself sitting in classroom number two all alone. "Infinity's waiting for his ones and zeros," the students joked. Kurlov spent the whole of the following day sitting patiently in his room too, and he made sure to write his name in the book, so that he would get paid. On the third day, he informed Mr Maurus about the situation. The next day Mr Maurus stormed into the classroom in a rage; the theology class was underway and they were in middle of crossing the desert on camels.

"Tigapuu, why have you been absent from the mathematics lessons?" Mr Maurus asked.

"It wasn't just me who was absent," said Tigapuu.

"Answer the question: why did you miss the last three mathematics lessons?"

"The whole class missed them," Tigapuu replied.

"Do you hear that, do you hear that?" the headmaster asked, turning to the teacher. "You're a clever man; you've got a good head on your shoulders. Did Mr Maurus ask clearly or did he not? He asked clearly. Very good! I thank you!" he said, shaking the teacher's hand. "So there can only be one man here who is completely mad, and that is this man Tigapuu. Because what did I ask? Who remembers? Who can tell me? Paas, you say it, you're the tallest one here. Or maybe you missed the classes together with Tigapuu? Do you understand Mr Maurus' question, or have you gone mad too, why did you miss the class?"

"Because that's what we decided," said Indrek.

"Who is we?!" the headmaster yelled. "Mr Maurus never decided that, and only he can decide such matters. Who is this 'we' who decides things here? Who?"

"All of us," Indrek replied. "The whole class, two classes."

"Do you hear that, do you hear that?" the headmaster asked, turning towards the teacher and shaking his grey head so vigorously that his pince-nez fell from his nose. "The whole class! Two classes! The whole of Mr Maurus's school! The whole school decides not to attend class! But that's a rebellion, that's socialism, imported to our law-abiding land by Russian students. That's Russian cabbage, that's warty cabbage imported with Russian grain, and now the students import rebellion and socialism. So that's what you and the duke go hunting for amongst the Russian students and their sweet-smelling women! Those stinking Russian women are teaching you socialism!"

But Tigapuu replied in a superior tone, "Mr Maurus, that's not socialism; it's the right of patronage,"

"What's that? The right of patronage!" Mr Maurus yelled, and started running backwards and forwards in front of the desks as if the ground beneath his feet were ablaze. "That man will drive me crazy, he'll drive me crazy! The crazy man will drive me crazy! The right of patronage he says, that's why they don't come to the lesson. Herr Schnellmann, Herr

263

Schnellmann, *sagen Sie mir schnell*,[45] which one of us is crazy, because one of us surely must be!"

But Mr Schnellmann just chuckled good-naturedly into his white beard, gave a slight shake of his head, and said, "Don't ask me, Mr Maurus, my old head can't retain anything anymore."

And so the headmaster didn't establish which of the two of them was crazy, Tigapuu or him, and just carried on yelling in a crazed tone, "Right of patronage he says, that's why they don't come to class! But even with his old brains Mr Maurus is clear on this point: right of patronage means that everyone must be in class! The right of patronage still holds force at my place, thank God, and whosoever didn't know that will be sure to know it now. At my place, order and subordination still rule. Tomorrow everyone must be in the class!"

With that the headmaster left. And since the bell had just announced the end of class, Mr Schnellmann said, "Next time we'll carry on where we left off, with Saint Paul, Saint Paul once more."

And then he picked up his Old Testament and headed in the direction Mr Maurus had gone. Tigapuu followed him to the door, but stopped there, straddling the doorway, and said, "Everyone stays put. There's a traitor amongst us."

"Not me!" yelled Lible.

"So it must be you," said Tigapuu, "because who addressed you? Boys, grab hold of him! Give him to me!"

But Lible had already flung himself under the tables, where he was writhing about, shouting, "It wasn't me; it wasn't me!"

"Yes it was," said Tigapuu, trying to grab hold of the traitor before he could flee.

"Let him be, and what are you making such a fuss about," said Indrek, restraining Tigapuu. "It's better if old Maurus knows everything, then we don't need to explain it ourselves."

---

45 *sagen Sie mir schnell*: "tell me, right now"

"The traitor has to get his just deserts," Tigapuu retorted, clearly itching to get hold of Lible.

"If he's ready to strike with the rest of us, let him be," said Indrek.

"I'm striking too!" yelled Lible from under the table.

"Very well," Tigapuu replied. "You can come out from under their now. But heaven help you if you decide to attend lessons."

"I won't, I swear," Lible said, climbing out from under the table.

And so the strike continued, and Mr Kurlov was left sitting all on his own in the classroom. And although Mr Maurus managed to catch hold of a student or two and drag them to the classroom, they would say nothing more than: "Teacher sir, I've got no idea what's going on." And that was the totality of the wisdom which Mr Kurlov could squeeze out of his students. They messed about like that for another couple of weeks, until the teacher's patience finally ran out, and he quit Mr Maurus's establishment. That was solution which everyone had been hoping for, not just the students but the headmaster too, although he pulled a sad face when he spoke with Tigapuu and Indrek, as the initiators of the strike.

"You're clever boys, but you've got no idea what you've gone and done. You've driven away Mr Maurus's cleverest school master. And what's that clever schoolmaster going to tell everyone now? Isn't he going to tell everyone that Mr Maurus's school is bursting at the seams with socialism and rebellion?"

"But I said right at the start that it's not a rebellion, and it's not socialism; it's the right of patronage," Tigapuu explained in a knowing tone.

"Thank heavens for the right of patronage," said the headmaster, "otherwise God knows what could have happened. But I'll tell you one thing: you're wrong about the right of patronage, because a school is not a parish. Can you study Latin or algebra at a parish school? No you can't. You can't learn anything there. But here you've got algebra and geometry, Latin and Greek, Paul's journeys, and lots of other stuff too. That's why the right of patronage has to be preserved. And so I've found you a new teacher – he's young, tall and handsome, and clever too, even cleverer than the one who left. It's true he's been barred from teaching in the capital cities, but in our town he can still put his cleverness to good use, thank God. Just not at the state schools, because they can make do with any stupid teachers there, that's how they do things at state schools. Anyway, let's see how you get on with this new one."

The new teacher was indeed young and tall, but his looks were marred by his glasses, which he had to wear because of his weak, grey eyes.

"So you drove Mr Kurlov away?" said Mr Molotov, once the headmaster had left the class. "Who were the ringleaders?"

"Tigapuu! Tigapuu! Paas!" came the cries, and fingers pointed in their direction.

Mr Molotov approached Tigapuu's desk, and looked at him questioningly with his dull eyes. Then he did the same to Indrek. And then he turned round, stood by the blackboard, and hissed through his teeth, "Pigs! What pigs you are! But don't think that I mean it in a bad way," he said, addressing the whole class. "No, I mean it quite sincerely, quite sincerely. What pigs! Of course Kurlov is an idiot, I know him well; he's got the brains of a snowman and he doesn't have the slightest clue about maths! He's the ideal schoolmaster, you could even make him professor, that would suit him just fine! But I'm not here as your teacher, but as your comrade. Not as a friend, because I choose my friends, but as a comrade – any dimwit can be my comrade, because I'm a socialist. But I'm not here to teach you socialism, as your headmaster fears. He's a total clod, a total fool, you can tell him that from me, if you want. No, I'm not going to teach you socialism. But I'm a socialist by conviction, and I want to teach you mathematics. And so, let us start. Where's the textbook? The names of the students? Head boy, what have you covered already? Right. Let's see how much you know."

And so he asked the students up to the blackboard one by one. And every single one of them he sent back with the following words, "Idiot! You don't know the first thing about mathematics! Blockhead! This one has porridge for brains. The wits of a turkey, a turkey I tell you! Mathematical myopia! Sheep's skull! Off you go to knock about with the negros, that's the best place for you! A dead fish's fins for brains. You're about on a par with a tadpole, only you've got no tail and you don't know how to swim. Enough! A premature calf, a fly's sneeze for brains... is that all of you now? So, a classful of mathematical idiots? And you want to be my comrades, become my friends? What kind of friend can you be if you're a mathematical moron? What kind of comrade? Can we have any truth in this world without mathematics? Can we have any honesty without truth? And any sincerity without honesty? Would I be speaking to you like this if I were also a mathematical idiot? Did Kurlov speak with you like this? Did he call you pigs, or calves, or clods? No, he called you gentlemen, I know. Am I right? If Mr Kurlov were to call you a pig or a calf, then it would be offensive, but if I say to you: idiot or clod, then I'm speaking the truth, nothing but the truth, the pure mathematical truth, which is the purest truth there is, because it contains the truth, the whole truth and nothing but the truth. So I will nurture your mathematical brains. Come to see me at five today, because I want to make you into the first real men in Mr Maurus' school. You understand? The first ones to understand what kind of centipede 'pi' is and what kind of rhino a logarithm is. You hear me: five o'clock! Mäe street, number twenty-six. If I'm not at home, let yourselves in, the door's always unlocked, then wait for me to come."

And with that the class would have been over, if the question of the cost of private lessons hadn't come up. The students wanted to clarify the matter, but not one of them dared to ask Mr Molotov. Eventually, they managed to persuade Indrek to do so.

"What?! What did you say?" Mr Molotov yelled, rushing at Indrek and grabbing him by the shirtfront. Indrek repeated the question, and Molotov let go and bellowed into his face, "You're a useless idiot! You're all useless idiots! You deserved Mr Kurlov and you deserve Mr Maurus! But listen to me, you idiots, I'm telling you as a good comrade, come and see me at five o'clock. Let yourselves in, the door will be open, and wait for me there, because I want to give you a human face, I want to remove the mark of the beast from your brows. But the others, what good are they for? Blast and damn it! Who do you take me for? And you, pig snout, and you, grey barrow hog, weren't you ashamed to ask such a thing of me, your comrade? Were you not ashamed? Or you don't see me as your comrade? How am I supposed to make people of you, you quadrupeds on hind legs? Who would try to make money from turning animals into people? Even the German professor wouldn't do that, and the Germans will do almost anything for money these days. But not me, I'm a socialist, and I only mix with others of my kind. Even if women or rhinoceroses were sitting here in your place, I would still treat you as socialists. So I tell you in plain Russian: five o'clock, the door's open, wait for me. But look, they're already trembling with fear – he's going to rob us blind, we'll be seized by a cutthroat! But who's talking about money, you feeble-minded bacilli? Is there even a corpse's whiff of robbery, you numb-skulled specky boys? That's why in the future no one will ever hurt me, because I'm the senior representative of humankind in the music of the spheres. Five o'clock and straight through the front door. No need to knock. There's a lamp on the table, bring some matches with you. If there's no oil in it, you can pour some in, there's a bottle behind the door, by the wall. Make yourselves at home."

And with that Mr Molotov left his first class, followed by the cry of almost the whole class in unison: "Grey barrow!"

That nickname seemed just right for him, because he had coal-black curly hair, and black eyebrows and whiskers. But they all wanted to go and see Grey Barrow that evening, apart from Unter the German, who was the son of a Moscow factory owner, and who reckoned he could afford to take private lessons, where there would be less likelihood of being insulted than at Mr Molotov's.

Mr Molotov's apartment turned out to be on the third floor, an attic room, at the top of a steep, dark, flight of steps, which the students had to climb by matchlight, arriving in single file at the door which Mr Molotov had referred to. Not a single sound came from the room, and, peering through the keyhole, they saw it was unlit too. They deliberated as to whether they should go straight in or knock at the door as Molotov had instructed.

"Stand aside!" Tigapuu cried, shoving his way past the others and barging open the door with a loud thud. "Come in," he said, already inside. "I'm a socialist too, no need to knock," he said, having lit a match and confirmed that the room was empty.

The room was cold. The black iron stove in the corner was cold too. The match quickly went out, and so they decided to light the lamp, but there was no oil in it, as Molotov had warned. The oil bottle outside the door was also empty, with no cork in it. So they had to club together and go and buy some oil. And since Molotov himself had still not turned up, they started looking about for some wood to get the stove going. But there was no wood either. Eventually they got an armful of logs from the caretaker.

"Now we're masters of the house," said Tigapuu, sitting down next to the warm stove.

But the others couldn't feel themselves masters of the house because they had nowhere to sit. They either had to stand, or squat on the floor, while they waited for the teacher. By now the stove was ablaze and the room had warmed up, but they still hadn't seen hide nor hair of Molotov. Eventually,

Indrek said, "That Grey Barrow really is no better than a grey barrow."

And having reached that conclusion, they all tramped back down the stairs. Tigapuu wanted to leave the door wide open, and open the stove door too, so that Mr Molotov wouldn't be able to enjoy the warmth which had filled the room thanks to their efforts. But the others didn't agree, so they closed the door behind them, and left the stove door shut, just as they had found it.

"Did I invite you to my place yesterday?" asked Molotov the students in the next lesson. When they confirmed he had, he said, "So that's why! I racked my brains about it, who could have warmed my room for me, and poured oil in the lamp. So then! Now you see what a scoundrel man can be. Just think – I'm a socialist, I'm supposed to occupy the highest position on the scale of mankind – I mean that in the mathematic sense – and I behave like that. Just think what your everyday mortals, the petit-bourgeois and the bourgeois get up to, if the loftiest amongst us behaves in such a dastardly fashion! You take note of that, and bear it in mind, because it will stand you in good stead later in life. Man is a scoundrel, even if you put him in paradise. He was already a scoundrel, back there in Eden. Because you know where I was? I was walking round town and up on cathedral hill, and I was trying my hardest to remember something, because I knew there was something I was supposed to remember. I carried on like that until seven o'clock, but then I gave up; after all, how long are you supposed to carry on trying to remember something when you can't remember it? In the end you just decide that there probably wasn't anything to remember to start with. If you'd just put oil in the lamp, then I'd have known that you came for the lesson, but given the stove was warm, I didn't know what to think. What pigs you are to get my stove going like that, there's no formulas or theories which could explain it. But come to see me today, I'll definitely be at home today."

And with that he turned to Unter the German and said, "And you, you swine, you made a complaint about me to the headmaster, apparently I insulted you. So I insulted you, did I, you little blubberer? Do you have any idea, you anvil block, what it means to insult someone in Russian? Have you ever heard a Russian swearing, you dolt? When a Russian swears at someone, all the hair on his head falls out, and every single body hair too and he'll look like he's never been born. That's how a Russian swears. If he's a socialist, that is. But you, you rotten potato masher, you've still got all your hair, thank God, which proves that I never so much as thought about insulting you, you pathetic lamb. A couple of comradely, grammatical terms of art, that was all. And even Mr Maurus and his idiotic mug understood that. But as you wish, Mr Ober, with dolts we shall speak the language of dolts. It's all the same to me."

When the students went to see Molotov again that evening, he was sitting at the table, in heated debate with a bearded fellow. There was an almost empty bottle and two glasses on the table, and next to them a piece of paper with the remains of some food on it.

"Ahh!" cried Mr Molotov when he saw the boys. "My new flock, which I now have to transform into fully enfranchised and majestic human beings." And turning to his guest he said, "Bye for now then, I'm out of time today."

He shook the guest's hand and hurriedly saw him out the door. Then he put the bottle, the glasses, and the food at the end of the table by the window, and said, "Sit where you can. You will have to take it in turns to stand up and sit down, there aren't enough chairs for everyone. You can sit on the bed too if you want, there are no fleas in it; they don't breed in the cold, as they're such aristocratic creatures, the little devils. They prefer it where it's soft and warm. But it's neither soft nor warm here. Pull the bed closer to the table."

Seeing the boys hesitate, Molotov said angrily, "What are you waiting for, you dolts? A sofa? Only cutthroats sit on sofas, only bloodsuckers. You think there's riches enough in Russia to buy everyone a sofa? We should be thankful for a pair of felt boots or bast shoes."

Eventually Molotov started the lesson. But before he'd got very far, he said, "You know what, my brothers, I'm drunk. God help me! At first I didn't realise it, but as soon as the old grey matter came into contact with mathematics, I did. That's my measuring stick. Mathematics demands a sober head, because doing mathematics is a bit like downing one shot of vodka after another. Understood? It can't be helped; you'll have to come back some other time. Then I'll definitely be home, and sober too. There's no other way for me, I have to get into the flow, can you understand that? The first two hours are spent getting into the flow, then we start. Third time lucky!"

The boys descended the stairs with long faces, some of them laughing, others spitting. Then, on the third occasion far fewer of them bothered to turn up at Molotov's door. But this time the lesson did indeed get off to a good start, and Molotov managed to get into the flow. After a couple more lessons like that, there wasn't a single boy missing from Molotov's private lessons, even Unter the German came. It was as if they had found inspiration in mathematics, as if dreams really came true in the world of numbers, dreams which were perfectly formed and crystal clear.

"Stop me if there's something you don't understand," Molotov said to his students from time to time. "I've nurtured mathematical brains in all sorts of numbskulls, I'll do the same for you lot, until you learn the joy of it."

And everyone did indeed start to learn the joy of mathematics, as if something had fundamentally changed within them, or even in mathematics itself. It made no difference that Molotov carried on insulting them just as before; they soon got used to that, even Unter. But Molotov didn't find it so easy to forget that Unter had made a complaint against him, and he came back to it again and again. One time he said, "You little whippersnapper! Can't handle the Russian language! Even women can handle it, when I speak Russian with them. At first they make a fuss, but before long it's all well and fine. There's one I know: tall as a pole, almost reaches my fringe, and when she walks she bobs up and down like she's on springs. And what word do you think was too much for her? Only flaxen mane – nothing worse than that. She fainted! Just imagine! I said flaxen mane and she was down on the floor! Maybe not right down on the floor, because I managed to react her just in time and I sat her down on the bench. Such a fuss, moaning, crying, whining – an affront to her dignity, it was! Just little old me, and suddenly it's an affront to the dignity! But you know how it is now? She just blushes a bit when I say flaxen mane. She goes red all over, you can see it through her clothes. Heaven help me, that's what she does!"

Chapter 23

One day Mr Molotov turned up for class holding a small package wrapped in white paper. The boys tried to guess what it might contain, but to no avail. Normally Molotov bought only tobacco and rolling papers, nothing more, but recently he had stopped doing even that, because the boys had clubbed together and brought him a load of Fru-Fru cigarettes, right to his table at home, so he had one packet he could hold in his hand, and another which he kept as a reserve supply in his pocket. Of course, they suffered an earful of insults from him for that "swinish trick", but Molotov took the cigarette papers from the boys gratis, just as they enjoyed free classes from him. And so, it couldn't be cigarette papers or tobacco or filters in the paper package. Anyway, the package was the wrong shape for that. Then, at the end of the lesson, he opened it, and it turned out that it contained a paper shirtfront, a paper collar, and a new red necktie.

"Does anyone have a mirror on them?" Molotov asked.

Of course they did. Vainukägu was always sure to have a pocket mirror on him, without it he had to resort to opening the inner window, holding it with the dark wall behind it, and using that to admire his reflection. Vainukägu handed his mirror to Mr Molotov.

"Oh what a dolt!" cried Molotov as he took the mirror. "Going round with a mirror in your pocket, day in day out!"

"He has it with him at night-time too!" said Lible.

"You bunch of fops!" said Molotov, tearing off his dirty shirtfront, collar, and threadbare necktie, so that he could replace them with the clean new ones. And he carried on cursing as he did so: "What a bevy of fools these women are!

A woman's not a man, not a friend, nor a comrade. Only yesterday Madam Headmaster said to me, "Mr Molotov, you're a good-looking man, why don't you take more care of your appearance?" What do you think of that: a man, and good-looking she says! So I told her, "I don't have a mirror, and beauty is not the same as truth, and anyway you can't see the truth in a mirror." Do you suppose that turkey understood a thing I said? No, she just carried on cackling like a gander: "You really are a good-looking man, Mr Molotov." It was as if she wanted to make me an indecent proposal! Her with her false teeth and false hair on! But now I'm going to start taking care of my appearance. Look! Just like a slave labourer in his fetters!"

He wrapped his old rags in the piece of paper, and chucked them into the corner of the room.

"You can shove that into the stove," he said. "The paper is clean enough, you won't get your hands dirty."

A similar routine was repeated frequently after that, only with less misogyny or with no more than the obligatory minimum, for form's sake. Mr Molotov would even have shaved his beard in front of the class, but he couldn't, because neither he nor his students had a razor. So he had to do that elsewhere, and he started doing so with ever greater regularity.

"It must be something to do with him calling that girl 'flaxen mane'," Tigapuu said.

"No, it's because she fainted," said Indrek.

"Idiots!" cried Metslang. He was a boy of around twenty, stocky, with an old man's physiognomy, white eyebrows, beady grey eyes, powerful jaws, a large mouth and crooked teeth, and wherever he went he brought a smell of dough and freshly-baked bread; he spent all night at the bread trough with his sleeves rolled up, and came straight to school the very next morning. "You know nothing about women," he said in a worldly-wise tone. "Flaxen Mane is no big deal, nor is fainting, but you must never touch them. Our Grey Barrow put his hands on Flaxen Mane, when she was unsteady on her feet, that's why. You must never touch a woman with your hands, otherwise you're done for. Anyway, if you want to know my view, then I reckon that Flaxen Mane was only pretending to faint…"

"You really think so?!" cried the class in amazement.

"What do you think? That fainting fit was bait, plain and simple."

"So if Grey hadn't laid his hands on her, she would have just swayed a bit and then stayed steady on her feet?" Indrek asked, intrigued by Metslang's interpretation.

"Without a doubt!" said worldly-wise Metslang. "Grey is a pathetic little man who tries to sound tough by insulting people. Any girl can see right through him. And you mark my words, it won't end with that. Grey has to lay his hands on Flaxen Mane again. Women never settle for just once."

Indrek found Metslang and his worldly wisdom strangely persuasive, and from that moment on something close to friendship started to develop between them. They'd been sitting between the same four walls, at opposite ends of the same room for quite a while, but they'd never felt the need to become better acquainted before that. Then all of a sudden, it was as if they were the only two in the class who truly understood the situation with Molotov and his Flaxen Mane. It was only later that they learned that as far as this particular mystery was concerned, they'd got completely the wrong end of the stick. But for now, their friendship blossomed, for Metslang had found a pair of ears which were willing to listen attentively to his words of wisdom, especially on the subject of women, and from that wisdom Indrek wove himself a web of romantic fairy tales.

It worked best of all by the bread oven, in Metslang's little warm room, because no one came to disturb them there. A linden-bark mattress had been placed on wooden crates, and a feather pillow on top of that. Lying on that bed with his sleeves rolled up, his hands behind his head, Metslang delivered his lessons and shared his wisdom with Indrek, keeping his eyes fixed on the ceiling above, as if his whole life story were written up there. He kept returning to his main point: "Women want nothing more than for you to grope them. If you don't do that, then you're just a cowardly drip in their eyes, a wimp. They're all the same. If I could find one that wasn't, then I would fall in love with her right away, but I can't."

That was a revelation to Indrek, because he had never properly touched a single woman, in fact he'd already managed to convince himself that the woman who would let him touch her simply didn't exist.

"We've had them all in here," Metslang said one time, "some of them older, some of them younger, but they're all the same. And they've all paid a visit to my room. Sometimes I think – this one won't come – but I only have to wait a little, and there she is."

Indrek tried his hardest, but he couldn't remember a single woman having ever paid him a visit. And so Metslang had the upper hand in their relationship, and he always seemed to have some piece of advice for Indrek: "Have you been to our shop? How do you like that one behind the counter? You want me to introduce you? Next time take a look at her, and let me know what you think. Then just leave the rest to me."

But Indrek couldn't follow Metslang's instructions, because as soon as he entered the shop on the pretext of buying something, his throat felt hot, and when he tried to ask for what he wanted he could only do so in a strange croaking voice, which made him feel so embarrassed that he couldn't even manage to make eye contact, let alone try anything else.

But Metslang just laughed and said, "You let yourself imagine God knows what, but there really isn't anything so special about women. Believe me when I tell you, because I know. Only stupid people make some big mystery out of it all."

As Indrek listened to those words, he saw in his mind's eye a faded postcard scented with a lovely perfume, he remembered Maie, the girl who had kissed him in the dark causing his vision to blur, he remembered mug handles wrapped in tissue paper, and he listened to his companion's insights and explanations as if they were some kind of fairy story.

"Soon you will feel ashamed for having never known a woman," Metslang continued, "because you're already a fully grown man. You have to get to know women when the time is right, otherwise they're sure to have their way with you. They're sure to!"

And so it continued until spring with no hope of words turning into action. But when the classes at school had finished Indrek decided to stay in town to give some lessons to a couple of private students, and continue his own studies. One evening, Metslang invited him round: "You can stay here the night if you want," he said when the evening was drawing to a close. "Use my bed, I can sleep on the floor, I'll put some bags down to lie on."

This time Indrek could allow himself to stay, because Mr Maurus was away, and it was easy to talk Ollino round.

"Some new lass started work here the other day," said Metslang when they were both lying in bed. "I'm sure you'll like her, when you get a look at her. I'm sure of it! She promised to drop by here today, let's see if she does."

"But I'll be in the way," said Indrek, sitting up in bed.

"What do you mean, in the way?" Metslang said incredulously. "Don't be stupid! Stay where you are and relax, she might never come anyway. She would be here by now, if she was going to come."

Indrek still hadn't managed to decide whether he should stay or go when the door opened, and someone entered, wrapped in a large towel. They stood there for a moment, as if trying to get their bearings. And then, the very next moment Metslang sat up in bed, reached across and grabbed hold of the figure. Without saying a word, they fell onto the bed with Metslang, and now the large towel was covering two bodies, leaving only two pairs of feet visible, poking out just below the ankles.

Silence reigned in the small room. No one uttered a word. All that could be heard was muffled laughter, coming from under the towel from time to time. And as strange as it seemed, Indrek thought he'd heard the girl's laughter somewhere before, even though it was unlike any he'd previously encountered. And when she eventually fell silent, the silence was like no other silence that Indrek had heard. Indrek couldn't even hear her breathing, although he could hear his friend Metslang. His breathing was loud, as if something heavy was pushing against his chest, suffocating him. And it continued for a while, until Metslang seemed to get the better of his breathing difficulties, and then everyone was silent. Indrek listened hard, but he could no longer detect any sounds. How long he spent listening like that was hard to tell, but eventually he must have nodded off, because the next thing he knew, he was woken up by someone climbing into the bed next to him, someone soft and warm. She wedged herself between Indrek and the wall, then she manoeuvred herself so she was lying in his arms, pressing her legs in between his legs, which Indrek resisted, without being sure why. And so the intruder lay there nestled under Indrek's chin, and remained motionless for a while. Indrek could feel her breathing, the warmth of her body, he felt her hair, he could smell her hair and he even thought he could hear her heartbeat. Meanwhile, a loud snoring was coming from behind Indrek's back. He was sure that it was his friend Metslang. It must have been, although Indrek didn't dare turn round and look, because he was frightened it might stir his intruder into action. What action that might be was impossible to know, but he was sure it would have irreversible and fateful consequences, even if he were to move just slightly.

But as Indrek lay there like that it occurred to him that he could open his eyes without his new bed-companion noticing, because her head was under Indrek's chin, her head was resting against his chest. He opened his eyes, and to his surprise he saw that the room was much lighter than it had been when he'd been lying there, listening to his friend Metslang's heavy breathing. That meant that he must have been asleep for some time. He remembered the laughter of the visitor who was now lying under his chin, with her soft, rounded knees pressed against his thighs. Then he opened his eyes wide, and tried to look closer, but all his gaze could take in was a narrow waist and curved hips. The legs were nowhere to be seen, they were lost under the ruffled-up skirt. Her head was hidden under Indrek's own chin. But then, as if she'd sensed that Indrek had opened his eyes, the visitor angled her head backwards and smiled. At first, all Indrek could do was look at that smiling mouth in shock. Eventually, he said, "It's you!"

The girl looked at him quizzically at first, but then the sweet smile froze on her lips, she gave a barely noticeable nod of the head, and said, "It's me!"

Now Indrek cast his gaze behind his back, and saw that Metslang was lying there alone, facing the ceiling with his mouth open, snoring. Then Indrek looked down at the girl again, whose head was still in the same position, looking up at him. That's right! It was her, the same girl who had smiled at him when he first arrived in town, at the door of the inn, and then again in that little room with the windows which faced onto the yard, where the farmhands' horses were waiting, chomping hay. Yes, that's right, back then that smile had comforted him and given him courage, it was the only thing in those strange surroundings which had reminded him of home.

Without fully understanding what he was doing, Indrek got up from the bed and started pulling on his boots. "It's good I left my socks on, at least I don't have to bother with them," he thought to himself. And then, without saying a word he pulled on his clothes and got up to leave.

"The doors and gates are locked, and there are dogs in the yard," said the girl, who was now sitting upright on the edge of the bed, her hand resting on Indrek's arm.

Indrek approached the window and looked out. It was a little too high to jump down onto the stones below, he thought to himself, but he opened the window anyway.

Now the girl was by his side, her hands lifted under her chin in a strange gesture, a bit like a small child asking for something imploringly. "She must have been doing something similar when she was lying with me in the bed", thought Indrek, as he climbed onto the windowsill.

"Please, stay," said the girl, quietly and meekly.

But barely had Indrek heard those words when he found himself down on the stones below, a sharp pain in the balls of his feet; his brain was making sure he properly registered what had just happened. He got to his feet and started plodding home, without looking round once. When he got there, he found that all the doors and windows were shut, and since he didn't want to knock, or make a racket trying to let himself in, he had to climb over the high gate into the back yard. At the far end of the yard there was an old shed, empty apart from some bundles of straw and rubbish on the floor– that was where he planned to try and sleep.

A few days later Indrek met Metslang, who said, "Why did you run away like that? What a heartless brute! The girl asks him to stay, and he jumps out of the window! If you'd only seen how she sobbed. That's what women are like, if they take the initiative to come and see you and you jump out of the window then they sob, and if they let you in through their window, they sob too. That's why you have to show them a bit of kindness."

But Indrek wasn't interested in Metslang's worldly wisdom anymore. It was as if they were no longer friends, but total strangers.

And as it happened, Indrek's decision to sleep on that bail of straw in the shed that time was to set in train an unexpected train of events.

Chapter 24

For a long time afterwards, Indrek found himself thinking about how the girl had curled up under his chin, just like chicks shelter under their mother's wing, and how she had lifted her hands imploringly as Indrek had opened the window, climbed onto the windowsill, and jumped out. But the memory of the girl's first smile two years earlier at the inn door had faded. And even if it sometimes returned to him, it had lost all meaning, and so Indrek's world had become a little poorer; one less beautiful thing to comfort him.

Those thoughts and feelings occupied him constantly. He tossed and turned in bed at night, half-asleep, half-awake, and during the day he sought out a place where he could be alone. Strangely, there was nowhere he felt more alone than that old shed, where he had slept on the bed of straw, where the memory of that smile – that beautiful vision which had comforted him – had faded from his heart. And so he started sneaking back to that shed, to come and sit on those bundles of straw, as if memories of his childhood were drawing him back there.

The straw had been there for years. It belonged to another era, when Mr Maurus' establishment had still been going full steam, as Tigapuu and Ollino liked to put it when they recalled those bygone days. The straw was bought to fill the students' mattresses, because Mr Maurus didn't like mattresses which were hard to clean, when some mishap occurred. And given that some mishap or other was always occurring, the mattresses had to be easy to clean. The straw filling could be replaced every half year or so, and the mattresses themselves could be boiled clean, which was why Mr

Maurus favoured straw. Now and again, Tigapuu and Ollino would get carried away and start telling stories of parties which they'd had in the forest, by the river and on the ice, or recall concerts and evening dances. If they were asked, they would explain that the classroom partitions were constructed in such a way that they could be stowed under the ceiling, or removed completely, so as to turn the whole building into a single hall. Yes, if they were asked about those dances, or the straw on which Vargamäe Indrek now liked to sit, they would talk about times gone past and their eyes would light up, as if they had been times of great joy and happiness.

"Those days will never return," they would say, "those old students, those teachers have gone for ever now."

"The main thing is that old Maurus isn't the same man he was back then, that's the main thing," said Ollino as he paced up and down the room with his hands in his pockets, his head hung low, an extinguished cigarette between his teeth.

Indrek heard that kind of talk again and again; how could it be, he thought, that wherever he went, people would always tell him that the best times were in the past? It was true that he had arrived at the school later than most, he was almost a fully grown man, and so it was no surprise if the best times had passed, those few bales of straw left in the shed now serving as testament to bygone days. But what about back at Vargamäe? Had he been born in the wrong period of history, along with everyone else? It was true that the best times were over there too, by the time he'd left. There weren't as many grasssnakes as there used to be, and those that were left were smaller; there weren't as many duck nests in the riverside thickets; there weren't as many fish and crayfish in the river; there weren't as many slender, supple birches in Jõesaar. Less and less of these things were left now, it was as if the world was becoming more impoverished by the year.

Indrek felt that he had lost something too, as he sat in the shed on the bale of straw, where he had been joined by a brown and white tabby cat, which came to stalk the mice which were rustling about in the straw. Lucky for that cat that it wasn't born in Vargamäe, thought Indrek. It would have had a stone tied round its neck and been drowned in the river, and for no reason other than blind ignorance; old Mäe Andres reckoned that tabby cats were no good at catching mice and sparrows, all they did was scavenge for meat and milk.

One time when Indrek was approaching the shed he heard a voice coming from inside. He couldn't quite make out what was being said, but the tone of the voice drew him in. He sneaked inside as quietly as he could, and found a girl of around seven sitting on the straw. She had the tabby cat in her lap, and it looked like she was trying to teach it a lesson in good manners. But as soon as she saw Indrek she let go of the cat and ran off – not upright, but in a strange hobbling motion – to the corner of the shed, which adjoined the neighbour's fence. There she pushed the planks to one side and disappeared through the gap, leaving Indrek looking on in surprise. But as he stood there in the middle of the shed, he felt something brush against his leg, and looking down he saw the tabby cat, rubbing itself against him, its head arched back, its tail curled upwards.

"Don't let it, its fur is moulting," the child warned from behind the wall of the shed, her large brown eyes peering through the gap.

"Come back here!" said Indrek.

"I'm not allowed, I was only there secretly, it's not our shed," the child said. "I used to come more often, but now I can't, you're always there."

"Do you know me?" Indrek asked.

"Of course I do. You're the lanky one. Molli called you the lanky one, and now everyone calls you that."

"Who's everyone?" Indrek asked in surprise.

"Mother, me, Molli, Vanda, Paula, everyone, absolutely everyone."

"Who's Molli?" Indrek asked.

"My sister. She's grown-up already, and she's fit and healthy – she's a seamstress. Arno doesn't live at home anymore, he's training to be a locksmith. When I get better, then I'm going to leave too, what's the point of staying here, when I'm fit and healthy."

"What's wrong with you then?" asked Indrek, approaching the gap in planks which the girl was peeking through.

"Don't you know?" asked the girl in surprise. "My legs don't work right, I've got crutches, look over there by that bush." Indrek squatted down in front of the fence and tried to look through the gap. "When I grow up, God will fix my legs, he'll call an angel, and he'll say, Tiina's legs are poorly, now make them better. And if that angel can't do it, then he'll send another angel, and another one, he'll keep sending angels, until one comes which knows how to fix my legs. But the angel will come in secret, when everyone is asleep. Angels always come in secret. He'll come and knock, and ask my mother: where's that little Tiina, with the poorly legs? And mother will point and say: look, behind the stove, on the floor, that's where she sleeps, on her mattress. But it might well be that the angel doesn't knock or ask, he'll just come through the window or through the gap between the door and the doorframe, because God has already explained everything, the angel will just come in, because he can fold up his wings, and get through any gap; he will come, read the Our Father, and then fix my legs. He'll definitely come, because I can't crawl about on all fours like this when I'm older. Mother says that's it's not decent for a big girl to crawl about like this."

"I'm sure that's right," said Indrek.

"It is," Tiina said. "Mother promised she would keep praying to God until he sent an angel. I pray as well, the two of us pray together, because Molli can't be bothered. She always says: no one could ever pray enough to make Him listen. That's what she says about God. Arno doesn't pray either, he's studying to be a locksmith and doesn't have the time. Whenever mother tries to make him, he says what's the point of studying to be a locksmith, if he still has to pray to God. In that case it would be better not to study to be a locksmith at all. So it's just me and mother, me lying down in bed, and mother next to the bed on her knees; that's how we pray every evening and every morning. Sometimes I miss out a prayer, I forget if mother doesn't remind me, but she never forgets and always says, 'How else are you going to get up on your own two feet! And me and mother aren't going to give up until my legs are better, we won't give up because God has to see that we mean it, mother says. And aunt prays too. She lives on the other side of the red church, next to the graveyard, where all those crosses are. That's where father's grave is, mother takes flowers there... and so the three of us pray, mother, me and aunt. When mother's rich she'll have lots of money, then she can ask the pastor to pray too, that will help even more. But we're poor now, so only the two of us pray. Aunt helps a bit, but mother doesn't pay her, she prays anyway, because she's my godmother."

"Where do you live?" Indrek asked.

"Over there, look, in that house with a red roof, you can see it through the fence. This is our fence. We live in the cellar room. Our Germans live above us, and there are some other Germans living at the other end, in the cellar rooms too. Mother works for them."

And that was how Indrek made a new acquaintance, which soon became a friendship. It turned out that it was much easier to listen to a child's dreams about how her legs were going to be fixed than to put up with the thoughts which were teeming in his own head. And it made a nice change to listen to someone who truly believed in God, because he'd already heard plenty from the doubters.

One time when the two of them were talking – it was later afternoon – they heard a clap of thunder, and a black cloud appeared to the northwest, accompanied by zigzag flashes of lightning. The sun was still high in the sky, but it suddenly became dark, as if night had fallen. A tense silence came over the town. Even the swallows seemed to call with their beaks half shut, as they fed their young. It was as if all of them were awaiting some impending doom. The wind died down completely. The air was warm and close, as if some heady vapours were seeping from from the old wooden walls of the shed.

Indrek and Tiina sat by the door, so that they could watch the flashing lightning as it got closer, and wait for the thunder to follow. As the storm gathered strength, the little girl huddled up closer to Indrek.

"I'm frightened," she whispered eventually. "Arno is never frightened. When there's thunder, we can go and hide at his place. If Arno isn't there, we'll have to go and see mother, there's nothing else for it. Mother says she's not afraid, but I don't believe her. She only says that for our sake, because she knows that me and Molli are afraid. Whenever we try to shelter from the lightning, hide our heads under a pillow, then mother calls us to her bed and says: 'Come here, if the lightning strikes, we'll all die together.' Why would she say that, if she's not afraid? She must be afraid. Aren't you afraid?" she asked.

"No, I'm not afraid," said Indrek.

"Really, truly?" Tiina asked.

Indrek assured her that he wasn't, and then Tiina said, "In that case, I'll sit in your lap to shelter from the lightning. And do you know why I'm so frightened? I'm frightened that it will strike me dead while my legs are still crooked. If my legs had been fixed, then it wouldn't matter, it would be fine, let the lightning strike me dead; but not now, because then I'll go to heaven with crooked legs. Once God has fixed my legs, then let the lightning strike. But why does God frighten us with lightning like that, if he's not going to strike? Why? Mother says that it's to punish us for our sins. Is that true?"

"If she said so, I suppose it must be," said Indrek.

"So is that why my legs are like this, to punish me for my sins?" Tiina asked.

But before Indrek could reply, the first strong gust of wind rustled through the trees and burst in through the gate. The very next moment there was a flash of lightning, followed by a crash of thunder, which dislodged some fat raindrops from the edges of the clouds. The swallows cried out in alarm, "What are you doing? What are you doing?" and Tiina had huddled up close to Indrek. At that moment they heard a girl's voice, calling out.

"It's Molli," whispered the girl, pressing closer to Indrek. "We'll keep quiet, let her call."

But the voice got closer, and then stopped right behind the wall.

"Tiina, where are you, why don't you answer?" came the voice, and a pair of eyes peered through the gap. "Come home, it's about to start raining, come quickly!"

At that moment there was another flash of lightning, followed by a crash of thunder, and then it started pouring with rain.

Indrek and Tiina got up, and Indrek approached the wall, where the voice had come from.

"I'm sorry, young lady," said Indrek, "but you should come and shelter from the rain too, otherwise you're going to be wet through."

The girl hesitated a moment, but Indrek held the planks open for her, and she slipped through the gap too. She joined her younger sister, and the three of them sat there, waiting for the downpour to stop.

"Sit closer to us," said Tiina to her elder sister, "we're not frightened of the storm."

"That's right, young lady, come and sit closer, if you're afraid," said Indrek.

And so they sat there together, huddling closer with every crash of thunder, as if together they had no fear of dying, if a bolt of lightning should happen to strike. Although it was unlikely that they were thinking about death at that moment, or at least Indrek wasn't. He was thinking only of the girl sitting next to him, and all her perfect roundedness. Her round black eyes, her rounded face, with its smoothly rounded features – her chin, cheeks, brow, even the nose, the rounded head and neck, the rounded shoulders, wrists, waist, and hips. It was as if her gait and her voice were rounded too; at least that was how it seemed to Indrek, when he watched her moving and talking, and he was amazed that such a rounded being could be sitting on the bale of hay next to him without rolling away somewhere. The one who was sitting on his knees was another story: she felt angular and bony, especially her long, crooked legs, the legs that refused to carry her.

"We've known you for quite some time now," said the girl called Molli, placing her sister's limp legs in her lap, so that she could sit closer to Indrek.

"From your boots and trousers," Tiina added by way of explanation.

"Is that right, just from my boots and trousers?" Indrek said in surprise.

"We can't see anything else out of our window, that's why," Tiina said.

"That's right, we live in the cellar room, and we've only got tiny windows," said Molli. "When someone walks past, you can't see anything but their legs, even if you put your head right up close to the window, crook your neck, and look upwards. That's all you can see. Apart from if they're walking on the other side of the street, then you can see the whole person."

"I climb up onto the windowsill, there's a better view from there," said Tiina, looking upwards, as if she were sitting on her windowsill right now, although she was still sitting in Indrek's lap.

"We're not all little swallow chicks like you," Molli said to her sister. "That's right, we can only see the legs from the knee down, or a little higher. So we've learned to recognise passers-by from their legs, boots, trousers, coat hems, dresses, walking sticks, umbrellas or their gait – how they place their footsteps. To start with it was terrible, because we lived on the second floor, when daddy was still alive. But now we've got used to it, and it's actually quite good fun. You see someone's legs, and you try to imagine what kind of face they might have. You see their boots and try to guess what kind of hat they might be wearing. You estimate the length of their calves, or the length of each footstep, and you try to say what kind of person it might be. Sometimes, you see two pairs of legs together, and you try to work out if they're old legs or young ones. If they're old ones, then you just let them pass, after all, those old legs can't be going anywhere interesting. But if they're young legs, then you start to wonder, you might wonder for half an hour or more where those two pairs of young legs are going. You can tell easily enough whether it's a married couple, or whether they're just flirting, because they walk quite differently. And then if you hear laughter or the odd word, you can be quite sure. I'll tell my mother that a yellow pair and a pair of shiny black ones went past today, and the yellow pair said quietly to the leather ones: 'See you tomorrow then' and the leather ones answered: 'at eight'. But you know what, people's feet make me sad. Some of them go backwards and forwards for a while, laughing and flirting as they pass, and then suddenly they stop going past and you only ever see them on their own after that. Sometimes both pairs disappear, they never go past our window again, and I wonder where they've got to. Have they gone to another street, another town, or even some foreign country, maybe even the cemetery, which means you'll definitely never see them again. It's sad, isn't it?"

"It's true, it is sad when a familiar pair of legs stops walking past," Indrek said, and then he noticed that Tiina's head had slumped onto his chest. "She's asleep," he whispered to Molli, who was still holding her sister's legs.

"It must be nice and warm, sitting on your lap," said Molli. But her next comment made Indrek start: "Miss Maurus never walked past our window, she always walked on the other side of the street. When she comes back from Germany, she will probably carry on doing just the same."

"Did you know her then?" Indrek asked, and suddenly it felt odd to be sitting there with that girl he had only just met sitting on his lap, and listening to the rounded girl's chatter. Suddenly he remembered that Ramilda had also talked about something rounded, but now he couldn't remember what it was.

"We've known her for years," said Molli. "She was so pretty. Everyone was in love with her. All the boys were crazy about her."

"How do you know?" Indrek asked, as if he might have been one of those boys who was crazy about Miss Maurus. And as soon as he said that, he added to himself: "That's right! A rounded eternity, a rounded eternal life, a rounded life. But how could life be rounded, if Ramilda was in Germany, and he was sitting here? Surely that meant that life's path followed sharp angles?"

"We know everything," Molli continued. "Through Jürka, he likes to talk. Not to us, but to someone else we know, and then we hear from them. But even before we'd heard anything, mother used to say: All the boys must love that Miss Maurus. How do you know, I would ask. Just look at how she walks, how she carries herself, mother said. She's got a spring in her step, and she holds her head perfectly straight. There's no way they couldn't love a girl like that. I used to try and walk like Miss Maurus, so that everyone would notice me, and believe in me, so that everyone would love me too, but I couldn't, I still can't to this day. Back then mother told me it was best not to try, because I couldn't pull it off right. First wait for love to come, then everything else will follow, she said."

"The rain is starting to pass," said Indrek.

"That's right, and the thunder is growing more distant too," said Molli, gazing through the darkness at Indrek with her round eyes. "I wonder if there are cellar rooms in Germany, so that Miss Maurus could walk past a window there too. What do you reckon, do they have houses like that in Germany? Mother says that they don't build houses like that there."

"I reckon they do," said Indrek.

"Do you ever think about Miss Maurus?" Molli asked.

"Me?" asked Indrek, a little taken aback.

"You and the others, whoever they are," Molli said.

Indrek breathed a sigh of relief. But he was surprised at how little he had heard Ramilda's name recently. It was just as always: out of sight out of mind.

"There are a lot of new students who have never met her," said Indrek.

"But what about those that do know her – you, Tigapuu, Mr Ollino and the others?"

"You know them all?" Indrek asked in surprise, without answering the question.

"Of course," said Molli. "Tigapuu always has crooked heels, that's how we spot him. We always say, look there goes that Crooked one. Mr Ollino wears a brown coat, we call him Tawny. We know Vainukägu too, he's the only one whose trousers are always pressed and whose boots are shiny. So we call him pressed-shine or shined-press, depending on how we're feeling."

By now the rain had stopped completely. In the garden behind the fence, gusts of wind were blowing drops of rain from the branches of the trees.

Molli stood up and, pointing at her sleeping sister, asked, "what should I do with her? She falls asleep in mother's lap too, whenever there is a thunder storm."

"I could carry her home, but the two of us won't fit through the gap in the fence," said Indrek.

"We will somehow," replied Molli, "we can push the planks aside. Our Germans are all away on their summer holidays, so there's nothing to stop us."

And so Molli held open the planks, and Indrek squeezed

through the gap, holding the sleeping Tiina in his arms. They passed through the garden, under the dripping apple trees, heading towards the house. As they went, a couple of cold drops of water fell on Tiina's legs, and she woke up.

"Where am I?" Tiina asked, opening her eyes.

"You're in Lanky's arms," Indrek said with a laugh.

"It's not thundering anymore?"

"No thunder, or lightening."

"Now come this way please," said Molly, who was walking ahead. "Watch out that you don't trip, or hit your head – the ceiling is really low, and it's so dark."

But there was no helping it, Indrek couldn't dip his head low enough, and a couple of times he knocked into the ceiling. He also felt something rubbing against his shoulders and his torso. The narrow stone-floored corridor led diagonally under the house, passing some rooms on the left, while on the right there was first a laundry room, and then the caretaker's rooms, with its little window looking out onto the street, just as the girls had described. The living room was divided in two by a wooden wall, with a doorway which had reddish-brown curtains hanging across it. In the first room there was a stove, with patches of red bricks visible under the grey paintwork and a hob in front of it.

Indrek looked about for somewhere he could put Tiina down.

"Come round the back," said Molly, pushing the curtain to one side, but the very next moment she let the curtain fall again, and stood with her arms spread wide and a smile on her face: "Mother's Noah's Arc is full...., you can't put her there. Put her down here."

Indrek put Tiina down on a chair with a wicker seat, near the stove.

"You sit down too please," said Molly, offering Indrek an upholstered chair which she had brought from the back room. "The pride and joy of our house," she said, smiling as she pointed at the chair. "Only our most beloved guests get to sit on this one."

"That's daddy's chair, the one he always sat on, before he died," Tiina explained. "Mummy had one like that too, but it broke, woodworm destroyed the legs, it's in the shed now."

Now mother appeared in the doorway.

"Look, it's Lanky!" Tiina cried, before anyone had time to introduce themselves. "He carried me home in his arms, but the raindrops woke me."

"We've known you for a while now Mr Paas," said Mother Vaarmann, and she smiled in a way which was supposed to convey to anyone with any sense that neither she nor her children really belonged in this place, but should really have been somewhere else altogether, somewhere much better, much higher class. "We've heard so much about you, about you and Miss Maurus."

"That's strange," Indrek said, a little taken aback again; he was grateful that twilight had fallen in the room, because otherwise they would have seen him blush.

"You're sitting here by the door," mother Vaarmann fussed. "You could have invited the guest to the back room," she said to Molli.

"I wanted to invite him in," said Molli, "but your Noah's arc is full to the ceiling."

"Oh heavens, my Noah's arc!" said Mrs Vaarmann, flinging up her arms, and turning to look apologetically at Indrek: "If only you knew how much trouble I have with the two of them. Wherever they take anything, they just leave it right there where they took it. And I have no time to tidy up properly, I just have to rush about after them, trying to clear a little space by the door for myself and whoever might drop in. And we've got so many rags and so much junk that I don't know where to put them. I've got nothing to wear myself, but I tire myself out tidying up and picking things up after them."

"Mr Paas," said Molli, "if you knew our mother, then it would all be very clear. She never throws anything away, she never gives anything to the ragman, she hangs on to everything, she says that in a household with young children you never know when it might come in handy."

"But it does," mother Vaarmann insisted, as her daughter continued.

"Do you want me to show you the dresses, the pinafores, the stockings, the shoes which I wore when I was four, five, six or seven. All those old rags are still here somewhere. And whenever Tiina is in the mood she digs them out of some bag or basket and chucks them in a heap in the middle of the floor."

"But don't you go thinking that we're messy, Mr Paas," Mother Vaarmann said. "We're clean and decent folk. Because when we take matters in hand and start airing the room, and dusting it, we always do such a good job that dust billows out of the windows onto the street, like smoke from a chimney. And in the end, everything is spick and span, from the bottom of the chests to the back of the cupboards. Of course, then everything carries on just as before, until we end up having to do another clean. That's how us poor folk live, it's a real shame. But back when my husband was still alive…."

And now mother Vaarmann had started on her favourite subject, the subject that she couldn't resist, the subject of her past life when she had known no troubles, she had wanted for nothing and there wasn't a wish she could have wished which wouldn't have come true.

Her husband had been a skilled carpenter, almost on a par with a German cabinetmaker, and he had earned enough to meet all their needs. They were friends with the most refined class of people, all of them professionals, not a single labourer or hired hand, only cobblers, carpenters, saddlers, tailors and one coachman who drove his coach with two horses, while his son drove another. But then her husband had died, and the course of their life had changed abruptly, as if a knife had cut it in two. And they'd been living like this ever since.

That first visit of Indrek's was soon to be followed by others. And although he had no grounds to boast about his new acquaintances, he was pleased that he had some place outside school where he could drop by whenever he wanted. Most of the students didn't even have that.

The new acquaintances had an unexpected affect on Indrek. Until then, he'd felt like a complete stranger on the cobbled streets of town, it was only out in the countryside, amidst the fields or the forest, that he felt at home. But now the lamp-lit streets and the rows of houses started to feel more familiar, especially in the evenings when he crept out through the back gate to go and meet his rounded Molli. Now his companions were the roads, the street corners, the lanterns hanging in front of the houses, various out-of-the-way alleys or avenues, each of which offered another perspective on the town which he and Molli enjoyed together, along with the chimes of the townhall bells, the brightly lit shop windows, and all the other experiences and impressions, some of which were preserved in their memories, others which proved only fleeting.

And there was something else which helped to strengthen Indrek's bond with the town and its cobbled streets. It first became clear on one occasion when Indrek turned up at the Vaarmann's to go for a walk, and he found Molli getting herself dolled up, as she liked to say herself.

"You have to when you go to town, there's no other way," said mother Vaarmann, partly by way of apology on behalf of her daughter, partly as a reproach to Indrek. "All the young folk, whether they are men or women, have to take care of their appearance when they go to town, that's the civilised way."

And as she said that she let her gaze pass across Indrek's home-stitched clothes, his shabby shoes and his collar, which he'd been wearing for a week already. Compared to Indrek's, Molli's cloths were downright festive.

Indrek's clothes looked particularly shabby alongside Molli's because she had the knack of making something out of nothing, if she had to dress up for some occasion. Just a ribbon, a couple of curled locks, or a flower in her hair, and

Molly already looked like she was dressed up, which made Indrek blush from embarrassment, because he had no idea what to do with himself, although he would have very much liked to do something. But luckily enough, Molly came to the rescue with her feminine wiles and ways. She would stop, as if by chance, outside a shop window displaying endless rows of shirtfronts, neckties, braces, gloves, handkerchiefs and other knickknacks, pointing out this or that item to Indrek, and assuring him that it wasn't really all that expensive, and that it would be sure to be long-wearing. And unsurprisingly Indrek found himself acquiring quite a few of those inexpensive and long-wearing items. Sometimes he found himself overcome with a strange desire to cast off everything which reminded him of Vargamäe and its surroundings, to turn himself into a completely new person, to change his outward appearance just as he found his inner self changing by the day.

Whether he liked it or not, his bond with the place he was born was growing weaker by the day. He had stopped writing home, and no one wrote to him; it was as if they no longer had anything to say to one another. Then, towards the end of summer, Indrek got the first letter from his brother Andres, which informed him that he had stopped going home too, even though he had promised that he would go back regularly. So Indrek could comfort himself with the thought that he wasn't the only one who was becoming estranged from his former home. The reason that Andres hadn't gone was that they were sure to ask him whether he planned to come back to live in Vargamäe after finishing his military service. But he didn't want to, because he'd seen a bit of the world now, and was living in northern Poland, where they had the prettiest girls. "I wouldn't admit that to anyone else but you, my dear brother," Andres wrote, "because you've seen the world for yourself, you're educated now, and you know our home, and you know Vargamäe, the place where we both grew up and tended the flock, and broke our backs working so hard, although you not quite so much as me; the place where our mother and father and little brothers and sisters still slog their lives away. But I've got my own plans now, and if they work out, then I'll bid farwell to Vargamäe. If they don't, then I don't know what I'll do, it's hard to say. And I'm only telling you and not the others, because I'm your elder brother, so that you would know not to lose hope, because my life is no rose garden either. But if they ask you whether I've written, then tell them that I did, but that I couldn't come home because we're on manoeuvres and all the rest of it, because it's not as if we're here getting a free dinner at the Tsar's expense, we're earning our keep with the sweat of our brow. Tell them that, my dear brother, and bid them farewell without a handshake, without looking them in the eye, because Poland is no Jõesaar, and there's a long way to travel from here before the dear homeland comes into sight, the place where we were all born and grew up. They wrote to me about Kassiaru Maali, that she's already planning her wedding, and that she'd been round to ask our Liine to be her bridesmaid, and that Liine didn't agree, because she and everyone else reckon that I should be the one getting wed to Maali. But they don't understand that I've seen the world now, that I've been to faraway places, and what's so special about some Kassiaru Maali, when you've been so far afield and seen as much of the world as I have, because here there are forests of plum trees as thick as the alders in our pig paddock, you can stuff your mouth full of as many plums as will fit, and you don't even have to bother removing the stones, you just gulp the whole lot down in one, because they're no bigger than salted sprats anyway, and I could swallow those whole too, as you'll very well remember. And so health and happiness to you, until the next time we meet face to face, and we can shake each other's hands like good brothers should, for I consider your mother to be my mother too, she suckled me when my own mother died, the mother whom I remember no more, that's why your mother is the only mother I know. I wrote to her and said, dear mother, don't worry so much, there in my distant, beloved motherland, I'm sure we will all live to see better days, just let me try and fulfil my hopes and dreams, which I'm still keeping under a veil, because I don't want to talk about them yet, it would be too soon anyway. And you should know, my dear brother, for all I care Kassiaru Maali can have her wedding right away, although I don't believe she really wants to, because she was only trying to frighten us, that's why she went to ask Liine to be her bridesmaid, because she's not going to get me to ask for her hand, here in north Poland, where the girls are more beautiful than anywhere else, whence your dear brother Andres wishes you peace and good health."

Indrek read his brother's letter through a second and then a third time, but he couldn't shake off a strange sense of melancholy. His brother spoke of a forest of plum trees like the alders in their pig paddock, about Kassiaru Maali and her wedding plans, about Poland, which was nothing at all like Jõesaar, about bidding farewell without shaking hands or looking each other in the eye. But the whole time he was reading, Indrek saw before his eyes the image of his father's gnarled fingers from the previous summer. And for the first time in his life he felt that he could truly understand what it would mean for his father, his mother, and for the whole of Vargamäe if his brother chose not to go back there after his military service. Now his sisters had gone, he had left, Andres too, and Ants wasn't planning to stay either. It was as if everyone one of them was sure that they were more likely to find happiness anywhere in the world apart from home. And now Kassiaru Maali was planning her wedding! Indrek hardly knew her, but her name always seemed to cause him distress. Everyone seemed to think that Andres and Maali were meant for each other. It was even said that the only reason Andres might not return to Vargamäe would be because he'd chosen Kassiaru as his wife, and was planning to live with her at her parents' house, because Kassiaru meant more to him than the whole of Vargamäe. But it didn't take more than a couple of years for Andres to abandon that plan because he'd seen the world, as he put it, and now he was living happily in north Poland, where they had the most beautiful girls in the world. It seemed that everything happened a bit too easily and a bit too quickly out there in the big wide world, not like back at home amidst the bogs and marshes. It was only back there that people felt eternity within them, a true eternity, not the rounded eternity which Ramilda had spoken of, and they lived their lives accordingly.

Chapter 25

The mood which Andre's letter aroused in Indrek remained with him into the start of the school year. The mood matched the overall situation which he found himself in, because laughably little of what Indrek had hoped for when he decided to stay in town over the summer had come to fruition: the private lessons had soon come to an end, and all his plans for reading and studying had fallen prey to silly adventures and new acquaintances.

Every day, Indrek waited for the moment when Mr Maurus would put on a wounded demeanour, invite him up to his room or take him to one side, and pat his trouser pocket with his right hand and hold out his left hand, rubbing his thumb against the tip of his index finger, in a gesture which could mean only one thing: money! And when that moment arrived, Indrek would cease to be a student with full rights and entitlements, but, just as he had been the previous year, an errand-runner, a bread-cutter, a table-layer, an order-keeper in the little boys' class, a guard, a doorman, and a meeter-and-greeter.

"You're my minister," said Mr Maurus, confirming Indrek in office again, "because you're taller than the others, just like Saul, who was chosen over Jehovah to be king. I can't make you king, because I am king in my house, but I'll put two people under your command, and you can be king over them."

One of Indrek's subordinates was the pious Mr Vainukägu, whose parents had run out of money before their son could train as a teacher or a sexton. But he still took great care to make sure that his trousers were always smartly pressed. And he occasionally made an attempt to read out the scriptures to the students.

"I will hold you responsible for the maintenance of order," Mr Maurus continued, "and you in turn must hold these two responsible," he said, gesturing at Indrek's assistants. "Someone has to take responsibility, if Mr Maurus himself doesn't have the time. Just hold your head up high and push out your chest!" he said to Indrek who was standing with his shoulders sagging slightly and his head bowed, as if burdened by life's troubles. "Look at Vainukägu, that's how a real man should hold himself. A king should be able to learn from his subjects how to hold his head up and keep his chest out."

Those were the instructions Indrek received as he took on his new duties, which quickly got him caught up in all the ins and outs of school life. In the dining room he encountered Mrs Malmberg, who immediately raised the topic of Ramilda.

"She was asking if you are still here," she said, before adding: "She often asks after old acquaintances. Her health is better now, and if it continues to improve, she should be able to come home for a visit in spring. But it's very likely that she won't leave Germany, and will make a new home for herself there."

Indrek didn't know what to say to that and all he did was smile awkwardly, as if he was being told something quite fantastical.

"Could I pass on your greetings to her?" Mrs Malmberg asked in a tone which suggested the question was no more than just a silly joke.

"If it's permitted then I would be most grateful," Indrek said.

"Very well, I'll write to her and tell her that you're still here helping and supporting me, and that you've now managed to break every handle on every mug."

"But it wasn't me!" Indrek cried, turning bright red as if he'd been accused of some shameful misdemeanour.

"Of course not, but I can still put it in the letter; I'm sure you won't take it the wrong way. I'll also put that you've grown more serious and more manly, and that we speak only German; let her think that we're flourishing here. I've got to write something after all, and she keeps going on at me – write, write about everything, she says, the more the better, and the more it's inconsequential the more interesting it is, that's what she says."

The atmosphere in the lower realms of the house was now very different from before, because the corpulent Mr Slopashev had shaken the dust off his boots and moved to new lodgings. For that reason, Mr Voitinski was slinking about like a shadow which had lost its owner: there was hardly sight nor sound of him (either that or people simply didn't notice him anymore). It was only when he'd visited Slopashev that his dull eyes would light up and he would become talkative, which soon gathered a crowd of students around him.

Slopashev's room was now filled by a skinny pock-marked man called Kulebyakov, who walked about with his coat collar turned up, as if he wanted to conceal his intermittent facial twitches from the world. He taught history to the older students, and by way of introduction to the subject he once told Indrek all about the French Revolution, which was one of his great passions. As he spoke about it he would become so enthusiastic that his features contorted, and his stumpy nose moved up and down. His eyes grew watery, as if a strong gust of wind had blown right into his face.

As it transpired, that quiet, skinny bumbler, with his weak eyes and feeble, dull voice, was passionate only about the major, heroic events of history, the most cataclysmic turning points. As he described various battles he would clench his bony little hands into fists, and then push them together, as if he were crushing some large, hard object into smithareens. In spite of this, he was of course a convinced apostle of peace himself, and was opposed to war in principle.

"But peace, by which I mean eternal peace, won't come

until the ferocity of conflict and the destructive force of the killing machines is developed to the absolute maximum. Have you understood me, max-i-mum," he said, stressing each syllable, as if that in itself would help to bring forward the arrival of eternal peace. "Do you know what that means?" he asked. "No, you can't possibly understand that, because no one understands that yet. And yet we can say so much: if we want to achieve eternal peace – and we must do eventually, because it's humankind's most sacred and noble goal – yes, if we really want to realise the ideals of peace, we must avoid the temptation of feeling the slightest mercy or sympathy. We must make conflict so terrible, so awful, so horrific that the very thought of war will make people's blood curdle. As it stands, the awards are being given to writers and suchlike who natter about the ideals of peace, but it won't be long before those very same awards rightfully go to those who invent new explosives, some new laser ray or any kind of killing machine, as long as its destructive force is maximal. There's no point even thinking about weapons of defence, because the perfection of killing machines is always going to advance more quickly than that of weapons of defence. Reason is the slave of the passions, and given that man's greatest passion is death, then reason should be devoted to devising new killing machines. And so there is no chance at all of achieving eternal peace with the help of some kind of wish-washy psychology, the only path left to us, as I have already said, is the path of maximum destruction, and through that, the maximum achievement of the ideal of peace. I heard that from an apostle of peace in Paris once. They know about that stuff there, because they had their revolution, then the commune, the guillotine and the barricades. We make peace with words, we make it with the words of the one who we nailed to the cross. You follow me? But what did we say, through the mouth of the high priest, to the Roman, to that sober and masterful bloodletter? His blood will be on us and on our children, that's what we said. And that's what happened to us and to our children, and it will continue into the future, until we learn to speak of mercy and sympathy. What good do words do, if man is bloodthirsty. Humankind can be saved in this mortal life only through mercilessness and brutality, the same way that salvation was achieved. Everything else is just pure fantasy, because *homo homini lupus est*."

Mr Kulebyakov spoke those words quietly, as if he was afraid that some passer-by might hear him. But a passion burned, a flame must have been smouldering in those skinny insides of his, otherwise his eyes would not have been ablaze like that. He finished and fell silent for a while, almost as if he was ashamed of his words. Then he added, "Of course the truth, the maximum truth which one can say about man, and his striving for peace, would be inopportune here. But I have spoken to you as a friend, who wishes only to arouse in the young a belief in the ideals of peace. The truth is usually hidden from us, but I don't want to hide it from you. Time will tell if you are able to respect my choice."

Oh, Maurus's boys could respect it alright, because it wasn't the first time that things had been kept from them after having been stamped with the seal of silence, and it wasn't the last time they would hear Kulebyakov's revelations. It was particularly important for Vargamäe Indrek to hear these things, and Mr Voitinski made sure he would.

As has been mentioned, Slopashev's departure left Voitinski a virtual widower. To start with, he attempted to establish a similar relationship with Kulebyakov, but his attempts failed dismally – maybe because Voitinski was in a state of physical and spiritual decline. His clothes were threadbare, and you couldn't help noticing the grease stains across his chest, marks left by the bits of food he'd dropped there. Before long he went the way of every wretched beast – his body became a feeding ground for other living organisms, and this became more and more evident by the day. There was nothing for it but to take him, and all his clothes for a thorough spring clean, as Mrs Vaarmann liked to put it. They would take old man Voitinski to the sauna, hang his clothes up on the beam, and then hurl water on the sauna stones until the clothes, and the surrounding area were enveloped in scalding hot steam. That responsibility was placed upon Jürka's shoulders, because he had completed his military service, and was therefore supposed to know what he was doing. That might have been true, but Jürka treated Voitinski as if he was such a dirty animal that if any of his own clothes came into contact with the teacher, they had to be hung up in a steamy sauna. In other words, he treated Voitinski like some mangy dog, and when he brought him back home he would say, "Now the old man can sleep a couple of nights without scratching."

But then one Saturday, when the visit to the sauna was fast approaching, Mr Voitinski started to behave strangely, following Indrek around as if something were weighing on his mind which he was too ashamed to mention. Eventually he said, "Mr Paas, I've got a big favour to ask."

Indrek realised immediately that it must be something important, because Mr Voitinski never called him "Mr", and so he stopped and looked expectantly at him. But instead of revealing what the favour might be the old man seemed to be lost for words. He stood there, sucking his lips and forlornly treading the ground with his feeble legs, his knees knocking together.

"How can I be of service to you, Mr Voitinski?" Indrek asked eventually.

"We're going to the sauna soon," said Voitinski, despondently sucking his lips again. "I have to go to the sauna with Jürka," he said after a short pause, "but it's horrible. Do you understand me, horrible!"

"So why don't you go on your own then, Mr Voitinski?" Indrek asked.

"Mr Maurus won't let me," Voitinski replied. "Someone has to go with me, but there's no one else who will go, only that vicious bumpkin Jürka. I wanted to ask, if...."

"If I would come in Jürka's place?" Indrek said, completing Voitinski's sentence for him.

"Forgive me, but that's exactly what I wanted to ask," Voitinski said in such a meek tone, that it almost caused Indrek physical pain, and he felt unable to answer straight away. At that moment, Jürka arrived with his knapsack.

"You ready then?" he asked Voitinski in a pushy tone.

"I'll be going to the sauna with Mr Voitinski today," Indrek said.

"You?" Jürka said in a challenging, mocking tone.

"That's right, me," said Indrek.

"That's probably for the best then," said Jürka and he turned to leave. But before going he turned back and said: "Make sure you do go, otherwise old Maurus will give me what for. And one hundred degrees centigrade, no less, otherwise it's no use."

"I'm going, don't worry," Indrek replied.

Indrek and Jürka were speaking Estonian, so Voitinski couldn't understand. But when he saw that Jürka had left and taken his knapsack with him, he guessed that the favour he'd asked would be granted, and so with trembling fingers he took hold of Indrek's hand, looking as if he was on the verge of bursting into tears. Indrek was moved too, because for some reason Voitinski's hands reminded him of his father's, even though they were smaller and less gnarled.

In the sauna, Indrek had to witness extreme human wretchedness, the like of which he had never seen before. It made him so depressed that he didn't even notice the dirtiness and slovenliness which went with it. All of Voitinski's clothes were shabby, worn down to the last thread, from his shirt to his socks, and there were little bugs crawling about all over the place, bugs which gave him no peace by day or by night. They were tiny, skimpy, pale-white things, and they looked like they were worn out too, tired of life, as if their master no longer had the energy to feed the whole herd of them.

Indrek did as Jürka, in all his expertise, had ordered. First, he had to give the clothes a burst of one-hundred-degree steam. Only then could he walk the old man to the sauna bench, holding him by the wrist, which seemed to be little more than bare bone with thin skin hanging loosely from it. Indrek had never seen such a thin wrist, and either out of curiosity or in horror, he couldn't help but look at the other limbs, although he didn't have to touch them yet. Before him he saw a skeleton in which it was possible to make out every bone distinctly: the ribs, the shoulder blades, the vertebrae, the joints of his hips, knees, ankles and toes. His cheeks – both front and back – had sunk so deeply that they were hopelessly lost from sight, as was anything else which would normally adorn the angular, bony, human frame. And here in the sauna it was strange to think that this skeleton bore the name Voitinski, and that the name could be preceded by Mr or Sir. Voitinski probably thought something similar, because he said, "Mr Paas, please don't call me Mr Voitinski, just call me Ivan Vassilevich. Once people have been to the sauna together, they always grow closer; they become friends even. The sauna is a great leveller. Just like the grave."

And so it was from that moment on. And then when Indrek swished Ivan Vassilevich with a soft, aromatic birch-leaf brush – he had found some particularly soft, leafy branches – the old man said, "Ah, I could do with a bottle of beer right now! But I've got no beer, and no money to buy it with. Mr Maurus, the good-for-nothing, won't give me any. He gives me a bit of food to eat, and he heats the room, but he doesn't give me any money. I can buy cigarettes, but no beer nor vodka."

"Would you like me to have some beer brought here, Ivan Vassilevich?" Indrek asked.

"It would be like the second coming of Christ, if such a thing were possible," said Ivan Vassilevich, visibly excited by the prospect.

"It's possible," said Indrek, as he came back with the beer. "But it's a bit cold," he warned.

"Cold is good," said Ivan Vassilevich, reaching out for the bottle. "Cold beer and a hot sauna – heavenly!"

He seated himself on the highest sauna bench, and started drinking the beer straight from the bottle, until Indrek poured it into a glass for him. Then he sipped at it slowly, savouring the flavour.

When the beer was finished, he stretched out on the sauna bench, and asked to be whipped with the birch leaves again, only properly this time, not like the first time. He also wanted more water to be thrown on the stones, to make the sauna hotter. When Indrek started to whip him, Ivan Vassilevich croaked from pure pleasure, and cried out, "What a good-for-nothing I am, one bottle of beer and drunk already!"

Indrek noticed that the beer had had an effect on Ivan Vassilevich, because he became more talkative. He carried on prattling away while Indrek rubbed him with the sponge.

"Careful," he warned Indrek, "not so hard! Old skin is thin and flaky, it splits so easily, I'll lose the few drops of blood I've got left."

The warning came just in time, because spots of blood had already appeared at various places, particularly the nobbliest bits, where the bone appeared to be protruding through the skin.

"Jürka, that dolt, he used to scrub me so hard that I was covered in blood," Ivan Vassilevich continued. "That's right, that's good, that's just right. A little bit harder right there, that's it, like that. Because it's no joke if your skin splits and blood starts to flow. Although what's the likes of me needing blood for, what am I holding on to it for? Do I still have a reason to live? Who needs me? Who would miss me? Who would ask after me? They're more likely to ask after some dog than after me. Am I even a human being? Or better still, do you believe that I've ever been a human? Do you believe that I used to teach dukes and grand dukes, that I used to get gold medals for it? That I used to mix with high society, that I used to go to balls where fine ladies held me by the hand, that I danced with them, put my arms round their waists, whisked them round the mazurka, I was the best mazurka dancer in the whole of St. Petersburg you know, the whole of St. Petersburg, can you believe it? I know you won't answer me, because you're an honest person, who doesn't speak untruths, and you don't want to speak the truth, because the truth can hurt. Yes, the truth can hurt, the truth is inconvenient. That's how man is with truth. That's why it doesn't do to speak the truth to any man, it's better just to love him. But you can tell me the truth, you can tell me, because I'm not human anymore. One time last summer I went out of town to the riverbank and stripped naked there. And do you believe it, when I saw my own shadow on the nice soft, lush, green grass, then I didn't recognise it, I didn't realise that it was my shadow. I turned and looked behind my back to see who it could be, and when I saw that there was no one there, I realised that I was no longer human, because I no longer had a human shadow. That's the state of affairs with me. So that's why you can speak the truth straight to my face, and it won't hurt me one little bit, the truth will just make me laugh. What have I got which could be hurt? Just a sack of bones. But who could hurt them? They're just the same as anyone else's bones. It's only the stuff round the bones, the stuff which casts a proper human shadow, which can be hurt. When I still had a proper human shadow, then I was easily hurt, because I was a Pole. Now no one can hurt the Pole in me. But earlier they could, and I have duelled twice in my life. With pistols. The first time it was just a silly game, the second time it was serious. Look at my left shoulder, you can see the scars on the front and back, that's where the bullet went through. You can't see? Well then it's surer than sure that I'm not a human any more, if the bullet scars have disappeared. That's because there's nothing left of the stuff which the bullet passed through, back then."

On another occasion, Indrek bought Ivan Vassilevich two bottles of beer, because he asked so insistently. He had already started talking about it at the school, and in order to save his money for beer, they didn't go by coach as usual, but plodded on foot through the blizzard.

Those two bottles did double the work on Voitinski's weak organism. The beer loosened his tongue to such a degree that instead of just talking he started to babble. But the less capable his tongue became of expressing his thoughts, the more his imagination soared.

"When a man is young, you understand, young," he said, sucking his lips, "then the main thing for him is women, curiosity, passion, sin, craziness. That's when a man is young, you understand. But I'm nothing now, no longer old or young, you understand, nothing. An animal can still be old or young, but not me, because I'm already standing on the other side of time, outside of time, you understand. I'm like a star in the sky, a star, you understand. Examine me carefully, under a microscope. See if there are any signs of humanity left. There are none, not if you look with a microscope, not even a telescope!"

He sucked his lips heartily and then started laughing, wheezing heavily, as if some mischievous thought had occurred to him.

"You remember Solomon?" he continued. "In his old age he sought warmth from a young lady, warmth, you understand, nothing more. But what do you reckon, isn't a dog warm too? So why didn't the king of Israel hug a dog, if he was cold, a young dog, eh? Why? You tell me. Clever Solomon was stupid, that's why. Is a woman a stove or a sauna, which you go to for warmth? Even vodka gives an old man more warmth than a young woman. Vodka can warm you even when there's nothing left of you. Vodka and beer, you understand. Sometimes when I'm in bed at night, in the dark and under the sheet, I try to think of a woman if I can't get to sleep, I try my hardest to see a woman just as she is, you understand, with everything she is endowed with, her figure and everything else that makes her a real woman. But I can't, my eye can't discern it, I can't see it, my eye doesn't make out the shape. You know what I see? I see a bag of bones, nothing else, I see a woman just as I am myself, I see a young woman like that, you understand..."

One time at the sauna, after Indrek had brought Voitinski two bottles of beer again, and whipped him with soft birch branches, he started sharing his views on various countries and nationalities.

"You're a fortunate man," he told Indrek. "The Estonian people are fortunate. They can't be unfortunate, there's nothing to take from them. You've got nothing to hope for either, after all what can a small nation hope for. But us Poles, we hope and we wait and we believe, you understand. And you mark my words, you listen to what I say: things won't remain as they are, things can't stay as they are for ever. The Poles will become masters of their own lands again, the Polish *pani* will be his own master, the Russian oppressor will go. Poland will get its lands and its rights back, it will get everything back; he'll come to Estonia again, the Polish king will come to Estonia. And when the king comes with a large army, and the music plays, the cannons rumble, you understand, rumble, that's how our king will arrive, then I, *pani* Voitinski will go, I'll go with you, hand in hand, as an Estonian and a Pole we will go together, and I'll take you to the king, and say, 'I am *pani* Voitinski, and this is my friend, my Estonian friend. Make it so, my majesty, make it so that my best friend, who kneels before your golden throne with me, make it so that this Estonian here, the whole Estonian nation, are masters in their country again, and not just lowly serfs! Your loyal subject and native nobleman *pani* Voitinski asks this of you, oh majesty!' That's what I'll say to my king, when he comes here with cannons rumbling. And what do you reckon, what will the king do? The king will rise from his throne, reach out his hand, and the cannons will fall silent as quickly as if a mother had shoved her breast in her crying child's mouth; they'll fall silent and wait for the king to speak, and then he'll say in finest Polish: 'Pani Voitinski, it will be thus, now go in peace!'"

Voitinski fell silent for a while, but then he resumed in a tone which suggested he wanted to make a joke out of it all, "And so we will rise from before the golden throne and return to the sauna, and you will hang my clothes from the beam, and start to beat me, yes like that… just like that. You mark my words, it will happen just as I say," he said, now in a more serious tone of voice. "But I won't live to see it, I will die before it happens, I will die pretty soon. But you won't die before it happens, you are more fortunate than I."

To these heights were Ivan Vassilevich's spirits raised, and such were his powerful feelings of friendship and gratitude towards Indrek who had only brought him a couple of bottles of cold beer and was now beating him with birch branches in that hot steamy sauna.

Chapter 26

But their friendship didn't cool off, even outside the sauna. It was particularly in evidence at Voitinski's name day, which was celebrated at Slopashev's place with the participation of Kulebyakov, Molotov, Koovi and a few others; Indrek was the only student to be invited.

The atmosphere was not dissimilar to the sauna, and the absence of steam compensated for by multiple bottles of alcohol; the imagination and emotions ran high here too.

The guest of honour was sucking his lips, as if preparing to say something, but his speech was already slurred, and he didn't appear to understand much of what the others were saying. He raised his right hand, trying to beat time, and he even started singing a tune in three-four time but that made him break out into a cough.

"La la laa, la la laa," he intoned. "Strauss, you know. The waltz, with the violin. Vienna, you know. The public, the ladies… standing ovations…" he raved, already slurring his words.

He tried to raise both hands and move them backwards and forwards as if he were gliding across the ballroom floor. He did it more for his own amusement, without expecting anyone to pay attention, because clearly they weren't interested..

Molotov was trying to persuade Indrek of the benefits of alcohol, arguing that it was vital to the formation of close friendships. It seemed that Molotov had decided that Indrek should be his friend, whether he liked it or not. And why on earth shouldn't a man drink, if the animals, plants, and even the stones drank, as Molotov insisted: "But do the stones, the animals, and plants have monopolies, vodka refineries, pubs, inns, excise duty to pay for the military and an orthodox state, which distributes alcohol to the people only to wages war against it with temperance campaigns?" he said, his voice having risen to a shout once he'd got to the point about stones drinking. "Have you heard of such a thing? No? Me neither. There is no such animal within the animal kingdom, and no such crawler amongst the plant kingdom, no animal or plant which would feed off itself, devour itself, which would saw the branch from under its own feet, leaving itself high and dry. Only an orthodox believer could do such a thing. And so the defining characteristic of an orthodox human is that he is in a state of conflict with himself."

"There are no real humans in Russia anyway," Kulebyakov said, his face bright red. "In Russia there are only subjects. The orthodox human isn't a real person, he is only a subject, a true subject. There's only one real person in the whole of Russia."

"Two!" cried Molotov, banging his fist on the table, which caused everything on it jump in the air.

"One," Kulebyakov argued back. "You're not cleverer than Tolstoy, and he said that there was only one."

"Tolstoy never said that!" Molotov cried.

"He did," Kulebyakov said. "Otherwise, why would he teach us not to fight evil. Man always fights evil, otherwise he wouldn't be man, but if there is only one real person in a country like Russia, why should he fight evil! No, there's no point fighting evil on your own in a big country like Russia, evil only arises when there are lots of people together in one place, and there's not enough room for all of them. Even Tolstoy didn't realise that, and do you know why? He was the wrong person to do so, otherwise why would he have said that if the evil is in you, then fight it, but if it is in others, then don't. Could anyone really have said something like that, if they were the right person? So if there is anyone in Russia who thinks he's a real person, do you know what that means? Do you want to tell me what that means?"

"You think it means he's a dolt, don't you?" yelled Molotov.

"A dolt or an underground revolutionary," said Kulebyakov, quietly but with conviction.

Kulebyakov's quiet voice was lost in the general racket, which only made him get more and more worked up, until he yelled in mid-conversation, "Do you want to know when peace will come, eternal peace..."

"When we're dead," Molotov suggested.

"Of course – when we're dead!" Voitinski piped up.

"Let me speak!" yelled Kulebyakov again. "Who can prove that death brings peace? Who? What do we know of death?"

"The dead don't fire cannons or drop bombs!" cried Molotov.

"Do you really believe that without cannons there would be no war? It wasn't so long ago that there were no cannons, and we still had wars. And so we should leave the dead and their cannons completely alone. We know nothing about them. We don't even know if we might be reborn eventually."

"Nonsense!" cried Molotov, and took a hearty swig of his drink.

"Let me speak, I say," said Kulebyakov. "So, this means that it's no good relying on death. So what should we rely on? What?" He waited a while to ensure that everyone was paying attention, and then delivered the answer to his own question with the sureness of a blacksmith's hammer striking the anvil: "Maximum destruction. Do you know what that means? The max-i-mum!" He stressed each syllable just as he did in class with his students. "When the maximum is achieved, then there is peace, eternal peace. The maximum..."

"So our maximum means blowing the planet to bits!" Molotov cried.

"Oi, oi, oi," said Voitinski, choking from laughter and leaning back in his chair. "Blow the planet to bits! That's idiocy of rare genius! Heaven help us, pure genius! Let's crash it into the moon! The sun! Into the constellation of Hercules! That's right!"

"Please let me speak, listen here!" said Kulebyakov, "That's just not logical."

"It is logical," Molotov argued back, and turning to Indrek he said, "We're all as drunk as pigs in a Chicago slaughter house – death makes pigs drunk, you know. You're the only one of us who is sober. So you tell us, is it logical that we blow the planet up to high heaven, if we've achieved the maximum? Yes or no?"

But Indrek had no idea what to think about the maximum, and so Molotov concluded, "The only sober one here, and he's a total idiot; he doesn't even know if it's the maximum, if we blow ourselves up to high heaven."

"Please let me speak, I need to explain," said Kulebyakov, trying to make his feeble voice heard.

"What more is there to explain," shouted Molotov, "Blow it up and job done! Maximum!"

"Blow it up and job done! Maximum!" repeated Voitinski, choking from laughter and smacking his lips.

"That's no answer," said Kulebyakov. "You forget about the human factor, about human psychology. Peace isn't a fact, it's a psychological fiction. But the planet is a fact, blowing it to bits is a fact. We who struggle for peace don't seek the fact, rather the possibility of a fact. Do you know what that means? Only the naked possibility! We're not planning to blow up the planet in order to achieve peace, because that would achieve nothing, other than creating another cosmic graveyard. All we want is that, *a priori,* any opposing, warring parties would have to reckon with the possibility that the other side could annihilate them and the whole planet along with them. What do you reckon, would anyone dare to attack, if, in a single act of folly they could end up destroying the clod of earth which we call mother earth? Of course they wouldn't. This would mean that in terms of their size and strength the parties could be as badly matched as the planet and a single, tiny atom, but they would still be on an equal footing. What would follow? The problem of large and small states, large and small peoples, would be immediately resolved. Moreover: all kinds of intractable economic problems would be resolved too. After all, what kind of factory owner would choose not to look after his workers and share his profit with them if any one of those workers could decide, as soon as his rights were violated, to destroy the factory owner together with everything he owns. I repeat: rights violated, because rights are the most important thing here. The logical development of my idea means that justice will be honoured, not only between peoples and exploiters, but amongst the exploited themselves, at school, and at home. Tyranny and cruel, brutal abuse would be kept in check by the sheer possibility that the planet could be blown to high heaven by the lowliest amongst us as soon as he is mistreated. There would no longer be any place for unfaithfulness in marriage, or lies between friends and acquaintances, because no one would be afraid of speaking the truth, or of thinking the truth, of living according to the truth, because each one of us would be adequately protected from our superiors, and from society. This would bring an end to the dark ages, once and for all."

"So that means that if a student is an idiot and I call him a dolt, he could respond by blowing the planet to bits?" Molotov asked.

"He could," said Kulebyakov.

"Oh how wonderful!" chuckled Voitinski, smacking his lips. "Dolt and then maximum, straight off! Oh dear me!"

"But what happens if someone has grown tired of living, and they blow up the planet just because they want to take their own life, what then?" Molotov asked.

"There won't be any more suicides," Kulebyakov said, "because the reason for suicides are economic strictures, the trampling of rights, the trampling of the truth, the impossibility of expressing the truth within you, of doing justice to the truth. But all of those causes will be liquidated."

"But what will become of God and of faith?" Slopashev asked.

"They will be pronounced independent and enjoy the full range of rights, they will be autonomous, so to say, and they will be released from any patronage or care," said Kulebyakov.

"What?" Slopashev bellowed. "God will be released of patronage? God will become independent, autonomous?!"

"That's right," Kulebyakov confirmed, "because God has always been, and remains to this day, a ward of care, especially our Orthodox God. Just try to touch him and you'll see what happens. Does God himself raise a hand or a foot? Do his angels appear out of nowhere? No, only priests, the police or the gendarmerie. Which means, his carers! And moreover, God has always been associated with faith, and faith associated with God. But you tell me, what have those two things got to do with each other? It's written in the scriptures that if you believe you can move mountains, but nowhere is it written that if you believe in God, then those mountains will move. Which means that faith can move mountains on its own, without the help of God. So why are those two things bolted together? It's not important what you believe in, or in who's name, the main thing is that you really do believe. For example, the Chinaman carries his God in his pocket, but his faith has performed miracles: the Great Wall of China, silk, opium, the population of five hundred million, and so on. I happen to believe in a little mottled stone. I found it a few years ago on a beach in Brittany. And as soon as I saw it, I felt, here is the object of my faith, the thing which will affirm my faith. One of my old friends has a pair of old galoshes to affirm his faith. You find that funny? Please do, those galoshes are full of holes, but he packs them in his suitcase and takes them everywhere he goes. And so these days no one can be prevented from believing whatever they please, there's only one thing that's important: he really must believe, otherwise those mountains won't move anywhere."

"But what about salvation then?" Slopashev yelled. "Does mankind still await his salvation?"

"If mankind can blow up the planet, then why would he be in need of salvation!" said Molotov. Then he turned to Indrek and added: "Look at them, the drunken swines, and they still demand salvation."

"The planet has nothing to do with mankind," said Kulebyakov, "because the planet is a chance phenomenon, whereas mankind is eternal. Faith makes him eternal. But the planet believes in nothing. Or do you think the planet believes in something too?"

"Oh dear me!" said Voitinski, choking and coughing from pleasure. "Some birthday party this is! Killing with a smile! The planet earth believes in something! Are you listening to all this, Master Paas!" he said, turning towards Indrek, who the others had been ignoring. "The planet believes! *Credo quia absurdam!* Faith takes on planetary proportions! Cosmic proportions, understand?"

He sucked his lips for a while, as if speechless from amazement.

"Everyone has to believe, if they want to achieve anything in this life, and if they want to achieve something big, they have to believe big," said Kulebyakov.

"I don't believe!" Molotov shouted and banged his glass down on the table with such force that it smashed into pieces.

"Then you won't achieve anything," said Kulebyakov.

"I will!" Molotov shouted. "But I will do so with reason, I will do so with science."

"Then you believe in reason, you believe in science," said Kulebyakov. "Everyone has to believe in something. Even God, if he exists. Listen to me: I don't say that He does exist, I have no need to say that, because God is a completely irrelevant character for me…"

"A dyed-in-the-wool atheist!" Voitinski squealed, and smacked his lips.

"Poppycock!" said Molotov. "He goes to Holy Communion several times a year."

"You heed my words: even God has to believe, if he exists," Kulebyakov continued, "or if he ever existed, in order to create this heavenly body and the rest of them. Yes, even God had to believe, when he set about creating this world. And there is no difference between God and man apart from the strength of their belief, because if God really exists, and if he created this world, or some other world, then he had to have the strongest of faiths. He had to have absolute faith, do you know what that means? No human has ever had that kind of faith, otherwise he would have created some world as well…"

"How do you know that he hasn't?" Molotov asked, his voice hoarse by now. "Who told you that man hasn't created a single world? What book did you read that in? What if man in fact created everything, and there is no God or anyone like him. There is only man, and he sometimes appears as God, sometimes as man, sometimes as an animal, or a flower, a rock, or the sea? Man is eternal, as you said yourself. So what can we know of him? Ten million years ago man might have believed so surely that he created new worlds, and a hundred million years from now he will believe so surely, that he destroys everything with pure belief. You see – pure belief! The only thing he won't destroy is himself, if he's eternal, otherwise it would be possible for God to destroy himself; if he exists, that is."

"Allow me to ask one thing," Slopashev growled. "Just one little question. You tell us that God had to believe when he created the world. But did God have to believe when he created man? Did he? You tell me that," he shouted, staring straight at Kulebyakov from across the table.

"How could it be otherwise," Kulebyakov replied.

"But man can create other men without any faith," Slopashev thundered, "which shows us that man is more powerful than God."

"But man didn't create the first man," said Kulebyakov, "and he probably won't create the last one, because God will create him with his faith."

"Wait a moment, wait a moment!" yelled Slopashev, as if he had suddenly remembered something important. "With his faith you say. So is God's faith in man so certain?" But why did man do evil, when he fell into sin, if God's faith in him as his own creation was so strong? Man couldn't have gone astray, if God's faith in him hadn't faltered. And do you know who did in fact believe in man? Satan believed in him, and that's why man did just as he wanted. Man will always perform the wishes of whosoever believes in him. And in order to confirm his faith, God was born of a virgin, and died on the cross. And so he proved to himself, to man and to Satan that his faith was surer than anyone's. Because Satan has never appeared on earth, nor died on the cross, nor in any other way. Although he could have done so. He could have come, born of some three-toothed witch, and allowed himself, in the guise of a horse thief, to be thrashed to death by some drunken peasant. The main thing is that he would be dead, and he would be able to say: look what you did you drunken fools – you beat Satan to death. But Satan never did anything of the sort, he never did! Only God came and died, in order to believe unfalteringly in man once again, to believe in him so surely that only love would come from faith. Love, I tell you! Otherwise, evil and hatred come from faith, only evil and hatred, but from God's faith on the cross came only love. Love for mankind. And it makes no difference if man is religious, if he is Christian, Moslem, pagan, whether or not he is good, honest, truth-loving; it's quite enough that he is a man. Can't you see that! That's all he needs to be, nothing else! A man must be believed in, must be loved!" bellowed Slopashev, as if he wanted to whole world to hear. "And if God had always believed in man as he did when he was on the cross, then…"

At this point several voices interrupted Slopashev and a terrible war of words ensued over the question of man and God, "who might exist, or might have existed", as Kulebyakov maintained. But Indrek couldn't wait to find out who's faith would turn out to be the stronger, whether man's or God's. As the only student there he had to leave, because midnight was nigh.

The next day he asked Mr Koovi about the outcome of the argument, and he replied with a grin, "That Russian God and the eternal man have got to you." He then added in a more

322

serious tone, "Why do you waste your precious time on such tittle-tattle. Leave God in peace. He doesn't bother you, so what do you need of him? You didn't create him, and he was around a long time before you came along. He's not to blame for the fact you were born, you have your own parents to blame for that. And that eternal man who is the fruit of those drunken minds... how can we know if man is eternal or not! They're just big words spoken by people who sit around doing nothing all day."

But Koovi's thoughts on the matter meant little to Indrek. He was much more interested in the eternal than the transient and mortal. It felt good to believe in something, to yearn for something eternal. And he promised himself he would search for it, even if Mr Koovi had no intention of helping him. Not before long he would come to understand what a vicious battle raged between the eternal and the transient in everyone's heart, and in his own heart too.

Chapter 27

And yet of course the everyday and transient are in the habit of displacing the eternal, as if the latter had no sway at all in man's life.

A circus had come to town, and everyone got carried away by the fun. The excitement grew to even greater proportions when the wrestling got under way; the famous wrestler Lurich had come to take part too. Even Mr Maurus visibly lost his usual comportment. Being in the habit of giving his charges dinnertime guidance in life's most difficult questions, seeking to rouse them to higher ideals, he couldn't avoid addressing the question of the circus once or twice. In one of his speeches, which he made a point of concluding in Estonian, he said, "And now I shall tell you, those of you who can understand, that a count from the house of David has been born here too. The star of Bethlehem has begun to shine here too, and its light reaches far across our homeland. You know who I'm speaking of, and whosoever of you should like to acquire a circus ticket should come and see Mr Maurus, and he'll make sure you get one at a reduced price. Mr Maurus buys a ticket every evening, because he wants to see our count, the one who has come from the house of Kalev and is going to strike down all the Moab kings and counts. And so whoever wants a ticket, come and see me as I get them for half price. Mr Maurus doesn't say to his boys: bring me your money, I'll buy you tickets to the circus, because they're riding horseback there and a naked lady is walking the highwire holding a pink parasol in her hand; no, Mr Maurus will never say such a thing, because he knows very well that his boys' parents are poor, that they can't afford to pay to watch horse riding and naked women. No, what Mr Maurus says is: he who wants to see our Bethlehem count, our sword of Kalev, acquired from a Finnish blacksmith to mow down men, then come. And if there are those amongst you who don't even have the money to see our very own count, then come and see Mr Maurus and say to me: 'Mr Maurus, my mother and father would be very sad if I couldn't come to the circus to see our Aaron's rod, but I just don't have the money, so I ask you, Mr Maurus, won't you please buy me one and make a note in the book, then I'll go home and bring back some money, or my father will bring some when he next comes to town, and then we can pay for it fair and square.'"

The result of this explanation, which was repeated more than once, was that a whole herd of students went to the circus, with Mr Maurus heading up the herd. Of course it wasn't only the Estonian boys who went, but the foreign students too, often provoked into doing so by Mr Maurus, who said, "Let them come too, let them see what kind of men we are, let them see us, so that our name is on everyone's lips. Let them know that the Germans might have fed us bran for seven hundred years, but still their men are no match for ours. What of it if we have to eat God's grain for another seven hundred years? Why shouldn't we have our own Luther, Goethe or Schiller? If animal fodder has made us brawnier than anyone – yes, animal fodder gives more brawn than any human foodstuffs can, because no man is a match for a bull who's been fed on bran, straw and chaff – if we got brawny on bran, then we can get brainy on bread too. And just as our Estonian brawn will get the better of them all, we can better them all with our Estonian brains too, once we've eaten God's grain for another seven hundred years."

Soon all the students got carried away by the circus, Indrek too, as if the smells and the music there had something of the eternal in them. The circus had some sort of mysterious aura, which seemed to intoxicate everyone. Wrestling and many other kinds of trials of strength became the students' daily bread and butter. Until then, only Sikk had pounded his chest and biceps with his fists, pumped up his muscles by lifting himself up on bedsteads, chairs and tables, picking up chairs in each hand and holding them up with outstretched arms, but now almost the whole establishment started doing exactly the same, and even Indrek was no exception. So intoxicated were they all by the circus that if it had stayed in town much longer and the wrestling matches had carried on, then even Mr Maurus would have put his old muscles to the test, after all Mr Koovi had already done so twice – maybe just for fun, but he'd done it all the same.

A strong neck and upper back were now de rigour; it meant that if you went down on all fours to wrestle, no one could push your head onto the floor or twist your neck sideways, and you could form the bridge too; for a while there was such a fashion for the bridge and the full nelson that some of the lads would have liked to live their whole lives in the bridge position whilst performing a permanent full nelson, rather than settle for walking about on two legs with no nelson at all. For a while Indrek, went around with permanently swollen neck veins and aching muscles. His head felt heavier than usual, and he was dazed, dull-witted, as if his brain had been replaced with a jug of soured milk. And at night his ears were burning; after all, what sort of wrestler were you if your ears didn't burn like Lurich's. That wasn't Indrek's view, but the company he kept and society at large forced it upon him, arguing that a real man had to be not only tall, but strong too. And so Indrek wanted to show everyone that a tall lad like him could be brawny too, just as if he'd also been raised on animal fodder, which was sure to make you strong, or so Mr Maurus claimed.

The craze for strength lasted for a while after the circus had left town, and plenty of knees and elbows got smashed against hard wooden floors, but before long the excitement abated, the earlier intoxication gave way to a quiet, empty apathy.

After Christmas, a new student joined the seventh class,

whose name was Pajupill. He had a dark complexion, a moon-shaped face, a protruding forehead, fleshy lips, strong teeth and thick hair, and he was short in stature, stockily built, and around seventeen or eighteen years old. He wore a grey overcoat, with faint square marks on the lapels, revealing that something had been there once but was now missing. It was in fact the overcoat of a state gymnasium student, the official insignia having been removed from its lapels.

No one knew for sure why Pajupill had left the gymnasium. He himself spoke of books of some sort, banned literature, nationalist sentiment, some irreverent verses about his seniors, religion and even God. In other words, Pajupill was a pretty daring chap, if you were to take his word on the matter.

But his self-aggrandisement didn't wait long to be corroborated. Pretty soon, salacious verses started to circulate at Mr Maurus' establishment too. Those who got closer to Pajupill discovered that he had notebooks full of poems and other kinds of texts. That discovery seemed to raise the school from its slumber. It soon transpired that some of the other students were no strangers to the muse, some of them had been secretly knocking out verses themselves, others had even attempted to translate Pushkin and Lermontov. They'd kept quiet about it because writing poetry seemed a little ridiculous, shameful even. Although it wasn't that poetry was ridiculous in the wider world, only at Mr Maurus' establishment. And as it turned out, that very same establishment was teeming with poets. They even plucked up the courage to take their verses to Mr Koovi, hoping for his opinion. But Mr Koovi, who was a quiet and reserved man by nature, just told them, "I know nothing about poetry, especially Estonian poetry. All I know is that Estonian poetry has to be patriotic, and I can't boast of being particularly patriotic myself. You should go and see Mr Maurus, he once won a prize in a poetry competition organised by the Society of Writers, and he'll be able to tell you what's right and wrong. Write something in Latin or Russian, then I'll read it."

327

That way Mr Koovi hoped to politely excuse himself from the attention of the poetry enthusiasts. But no such luck, because a couple of days later a group of them turned up with folders full of poems written in Russian; Mr Koovi couldn't get out of reading them now.

Pajupill, who had gained ascendency with his Estonian-language verses, was now swiftly forgotten, as those who could mangle the Russian language found that their star was rising. But then a verse appeared which had somehow been knocked together from Estonian, Russian, German and Latin; it even had a Greek title. Everyone found this verse very funny, but it also set off a heated debate about the very nature of poetry, its opacity and its profundity, its meaning and feeling, its rhythm, rhyme, language and mood. In the end Mr Maurus had to intervene.

"I've heard people say that foreign languages are profounder than our native tongue," he said one day. "But what is it that makes things meaningful and profound? Love, of course! You listen to me: love, and nothing else. And what makes things beautiful? Love, once again. Only love. Because without love everything is empty, it has no soul. Only love brings things to life. That's why the poet must speak in his mother tongue, otherwise his words are like the dull ring of copper or the tinkling of bells: there is no love in them, and where there is no love, there is no profundity, you can make it as opaque and incomprehensible as you like. So love is the only thing which gives the eye, and the word, profundity. He who doesn't love, his gaze is shallow, his word is hollow, and even if he speaks in the tongues of angels, he will never win over the hearts of men."

That was Mr Maurus' view on the opacity and profundity of poetry. And although everyone laughed, his words did not fall on deaf ears. The students didn't stop knocking out verses in foreign languages, they didn't give up their brash but awkward rhyming, but alongside that there was a powerful welling-up of love for the mother tongue and everything to do with the motherland, a love which threatened to engulf Mr Maurus' educational establishment just as it was threatening to engulf the world beyond its doors.

Indrek didn't belong to the guild of poets himself, but he still found himself pondering Mr Maurus' words. "So, love is the only thing which makes the gaze and the word profound," he repeated to himself. Now, he finally grasped the truth! Now he knew why a gaze could sometimes be so deep: love! Only love!

Whether it was due to that sentiment or for some other reason, Indrek started to visit the Vaarman family more and more often, as if that was the only place in the world where he might find love. Here there was so much poverty and wretchedness that without love to counterbalance it, life would have become totally unbearable, especially for Tiina, who spent whole days on her own, because mother and Molli were out, performing their washerwoman and seamstress duties. Indrek sometimes dropped in for a moment, sometimes for longer if he could, to check if the crippled girl hadn't turned the dwellings head over heels and then, bored and tired, curled up on a heap of rags in the middle of the floor and fallen asleep. Even in the evenings, Tiina's mother and sister had no time for the poor child, because there were always at least ten other things which needed doing.

Among their duties was clearing snow from the street into the back yard and garden. That often had to be done in the evening, or in the middle of night, if it hadn't proved possible to do it earlier. One time when the snowdrifts were as high as haystacks, Indrek went to help clear them, and before long what started off as a bit of fun became an established routine. To make sure that no one would recognise Indrek out on the street, Molli gave him her father's old coat and hat to put on; the hat was so big that it almost completely swallowed up Indrek's head. His eyes were hidden under the brim, and all he could make out were the snowdrifts and Molli, who was working hard next to him. Molli always made sure she was close to Indrek, while Indrek's shovel found no better spot to attack the snow than next to Molli. He would drive it deep into the snow, and then lift out such a huge lump that Molli was incredulous, Molli could only ooh and aah, giggle and squeal.

The work brought a pleasant ache to Indrek's limbs, a feeling which wasn't so different to the circus intoxication which Maurus' boys had experienced, or their craze for poetry. It felt so good, the way it oozed like some kind of viscous substance through his limbs, to every cell of his body, it seemed to soak into his whole being, to penetrate every hair, how else could you explain that crazy, sweet, intoxicating feeling when Molli and Indrek's clothes touched in the heat of work, or when a gust of wind blew a light covering of snow onto Indrek's face and with it some strands of Molli's hair, which refused to stay put, whatever she tried; for Indrek, working like that, shifting the snow on a city street, out of view of everyone he knew, was indescribably fun, and he started to envy people who did that kind of work for a living. Once Indrek had graduated from Mr Maurus' establishment, when he'd read his geometry, algebra and Latin grammar from cover to cover, then maybe he would find work as a caretaker somewhere, so that he could mess about in the snow all day long, or at least as a snow clearer, driving about here and there, sitting atop a bag of hay or just on a mound of pure white snow, once the bag of hay was empty, or had been left behind somewhere. Yes, that's what he would do once he'd read his Latin grammar from cover to cover.

Mother Vaarmann and Molli usually cleared the snow between them, while the younger daughter stood on her toes, or climbed onto the windowsill, to look through the window at what was going on outside. But as soon as Indrek turned up to clear the snow, Mrs Vaarman always found she had something vitally important to do somewhere else, and she hurried off to do it. In any case, the Vaarmanns only had two decent snow shovels, the third one was a spare and it wasn't much fun trying to shovel snow with it. And so there were still two people outside clearing the snow, with poorly Tiina the third, left inside, hunched up on the windowsill.

To start with either Indrek pulled the sledge, while Molli pushed from behind, or vice versa, but pretty soon Indrek and Molli realised that this wasn't the right way to handle a sledge piled high with snow. The right way to do it was for one person to pull from the front, tugging with almost all their might and laughing with joy, and then the other could come and help them tug. And if one of them was pushing from behind, groaning, panting, squealing, and yelping, then the other one would have to come and help push and yelp, because two was always better than one. Of course perfectly-rounded Molli knew that very well, because she was much more experienced than Indrek, and she could teach him how to clear snow properly. And so it came about that the two of them were in the garden, dragging a load of snow – it was an unusually heavy load, especially heavy – and the two of them stumbled in the deep, soft snow, and fell over. And why shouldn't a person stumble, if the load of snow is heavy, and the snow is deep, soft and crumbling underfoot: it can easily whisk you off your feet. And that's exactly what the the snow was like in the Vaarmann's garden, under the old apple trees, in the spot where they were dragging that heavy sledge.

In fact it was Molli who was the first to stumble and fall, to be followed very soon by Indrek, and he fell so awkwardly, that he almost fell right on top of Molli. Then he tried to stand up in the soft, crumbling snow, and Molli tried to do the same, laughing as she did so, but their legs somehow got tangled up, and they had to hold onto each other for support, and then they both fell over again, only that this time Indrek fell even more clumsily, right on top of Molli. It all seemed to happen in a dream, because the intoxicating warmth of their work had washed through their bodies. There was one thing which Indrek noticed: Molli was just as warm and soft in the cold, crunchy snow; he could feel her warmth and softness through her clothes. Then, when he tried to stand up, he noticed they were under that same old apple tree, the one he had passed with the sleeping Tiina in his arms, the tree which had shed a couple of drops of cold rain water, causing the child to wake. As Indrek fell, a vision flashed before his eyes, of that apple tree in autumn, laden with red apples. And then the very next moment he noticed that his face was very close to Molli's, and that she was smiling, her lips parted, and that he could feel the warm breath coming from her mouth, and her round eyes were narrower now, and they were shining in the dark. And then Molli put her arm round Indrek, and Indrek fell onto her, his lips meeting her lips, only that he fell a little awkwardly again, so that his mouth didn't quite cover Molly's. It should have covered her mouth, because she had such a small, rounded mouth – or was it because she still laughing, her mouth half open? Those were Indrek's thoughts later, when he tried to recollect what had happened, but he must have thought something similar there under the old apple tree, because he had tried to manoeuvre himself into a better position, but before he could do so Molly's mouth disappeared from underneath him and he found himself with a mouthful of cold snow instead.

"You're so big and tall that you'll suffocate me," Molli said, and she started struggling with all her might to stand up. Molli's words, and her innocent tone of voice brought Indrek to his senses, and now his limbs felt numb. Once he'd got to his feet, he felt he should say something decisive, but he ended up saying and doing nothing at all. Molly was left to speak for the two of them.

When they finished clearing the snow, and it was time for Indrek to go, Molly saw him to the gate, and there they found themselves, as if by silent agreement, standing near the wall, the gate open, holding each other tight, their eyes and their lips yearning for contact. Now their lips didn't miss each other, but pressed together firmly and surely, and Indrek could feel Molly's teeth against his lips, and then the

332

slightest taste of blood on the tip of his tongue. It didn't hurt, it didn't hurt him one bit, and Indrek would have been happy if their lips had pressed together even harder. But Molly had no strength left, and so Indrek had to use his strength to help her, just as if they were still dragging the snow sledge the other side of the gate, the sledge which had somehow got stuck, but now just didn't want to come unstuck. Yes, clearing snow secretly in the dark was so incredibly enticing, so bewitching, that Indrek was sure that he would become a snow clearer, just as soon as he'd finished his Latin!

Eventually Molly worked herself free from Indrek's grip.

"You'll swallow me whole like that," she said, reproachfully. "You'll suffocate me, you'll squash my nose, how am I supposed to breath!"

But without saying a word Indrek grabbed hold of her again and kissed her until her legs started to give way under her and he had to hold her up, until she had become soft and supple in his hands. He could no longer feel her teeth, he couldn't feel her body, all he could sense was something soft and scented, which he wanted to drink down in great gulps, because it was so sweetly intoxicating.

The memory of that kiss shone like a star above Indrek's existence from that evening on. Nothing in his life had any meaning apart from his one and only, the one that made his gaze and his word profound, as Mr Maurus had said. He still carried on with his day-to-day business, but it was as if his only purpose in life was to see Molli. All the days and the weeks in his calendar were devoid of meaning if he couldn't meet Molly, if only for a few minutes.

"Did you know that this would happen?" Molly asked Indrek one time.

"No," he said. "How was I supposed to know?"

"I knew," said Molly. "I already knew back then when we were sitting on the bales of hay while Tiina slept."

"How did you know?" Indrek asked.

"I just had a feeling," Molli said. "But I believed it would happen much sooner; I thought it could have happened there on the bale of hay, while Tiina was asleep."

From what Molli said Indrek realised that she was much more relaxed about the whole situation than he was. As far as Indrek was concerned, something incredible had happened between them, something which was hard to put into words. It was something which was possible to do, to feel, to think about, to dream about, but it wasn't possible to talk about it, because there weren't words which were profound enough to express it. Mr Maurus must have been mistaken when he'd said that love made the word profound. Love had come, but there were no profound words.

And yet in the end it made little difference whether Indrek could find the right words or not, his secret started to come out. To start with, his marks at school started to suffer.

"You in love or something, you good-for-nothing, eh?" Molotov asked him one time, when Indrek had dazzled them with his ignorance once again. "Some mother turkey got to you, has she?"

But instead of answering, Indrek blushed from ear to ear, and so Molotov continued, "You keep away from the ladies, I tell you. Mathematics has no love for women, where there are women, there is only silliness. Women make you stupid. The purpose of women is to make men stupid. God only knows how far man would have gone if he didn't have to bear that cross."

Indrek almost wanted to tell the class that love makes the word and the eye profound, and that without women there could be no love in the world.

The strange intoxication lasted until early spring, with no abate. But then gradually, there were more and more occasions when Molli couldn't come out to stroll with Indrek when he invited her. And sometimes she wasn't at home, when she could have been or when she should have been, in Indrek's view. On those occasions, Indrek had to make do with Mother Vaarmann and her younger daughter, and he had to listen to the same old stories about Mother Vaarmann's old life, about where she had lived, whom she had associated with, how she had laid the table, what they had eaten, what they had worn, and how she had brought up Molli, so that she would find herself a good man.

"My daughter is looking for a man who earns a hundred roubles a month, and is home in time for lunch" Mother Vaarmann said. "Of course, no young lad is ever going to earn that kind of money, but then there's no need to get married to a young lad is there. It's fine to be a bit flirty and galivant about with a younger man for a while, but a girl should get married to a fully-grown one. And it's no problem if the man's a bit older, the older ones love you more than the young ones. That's why I always tell my daughter, find yourself an older one, he won't chase the skirts and he'll earn more money; he might earn as much as one hundred roubles a month and he'll be home in time for lunch."

Whatever subject Mother Vaarman started with, she would always end up at the same place: an older man, who earns a better wage, as much as one hundred roubles a month, and is home in time for lunch. Once he'd heard this a few times Indrek couldn't escape the conclusion that Mother Vaarman was trying her hardest to make a point, which made him want to see Molli even more. But for a long time it didn't happen, which gave the pain plenty of time to gnaw at his sensitive heart. Only when there were important events for him to take part in did the pain stopped gnawing for a while, as if it were taking a break, having worn its teeth blunt.

Chapter 28

One such event was the spring graduation party for the final class. The headmaster, teachers, and the class immediately beneath them were invited, so that the links between the establishment and the graduates would continue. By way of refreshments, there was a cold spread, hot tea, vodka and beer. But the practical arrangements were secondary to the cultural programme. The students of the final class would themselves be responsible for that, given that they were organising the party. They held discussions for weeks on end, arguing over who should speak and what they should say. That livened things up a bit, because all the other classes were thinking about was that sooner or later they would also be the final class, and would face the same challenges. The main point of contention, just as it had been in previous years, was whether they should use their speaches to tell the truth to the headmaster and the teachers, or whether they should stick to the "usual lies".

"If I'm not allowed to speak the truth at the leaving party of all places, then I'm not going to say anything at all," said Vellemaa, who was fond of knocking out verses in Russian. "Over the years we've lived and studied here, we've always had to refrain from speaking the truth, otherwise it would have been impossible to get an education. You know what I mean? In order to receive an education, we had to hide the truth. But now, now that we have already got our education, and now we're going to try our luck on the final exam, now I finally want to speak the truth, because the truth is profound, and I want that profound truth to be my first step towards passing the final exam."

"But what happens if you fail?" someone asked.

"If I fail, then obviously I won't ever come back here," said Vellemaa, "because a man should never return to the place where he has spoken the truth."

"But how do you know that what you want to say is the truth?" they asked him. "Surely you don't believe that your opinions and the truth are one and the same thing?"

"There are two kinds of truth," Vellemaa argued. "Objective and subjective. It goes without saying that I don't plan to proclaim any objective truths in my speech, because the teachers know them better than we do. But they don't know our subjective truths, they can't know them, and in that respect they're stupider than us. In other words, they've been teaching us objective truths for the last few years, now we'll give them some subjective ones. That's what I reckon."

The day of the party neared, but the students had still not come to any agreement as to whether they should speak the pure, bitter truth at the leaving party, or whether they should mix in some sweet lies, so they elected a commission consisting of two members, who would go and ask Mr Koovi's opinion on the matter. In fact, they already knew what Koovi would say, but they still wanted to talk with him, maybe with the hope that he had changed his mind over the course of the year. But no, Koovi hadn't changed his mind. He was still of the view that the students should show some mercy to the teachers, the headmaster, maybe even to truth itself.

"Why won't you leave the truth in peace! You've done very well without it over these long years, can't you wait just another day, just a few hours! People are coming together to eat and drink, and to chat, not to hear the truth. Anyone who feels such a desperate need to search for the truth should stay at home, alright? In any case, what kind of truth could you possibly tell Mr Maurus that he hasn't already heard? Do you think he'll take your truth seriously? No, he'll just turn it all into a silly joke."

"Very well," said the two-member delegation, "but

whatever is forbidden in the speeches, is allowed during the eating and drinking."

"That's another matter altogether," said Mr Koovi "In vino veritas! When a drunk man speaks the truth, it doesn't offend anyone. A drunk man is a bit like a madman, and madmen can always speak the truth, no one will reproach them for that. It can even be quite funny, when madmen speak the truth!"

"OK boys, let's have a proper skinful then," said Vellemaa, when he had heard Koovi's view, and everyone agreed that it was the only true path to follow at a juncture as important as this graduation party.

And so the difficult question was resolved to everyone's satisfaction, both with regards to the objective truth and the subjective truth. The organisation of the party was placed on Indrek's shoulders – as a student in the year below he would have to come to the party too.

"You've got the knack of bread and butter," they told him, "so now you can show us what else you've learned at Mr Maurus' first class establishment. You might not have got your hands or teeth on much sausage or ham, but whosoever has a thorough knowledge of bread and butter should be able to handle sausage and ham and other such stuff without too many problems."

Among the planned hors d'oeuvre, caviar was to take pride of place, intended as a symbol of the success which this year's finalists had achieved. Finishing school – reaching academic maturity – only happened once in a person's life, just as he was only born and died once, which was why this event was deemed as important as life or death. And so it was not excessive to celebrate the attainment of maturity with caviar, just as people did to mark births and deaths.

And so they waited for the important day to arrive, full of great hopes and expectations. They removed the table from the classroom which the top class had been using, and they brought some different tables in their place, which they arranged in a horseshoe shape. To start with they planned to cover them with paper, white paper, but Indrek took the initiative of procuring some bright white table clothes from Mrs Malmberg, which she gave him with the instructions that if they had any accidents with the wine, then he should pour on some salt, plenty of salt. But the instructions were pretty pointless; there could be no accidents with wine, because they had no wine, only vodka and beer. And anyway, what was the point of wine, or other sweet drinks, if only men were going to be there, and not a single woman? The cups and glasses, dishes and plates which they placed on the tablecloths were generously donated by Mrs Malmberg, just like the white tablecloths. They laid out some long benches and a few wooden chairs. The only armchair in the room was there for Mr Voitinski, and it was provided by Mr Slopashev, who was well aware of his friend's weakness for merrymaking, and wanted to make sure he had a sturdy chair to sit on.

The party was supposed to start at seven o'clock, but the guests were so late that Vellemaa couldn't start his opening or greeting speech until around nine. He'd made it clear that he was against talking in principle if he wasn't allowed to declare some subjective truths, but since he was sure there wasn't a single soul there who was worthy of standing in for him, he abandoned his principles for the sake of the collective good. In fact, he managed to sneak around his own principle, amazing everyone in the process. He wrote the speech in advance of the party, and read it out to the whole class, making a few changes to it here and there on their advice, but then on the night before the party Vellemaa became quite inspired, and so he turned his whole speech into a poem in the Russian language, for which he was showered with praise from all and sundry. And so he didn't betray his principle – his speech might not have contained any truths, but then it wasn't a speech, it was poetry. There was only one thing which he later regretted: why hadn't he used poetry to express all the truths which he couldn't express in prose.

After all, poetry resembled a drunkard talking, a bit like the talk of a man who'd taken leave of his senses, and so any truths told in that tongue couldn't have offended anyone, be they subjective or objective.

But the regret came later, after the party. That was why the cultural programme was so boring, even though weeks, even months had gone into preparing it.

There were a few responses to the opening speech, but they were more for form's sake, they didn't address any matters of substance. Even when the food was brought to the table it didn't seem to liven anyone up; no one seemed to be in the party mood.

Only Mr Slopashev's voice grew louder, and that seemed to put Voitinski in a good mood too. He sat there in his personal armchair, croaking with laughter and beating time with one hand, as if in his mind he was elsewhere, at some concert which he'd attended decades earlier. In a similarly good mood, Slopashev stood up from behind his table and yelled at the top of his voice, "My friends in food and drink, my companions in work! Everything has been spoken of here, but not of man himself. But I ask you: what is man? Where is man? Am I a man? Is my best friend Ivan Vassilevich a man? And all the rest of them – are they men? But if we're all men, then what is man? Man is a bomb, man is dynamite. So let's avoid the subject of man. My best friend, our oldest man, Ivan Vassilevich, he's our biggest bomb. His earthly form is almost completely dead, all that is left of him is a bomb, holy dynamite. Ivan Vassilevich, everything in you which was transient has died, all that is left is the ideal and eternal. That's the kind of model man which my friend Ivan Vassilevich is, and I ask all of you to raise your glasses to the health of the oldest and most exemplary of men. Long live Ivan Vassilevich!"

Everyone stood. Even Voitinski tried to stand, attempting at the same time to lift a full glass from the table, but he didn't quite manage to grasp it, and the glass tipped over, while

Voitinski himself fell back into his armchair.

"Our eternal man must be tired," someone joked.

"To tire is human," someone else cracked back.

"Ivan Vassilevich!" cried Slopashev. "Let's drink to your health."

But it looked like Ivan Vassilevich hadn't heard them.

"Wake up, Ivan Vassilevich, we want to drink to your health!" Slopashev bellowed again, but since his friend again failed to answer, he drained his glass, and the others did likewise.

"Now then, now the bomb has been soaked, the dynamite is damp, now it won't explode in him again," Slopashev speculated in a philosophical key. Then he stood right in front of Voitinski and asked: "Ivan Vassilevich, are you asleep or are you already dead?"

The word "dead" had the effect of stunning the whole room.

"Our eternal man is dead," said Molotov, who was standing in front of Voitinski and inspecting his face.

Maurus placed his hands either side of Voitinski, as if he was about to shake him, but then Voitinski's head slumped onto his chest.

"Ivan Vassilevich, listen to me, what's the matter with you?" Slopashev asked, holding the deceased's head between his hands and looking into his eyes as if he were hoping to find signs of life there. And when he failed to find it, he said: "Are you really dead then? Your bomb has exploded."

Then he stood up straight, turned to face the students who had gathered around, and delivered a line from Derzhavin, "Where there were was a table of viands, now stands a coffin...."

And without any further ado he lifted the corpse from the chair, and started to make his way towards the door.

"What are you doing?" asked Mr Maurus. "Where are you going, Mr Slopashev?"

"Home... I'm going back to my place, Ivan Vassilevich will

be more comfortable there," he said, and carried on walking with a determined stride. Mr Maurus tried to block his way, but Ollino stepped forwards and put his hand on the headmaster's shoulder, and now no one obstructed Slopashev's path. Quite the opposite: they opened the doors, and stood in two lines on either side of the corridor, allowing Slopashev to make his way out. He left the building by the back door, which was a shorter distance from his lodgings, and the students followed him, without putting on their hats. The night sky was cloudless, and a multitude of stars twinkled in the moonless darkness. They proceeded with their bare heads under the glittering stars. But Slopashev couldn't help addressing his dear departed friend, making recourse to Pushkin: "Farewell my comrade, my loyal servant, it is time for us to part. Now rest in peace."

And so ended the party which they had put so much effort into preparing, because there wasn't a single person who wanted to remain in a room which had just been visited by Death. Moreover, a good number of them had to help deal with Mr Voitinski's corpse. People rushed about here and there, and they completely forgot about the graduation party, as if it had never happened, as it there were no longer any reason to have a party. There was one, but they were fetching a coffin for him.

The party organisers couldn't help wondering how it could be that they had thought of everything apart from the possibility of death. It was true that even the caviar had been more prominent in their minds than death. But now most of the caviar was left untouched, and they were all bustling about because of death, because death had drawn a big cross through everything. This was the moment when Vellemaa started to regret he hadn't had the guts to speak the truth even in poetic form, and there were others who also regretted it, having prepared plenty of truths to tell the headmaster and teachers. But there was nothing for it, death had beaten them to it, and it was unlikely they would ever have a chance to reveal those truths.

"He could have shown the consideration of dying a couple of hours earlier, or later, and not at that precise moment," said one young disciple of the truth reproachfully.

"Death is such a silly thing in general," said another student.

Death seemed the strangest of things to Indrek, when he thought about how it had come today. He was probably the only one of them who had heard death's footsteps approaching, but at that moment he hadn't realised that this was what death sounded like. For he had been to the sauna with Voitinski and washed him and his clothes in preparation for the party. He had done just as he had many times before, but Voitinski had never spoken to him as he did that day.

"This is probably the last time you'll wash me," Voitinski said, once he drank his customary bottle of beer, and was sitting on the bench in the hot sauna.

"What do you mean?" Indrek asked, failing to understand. "Are you planning to go away somewhere?"

Voitinski just laughed and said, "Of course I am, how could it be otherwise. Or do you think that I'm eternal?"

Only then did Indrek realise that Voitinski was talking about death, and there was nothing he could say in reply; it was almost as if he agreed with Voitinski that now was indeed the time for him to depart.

"You'll be rid of my sorry old hide," Voitinski continued after a short pause. "And you know what? You're a fortunate man, God knows how fortunate you are!"

"Why's that," Indrek had asked, and now he heard the answer, "How couldn't you be? A young man, who is willing to help someone like me as you do, has to be fortunate, he is sure to be happy, very happy. The women must really adore you, and nothing makes a man happier than a woman's love. There's more happiness to be had from a woman than anything. I'm a Pole, I know these things."

That was what Voitinski had said on the sauna bench, once he'd drunk his bottle of beer. And now he was dead. Indrek even felt a little sad that the wretched old man was no more, that he could no longer help him in the sauna, and listen to what he had to say. Gone was the man who'd predicted his happiness, who'd said that he believed in Indrek's happiness. And so his own faith in himself had taken a blow. Indrek felt it pretty soon, as soon as the fuss had died down, because by then his pain had rested a while and could start gnawing away at his heart once again. The departed Voitinski had contributed to that, by speaking of happiness and the love of a woman.

Chapter 29

Nor could Indrek forget what Mother Vaarmann had said about a prospective groom for her daughter: "one hundred roubles a month and home in time for lunch." Once he'd thought her words over he said to himself, "But what if I take matters in hand and start swotting from this very day, I'll swot the whole summer through, I won't do anything but swot, and then in the autumn I'll do the private teacher's exam! Maybe then I'll be able to earn 100 roubles a month and be home in time for lunch? Will I or won't I? If I will, then what will Mother Vaarman and her perfectly-rounded daughter Molli say to that?"

This was definitely the right idea, it was a great idea, it was a wonderful idea, and so Indrek started to investigate various teacher training programmes in order to try and select the most suitable one, the best value one. And he would have come to a decision and started to implement it, if something hadn't got in the way. The first stumbling block was an invitation to a party at the Vaarmanns' – a birthday party or some other sort of anniversary, Indrek wasn't sure.

The Vaarman's standard of living seemed to have changed for the better, as if they had got the better of their privations. They had started having more guests, and Mother Vaarman always had a little something to offer them, whether a cup of coffee or tea, a piece of bread or a biscuit, a boiled sweet, or even a piece of chocolate. And there was always a joyful mood in those cellar rooms, because the guests were usually young, and full of the joys of life. There were seamstresses and sales girls, shop boys and craftsmen, acquaintances of her son, and sometimes a junior official or student who might have got caught up in the fun as well. It was wonderful to see how many smiling faces and shining eyes could fit into the cellar apartment.

When Indrek entered there was already dancing in both rooms, and the squeaky violin could hardly be heard amidst the din and commotion. It was as hot as a sauna, but the smells weren't sauna smells, the smells were quite different. Indrek quickly got stuck in too, because Molli greeted him as if everything was perfectly fine between them, as if only a day or two had passed since their last meeting. But whenever Indrek was in a good mood, when he had more joy than he needed for himself, then he always tried to share it with someone; he would never hold that supply of joy in reserve, he would never hold on to it for some future day. And so he grabbed hold of poor Tiina, who was sitting hunched up on the bed, and started dancing with her. He had no desire to dance with any of the able-bodied girls, and Molli couldn't be expected to dance with him non-stop.

"You must dance," Indrek said to Tiina, who had put her spindly arms round Indrek's neck and was holding on tight. "It doesn't matter if your feet can't reach the ground, just hold on as tight as you can. Mosquitos don't touch the ground, but they still dance in the sunshine and hold on tight to their wings. Just don't look about too much, otherwise your head will start to spin. Don't worry about your feet, they won't start spinning."

"My head isn't spinning yet," said Tiina.

"Isn't it?" Indrek asked, performing a full circle in the middle of the floor and whisking Tiina round with him. "How about now?"

"It is now," said Tiina. "Do it again, it feels so good. More, more!"

That moment they heard agitated cries coming from the next room, and then a familiar- sounding voice joined in. Indrek hurried off with the others to find out what was going on, and ran straight into Mr Maurus, bareheaded, dressed in night gown and slippers, and holding two girls by the hand, evidently two of the partygoers, both of whom were crying. Tigapuu, Vainukägu and Vutt were looking on over his shoulder.

"Here they are!" Mr Maurus cried triumphantly. "I caught them! These are the ones!"

But at that moment he noticed Indrek among the other guests. He left the girls where they were standing, and made straight for Indrek.

"You imp!" he cried. "What are you doing here? Whose house is this? Who is that girl? Put her down! Put her down right away, I tell you!"

Indrek turned to put Tiina back down on the bed.

"Where are you going?" yelled Mr Maurus. "If I tell one of my boys to do something, then he does it right away: put that girl down, I say!"

Indrek sat Tiina down on a chair.

"Who are you?" Maurus asked her.

"My name is Tiina," she replied.

"A polite child stands to address her elders," Maurus said. "Don't you see that my beard is grey? A child must stand when she sees a grey beard."

"Mr Maurus..." Indrek started.

"Do not interrupt when Mr Maurus is talking," shouted the headmaster, and turned to Tiina again: "Why do you not stand before a grey-beard?"

But now Mother Vaarmann intervened, "Mr Maurus, my daughter cannot stand on her own feet."

"Who are you? How do you know my name?" Maurus asked.

"Well, Mr Maurus, everyone knows you," said Mrs Vaarmann in as refined and flattering a tone as she could manage.

"Of course they do," Mr Maurus replied, "me and my grey beard. But what kind of house is it you're keeping here? Who are all these people?"

"Mr Maurus!" mother Vaarmann cried. "I'm not keeping

any kind of house, these people here are my guests, and all of them are decent respectable folk. And I would ask you, Mr Maurus, not to...."

"What!" cried Mr Maurus in response. Now the reason he had come suddenly came back to him in full clarity. "This woman is becoming insolent. Do I have to call the police? Tigapuu!"

"Yes, Mr Maurus," Tigapuu replied tersely and stepped forwards.

"Very good," said Mr Maurus. "Wait! When I say, then bring the guardian of law and order."

Then he turned to Mother Vaarmann again and said, "You're corrupting the young here. In the dark of night you send young girls to ring Mr Maurus' doorbell. And do you know what happens to my boys when young girls ring my bell? I have to chase after young girls in the dark street – an old man like me – because I can't very well have my boys chase after young girls, can I? And how am I supposed to chase after them? I'll show you how!"

Mr Maurus opened his night gown, revealing his underwear to all and sundry, and he was in such a state of disarray that he inadvertently revealed much more than Mother Vaarman's partygoers were prepared to see.

"Look, this is how I have to chase after the young girls in the dark street, after they've come to corrupt my boys with their ringing. My boys are decent, honest boys, but if these girls come ringing at all hours, what good is all that decency and honesty! That is why I ask you: what kind of house is this, and what kind of woman are you, Frauenzimmer, if you let your girls come and ring my bell like that? Mr Maurus refuses to leave this place until he knows what kind of house this is and what kind of girls these are who come ringing for my boys, and force me to come chasing after them. Answer me now, Mr Maurus is waiting, Mr Maurus and his decent boys."

Of course, old Mr Maurus and the "decent boys" who were giggling behind his back found out everything they needed to know. Mrs Vaarmann had put on a party, and a couple of girls wanted to have some fun with the Maurus' boys, by pulling the doorbell, then bunking off and hiding. Their trick worked a couple of times, and no one knew who had rung. But the third time they came Mr Maurus and his boys were waiting, and as soon as they saw the doorbell-ringers they flung the door open and chased them as far as the Vaarmann's yard, where they had caught them.

"Do I have the right to know whose house this is, yes or no?"

"Yes, Mr Maurus has the right to know," Mother Vaarmann said, "but we are all decent, respectable people."

"There you go then," said Maurus triumphantly. "Mr Maurus does have the right, Mr Maurus and his boys have the right. They wouldn't normally chase girls, when they ring. But then gotcha! Two girls at once!"

Mr Maurus raised his hand to his brow, as if he had suddenly remembered something. Then he turned to Indrek, and asked:

"Where is that girl. That girl of yours?"

Mrs Vaarmann picked up Tiina and stood with her in front of Mr Maurus.

"Here is my poor child, Mr Maurus."

"Put her down," Mr Maurus instructed.

"Her legs won't support her," mother Vaarmann replied.

"You're a brazen woman. Don't you understand what Mr Maurus is saying? Mr Maurus is speaking clearly, clearly and to the point as always: put her down. Is that clear enough for you?"

"It is, Mr Maurus," Mother Vaarmann replied, "but our floor is…Mr Maurus you can see for yourself what a poor family's floor is like…."

"Then sit her down on the chair," instructed Mr Maurus.

Mrs Vaarmann did as he asked and Mr Maurus set about examining Tiina's legs, touching them here and there, as if he were some kind of expert. Then he took hold of her hands, and said, "Right, now stand up, I'll help you, Mr Maurus and his grey beard will help."

"I can't," said Tiina, making no attempt to stand.

"You have to believe that you can, then you'll be able to. Learn to believe, then you'll get better," Mr Maurus explained, much to the mirth of his "decent boys".

"She hasn't yet learned to believe strongly enough," Mother Vaarmann said.

"So how do you get around then?" Mr Maurus asked.

"With crutches, Mr Maurus," said Mrs Vaarmann on behalf of her daughter.

"Don't interrupt when Mr Maurus is talking. Mothers do have the habit of talking when one wants to talk to their daughters, as if they wanted to take their daughters' places. But Mr Maurus asks you: how do you walk?"

"I use crutches," Tiina replied.

"So, you've got crutches have you. Where are they?"

The crutches were produced for Mr Maurus to see.

"Now show us how you walk with them," said Mr Maurus.

Tiina demonstrated, hopping around the room on her crutches.

"Very good," said Mr Maurus. "If God decides to take away our legs, at least he gives us crutches, he never leaves anyone completely wanting."

"When I'm bigger, then God will fix my legs, He'll send an angel to do it, otherwise no one will ever want to marry me," Tiina explained.

"That's right, that's right," said Mr Maurus approvingly, "God will send an angel, who will make sure you get married. And if you were a boy, then Mr Maurus would tell you: I've got a big school not far from here, and there's lots of other boys there, you come with me, you come with me and while God's angel is on his way you can study mathematics and Latin. You would be a real boon to my school, because I've got boys of all sorts there, but not a single one with crutches. You come and study ancient Greek, crutches don't stop you studying Greek. Yes, that's what Mr Maurus would say if you were a boy. But you're a girl, and Mr Maurus can't admit girls to his school, because the boys would run you off your crutches. Yes yes, the boys would always be running around a girl with crutches, so.....*Warten Sie, warten Sie…*" Mr Maurus paused and looked around for a moment.

"Paas!" he yelled. "Were you dancing with this child?"

"Yes, and she was enjoying it very much," said Indrek.

Mr Maurus looked him questioningly in the eye and said, "Then let her enjoy some more of it, until God sends his angel, because she won't be able to study Latin and Greek anyway."

Then he turned towards the door and started to leave, but when he'd reached the threshold he stopped and said, "But don't come ringing Mr Maurus doorbell anymore, because it corrupts his honest and decent boys, when young girls come ringing in the dark. But you, Paas, once you've had your fill of dancing with the girl with crutches, then you come on home, there are plenty of girls with good legs, they can even dance on them too. Oh yes, those girls had good legs but Mr Maurus' boys were quicker; his boys were quicker than them!"

And then, much to everyone's relief, Mr Maurus left. But he still couldn't let the business go, because he was sure that the girls hadn't come to ring just like that, for no reason, he was sure that they must have already known some of the boys, especially after he'd caught Indrek red-handed, dancing with a girl. Although only with that crippled girl, only with her, otherwise…

After that Indrek's name was on everyone's lips, and there was no end to the teasing and mockery he had to suffer, and this was at a time when he'd already been going around with his head hung low. For he'd now had the explanation from Molli which he'd been longing to hear for so long. Molli had taken the initiative, since things were much clearer for her than for Indrek. She took Indrek's hand, looked at him with her round eyes, and asked, "Don't you trust me? Don't you trust me just as I trust you? Completely and with your whole heart? Recently I've had the feeling that you don't trust me anymore. And I know why: it's because of what my mother said: 'one hundred roubles and home in time for lunch.' It was because of that, wasn't it? Tell me truthfully."

"Partly because of that, and partly…" Indrek tried to reply.

"I know, I know!" Molli cried. "And partly because we haven't met so often recently, that's right, isn't it? You see, I know everything. But it's not my fault, believe me. And it's not my mother's fault either. It just so happened that my mother got a new job, you must have heard…"

"I've heard nothing," Indrek said, shaking his head.

"Did mother not say anything? Nor Tiina? Very strange. They must have forgotten then. You know that Slopashev, the Russian, left your place, and then he moved in next to us. He knows you, speaks very highly of you. He was the one who told me that you'd been going to the sauna with Voitinski, the one who died recently, at the party."

"I was the one who told you about the sauna," said Indrek.

"I don't remember that," said Molli, "but I do know what Mr Slopashev said. I know from him what sort of person that Mr Voitinski was, and that you went to the sauna with him to wash him. That's right, isn't it? You see, I do know. Of course you're surprised that Mr Slopashev should have told me such a thing. But the explanation is very simple: I've started having Russian lessons with him, although I'm not too good at it yet. It came about because I went to interpret for my mother one time, and that's how it happened, that's how I started taking lessons. I have them every evening now. You don't believe me? I swear to you, I do! Mother started working as Slopashev's housekeeper. And when she didn't have the time to go, I went there instead, and used my Russian there. That's how the lessons started, and now he's my teacher. He said to my mother: 'You're a pretty well-educated person, and your daughter is pretty educated too, but it's a real shame when an educated person doesn't know Russian, it was the language of Pushkin after all.' You see, that's how I know! And so I started studying Russian. And when I get good enough at it, then I might even be able to marry a Russian. What do you think, will I be able to marry a Russian, if I speak Russian well enough? Mother reckons I will, and I think I will, and so does Mr Slopashev. But I can never be your wife. To start with, I'm a year or two older than you, and a woman must never be older than her husband, that's what mother says. And then the next thing is that I love you, so I can't because I love you too much. Mother always says: don't marry someone you love, it will only make you unhappy, because love makes you unhappy. My mother told me that men die when they're loved, they die from love just like flies, my mother says. So you should learn Russian, she says, and marry a Russian man, because you won't ever love him as much as one of your own kind. That was what I wanted to talk to you about, I wanted everything between us to be clear and honest, because I can never be your wife."

Indrek's head was spinning from what he'd just heard. He had wanted to talk about the teachers' exam which he was planning to take in autumn, and the university which he was going to get into, come what may – he was planning to stress the "come what may" – but now he dropped all that. Instead he said, "But I never wanted you to be my wife, because…"

"You men are all the same!" Molli cried, without waiting for Indrek to finish, and got up. "I talk about love, nothing but love, and he says: but I never wanted you anyway. Like a snow shovel to the head!"

"Please let me finish," Indrek said.

"No, I don't want to hear another word, that's quite enough. Mother was right when she said: 'Why are you messing around with that boy, he'll never take you to be his wife!' That's the fate we women must suffer. We give so much love, but we never get any love in return. You keep your mouth shut and listen to me! There is no love between us, none, none at all!

I already knew that back then under the apple tree, that it wasn't right. Now keep your hands off me, keep them off me! And you know what? The thing with love is that if it's not here already, then it will never come. Friendship is another thing altogether, it's quite possible to be friends, even if there is no love. And we will remain friends, friends for eternity, because man is eternal. You see the things I know now. That comes from my Russian lesson, that Russian is always talking about the eternal man, especially when mother brings him a bottle of beer. And so we will remain friends. Tiina will be pleased, she's always happy to see you here. You know something, she laughs in her sleep, she laughs when you have been round, she's really taken to you. Tiina is different to me, because her legs are poorly. She's always reproaching me, why I'm like this, why I'm like that. There's no point trying to compare me with her. Of course you won't believe me, because you don't love me. But I love you, and that's why I believe…."

Molli whirred on like a spindle, going on and on about love and faith, and that you mustn't get married to a man if you love him. Indrek listened until finally he said, "Love is indeed a strange thing, I certainly don't understand it one bit."

"That's right: it can't be understood," Molli said. "Love can never really be understood, can it?"

But later Molli spoke to her mother about it, who didn't bother her old head one little bit about the question of love. She'd said, plain and simple, "It makes no difference if you understand it or not, life doesn't come to a standstill, life goes on. It's down to your dad that you pay too much attention to things like that and repeat whatever you hear. He would also hold his head in both hands and moan: 'I don't understand, I simply don't understand'. You're just the same with all that talk of love, taking it all too seriously. What's the point of talking about, discussing it, if there's hardly any of it to go round in the world in any case?"

That's what the worldly-wise mother Vaarmann thought; as far as she was concerned, thinking played no role in love.

But when Indrek later tried to recall his conversation with Molli, he couldn't shake off the feeling that his own thinking had somehow been out of kilter. It was stupid of him to try and sound clever when his heart was aching and his passions inflamed. And it would feel just as stupid to step across the Vaarmann's threshold again, because love would flee the place where it had been talked of so much. But Indrek couldn't help himself going back to the place of love once or twice more. It was embarrassing and difficult but he still went, as if he was looking for burning embers in an extinguished fire or as if he were an inexperienced crook, drawn back to the scene of the crime again and again.

One time he found little Tiina alone at home. The "Noah's arc" had been crammed full of all sorts of junk, and Tiina had climbed onto it and was messing about there. She was overjoyed to see Indrek and collapsed into his arms in a blissful delirium.

"It's good that you came," she said. "There's no one else around today. Now I can tell you everything. You know what: Molli is lying when she says she loves you. She loves that Russian who lives in that other house, that fat one, not you. She's only telling you that because mummy told her that if anything happens to the Russian, then you would be the next best choice, because she loves you. But she wants to get married to that Russian, that's why she's learning Russian. To start with Molli didn't want to, she said he's as fat as a barrel, and he drinks too much. But mummy said it doesn't matter if he's fat, at least he's more likely to stay at home. She said that if a man doesn't drink or smoke, then he's going to be bad tempered; he'll always be keeping check on his wife. That bad-tempered man means you. But I don't believe it, and when I'm bigger and God fixes my legs, then I'll come for you myself. I'll love you, and I'll come. You can trust me, I'm not like Molli, who just lies all the time. I'm not lying when I say that I'll come to love you, to be your wife, I'll definitely come. And don't you think that I don't know what it means to get married. I know very

355

well. I'm not as silly as Molli and mother think. Being married means that the man goes to earn money and the woman stays at home and cooks, otherwise where would the man eat, if his woman doesn't cook for him. Isn't that right?"

"Exactly," said Indrek.

"And the man has to earn the money, otherwise the woman wouldn't be able to cook the food for him."

"That's very true," Indrek said.

"And you know what mother and Molli think? That you won't ever be able to earn a hundred roubles a month and won't be home in time for lunch, but that the Russian man will, and he'll be home in time too. That's why Molli loves that Russian. But I'll be your wife even if you don't earn a hundred roubles, and it won't be any of mother's business. You will have to be home in time for lunch though. When I grow up and get married, then my legs will be alright, and I won't want to be alone anymore, when I have a husband to take care of me."

"Of course," said Indrek.

"There you are then, you see that I'm not as stupid as the others think."

"You're a clever girl," Indrek said, feeling as if he had a block of ice pressing on his chest, stinging cold.

"Now don't you go telling mummy and Molli that you know everything," Tiina said, "because then I'll be given what for. And it's easy to give it to me, because I can't run away on my crutches. All I can do is hide under the bed or behind the cupboard. So you think about me, and keep coming here, and keep pretending that you believe what Molli tells you, because now you know what I'm going to do when I'm bigger and my legs are alright. Will you still come to see me?" Tiina asked, as if she wasn't sure whether to trust Indrek.

"I'll come," Indrek replied. "I'll definitely come," he said, telling himself that he would never set foot in the cellar room again. But of course, things would turn out differently.

Chapter 30

Oh yes, life turns out to be quite different from how we imagined it, or how it is presented to us in books, which are most probably products of the imagination anyway. In books, if its springtime, the trees are in full bud and there's birdsong in the air, then love will most probably be in the air as well. But real life can be quite different. Spring may well come and yet there is no love in the air, because love was over long before. And then all that is left is mourning. Because there is nothing harder than seeing bursting buds when you feel that something is constricting your heart ever tighter and tighter, like a coiled snake suffocating its wretched prey.

The town had grown empty and Indrek found it eerie now. He decided he would go to Vargamäe – either for the whole summer or just for a few days, he didn't know, but he had started to long for the place he was from and the person he had once been.

And then his plans were derailed by another letter from his brother Andres:

> Dear Brother, don't you go thinking that I am doing this deliberately, to spite someone, for in truth my sole aim in being here is so that this foreign land and all its people, and those other foreign lands and their people shall know very well how a steadfast Estonian man and a son of the Estonian nation is willing to struggle in the name of his family in a distant land. And so God be with you, my dear homeland. God be with you, my dear brothers and sisters because I want to make you proud of me with the strength of my body and with all of my might. And let there be no one under this grey sky who can stand against me when I'm fighting in the name

of my people. For I have put them all on their backs, just as the law requires, and just as I did to the strongman Mätlik Eedi at his confirmation, when I wanted to knock his head to high heaven and his head split wide open. Now I'm training with this Latvian, he's a tough bastard, but I'm still loads stronger than him and he can't stand up to me when I go at him full steam. He can stamp on my neck if he wants to, but my neck won't bend, the whole lot of them, the company, the battalion, the regiment, they can all come and try my neck in turn, and they won't be able to bend it, and I tell you, my dear brother, the whole corps could come if they wanted to, but my neck will stay straight, because it is my neck and I'm the only one who can bend it, as is my duty and right as a steadfast man of our family. And then this autumn we were reading a newspaper, because we order one paper here for all of us, and we club together to buy it, and then we use it to make roll-ups, because there are no rolling papers to be had here, and so we were reading it together, and we read about the feat which Georg Lurich pulled off in the dear homeland, and how they carried him aloft, just like our very own colonel, who we carried aloft too, when he left us on promotion. And so I told everyone, when we were making roll-ups from that newspaper, that Lurich might be number one, but I wouldn't ever be the last, because others would have to come after me, whose shoelaces I wouldn't have the strength to undo. But I've written home and told them everything I've been thinking about and about how I'm training every single day. And I wrote to father too, I wrote oh dear father, it's a sorry state of affairs that an old man like you has to take a plough handle in his hand, and fix the harrow blades, and fix the blade on the scythe, and then sharpen it too, but it can't be helped, if it's God's wish that I have to eat the Tsar's bread here on military service, which has made me much bigger and much stronger than I was from walking and singing in Vargamäe, and so I have to carry on using my brawn to show the Russians and Germans, who are both our masters – to show them that they really are our masters, and we have to do their bidding, and we can't do anything to resist. And so, dear father, don't be sad, but be glad, and dance there on Vargamäe like David before the arc of the covenant, because your son Andres hasn't hidden his light under a bushel, but has used his strength, which he used at Vargamäe to break the pitchfork handles as if they were made from wood splinters, not solid and gnarled birch wood; he has used his strength for your glory, and for the fame of your dear family, and it's taken him to this foreign land where he lives amongst foreign folk, and where he is paid so much money that we'll be able to build that town at Vargamäe, which we spoke about when we were levelling the mounds of earth on the marshes, and digging up willow roots, and clearing the undergrowth from around the dwarf birch with our scythes. And I don't want to think about anything other than that, for I have come from Vargamäe and that's where I want to return. And when I come to die, then I will make myself a beautiful grave on Jõesaar and put an iron fence around it and a tall tower with a cross on top, which will glitter in the sunlight, while the cow bells jingle and the birds sing overhead. And I will build a nice path to it from the house, with a ditch on either side, a layer of juniper and fir branches on the bottom, and a thick layer of gravel on top, because thank the Heavens there is no shortage of that at Vargamäe, and anyone will be able to walk down that road without getting their feet wet, oh dear father, and they will go and visit the resting place of your dear son Andres, the son who was supposed to be the next master of Vargamäe, but went to struggle for the renown of his father's house and his family and brothers, so that the whole world would know what kind of people we are and what kind of men we are, because man thinks, but God guides us. That is what I wrote to my father, but he won't listen, because what are you supposed to do with an old man, when he doesn't think about his family, but only about his Vargamäe, and mother sent me word via Liine, that I should

359

think about my old grey father, for father had indeed started to go grey, because his life was so hard. But you've been going to that big school for a few years now, and you've learned a lot of clever stuff, and so you should understand, and believe me when I say, that I'm thinking about my old father and home, because I truly think that when I get released from military service I will go and join a circus, and wrestle, and put all my opponents on their backs, and when they start paying me a lot of money for that, like they do here in this town, then I will want to tell everyone that I'm my father's son and Young Andres of Vargamäe, so that father won't have any reason to be ashamed of me. But the trouble is that mother and father don't understand me, and don't believe me, because they're old folk, and we're all young, and so I wanted to ask you, my dear brother, because you're closer and can pop home more easily, I wanted to ask you to go and talk with them, mother and father that is, because they'll listen to you and believe you sooner than they would me, because you're cleverer than them, and cleverer than me. You are no match for my brawn, you never were, and you never will be, you should see my wrists and my chest now, I've had to replace my overcoat and my jacket twice already, and they were still too tight, the sleeves as tight as flower buds, the buttons bursting off, so your strength is nothing besides mine. But my intelligence is nothing besides yours, so the both of us are better than the other, each in his own way, but now it's not just me that's better than you, as I was before, when you still had no intelligence, and no strength either. Now I don't want to repeat what I did back then, on the potato field, when mother was digging for potatoes and I filled your hat full of earth and threw it deep into the potato plants, which made you so angry that you tried to throw a stone at me, but the stone hit mother instead, and she fell to the ground, because she was so badly hurt. You probably think that I'd forgotten that, but I haven't, I'll remember it until the day I die, and I've often thought that it would have been better if that stone had hit me and not mother, because I deserved it, and she didn't, but I can't change anything now, and mother is still hurting where the stone hit her, you have to know that, and keep it in mind, just as I do, because we are both to blame, although I am more to blame than you; and we have to live with the knowledge that mother is suffering because of us and that we can't do anything about it, only God can, if he so chooses. And you should know that it makes no difference if she's not my real mother, I consider her to be realer than any, because I don't have any other mother, and when father once called her Sauna Mari, then I said to mother when the two of us were alone, and she was crying, I said to mother, don't cry, father can insult you as much as he likes, but as far as I am concerned you are just mother to me, and to all the rest of us here, for whose sake you worry so much, and work yourself to death, and for us you're no Sauna Mari, that's just what father calls you when he's angry. And I know that the mood has been gloomy at home since I wrote to them, and that's why I wanted to ask you to go and see and speak to father and mother, if necessary...

That's what Andres wrote from "north Poland", and the letter immediately put paid to any desire Indrek might have had to go home, because it brought back so many sad and troubled memories from his past, and it felt impossible to go straight back into the midst of things in his current mood.

What was more, one fine day the rumour reached Indrek by word of mouth that Miss Ramilda had come home. For some reason, Indrek's legs started trembling as soon as he heard that news, first the knees, then the shins, and then the thighs and feet too. He could be standing quite at ease and then suddenly he would feel his legs start shaking. And it wasn't worth trying to put up any resistance or calm himself down, his body just didn't want to listen, there was nothing he could do.

Indrek sneaked off to hide behind the curtain in the cellar

room, and then sat down on his chest, where he remained sitting for a while, resting his back against the wall. As he sat there, past events, experiences, facial expressions formed in his mind's eye, and he heard familiar voices, but they were all happening at such a crazy speed, through such a thick fog, that all he could hear was a hubbub of noise, and all he could see were hazy apparitions.

Tigapuu had spoken with Ramilda and was mouthing off about it with anyone who would listen.

"That young lady is even finer than she was," he opined. "You can tell right away that she's been living in Germany. She's only going to be around for a day or so, then she's going to the countryside, and in autumn she's probably going back to Germany, because it's just so boring for her here. When I've finished university I'll go abroad too, and I won't show my face round here again, after all why would an educated person live in their home country."

If doubts were expressed about this plan, since a lot of money was probably required to go and live abroad, Tigapuu said, "Money?! You're talking to me about money! When I've finished university I'll find myself a rich wife. And why would anyone suffer from a lack of money if they've got a rich wife?"

It seemed that everyone was happy with that explanation, because they all agreed that if he had a rich wife, then Tigapuu himself would no longer be poor. But it suddenly occurred to Indrek that Tigapuu's rich wife might well be none other than Ramilda. It had to be her! Why else would she be talking to Tigapuu and not with Indrek, as if it were not Indrek, but Tigapuu who was keeping those mug handles in the bottom of his chest. Indrek felt pretty silly thinking like that, but he couldn't help himself.

But it soon came about that Miss Ramilda talked with Indrek as well, and they talked for quite a while. She came downstairs looking for Mr Maurus, but happened to find Indrek there instead, on guard duty because no one else could be found for that shift.

"It's you, is it? Still here?" Ramilda said in surprise, approaching Indrek as if she was going to shake hands with him, although she didn't, which Indrek was quite relieved about, because he had suddenly come over in a cold sweat, and his palms were clammy. He was loath to offer Ramilda his sweaty hand to shake, but even more so to dry his hand on his handkerchief, because he'd suddenly remembered that the handkerchief he had in his pocket looked more like a rag you'd use to wipe the blackboard.

"That's right, I'm still here," Indrek blurted to Ramilda, as if embarrassed that he was indeed still there.

"You're still slicing the bread and breaking the handles off the mugs, are you?" Ramilda asked, now in a more relaxed and warmer tone, which made Indrek come over in a hot flush.

"There's nothing left to break, they're all broken already," Indrek replied, making Ramilda laugh. She sat herself down impatiently on the edge of the table.

"Is anyone else here?" she asked.

"They're all in class apart from me," said Indrek.

"Thank heavens!" Ramilda sighed, as if she was greatly relieved. "Have you thought about me at all, while I've been away? I've thought about you. It started to get a bit boring living amongst strangers, and so one day I said to myself: it would be better if I thought about home and the people back there, and so I thought about you. What do you think, have I changed a great deal?"

"It seems that you have," said Indrek, unable to think of anything better to say.

"I have, haven't I. I look a bit older, don't I?" said Ramilda.

"I'm not sure," said Indrek.

"Everyone tells me that I've taken on airs. But you know what, if you want to get rid of people, then it's good to take on airs. I don't like people much. Humans are the only animal I don't love. If you only knew how tiresome I find people sometimes. Even my own father and aunt! They all play games, hiding their thoughts and deeds behind fancy words. My own father too, he's worse than anyone. In the end you don't know what's up or down. And you know why I can't tolerate it anymore? Just as people cunningly use words to conceal their true intentions, so death sneaks up on you cunningly too. But it never arrives! It deceives and mocks you! Everyone! Me too!"

"You too," said Indrek.

"Me too," Ramilda said, sitting on the edge of the table, sideways on to Indrek, with her head hung low. "I was terribly bored, when it first happened," she started, but then she stopped, turned to Indrek and asked: "Do you know what it means to be bored? Do you know what it's like when someone tells you that tomorrow some great fortune awaits you, some incredible happiness, enough to make you lose your mind, and all you can do is reply indifferently: let that incredible fortune come, I'm no longer in need of any happiness great or small, because I just want to die, I want to die right away, because I don't believe in anything which might make me in the slightest bit happy. Even if God were to come, the one who created heaven and earth in seven days, and were to say: make a wish, I'll grant you any wish, then you'd reply to the creator of heaven and earth quite calmly: my dear heavenly father, you're a little late, if only you'd come a day earlier, because yesterday I still had a load of wishes, but today I have only one – to die. That's how I felt. But they saved me, against my own wishes. I really didn't care anymore. Then aunt's letter arrived. In fact it had arrived much earlier, but they hadn't given it to me. She wrote about you in that letter, there was mention of you more than once. And when I saw your name, I had a good idea. I said to myself: if Mr Paas had been here then it would have been even easier for them to save me. You know what the doctor asked me: do I know anyone who feels almost like a blood relative to me, and would that person want to lend me just a little bit of their blood? That's what he asked. At first I couldn't think of a single person. But then when I saw your name in aunt's letter, and I thought to myself: that's the one. And I truly believed I was right. I thought to myself, if I should ever meet Mr Paas again, then I'll be sure to ask him, was my supposition, my belief back then right, or was I mistaken? You can be quite forthright with me, because this matter is long behind us now and all I want to do is know whether the feeling I had when I read that letter was right or wrong? And don't try and hide what you really think behind words, you understand me? Was I right or wrong?"

"Madam, how could you ask such a question?" Indrek replied.

"So I was wrong then," said Ramilda, looking at Indrek despondently, before sliding down from the table, and turning to leave.

"No!" cried Indrek taking a couple of steps towards Ramilda, his eyes full of tears. "It goes without saying that I would have agreed to everything. Open up my veins right now if you want, take as much blood as you want, you don't ever need to ask again!"

Once Indrek had overcome his tears, he saw that Ramilda was standing in front of him and making some strange movements with her hands, as if she was about to touch Indrek or something. But as soon as Indrek could see clearly again, all of Ramilda's strangeness disappeared, and she said, "I'm so happy that I wasn't wrong about you, even if I was wrong about the others. It's such a wonderful feeling to be able to trust someone, to rely on them. Even if you never need their help, it's still good to know that help is there if you need it. That must be why people believe in God, so that help is always at hand in times of need. But let that stay between the two of us, just like those cup handles which we broke back then. Where did you throw them in the end? You don't remember any more? It makes no difference now, the whole thing was crazy and stupid anyway. But I'll bid you farewell for now, because the class will be over soon. Tomorrow I'm going to the countryside, to stay with my other aunt, papa thinks it will be best for my health. Neither he nor my aunt here have a moment to spare for me, they've got their boys to worry about, and all their boys' problems, it's just the same as ever! They say to me: you're old enough to look after yourself. But they're only saying that, in reality they think I'm still a little girl. They say that just to release themselves of any responsibility. But as soon as their boys leave, then they'll take me in hand again – they'll pack me up and take me back to the place I once fled from of my own volition. Oh well, if that's how it must be! At least they'll give me a little bit of attention for once. If you knew how lonely I am there! It can be quite awful sometimes! But the things I miss the most might be some piece of old furniture, a wall, the corner of some room or some street corner, more than I miss any people. That's just between you and me, please remember. Have you ever felt anything like that? Have you?"

"If you put it like that, then I think I have," said Indrek. "When I feel homesick, I think less of people than of certain things and places: trees, bushes, some old hedge, or a dent in the hedge where I've climbed over it countless times, a creaking gate, which has been opened and closed a million times. And you know what, miss, there are some old pine trees on the higher ground back home, they're what I think of most of all."

"But do you know why that is?" Ramilda asked. "It's because things mean more than people, that's why. Things are truer. They have a reliable character, whereas people don't. You can't rely on people at all. You might see your friend today and everything is just fine, then you meet up with him tomorrow and he's a complete stranger. That's what people are like. I'm like that myself, because all I have is moods and illusions. That's right, moods and illusions, I've got them in abundance. You don't believe me? Oh, you don't know me well enough! You don't know me one little bit! But then my father doesn't know me either. He understands other women, that much is clear, that's clear to me now, but he doesn't understand his own daughter, because a daughter isn't a woman, she's just a child. And yet it's possible that he's just pretending not to understand me. My father can't be trusted, he's the most untrustworthy person in the world. I'll tell you a story about him if you want...."

But the story was not to be told, because somewhere in a distant corridor a bell started to ring and the whole house started buzzing like a beehive. Ramilda ran off, stopping for a moment in the doorway to smile and wave at Indrek. She did it in such a relaxed, light-hearted way, as if they would be sure to meet a few moments later, to carry on chatting. But that was to be the last time she smiled at Indrek, the last time she waved to him. And Indrek must have sensed that, for otherwise he wouldn't have felt so hopelessly sad and such a pain in his chest, nor would that feeling have lasted for days and weeks.

Chapter 31

That feeling of great sadness was probably what made Indrek start to frequent the graveyard. One day, for no reason, he went there, and spent a long time walking up and down between the gravestones. He felt a sense of relief when he saw those mounds of earth, side by side, containing so much pain and sadness, and the pretty flowers, watered with tears of sadness. It felt good to think that there were large fields full of such mounds, and that people would stand over them, mourning the dead, and yet life still carried on. If it were possible to gather together all the tears shed by the deceased and all the tears cried over them, and send them gushing down from the nearest hilltop, it would cause a spring flood of such proportions that it could engulf a whole town, together with all its crying and laughing inhabitants. But Indrek was glad to know that life in the town would carry on. And he was even glad to be feeling sadness and pain. In that way he would become closer to other people, he would become a real person himself, because true personhood was borne of pain.

Several times Indrek came across funeral parties at the graveyard, and if the group was large enough for him to go unnoticed, he would join them. For some strange reason, the grief of others passed him by, as if he had some protective shield around his heart. But then he would sometimes see someone being buried in a long black coffin without a single mourner walking behind it. There were just two or three men sitting on the cart besides the coffin, their legs dangling off the edge; there had to be someone to lower the coffin into the grave and toss the soil on top, the corpse couldn't do that for itself. That's right, someone had to be there, Indrek thought to himself, observing the scene. It must be some old man, because women aren't usually so tall. And it if it was a young man, then why would the coffin be black? In any case, the young would always be accompanied by someone; there would always be someone, but old men are always on their own, in their long, narrow black coffins. They don't need a wider one, because they've no longer got any flesh on them, just like Voitinski, who was nothing but skin and bone by the end, and so they would fit into a narrow coffin like this one, this black coffin with a yellow body lying inside it, which had probably looked even more corpse-like before death than it was now, now that it was being buried. Indrek stood and watched from a distance as the men busied themselves with efficient indifference around the grave, and suddenly he felt great pity for the old man. And before he even realised what was happening his eyes filled up with tears. He thought to himself: it doesn't matter how indifferently they chuck that soil on top of him, at least now he's been grieved for too, he can't grumble too much.

Who knows how long Indrek would have spent hanging around the graveyard if he hadn't met Mr Schulz, his former German teacher, also known as Copula? Indrek noticed him from a distance and wondered for a while whether he should greet the old man, because he wasn't sure whether he would remember him. But then it came back to him in a flash, his last conversation with Mr Schulz at his house, and without fully knowing why he removed his hat. That seemed to rouse the old man from his thoughts. He recognised Indrek straight away. And, as if they were old friends, he reached out to shake his hand.

"I haven't seen you for ages," he said. "The last time must have been when the two of us were conversing at my place, you remember. My old father was sitting in the summer sunshine, waiting for me to take him back to the homeland – back to the banks of the Rhine, where we hail from. But now he's lying at rest right here, that's his Rhine and homeland for him."

Mr Schulz paused for a while, as if he were unsure of himself. But then he continued, "Would you care to see my father's grave? Afterwards we could walk back to town together."

And without waiting for Indrek to answer, the old man set off. He was small of stature, and he walked with hunched shoulders using his umbrella as a walking stick while locks of grey hair dangled from under his old, dirty hat. Indrek felt that he couldn't say no, and so he joined the old man to say the Our Father at the grave of the old man he'd met only once before. And yet it seemed strange to recite the prayer in a language which the person lying in the grave could not comprehend, and so he just mouthed the words instead.

"Yes, this is the bank of his Rhine," said Mr Schulz after reading the prayer. "The Rhine was the last wish of my father, and I was supposed to make it come true. I think I told you about it when you brought me Mr Maurus' letter that time. But please mark my words: if you ever have a dream, then do everything you can to make it come true, and if you can't do so yourself then give up on it, but never rely on others to help. Don't you rely on your brother or your son to say nothing of your sister or your daughter. My father relied on me, and what did he get for his troubles? His own son lied to him on his deathbed: he promised to take his father's corpse to the banks of the Rhine; yes that's what he promised. And I am that son. I lied, because I wanted my father to die peacefully, and I wanted him to die happy. And what do you think, did I do the right thing?"

"I think you did, Mr Schulz," Indrek replied.

"Do you really think so?" the old man asked.

"I really do!" Indrek confirmed.

"I thought the same thing to start with," said the old man, "but afterwards I started to have my doubts. I started to have my doubts when I saw that the flowers on my father's grave had bloomed. I asked myself: was the lie I told my father really a lie of love or just concealed egotism? I couldn't bear to see the imploring, reproachful look in my father's eyes, and so in order to spare myself, I lied; I lied just to make myself feel better. I was indifferent to my father's fate because I thought, he'll soon die anyway, what does it matter what happens to him. That was the first problem. But then I thought: even if my lie was a lie of love, even then I wouldn't have had the right to say it. Why? Because there are some things in the world which are greater, more exalted, holier than the need to comfort a dying man, even if the dying person is your father, mother, son, daughter or wife. Yes, even if the dying person were your lover – forgive me, because I know that you are still too young to understand such things – yes, even if she were your lover for the sake of whom you'd made your wife, your children and yourself unhappy, even then you shouldn't comfort her on her deathbed with a lie. Because man, his life, his woes and misfortunes in this world are entirely fleeting, transitory, but lies are eternal, after all lies are nothing more than topsy-turvy truths, you see. Truth is eternal! Truth per se, truth in itself. And so one must not err from the eternal for the sake of something fleeting and transitory. I'll illustrate my thought with an example. Again, I should warn you that this example is probably not best suited to someone of your age, but I'll use it anyway, because we're interested in the truth now, which justifies doing so. Namely: what would happen if, in some strange way, it were to turn out that – I won't say that this will definitely happen, I'm only supposing so, for the sake of example – what would happen if it were to turn out that on Judgement Day we are not resurrected, because there is no such thing as resurrection of the flesh or judgement, or anything like it, all there is are graves, like the ones here, and decay, and turning into soil, and that's all there is. That is the resurrection, the rising from the dead, just as these flowers here will grow if someone waters them regularly. And if that were to turn out to be the case, then what would become of God's word, the scriptures. It would mean that it's all a lie. God's word would be a lie, you understand? God would no longer be true! And yet man could take leave of his senses, if he were to think that God lies, that the source of all truth is lying. And what would follow? One thing only: if God can lie, then man is the only entity who must never lie, on no condition whatsoever, because there must be someone in this world who fights for the truth. That was the second point. And the third point: how can we be sure that when someone dies their consciousness is lost with them? What if they're right, those people who say that consciousness lives on; it's just that we don't yet know how to communicate with it. In other words, there is no way of establishing contact between the consciousnesses of the living and the dead. But the means to do so could be found, if not today, then tomorrow, because all sorts of things are invented in this world; why not this means of contact too? Just think what would be possible then. My dead father would come to me and say, 'Son, why did you lie to me then?' And what am I supposed to say to him, as an honest person? And just think about it, if I were to be buried here, next to him, and were to lie here for years, for hundreds of years, thousands of years, we might end up lying here side by side for millions of years, and my father would never stop asking me, 'Son, why did you lie to me?' What do you reckon, what would God have done, God who is supposed to embody eternal truth, but who turns out to embody lying too, what do you think he would have done if his son had lied to him? If he had promised to save the world, for example, but hadn't done so, and had just said instead, 'Father, I did promise, but now I've thought it over, and so please take me back to heaven anyway.' What would God have done in a situation like that? What do you reckon? I'll tell you what: he would have sent him to hell, that's what he would have done, to the same place he sent his first son." Now Mr Schulz leant in, bringing his mouth close to Indrek's ear, and he said the last words in a hushed, conspiratorial tone, as if God might overhear him. 'Yes, He would have sent His son down there, to be with his brother, because Satan was also God's son, you bear that in mind, Satan was God's first son, his elder son. His father sent him to save the world, but he didn't do it, he promised to, but he didn't keep that promise, he lied to his eternal father, and so he went down to the place where he remains to this day. Because it's not possible that God tried to save the world for the first time only a couple of thousand years ago, the world is so old, much older than salvation. This means that Satan was the first, the first time God tried to save the world, but now poor old Satan is sitting in hell awaiting his own salvation. And you mark my words: there's no use in trying to save man, there's no sense in it, if Satan hasn't yet been saved, because the whole world must be saved. But who will save Satan? God's second son saved man, but who will save Satan, who was God's first son? God can't do that himself, because his word and his will are unchanging. But who can save him then, what do you reckon? Man, man alone can save Satan, and only then can Judgement Day come, not before. But where is this man, who is capable of saving Satan? Will I do it, or will you? Would you care to take on the task of Satan's salvation. No? Me neither. And you mark my words: there's no way that any old person, like me or you, could do it. And even Superman, who has become so fashionable of late, can't do it, because all that is just a farce, it's pure humbug. You understand? Farce and humbug! Nietzsche is a linguistic ropedancer and a conceptual cardsharp, nothing more. Man must save Satan just as he is, *der Mensch an und für sich*,[46] you understand? Man as an idea. Man is searching, and will eventually find eternal truth, which must exist somewhere, otherwise we wouldn't already have the idea of it, the concept. And once man discovers this eternal and undeniable truth, then Satan is saved *eo ipso*,[47] because he is original sin himself, the sin born of the world's salvation. And thus it follows that man

---

46 *der Mensch an und für sich*: "man in himself and for himself"
47 *eo ipso*: "by the thing itself"

must not lie – on no account. Man must always nurture the truth, only the truth, so that eventually the original truth will be born which will save Satan, the only accursed one in this world. But there are few people who fully understand that, apart from me. Until recently I didn't understand it either, otherwise I wouldn't have lied to my father. Do you know now what all these graves are, lying side by side here? They are mounds of lies, one mound beside the other, because there is not a single person lying here who hasn't once lied on someone's deathbed, or who wasn't once lied to himself. Only lies, lies, and more lies, wherever you look. It's awful! But there is more awfulness still to come.' Now the old man brought his face close to Indrek's, his eyes glistening feverishly, and said in a conspiratorial tone, 'Those same lies await us. Even on our deathbeds we won't hear the truth. Do you understand? If you were to ask in God's own language to hear the pure, naked truth, then no one would hear your prayer. Even a servant of God lies on every single deathbed, even him. And God lets it happen. And what is man, if he is lied to like that, and if he lies like that? What is he? Whose face is this? Man has Satan's face, not God's face, much more like Satan's face. I am Satan's face."

By now the old man had turned towards the graves, as if he were addressing them. Indrek watched him for a while: skinny, hunchbacked, a small head, hooked nose, his mouth slack from talking, hairy pockmarked cheeks, glistening eyes – this was what a face made in the image of Satan looked like. But as Indrek stood there watching him, an image from his distant past came back to him. He was sure he'd seen something similar somewhere else before. That's what it was! That's what it was! Pearu's dog had looked just the same, that Christmas evening, when it had been tempted in by the smell of sausages sizzling on the hob, and father had beaten it mercilessly and used the stove poker to push it deep into the water barrel, after which it had fled for dear life, jumping onto the backroom table and leaving a dirty pawprint on the open pages of a prayer book, on the Immanuel prayer. That mark must still be there, Indrek thought to himself, suddenly feeling sorry for that hairy, long-dead dog, because he could still see its shining eyes in the dark gap between the barrels. Feeling upset, he got up from where he'd been sitting and planning to bid farewell to the old man, whom he could no longer bare to watch or listen to, because he reminded him too much of the smell of sausages and the dog which had been beaten to within an inch of its life. But Mr Schulz paid him no attention, he was still busy talking to the graves, those mounds of lies. Indrek started to leave, first taking a couple of steps and looking back at the old man to see if he had noticed. When it was clear that he was oblivious, Indrek left without saying another word. And from that moment on, the graveyard suddenly lost all its charm, even though he couldn't explain to himself why that should be.

But a feeling of despondency and yearning remained. They hung over Indrek for the whole of spring, and were part of the reason why he didn't go anywhere that summer. Of course he secretly hoped that he might be lucky enough to meet Ramilda again, but it was not to be, because she left the country as soon as her studies were over, without so much as setting foot in the dusty town again.

The summer was dry and hot. The sun rose red in the sky, and set just as red, as if it were pouring its blazing heat into the earth, and dust hung in the air like billowing clouds of smoke. The window shutters were kept locked for days on end to stop the sunlight entering the rooms, and at night the air was still suffocatingly hot: even when the sun disappeared from view, the walls of the buildings and the paving stones continued to radiate heat in its place.

Just like the previous summer, Indrek spent his days sitting on a bale of straw in the barn, where everything was exactly as it had always been, untouched by the events of the outside world. The tabby cat chased the mice just as it had before, and Tiina rattled about on her crutches behind the wooden wall, slipping in through the gap now and again to see Indrek. She always had some news to share with him, and it was most often news about Molli, which she clearly thought would be of interest to Indrek.

"Molli is making herself some new shirts," she said to Indrek. "They're really fancy ones, with embroidery and lacework and all. This cloth is snow white and as light as silk; she used to use yellow cloth, it's more long-wearing. I'll show you just how light and white it is, if you want. She hides the shirts in the dressing cabinet when she goes out, but I know where the key is. I can show you if you like. Mother says that the last time she wore shirts like that was when father was alive, and they were still rich. That was before I was born, mother said. By the time I arrived they were already poor, which means that I am the child of poor folk. But Molli was born before me. Molli says she's making herself shirts which are fit for her station, and mother said that thanks to Molli we'll be all be fit for our station. But Molli doesn't like that idea, she doesn't want us all to be fit for our station, she wants to be the only one. You two haven't got the right shirts she says to me and mother, what station can you possibly belong to! And it's true, have a look if you want." And with that Tiina lifted up her little skirt and showed Indrek what was covering her puny frame. Then she said: "now you know what station I'm from; but come with me, I'll show you Molli's station too, just so you know. Come, there's no one at home, and I know where the key is kept."

It was clear that Tiina wanted desperately to show Indrek Molli's "station", as she put it, but Indrek didn't want to look. And so the air was tense between them, because Tiina couldn't understand why Indrek wouldn't want to see Molli's new shirts, if Tiina knew where the key was kept. But Indrek had a story of his own related to shirts, which he didn't mention a word of to Tiina. He couldn't help wondering how it could be that he'd had a run in at home with his sister over some shirts, just now he'd fallen out with Tiina over

376

shirts, and that time at his friend Metslang's he'd jumped out of the window because of a shirt. That's right, Indrek thought, it had all happened because of the shirt which had been covering the shoulders and breasts of the girl who had curled herself up under his chin in bed that time. That shirt, covering that naked body, had had a strange effect on Indrek, that was why he had jumped down onto the stones and hurt himself. It was only now that Indrek could explain those events to himself.

But Ramilda must have a shirt too, she must have. It was strange that the thought had never crossed Indrek's mind before then. Although it wasn't as if the thought had come to him just like that, he was willing himself to think it. For Indrek, Ramilda was like some beautiful statue which was best left uncovered. Ramilda was like a painting which he'd seen in a gallery one time: an empty desert under a blazing red sky, some bones bleached white by the sun – nothing more. Or another picture: a tall tree, standing alone, with leafy branches, stooping over some low bushes. But high in the sky an eagle was circling, eying the bushes, as if some prey must be hiding there. The sky was an intense blue. That was what Ramilda was like for Indrek, and so he never pictured her in a shirt, he never thought about what kind of shirt she might have.

Chapter 32

When the last of the swallow chicks had left their nests, autumn came; only then did it dare to, no sooner. The tabby cat sat in the shed watching out for mice who had come to spend the winter there, because they had no wings with which to fly to warmer climes.

The new academic year started, and with it there were all kinds of activities to be involved in, arrangements to be made, and rushing about to be done – from morning to night, sometimes from night to morning too, as if in all the commotion night had swapped places with day. The doorbell rang incessantly, as if it had an electric charge running through it. But there was no electricity, there were only students, returning like migratory birds after their travels, bringing with them lots of new students too.

A week or so earlier Mr Miilinõmm had arrived; he was a former student of Maurus' establishment who had gone to Germany to continue his studies. It was true that he hadn't completed his studies at Mr Maurus's place, but then Germany was the kind of country where you could always find some way to edify yourself. Even if you didn't know what you were looking for, all you had to was turn up, and you'd soon find something, somewhere to edify you, and you wouldn't return to the homeland until you were fully edified, which was exactly what Mr Miilinõmm had done. Before he'd gone to Germany he'd had a fringe which fell over his left eye, but on returning fully edified he wore his handsome brown hair combed back, creating a modest bouffant, which, together with his clipped beard, had the effect of making his face seem longer and thinner than it was. This was supposed to demonstrate to everyone, including to Miilinõmm himself, that he had returned from Germany much more dolichocephalic than when he had left. A true European should be dolichocephalic, Miilinõmm reckoned, and not brachycephalic. And with this new-found conviction he returned to Mr Maurus's establishment, hoping to find some way of earning his daily crust, before fixing himself up with a position which better befitted a man of his calibre; it was well known that at Maurus's establishment an edified man could always find some way of earning his daily crust.

Miilinõmm moved in with Koovi, because no other room was available. They were both quiet, calm individuals, which was why they thought they would be well matched, and Mr Maurus thought so too. But for some reason the conversations between these quiet, calm individuals quickly got very lively, one could say agitated even, as if they were on the verge of falling out. And yet they didn't really have any reason to fall out, they were simply debating an academic point, nothing more. Miilinõmm had recently been pumped full of Marx and Nietzsche, whether more Marx or more Nietzsche wasn't clear, but it was clear that he'd had a good dose of the pair of them. And whenever someone learns something new, then he wants everyone to know about it, and so it was down to that natural human weakness that those lively conversations, verging on arguments, came about between Miilinõmm and Koovi. In fact Koovi didn't have the slightest clue about Marxism or Superman. As far as he was concerned those two things were antipodes, but Miilinõmm was sure that one had given rise to the other. In order to be a true Marxist or Christian one first had to be a Superman.

"We've been reciting the words of Christ for two thousand years now, but you'd be lucky to find a true Christian anywhere in Europe, or anywhere else for that matter!" cried Miilinõmm. "Before a Christian can become a true Christian, he has first to become a Superman, because being a Christian isn't any easier than being a Marxist. So, first Superman, then Christian or Marxist, or the other way around, it's not important. Sow a Superman and reap a Christian, that's the new Superman, or sow a Christian and you'll reap a Marxist, which is the new Christian, which is Superman. That's how it goes, in short, and in philosophical terms. *Negation der Negation*... seed, shoot, new seed. Superman negates man, his seed, the Christian negates Superman, his shoot, the Marxist negates the Christian, or the other way round. That's clear enough, isn't it? Christ had already realised that himself, which is why he talked about him who is not born of water and the Spirit. What does that mean? It means Superman, no less. First you have to be born of water and the Spirit, and only then..."

"First nothing, then you get something," Koovi interrupted him with a laugh.

"That's not relevant here, that's another category altogether," Miilinõmm replied. "A man already is something. Or you think he is not?"

"You could ask the same question of God," Koovi replied.

"Please don't get God and man mixed up!" Miilinõmm cried.

"Why ever not?" Koovi asked. "How do you know who created whom?"

"Why is it so important to know," Miilinõmm asked, "what came first, the chicken or the egg, the egg or the chicken? It makes no difference who created whom, what matters is that in the end the creature kills the creator. If God created man, for example, then the last man will kill God. You get it? I mean that in a philosophical sense, of course. If man's representation is extinguished, then God no longer exists either, however wide the world – the *Weltall* – might be."[48]

"So if man no longer exists, then the world no longer exists either, is that what you're saying?" Koovi asked.

"What are you talking about?!" Miilinõmm yelled at the

---

48 *Weltall*: "space"

top of his voice. Silly questions like that always made their conversations more heated, their voices louder, the tone more agitated; yet it was neither Marx nor Nietzsche who were to blame, but Koovi and his silly question. "The world is a fact, whereas God is not."

"How do you know that the world is a fact?" Koovi asked again. "What if the world were the creation of man's brain, just like God? What if it were just like mathematics or music or something? Or do you think that the world is the same for turkeys and earthworms as it is for us? What if there were creatures which experienced our world not as something tangible and certain but as some sort of empty space in the universe? Take for example that creature or character which we call electricity. He must experience the world roughly like that. For him the air is so hard that sparks fly when he comes up against it, as if it were firestone or something. And yet for him a metal wire is like a hole which has been bored into that hard substance, the same air which you and me breathe in and out. Is that not the case?"

"It's not as if man can think of all possible worlds; he's only interested in what belongs to him, what he can sense. A horse may have his own world and his own god, but that's got nothing to do with us, because we're humans. And so my point holds: the planet earth is a fact, but God is not. The planet earth makes flames shoot out from Vesuvius, but God doesn't."

"But how do you know?" asked Koovi, refusing to back down. "What if it is God who sends the flames shooting out of Vesuvius? What do you say to that? Has anyone ever been to the crater to see who's making all those flames?"

"There's no point trying to have a serious conversation with you," Miilinõmm said. "Everything is so prosaic with you; you turn it all into a silly joke. One starts to feel as if one is living in the kind of country where they argue over the relative merits of the economy and the higher ideals of humanity. Ideals all over the place, but alongside them collectives for agricultural workers, trade unions for bulls, the breeding of cultivars, recommendations for artificial fertilisers."

And with that Miilinõmm was finished for the day, because they'd started on subjects which were close to the homeland, subjects which always seemed too narrowly focussed and cumbersome, subjects which didn't arouse one to flights of fancy or to dreams. But Miilinõmm liked to dream, especially in a learned and philosophical key. He found himself awe-struck by thoughts such as the following, "It's such a shame that I won't be alive a thousand years or so from now, by then Superman will already exist. I wonder what he'll do with himself when he gets here? Will he become a writer or a philosopher or a poet or maybe a scholar? If I were a superman, I would become a scholar and I'd resolve all of the outstanding questions, then scholarship would finally have clear boundaries and goals. All that Marxism, Darwinism, Lamarckism, Nietzscheism, Kantism with its *Ding an Sich*49 – all of them would be resolved with one fell swoop, and we would see what poor mankind does when all those questions are resolved."

"You'd be better off finding yourself a rich woman to marry and enjoying life," Koovi advised. It was intended as a broadside across Miilinõmm's bow, because he was the one who believed that anyone with any sense should try their hardest to avoid work, and let others worry about things like that. Anyone with any sense would inherit money, win it, or marry for money, and live off it for the rest of their lives.

"Why does she need to start off rich?" Miilinõmm asked, as if he had completely failed to get the point. "She can always come by money later. She could go into business, some big business, some sort of super business, she could trade in expensive leathers, elephant tusks, ostrich feathers, opium or slaves, she could buy up all the other business, and then fix the prices as high as she wanted, as high as the heart desired."

"But where does that leave Marxism?" Koovi asked

---

49 *Ding an Sich*: "thing in itself"

"You're such a cruel man," Miilinõmm said. "I'm giving my fantasy free reign, but all you do is niggle and rile, first with your talk of rich women, and then Marxism."

"But that's the problem, all you do is fantasise," said Koovi. "You fantasise about things which might never happen. Maybe Superman will never appear, maybe Marxism won't either, just as Christianity never really came. All man does is talk, so as to avoid having to do anything. As you say yourself, we've been talking about Christianity for two thousand years, so much so that it's starting to get a bit boring, then we'll talk about socialism for another two thousand, that way we'll have put the whole thing off for a whole four thousand years. The question is, is it a good thing or not. I reckon it's a very good thing. Just think: Christ was a Jew, John the Baptist was a Jew and Marx was a Jew just like his apostle Lassalle. The aim of Christ's teachings was to make the masses stare at the sky so that their masters could take their pick from the bread bag more easily. But what if Marxism was thought up for just the same reason? The heavens no longer beckoned, they were too lofty, too distant, and so another Jew came up with Marxism, which wasn't up there in the heavens but down here on earth: just wait another two thousand years until everything has been collectivised, and the necessary organisational structures have been created, then the bread bag will open for the poor man too. Sounds great, doesn't it?"

"But what about when people get bored of Marxism, what do you think will happen then? And will it be some Jew's idea again? For the third time running?"

Of course Koovi had no idea how to answer that question, and so Miilinõmm carried on fantasising: "Something will definitely come in its place. Man is the kind of animal who always seeks solace of some sort. Other animals are happy just living their lives, but not man. Just think of the thief on the cross alongside Jesus! He robs, he murders, but he doesn't know how to die without seeking solace, he wants to go to heaven. Have you ever heard anything more crazy and stupid? Can you think of a better example of man demeaning himself? It shows how wretched man is and how much we need a Superman. If you've lived your life as a robber, then die a robber – let justice be done. But don't think you can go killing people and then, when you're staring your own death in the face, you start blabbing. Just like a little child, there's no other word for it. A sissy, not a real man! Pah!"

Miilinōmm spat forcefully to show the strength of his disdain for man at that moment, and how heartfelt was his yearning for a Superman.

But Mr Maurus wasn't happy that mankind was disdained and Superman lauded within earshot of his "honest and decent" boys. And so he went and asked Miilinōmm and Koovi to try and resolve their academic differences a bit more quietly. But Miilinōmm wasn't prepared to hide his light under a bushel, as he put it. Otherwise what would have been the point of him going to Germany to further his studies? And so the situation developed in the only way it could.

"You've heard that man," said Maurus to his boys. "He speaks only of Marx and of unification, as if that's all he knew how to talk about. But what good is unification to us? What's the point of talking so much about something which no one has seen, and might never see! Is this unification long or short, thin or fat? No one knows, not even Mr Miilinōmm, because there's been no unifications in Germany either. There haven't even been any in Russia. And it's such a huge country that somewhere, in some distant corner of it there could well have been some kind of unification, but no, there hasn't. A calf was born there with two, maybe three heads, but there still haven't been any unifications. And do you know who thought the idea up? Some German who suffered from a vile, dirty disease, and when that disease started to make him go mad, he came up with that unification idea. But why does Mr Miilinōmm talk about him? Has he got some vile, dirty disease too? He hasn't, because he goes to the same sauna as you do, just as any decent Estonian man should, and there's nothing wrong with him. Is he mad?

No, not yet. Does he want to go mad? Has anyone heard that Mr Miilinõmm wants to go mad? No? No one has heard that? But Mr Maurus knows what Miilinõmm does want: he wants to go to Siberia, not our own Siberia, but that other one, which is the other side of the Urals. But he doesn't want to go there alone, he wants us to go there with him. That's why he's always talking about Superman and about Marxism. Because Marxism and socialism and socialists get sent to Siberia. But the cold will get to those socialists in Siberia. Minus forty! Sometimes more! Fifty! Sometimes more than that! What use is socialism when it's minus forty? So let's look after ourselves. Mr Miilinõmm can go to Siberia if he wants, and we'll go to the madhouse, there's plenty of unification there."

Mr Maurus laughed. But at that moment the doorbell rang and a courier entered with a book for Mr Miilinõmm, which he'd ordered from Germany.

"What book is that?" Mr Maurus asked the courier.

"I don't know," he replied.

"What? You don't know what you're delivering?" Mr Maurus said, in a tone which mixed surprise and reproach.

The courier read from the delivery slip, "Sociology."

The word seemed to cut Mr Maurus to the quick.

"What was that?" he asked.

"Sociology," the man replied.

"Take that book back," said Mr Maurus. "Take it away right now."

"But why Mr Headmaster?" the man asked.

"Don't answer back when Mr Maurus is telling you to do something. Just take the book back!"

"But Mr Maurus, I'm under instructions, I have to…"

"What you have to do is take that book right back where it came from."

"But Mr Miilinõmm lives here, doesn't he?" the courier asked.

"That's none of your business," Mr Maurus snapped at him. "Take your book back!"

The courier left the book on the table and fled, as if pursued by demons. Mr Maurus made chase as far as the front door, but stopped there when he felt the cold late-autumn rain against his face. He called after the courier, but he just went on his way without responding, as if he had been suddenly struck deaf and dumb.

Mr Maurus ran back into the classroom and yelled, "Paas! Get your umbrella right away and take that book back to the shop!"

"I don't have an umbrella," Indrek replied.

"What is that supposed to mean? It's raining and you've got no umbrella. Why ever not?"

"I haven't got round to buying one yet," said Indrek.

"That's always the way," the headmaster grumbled. "Whenever Mr Maurus needs something, no one has got it. Who has got an umbrella?"

But no one possessed an umbrella, and even if they did, then they had lent it to someone.

"I'll go like this," said Indrek, "I'll put the book under my coat."

"Go and buy yourself an umbrella," said Mr Maurus after a short pause, and started looking for money in his pocket. But, failing to find the money required, he asked: "Who's got some money? Who can lend Mr Maurus some money? Come on, Mr Maurus doesn't have any time to waste."

But no one had any money, or if they did, they didn't want to admit it. Mr Maurus didn't have the time to go upstairs and fetch some money, so he said, "Give me some paper and a pen then. Or are you going to tell me there's no paper and pen in Mr Maurus' establishment either? No umbrella, no money, no paper, no pen, no ink, no nothing."

Some paper did materialise. An envelope, in fact. But it wasn't required, because Mr Maurus had already ripped a corner off a newspaper, and scribbled something in German on it: "One umbrella for Mr Maurus. Cheap but good quality. I'm waiting. Mr Maurus." Then he folded it several times and gave it to Indrek.

"Hold it in your hand and put your hand in your pocket, then it won't get wet," he said. "Now run, run as fast as you can, show us that there's some use to be had from those long legs of yours. But don't open the umbrella when you get it, Mr Maurus wants to try it out first!" yelled Mr Maurus from the doorway.

Returning with the umbrella, Indrek bumped into Miilinõmm just outside the school, and they entered together. As soon as he saw Miilinõmm, Mr Maurus forgot all about the umbrella and rounded on him.

"What's this?" he asked him, pointing at the book on the table.

"It's a book," said Miilinõmm, picking it up to examine it.

"What book?" asked Mr Maurus, pursuing his investigation.

"It's 'sociology'," Miilinõmm replied.

"Who gave you the permission to order books like this, for delivery to Mr Maurus' establishment?"

"No permission is required," said Miilinõmm. "It's not as if it's a proscribed book."

"This man can't speak German," Mr Maurus said to his boys in Estonian. "He's been to Germany to continue his studies, but he doesn't understand German. Mr Maurus asked him clearly and concisely: who gave permission to order the book? And he answers: it's not proscribed."

Miilinõmm was clearly offended, and he answered in Estonian.

"Mr Maurus, what do you want of me?"

"I want you to give me a clear and concise answer: who gave you the permission to order this kind of book to my school? Am I making myself clear enough?"

"You are indeed," said Miilinõmm.

"Then answer me with similar clarity: who gave you the permission?"

"But Mr Maurus, it requires no permission," said Miilinõmm.

Clearly incensed by that reply, the headmaster turned to

his boys and shouted, "You hear that? This man is crazy! All that unification has driven him mad, just like that other one. Unification drives everyone mad! I asked him, who gave him permission. He replies, it's not required."

"But that's how it is," explained Miilinõmm, "this book isn't banned in Russia."

"Now you can hear for yourself, this man is totally crazy!" the headmaster yelled at the boys. "It's not banned in Russia, which means that it must be allowed in Mr Maurus' establishment. Nice! Very nice! Horse dung isn't banned in Russia either, so anyone who cares to can drive into Mr Maurus' establishment and dump a load of it in the middle of the room. Is that really how things stand? You tell me, is this man crazy or is he not, talking the way he does?!"

"Mr Maurus, I've been to Germany to further my studies and I know very well what horse dung is, but that book isn't dung, if it were I wouldn't have ordered it, because we've got quite enough of our own dung here as it is," said Miilinõmm, raising his voice.

"I ask you not shout in my school!" yelled Mr Maurus.

"You're shouting yourself," said Miilinõmm angrily.

"But I am allowed to shout, because this is my school, these are my boys, and I am their headmaster."

"And that's exactly why you're no longer my headmaster," Miilinõmm snapped back.

"As long as you live under my roof I am your headmaster, and you're not allowed to order these kinds of books, because they will corrupt my school. Do you understand what I'm saying? Anyone who doesn't care to abide by the rules can leave Mr Maurus's school right away."

"Mr Maurus's school is a heap of dung!" shouted Miilinõmm.

"Do you hear that, do you hear!" Mr Maurus wailed. "My school is a dung heap! Said by a man who has no dung heap of his own, and so has to use my school for that purpose. Get out of here this very moment!" he shouted in Miilinõmm's face.

"I'm gone," Miilinõmm replied.

"Get a move on then!" shouted Mr Maurus.

Miilinõmm went to his room to pack his things, while Mr Maurus continued addressing his boys, "That man is totally crazy. Not banned indeed! Everything is banned in Mr Maurus's establishment if Mr Maurus hasn't expressly allowed it. So what if it's allowed in Russia. In Russia you're allowed to blow your nose into your hand, but that's because the Russian state is so huge and so populous that if you were to try to give everyone handkerchiefs, then you'd quickly run out of cloth. His Majesty the Tsar knows that all too well. But is Mr Maurus' state also so huge, that he'd run out of cloth, if he gave handkerchiefs to all his boys? No, there wouldn't be any shortage of cloth here. That's why blowing your nose into your hand is allowed in Russia, but banned in Mr Maurus's establishment. Understood? But why is the reading of sociology banned in Mr Maurus's establishment? It's because in Mr Maurus's establishment, no one knows where sociology ends and socialism begins. Just think for yourselves: one starts with 'socio', the other with 'socia', there's hardly any difference in it. 'o' in one, 'a' in the other, and that's it. *Der Unterschied ist ganz unbestimmt.*[50] It's just the endings which are different – 'ism' and 'logy'. So as soon as you start reading sociology, it's a short path to socialism, and from there to minus forty – Siberia. Understood?"

Of course Mr Maurus's boys understood, when Mr Maurus himself explained it to them. They even understood when they didn't have the slightest clue what he was talking about, as in this particular case. But one thing was clear: Miilinõmm had to leave, either because of sociology or because of socialism, which meant that both of these things must be pretty interesting. Both them and Superman, who would make you go mad with some vile sickness.

---

50 Der Unterschied ist ganz unbestimmt: "the difference is quite unclear"

Chapter 33

And so everyone at the school was burning with curiosity, a curiosity which became ever more intense, as if some bug had started to spread amongst the students. The most active carrier of the bug was a new student who had arrived from Saint Petersburg, an Englishman called Solotarski, who was eighteen years old, skinny and bespectacled with a hooked nose and fleshy lips. He somehow had a way of speaking and comporting himself which was intended to demonstrate that he was cleverer than everyone else. Whenever he parted his plump lips all sorts of "isms" sprung forth, from socialism, to nihilism and Superman, from Darwinism to atheism and the dinosaurs, especially dinosaurs, as a result of which he earned himself the nickname Saurus. Saurus loved nothing more than launching himself into vivid monologues about his long-extinct namesakes, standing on a chair, a table or on anything which placed him above his fellow students. He puffed out his cheeks, spread his arms wide, rolled his goggly eyes, gnashed his teeth one of which was gold (it was the only gold tooth in the whole school), stretched out his thin neck or retracted it back between his narrow shoulders as he crouched down, crawled on all fours, played the hunchback, thrusted his chest out proudly, threw his head back or let it drop onto his chest. In short, everyone found his performances pretty funny. And then, having caught everyone's attention he would suddenly ask, "But what is an animal's most important organ? What determines his standing in the natural order? Is it his length of fifteen *süld* or his height of five? Is it his five-inch teeth? His three-foot tusks? His horns or his hooves? No, my good sirs, none of these things means a jot. The most important thing is right here," he said, tapping his forehead. "This is where the most important organ is located, on which all else depends. Neither teeth nor tusks, fleetness of foot or wide wings, not even great bodily proportions can help, if there's nothing up here."

He tapped his forehead again, and he managed to do so in a way which suggested that he was the only one who had anything behind his forehead, whereas everyone else had nothing there at all, or at the very best a hollow cavity.

"But did the dinosaurs have anything up there in that upper cavity of theirs? What do you think? No, they didn't have much at all. And where are they now, with those massive bodies of theirs? Where are they now with their horns and their teeth, their legs and their wings? They've disappeared off the face of the earth! Gone completely! And it was because they had nothing up here." This time he patted his forehead with the palm of his hand. "But I've got something up here," he continued. "And so I can say with full justification: the real king of the dinosaurs is not some fifteen-*süld* atlantosaurus or seven-*süld* brontosaurus but me, Vladimir Solotarski. You may laugh that I call myself Saurus, but I'm thinking about the whole human race. Or is it wrong to compare humankind with the dinosaurs? Who rules the world? Once it was the dinosaur, but now it's me, Saurus, king of the sauruses. You laugh again? Once more you forget that when I refer to myself, I'm thinking of the whole human race."

Indeed, the listeners did tend to forget that the speaker thought of himself as a representative of the human species, and felt that he was comparing himself with the dinosaurs, which was what they were laughing at. And yet the speaker continued heedless, "Or does someone think of the elephant as more important than me, Vladimir Solotarski? Does the lion outdo me in some way? Or are you not familiar with the rifle? Have you seen a machine gun? So then, I'm more important than any boa snake. Have you ever known a dinosaur to make a pair of spectacles or have you ever heard a hippopotamus play the violin? But I wear spectacles, and I play the violin – better than any of you. And I tell you this: if my fingers were just a little bit longer then I would be world famous. I'm telling you – world famous! And it's just my fingers, not my talent, not my brain which are the obstacle. So I've decided to stand aside, make way for the rest of them, and I don't take part in any competitions. Let Hubermann or someone play, I won't play, his fingers are longer than mine anyway. Why do you think Paganini played so well? He had longer fingers than anyone else, that's why. There are plenty of others with enough talent, it's just that their fingers are too short, they can't reach the high notes. There's no shortage of brains out there. But animals lack them, which is why humankind evolved. Millions of animals were required, from the infusoria to the dinosaur, to eventually arrive at me, Vladimir Solotarski, by which I mean humankind as a whole. That was the end goal. Now it has been reached: here you have my head, my hands, my feet, my eyes, my ears, my brain and a million animals can get lost. There's no longer any need for them, no need to select for the human. Do you know who the father of that wisdom is? It's Darwin, Charles Darwin, and all the rest of them are rubbish. Nietzsche's Superman is total rubbish, without Darwin he would have never come up with him. If you take evolution away from man, then I, Vladimir Solotarski, would like to know how you intend to arrive at the Superman. Marxism is a pygmy alongside Darwinism, because one of them wants to seize the whole world in its embrace, while the latter just gives mankind a little crack of the whip. And there we have it: evolution is the wisdom which tells us that I, Vladimir Solotarski, am descended from dinosaurs which grew to be fifteen *süld* long and seven *süld* tall. You get it? Me, a man, mankind. There's nothing else you need to know. Whosoever understands that understands me and Darwin. But that Superman is just child's play – after all, it would be easy enough to turn me into a Superman, but just try and jump from a dinosaur to a human. That's the real difference between Nietzsche and Darwin."

With his small, puny frame, his weak eyes and his lacquered

hair, Solotarski stood amidst a crowd of students, presenting his wisdom tirelessly. While his companions laughed at him and joked about the incongruity of those enormous dinosaurs producing such a tiny son, they couldn't fail to respect him and be a little in awe of him.

News of Solotarski's cleverness and eloquence reached Mr Maurus' ears, because everything reached his ears, even much smaller things than dinosaurs. He couldn't treat him the same way that he had treated Miilinõmm, because Solotarski paid well for his place at the school; in any case, Mr Maurus didn't consider him to be such a dangerous influence as Miilinõmm. But he did know an effective way to reduce Solotarski's sway, which he soon put into play: he gradually let it be more widely known that Solotarski was in fact no Englishman, but a Jew, who had moved from London to St. Petersburg.

"You have to understand that he's an English Jew," he said to Indrek and Vainukägu one time, as if he were revealing a major secret. "Of course that's something altogether different from a Russian Jew, because an Englishman is not the same thing as a Russian. The Englishman lectures us about evolution, he teaches us that the bird evolved from the reptile, the animal from the bird, the monkey from the animal, and then man from the monkey, the European from the man, the Englishman from the European, and then the English Jew adds: the Jew from the Englishman. And that's the highest stage there is. But what does this highest of beings do? He gets up to monkey business, that's what he does. He lectures us about socialism, which is nothing but pure monkey business. But Mr Maurus knows all those old Jewish tricks. The Jew teaches us: don't worry about what tomorrow might bring. But what does he do himself? Oh, that Jew worries alright! He does nothing else but worry. While everyone else is busy not worrying, he worries double, to make sure that everything goes his way. The Jew wanted to gain salvation, so what did he do? Did he nail Christ up on the cross? No, a decent Roman had to do it in his place. The Roman had to spill innocent blood, while

393

the Jew got his salvation. Pontius Pilate, or is it Pilate Pontius, can wash his hands as much as he likes, but there's only one thing that really counts: the Jews had their way with him. And this is why I think that Judas was no Jew. A Jew wouldn't have let himself get caught in a trap, end up getting himself hung like that. A Jew always makes sure he has other options. But what options did Judas have? None at all. He didn't even gain salvation. Both he and Pontius perished because they were responsible for the sentencing and then the murder of Jesus. And so Judas fell into the Jewish trap just like the Roman, Pilate. We condemn them to this day, but the Jews, they gave the world Jesus, the bringer of our salvation! And so what does this tell us: some people do great things but get nothing in return, while others do nothing and get given everything. Thus is God's will to this day. And consider this: the Roman is dead, while the Jew lives on. I tell you: the Englishman will die out one day too, but the Jew never will. Do you know why? Because the Jew goes around teaching everyone: don't believe in God, don't believe in anything, but at the same time he holds on to Jehovah's frock for dear life, and that saves him, Jehovah will always save him. Such are the tricks of those Jews. That's why one should never believe someone if he tells you he is an Englishman, because an Englishman might well be a Jew too."

That was how Mr Maurus explained the difference between an Englishman and a Jew to his boys. And even if they weren't left any the wiser, and didn't take the headmaster's words seriously, because of all members of the establishment his words were taken less seriously than anyone else's, a shadow of doubt was nevertheless cast over Solotarski.

But that still couldn't dampen the boy's interest in all the grand ideas which had taken flight. The clearest evidence of that could be seen in the more senior classes, where the students' studies increasingly fell into neglect. For how could you carry on studying as before, as if nothing had happened, when your world now contained Superman and evolution, and when all the dinosaurs were long-since dead.

Chapter 34

Indrek was amongst those whose studies suffered, but he had his own reason besides the dinosaurs. He had received a letter from Germany, a simple, short letter, consisting of no more than a few lines. But somehow it upset him more than ever.

> Do you ever get bored? I do. Sometimes I get awfully bored. That's why I'm writing. Don't be angry, nor too happy either, because I'm writing out of boredom. I won't write too much today, but if it turns out to be of any use, then more will follow. I won't send you my address today, you don't need to know it. In any case, I'll probably be leaving this place soon, so the address would be of no use.
>
> Rimalda.

There was no subject line, nor name from which one could discern who those lines were intended for, as if it made no difference who read them, as long as someone did. And yet Indrek's name was written on the envelope in large letters, in plain sight. Judging by the handwriting, the address had been written by someone else and not Ramilda herself, because Indrek was sure that Rimalda couldn't have had handwriting like that.

Indrek read those empty lines again and again, pausing over each sentence, each word, each letter, as if they might reveal some secret to him.

Rimilda hadn't written her address, which could only mean that she didn't want Indrek to reply. That's probably for the best, he thought, and yet he couldn't resist writing, not with the intention of sending anything off straight away, but just for the sake of it, to see whether he was able to reply to a letter like that should he have to. But he found out that he couldn't; he couldn't do it at all. He made a lot of attempts, but he ripped every single one of them to bits. If only he could succeed in writing that one and only right reply, then he would keep it, set it aside somewhere, maybe even into storage together with the mug handles, so that later he would be able to take it out and read it, and maybe show someone, first the letter he'd received from abroad, and then how he'd replied to it. But now he had nothing, he had nothing to show for his week-long efforts, because sometimes you can write and write as much as you like, but it never seems right. Eventually another letter arrived, a long letter, this time signed Ramilda instead of Rimalda. The change of name in itself took its toll on Indrek. If the first letter had made him fret, this second one almost made him lose his mind. And the worst thing was that there was no one he could talk to about it.

The letter had mostly been written in pencil, and clearly not in one sitting, not even in one day, it was too long for that. It went as follows:

The first letter seemed to be some help, otherwise I wouldn't be writing again. Although to tell the truth, this is not really a letter, just a way of passing the time. Sometimes I feel the need to have a natter, but to remain silent at the same time, because I can't be bothered to open my mouth, that's why I've decided to write. That's why I didn't send you my address in that first letter, because if you'd replied it wouldn't be the same kind of silent chatter, would it? And it's hard for me to believe that you wouldn't have replied, if I had sent my address, because you're just too good a person not to. You would have been sure to reply. Of course there is another reason why I'm not going to give you my address in this letter either, and it's the main reason; as I told you in the earlier letter, I really do have to leave here soon, there is no longer any doubt about that. So I ask you to wait a little while, until I find a more permanent place to live, then

I'll tell you the address, I'll definitely tell you. Until then, please resign yourself to the fact that I'm chatting and you're listening, as if you were my friend. It's true that you're better suited to being my friend than anyone in the world. Because it looks like there aren't many people who care about me, no one really wants to be friends with me. What's more, I'm often in a bad mood, and if a girl is bad-tempered when she's young, what's she going to be like when she's older? But I've done a lot of things which you would need to forgive me for. "That's enough!" yelled Indrek. "I've had enough!"

Of course there's no point writing about that to you. In any case, I wanted to ask you something, it's just that the other thing got in the way. My question is pointless, but I'll ask it anyway. And please reply to me in Estonian, because I've noticed that people are much more honest and direct in their mother tongues than in any other. That's why diplomats – I've become acquainted with one here – have to know foreign languages, otherwise they wouldn't be able to lie so well. We've been lied to least of all in our mother tongue, because it's spoken by those who are nearest to us, people who have spoken the most heartfelt words to us, words which are so heartfelt that we'll never hear their like again. How could you lie in a language in which you've heard so much truth said and so much tenderness expressed? And even if you do lie, then before long you will remember that this is the language of your truth, your tenderness and so you hold back a bit. Don't you agree? That's the reason why writers and poets only use their mother tongue, because it's the language of truth and tenderness. I'm sure that is the case. It might sound silly, but I'm sure it is! That's why I'm so scared of fibbing to you, because I'm writing in a foreign language. Please bear that in mind – a foreign language, because I've come to the conclusion that German is a foreign language for me after all: I've noticed that it's much easier for me to lie in German than in Estonian. That's why. Remember what I once told you about the German language and love? You probably

397

don't remember, but I remember it as if it were yesterday. Back then I told you that German was the only language to use if you want to declare true love politely. Now I am of completely the opposite view. I hope you understand what I mean? Love is the most important thing there is in our life, that's my strong conviction, and just think, my views about declaring love have changed completely. And if I should ever find someone in this life whom I love, then I could only tell them so in Estonian. Only Estonian. Even if I were to love a German, and were to write to him, I would start the letter in Estonian: *armas, kallis*.[51] Any man who loves me should at least be able to learn those two words. He can write to me in Chinese for all I care, but I want those two words to be in Estonian. That's obligatory!

.... the first two times I wrote I didn't get round to asking the question I wanted to ask you, but I'll try to do that now. But please swear to me that you will honest and frank in your answer. My question is the following: am I too German? I'm sure you know what I mean? I personally don't think I am, after all, I wanted to use my mother tongue to declare love, which is the most important thing there is, and can anyone who wants to do that really be accused of being too German? After all, a truly Germanified Estonian grows up hearing only a foreign language. Can you imagine what it must be like for someone not to hear their mother tongue at home, school or church? I'm sure you don't understand me. But it's a very simple point. Tell me, does the Germanified Estonian really believe he is a German? Of course he doesn't. But how can German become his mother tongue, if he knows that he is not a German? In other words, what does every Germanified Estonian mother do to her children right from the very start? She lies to them; she lies to them when they're still in the womb, telling them: you're a German. Do you realise what that means, when a mother lies to her children like that

---

51 *armas, Kallis*: "sweetheart, honey"

from their earliest age? I suspect that as a man you don't fully understand that. What do you think becomes of that kind of mother and the child of that kind of mother? After all, it can't possibly be that all love of the truth, all honesty has been entirely extinguished in that mother, even towards her child, the person who she has brought into the world. Surely there must be moments when she can see more clearly, when she starts to feel pain and shame for herself and her child. And you understand that this lasts a whole lifetime, even after the child has realised that their own mother lied to them from an early age and is still lying? And that this goes on from one generation to another? But what then becomes of the human being who lies with full awareness that they are doing so, from the cradle to the grave? Just think what happens to people who come together in their masses as Germans, despite the fact that every one of them knows very well that none of them really are. And they go to church in their herds with this same lie, and they go to communion. They hope to gain forgiveness for their sins while continuing to lie. They receive Christ's body and blood from the preacher, but they carry on lying. I've lied like that myself, which is how I know. But what becomes of a person who lies like that from generation to generation? Nothing can become of them, because they have been poisoned, not as living beings, but for death. I've been told that there are poisons which dry out the corpse. The primordial lie seeps into the Germanified Estonian like a poison, drying them out spiritually and intellectually, so that they are like sponges, like living mummies. This is why the Germanified Estonian knows nothing of art and literature, because a mummy lacks the living organs with which to make spiritual or intellectual contact with the living.

.... You must have heard of Darwin, that Englishman who made human beings from monkeys. We have self-development lectures and groups here, and I sometimes attend them. Not that I go there to learn anything in particular, but just to listen for the sake of listening. I think that's why most people

399

go, because it's good for their health. Darwin is good for the health too, so I listened to the lecture about him as well. He teaches us that everything evolves. But if that Englishman had known about our Germanified Estonians then he would surely have said: everything apart from them. That's exactly what he would have said, and he would even have found a scientific term for it, in Latin of course. But that clever Englishman didn't know any of our German Estonians. And when I think that he studied all the forests, the landmasses, the seas, the flowers, the trees, the animals, the people, he studied them very thoroughly, but he left out the German Estonian, then I start to feel sorry for him, believe it or not. What good was all that knowledge of his if he overlooked the most obvious, the most important case – an animal which doesn't evolve. That shoots a big hole through Darwinism, and I just can't have any faith in it anymore. If Darwin were still alive, then I would definitely have written to him about it, but the lecturer said he was already dead. He died before his time! And Goethe too. Remember what I once told you about Goethe? It was so stupid of me! Just think! I'm much cleverer now. Much more! Now I think like this: what would happen if someone were to come up to me and say: Ramilda Maurus, rejoice and be well again, because Goethe lives and next year he's coming to this very place to recuperate. What do you think, is such joy possible, joy which could make a sick person healthy? Even if it is the kind of sickness which otherwise has no cure? After all, there are people who are so sick that they will never get well again. I'm sure you don't understand that, because you've never been sick. But I understand it very well. Not that I have an incurable sickness, but I was sick, and so I understand it much better than you. And what would happen if Goethe were indeed to come here next year, but I were to know in advance that I would no longer be here? Do you understand what I'm trying to say? I want to tell you that if someone were to come to me, today or tomorrow, with joyous tidings that Goethe is still alive and is coming to our sanitorium next summer, then I would be so afraid for my health that I would be sure to die. Without doubt! Because the thought that Goethe could be walking down the street, or sitting under the shade of some tree, and you're no longer around, that thought is so awful, that I start to feel dizzy and see stars. That's why it's a good thing that Goethe is no longer with us: I don't need to die for his sake. But I feel sorry for Darwin, truly sorry.

... Today I'm going to write to you about a lady who once saw Goethe with her own two eyes. She's here recuperating in place of Goethe. And I'm sure that when Goethe was alive, he didn't get nearly as much attention as this old lady gets now. She is the most famous woman here, but old age has made her so frail that she can barely stand on her own two feet. She is always surrounded by gentlemen and other ladies, who wait respectfully for her to say a couple of words about Goethe, whom she once saw with her own two eyes. But this old lady – I think she's called Schaumkropf – is sparing with her words, partly to make herself seem more important, partly because she isn't capable of saying much; she just puffs and pants under the burden of all those years. And you know what I think: this lady doesn't remember Goethe very well any more, she remembers only her own memories of him, so to speak. Do you know what I mean? In other words, she remembers that there was something she once remembered, and that she's spoken to others about it countless times. What do you think, is such a thing possible? I think it is. And do you know why? That woman knows so very little about Goethe that I just can't bring myself to believe that someone who supposedly remembers Goethe could remember so little about him. A person either remembers Goethe and therefore remembers so much about him that they could never run out of things to say, or they have long since forgotten Goethe himself and are now only repeating the things they once said, and with the years the sum of these things dwindles and dwindles until eventually the very last remaining bit disappears – after all, how long can you keep remembering the things you once said such a long time ago. And then comes death, it comes without fail. There's no longer any point in living if you once saw Goethe with your naked eyes but have long since forgotten the event itself, and even any memories you later had of it. And I think that's where that lady will be pretty soon, so she can try to recuperate as much as she likes, but death is not far away. Poor old lady! She once saw something beautiful, important, but now she has to die!

Have you ever seen anyone die? I haven't. If you have, then write to me about it. I did see a dog die once. It was last spring, out in the countryside. That dog was old. His time was up, but death would not come. Then they put a bowl of something down for him, and when he started lapping at it, the master of the house put a gun to his head and fired. The shot rang out and the dog fell to the ground, treading the air with his paws – he wanted to die, to die as quickly as possible, but still death would not come. So I said to the master: shoot him again, otherwise... but the master approached the dog and prodded him with his foot, and when the dog opened its dull old eyes and looked up, the master said, "it's a shame to waste the bullets, he'll be dead soon enough anyway." What do you think, does death sometimes treat people the way the master treated that old dog? Would death say it's a shame to waste the bullets, and then just make the dying person wait, wait next to their bowl. That's what I'd like to know.

Ramilda.

P.S. Of course you don't know why I want to know about death, but I'll explain everything in the next letter. And if not in the next one, then in the one after next, and at any rate, as soon as I tell you my address.

Yours faithfully R.

402

Chapter 35

By the time Indrek got through the letter he had lost all sensation of the head on his shoulders and the heart in his chest. He wandered around like a dozy fly, or he sat with his chin propped in his hands, groaning for days on end. He barely noticed what was going on around him, and if someone tried to make conversation, he couldn't at first comprehend what they were saying. It was only when he had the opportunity to read the letter again that he recovered his senses, his ability to focus on what was going on around him. But in lessons his performance dropped. The teachers had already given up on him, just as they had with several other students. This was standard practice in Mr Maurus's first-rate establishment. If he's not studying or answering any questions, let him just sit there – he's sure to start doing one or the other sooner or later. And if he doesn't, he won't last long; he'll sit there bored and embarrassed for a while, and then leave of his own accord. That was the accepted view. Only Molotov was of another view; he demanded that his students study. And so he gave Indrek no peace.

"Hey you, beanpole, you there!" he cried. "Don't you understand what the lesson is about?"

"No, I don't," said Indrek matter-of-factly.

"What do you understand then, your horse's dreams?"

"I don't know what I understand," Indrek said in a more serious tone.

"Listen to that dolt," said Molotov, turning to the class, "he doesn't understand the lesson, and now he's trying to make a joke out of it."

"I'm not joking," Indrek objected.

"Have you grown a tree stump in place of a head, or an anvil?"

"Maybe," said Indrek.

One time Molotov stopped Indrek in the street, peered at him with half-blind eyes through the lenses of his glasses, and asked, "Mr Paas, am I your comrade or am I not? Do you know what I'm referring to? Have I treated you as a comrade would?"

"You have indeed, teacher sir," Indrek replied.

"But why then have you stopped studying in my classes?"

"I've stopped studying in all the classes," Indrek replied.

"That's no kind of answer," Molotov said. "What you chose to do in other people's classes is other people's business: what I want to know is why you're not studying in my class. Have I offended you in some way? Because there are students who take God-knows what kind of silly things to heart, and come up with all sorts of strange ideas, and then they stop studying altogether, and they never study again. They just won't study, whatever you try and do with them. They'll go and study with someone else, but they won't study with you. Is that how things stand?"

"No teacher sir. I've got no complaints about your classes," Indrek said.

"But what the hell's the problem then?" Molotov asked. "You're one of the few students who I'd set hopes on. I thought that when the spring exams come round you would be one of the top students, and you could go and try your luck at the state gymnasium here. No one there has the damnedest bit of respect for you and the headmaster, you're just a joke for them; and that's why I thought we could go and show those state school brats how to do a final exam in mathematics. You with me? It would be in your own and your school's best interests. And in my interests too of course. But now you're giving up on me, and you're setting a bad example for others too. Tell your old comrade what's going on. Is it some woman? Those demons have done for more than one young soul. Is she old or young? She's old, isn't she? Older than the rest, otherwise she wouldn't be so cunning. But you know what I'm going to tell you, and I tell you this not as a teacher but as a comrade, and one who has more experience of life than you. Namely, don't believe in love. A woman's love is nothing more than a noose round a man's neck, it will choke him, just like a lasso! Stay free, stay free like me, your good comrade. And the best defence against falling in love – it's mathematics, nothing more, nothing less. I cure all my ills with mathematics. It works wonderfully well. I'm sometimes amazed at how quick and effective it is. Try repeating your times table for example, starting off with small numbers, then progress to middle-sized ones, then move on to equations, logarithms, sinusoids, co-sinusoids, tangents, co-tangents. It's a shame that you don't know your integrals and differentials – they work best of all. But there's one thing I'll tell you: beware of infinity, you know, the number eight lying on its side. Infinity ends with love, it's a real swine. It's both the mother and father of love, because love is always zero or infinity. That's love for you. So, just you remember that, the number eight on its side. As far as everything else is concerned, the harder, the more complicated it is, the better. Infinity in itself is not hard at all, which is why it always ends with love. Everything else is much harder. And don't ever just walk about without some activity to exercise the grey matter, otherwise that is sure to poison your life more than anything. If there's nothing else for it, try to count the people coming in the opposite direction, and those that overtake you too, see if you can keep both numbers in your head simultaneously. If you get mixed up, then start again from scratch. Once you've got the hang of that then you can make things a little harder for yourself: start to count the men and women separately, so that you have four separate numbers to keep in mind. Why not calculate pi when you get home? Make sure that you get, let's say, a twenty-four-digit number. But you can carry on until your reach two hundred if you want. You get me? Pi with a two-hundred-digit number. I'd like to see the grimace that your precious love pulls then."

And so comrade teacher tried to lift comrade student's spirits with recourse to mathematics. But strange things were happening to Indrek. It went something like this: one times one is one, two times two is four, two times three is six, two times four is eight... but the eight was on its side, not upright! Indrek could clearly see that the eight was on its side, lying there, fully stretched out. And when he inspected it a bit more closely, he could clearly see that it wasn't an eight, but an infinity sign, the thing which Molotov had warned him about, because infinity is love. Why? Infinity isn't mathematics, it exists the other side of mathematics. But love was now off limits for Indrek, because he had to study if he wanted to pass his final exams in spring. Love would prevent a person from ever being ready to do his exams, because love made you... what did love make you? Love made the word and the gaze more profound, which was what would stop you being ready for spring. So, start from the beginning again: one times one is one, one times two is two... one times eight is... on its side. Eight is on its side. Just as it was to start with. Which means that eight is love. If it's on its side, it must mean love, never-ending love, because love is always never-ending, until it ends, and when it ends, then it is no longer on its side, it's standing up. Love is upright, loves is... Rimalda, Ramilda, Rilmada, Ralmida, Ridalma, Radilma, Diralma, Darilma. Love is eternity. Love is Superman, riding astride a dinosaur's back, Indrek could see it very clearly, Superman astride a dinosaur's back. Yes, yes, that's how it should be, that's more natural, much more natural. When the dinosaurs still roamed the earth, then Superman must have been around as well, all the big creatures together. It's just that his bones are yet to be found, or if they have been found, then they have not yet been identified, and have been mistaken for those of some dinosaur, most probably a homohippus. That's right! The Homohippus was Superman.

And that's completely natural! Everything big is in the past, because the planet earth, and everything on it, is getting smaller by the day, smaller and smaller. In the old days there were dinosaurs, there were Toell the Great and Kalev with his sons and Linda, who cried a lake of tears, then Jakobson, and John the Baptist along with Jesus Christ, there was Goethe – and all of them were in the past, like the dinosaurs. And they all loved everyone, all of them! Christ loved everyone, because he said, "Woman, what have I to do with you?" That was how he showed his love, before dying on the cross. But what about Goethe? What would Goethe have done in Indrek's place? Goethe and Superman? If only Indrek knew that, then all his problems would be solved, he would do exactly the same. He would follow Goethe's example like that old lady whom Ramilda wrote about… or was it Rimalda, or Ralmida, Rilmada, Ridalma or Radilma?

These were the strange things which happened to Indrek when he tried to cure his love sickness with recourse to mathematics, as comrade Molotov had advised. But soon enough he saw that strange things happened not only with him but with comrade Molotov himself, who always had some integrals and differentials to hand. And then something happened to the caretaker Jürka which also required mathematical intervention. In general, Jürka was highly respected at the school and he often performed the role of Headmaster Maurus's right-hand man in maintaining "holy order", or helping to restore it when it had collapsed. At the same time, he managed to remain a true friend and a dependable comrade to the students whenever they wanted to pull the wool over Ollino's or Mr Maurus's eyes.

Recently Jürka's star had risen, because Mr Maurus required his help not only in his domestic arrangements, but also in his private life and matters of personal health: he would always take him with him to the sauna, because not only was Jürka an expert back-scrubber, but he knew how to "ruffle" other body parts too. The responsibility for "ruffling" Mr Maurus gave Jürka such airs of grandeur, so emboldened him, that he would sometimes thrash one of the students – or, as he put it, knock him senseless – for the most trivial of reasons. Of course, he didn't actually beat anyone senseless, that was an overstatement and self-aggrandisement, because in Jürka's language, beating someone senseless meant what the English call "knock out". And the thrashings were all the sounder because complaining about them wouldn't make a jot of difference. Even if you went to see Ollino, he would redirect you to Mr Maurus, and if you then got an audience with Mr Maurus he would advise you to speak to Mr Ollino. If you were lucky, then Mr Maurus would slip twenty kopecks into your palm, and for that you would get four slices of napoleon cake and two glasses of tea at the "Sobriety" canteen, with two kopecks left over, meaning that the next time Jürka thrashed you and Mr Maurus gave you twenty kopecks, you could have five pieces of napoleon cake and two teas, and still have one kopeck left over for next time. So much for Jürka with his "ruffling" and thrashing. When he handed out the damages, Mr Maurus would normally say of Jürka, "You stay away from him! He carries pails of water on a yoke, he carries lots of water, because we all need something to drink and to rinse our faces with. Understood? That yoke presses down on his shoulders, from which the neck muscles grow, and those muscles reach the head. And whenever anything reaches a man's head, we're done for – that's just man's nature. Man should look after his head. But Jürka can't look after his head, as he has to shift pailfuls of water with his neck muscles, so it's no wonder that he has a go at you."

That was how Mr Maurus tried to explain and justify Jürka's rough behaviour. And when it was so rough that neither napoleon cake nor tea were of much use, then additional compensation was discharged, enough to play a couple of games of billiards – that would heal all wounds and restore all rights. But now Jürka himself had pulled off a stunt which was impossible to treat with napoleon cake or billiards. Namely, he had brought a woman to his room who wasn't his own woman or wife, and he hadn't asked for permission to do so from either Mr Maurus or from anyone. And when that woman had already spent a couple of days and nights at the school, where she'd eaten and drunk everything which Jürka put in front of her, he let it be known that he had brought someone to the school who ate and drank everything which was put in front of her. And so a few of the boys had visited Jürka's den to have a bite of bread and a swig of something, as if they were celebrating Jürka's wedding. They'd celebrated with buns in Jürka's den even when Jürka wasn't there, when he was trudging backwards and forwards between the water barrel and the well in the yard with the water pails across his back. It was thanks to those uninvited wedding guests that the whole business came out into the open, and even if Jürka himself wasn't caught, he would have to answer for it. Some of the students who'd been thrashed by Jürka in the past reckoned that he was now for the high jump. But Jürka replied brazenly, "They can't touch me, because I'm holding all the trumps. Just one word and the old man is as quiet as a sock."

In that respect Jürka's behaviour was rude and provocative, so much so that it had Mr Maurus pacing up and down his room, running his hand through his hair, and yelling, "That man is crazy, that man is totally crazy! All that water and wood he's carried about has got to him, it's messed with his sanity."

"Me? I'm not in the slightest bit crazy!" Jürka replied.

"Now you can hear that this man is crazy," yelled Mr Maurus "He's turning my decent school, my first-rate educational establishment, into some sort of bordello, and still he maintains that he isn't crazy. Is this man crazy or isn't he?" Mr Maurus asked Indrek, whom he blamed for not knowing what was happening at the school, or if he had known, for not having said anything about it.

"I don't know," Indrek replied.

That was like a red rag to Mr Maurus. He started running round the room, shouting. "I'm going crazy, Jürka and my boys are going to drive me crazy! I let this one study Greek for all those years, and when I ask him, is Jürka crazy or isn't he, he replies: I don't know. You understand: this dog dares to tell Mr Maurus that he doesn't know. But what do you know, if you don't know whether Jürka is crazy? But what about Mr Maurus? Is Mr Maurus crazy or is he not? Am I taking leave of my senses?" he asked, stopping in front of Indrek.

"No, you're not," Indrek replied. But that answer must have upset the headmaster just as much as the first one, for he started rushing about witlessly again, and shouting, "It's not Jürka that's crazy, it's this one here, this one is crazy! He tells me, he dares to tell me, that Mr Maurus isn't losing his mind. But Mr Maurus really is losing his mind. After all, what kind of person would waste his time with this lanky one, or with someone like Jürka, if he was in full possession of his senses? Who would do that? No one! Which means that Mr Maurus is losing his mind. Here we have Jürka: he's been lugging water about for ten years so that some lanky boy could study Latin, but in the eleventh year he starts to go mad. What exactly has been going on in that poor feeble mind of yours, which would be enough to make you go mad like this, all of a sudden, out of the blue?" said the headmaster, stopping in front of Jürka and pulling a face which sought reconciliation, after all that running about and empty prattling, which was the best outcome he could hope for.

"I'm not crazy," Jürka insisted, in a tone of voice which suggested that he, for one, wasn't in need of any reconciliation.

"But then how could you think of bringing that girl to Mr Maurus's place?" the headmaster asked.

"So it's alright for some, but not for others," said Jürka, frowning.

"Listen to him, just listen!" yelled Mr Maurus, now at his wits end. "He'll drive me crazy!"

Up until that point Mr Ollino had been calmly standing

there, hands in pockets, eyes glazed over, observing the scene. But now he intervened.

"So what is it exactly that's alright for some, which you then went and did?" he asked Jürka.

"That's for someone else to know, not you," Jürka replied.

Ollino's eyes, which until then had been cloudy and indifferent, now blazed up and his gaze became as stern and hard as steel.

"I would ask the rest of you to leave, because I would now like to talk face to face with Jürka," Ollino ordered, and with that the boys left the room, accompanied by Mr Maurus himself, who made sure that the boys dispersed to the more distant parts of the building, so that they wouldn't be able to hear the words and deeds which ensued, which were supposed to remain between Jürka and Ollino. Later, they found that one of the legs of the large table, the one covered with the black waxed cloth, had been damaged, and two flimsier wooden chairs had been smashed to bits, as if something large and heavy had fallen on top of them. What was more, Ollino's left eye was bruised, and the white of the eye a little bloodshot. For his part, Jürka had two black eyes, and his face looked like it had been trampled on; it was swollen for several days, turning shades of red, blue and purple in succession. But for all that the two of them were fairly calm when the boys were called back in to be informed of the outcome of their discussion.

"We cleared the matter up," said Mr Ollino as calmly as before, although he was puffing at his cigarette a bit more vigorously than usual. "A simple misunderstanding, nothing more. Now Jürka's ready to ask for forgiveness, and if Mr Maurus permits, to carry on serving here."

"Yes, Mr Ollino," Jürka said. "I would indeed ask, if Mr Headmaster permits, that…"

"Very good, very good," Mr Maurus quickly intervened, as if he were afraid that Jürka might say too much. "The main thing is that you've recovered your senses, it's no good being witless, when there's other people around."

411

"I never really lost them, it's just that a crazy mood comes over me sometimes," Jürka said, as if he were trying to make a joke out of the situation.

"There you go," said the headmaster, turning towards Indrek, "that's the Jürka we all know and love, that's how he talks when that mood hasn't come over him. But it's no wonder if a crazy mood comes over us now and again: clever people are often in crazy moods. But a man should never be too clever, otherwise the crazy mood is sure to come over him. I trust that the crazy mood won't come over you again?"

Mr Maurus turned to Jürka as he said those last words.

"No, Mr Maurus," said Jürka.

And with that the whole business was finished, and no one was left any the wiser as to what had happened or why. Although Jürka did have a few words to say about it, when Indrek caught him one day in the warm laundry room, rubbing ointment onto his bumps.

"Blast and damn it, he knocked me senseless! I've believed all sorts of things in this world, because I'm a true believer, but I would never have believed that. Total knock out! But you know, when you've been knocked senseless, what are you supposed to do about it, what are you supposed to say! That's just the way it is, when you've been knocked senseless, blast and damn it!"

Meanwhile Mr Ollino went about his business, as calm and as immersed in his thoughts as ever, as if he had long since forgotten that he had beaten Jürka senseless. He went calmly about his business as if all he had done was discharge his duty to Mr Maurus and his establishment, in particular the latter.

But his black eye had still not properly healed when a new struggle loomed, this time with Molotov, who had started turning up and demanding payment for his lessons, often at the most inappropriate of moments, just as he done previously, because he seemed to enjoy that more than anything. Mr Maurus and Ollino tried to explain to him that "right away" would not be possible, only the day after tomorrow, because that was wage day for everyone else, although they could perhaps consider a small advance, but Molotov stuck to his guns: he wanted his money right there and then, and not just some of it, but all of it, and he started using the kind of language that he otherwise reserved for instructing Mr Maurus's boys in mathematics. When that didn't help, he grabbed hold of the new rush-seated chair, bought to replace the wooden-seated one which was destroyed in the course of Jürka and Ollino's discussions, smashed it against the floor, and made his point quite clear.

"Will I or won't I get my money?" Molotov yelled.

Mr Maurus took fright and ran into the room next door, but Ollino calmly stood his ground and said, "No, you won't, because we haven't got any money to give you today."

A second chair – identical to the first one – was smashed against the floor.

"Will I get my money?"

"No, you won't," Ollino replied, remaining perfectly calm.

At that Molotov rushed at the clothes rail, grabbed hold of it, and started snapping it into bits, some longer, some shorter, producing a snapping sound like someone munching cranberries, until eventually all the clothes were scattered across the floor.

"Give me my money, damn it!" he yelled.

"There is no money, you can smash up the whole school if you like, there still won't be any money," Ollino replied, his continuing calmness only driving Molotov wilder. He looked around the room with a crazed gaze, trying to find something else to smash to bits, then he rushed up to the large cupboard, the one on which Goethe and Schiller had once sat atop side by side. He started trying to push it over, as if he'd decided that if Goethe and Schiller were no more, then this cupboard had no right to be standing there either. But Mr Ollino managed to get hold of the cupboard just in time, and the two of them strained, one of them on one side, the other on the other side, and the cupboard creaked a bit, but didn't fall over. After huffing and puffing like that for a

413

while, they found themselves face to face at one corner of the cupboard. Molotov shouted at Ollino, his face red with anger: "You incorrigible dog, I ask you again in Christ's name, is there really no money to be had today?"

"In Christ's name there's none," Ollino replied sternly.

"So, nothing will help, even if I push this over?" Molotov asked.

"Even if you push it over, it won't help," Ollino confirmed.

"So what should I do then?" Molotov asked despondently.

"You'll have to wait, until tomorrow at least," Ollino said.

"It's just not possible, do you understand," said Molotov, picking up a chair which he'd smashed the feet off, placing it on its side, and somehow managing to sit on it. He stared straight at the floor for a while, and when he eventually raised his half-blind eyes to look at Ollino, tears seemed to be glistening behind the lenses of his glasses.

"Whatever is the matter, Mr Molotov?" Ollino asked, moved by the sight of Molotov in distress.

"Be an angel and try to get hold of some money for me today," Molotov pleaded.

"Very well, I'll give you some money from my own funds, as much as I've got," said Ollino.

"Heavens, you're Jesus Christ himself and no mere human, you're the deliverer!" cried Molotov, jumping to his feet. "And I am the thief on the cross, the one who got into heaven."

But Ollino didn't have as much money as Molotov needed, and so Mr Maurus, who had ventured into the room again, had to empty his purse too. So great was Mr Molotov's joy that he couldn't help throwing his arms around Ollino and the headmaster, and repeating, "You're angels, God knows, you're angels! I would never have believed that you could be such angels!"

Then he ran out of the room.

"That man has gone crazy," Mr Maurus said. "Everyone has started to go crazy here. Let's see how long we old folk can hold out."

"We'll try to hold out as long as we can, Mr Maurus," said Ollino before adding, "but he smashed up the chairs and clothes rail."

"That's right, and the chairs were brand new as well, a rouble a piece, you should have taken that off his wages," said the headmaster.

"Some other time," Ollino replied.

But that other time was never to come, because this turned out to be the last time that they saw Molotov. The next morning Mr Maurus received a letter from Molotov informing him that he could no longer teach at the school. Included with the letter was his evaluation of the students academic attainments in the form of a list of grades. Solotarski's and Indrek's mathematical prowess over the last quarter were assessed as zero to the nth degree.

"That man really has gone crazy," said Mr Maurus, showing the zeros to Ollino.

"Either he has or the students he's given zeros to have," said Ollino.

True! That thought hadn't occurred to Mr Maurus. Very true! Solotarski's mental state didn't matter much to Mr Maurus, but he would have to take Indrek to task – he would have to ask him some questions.

"Mr Molotov has given you all zeros, what's the meaning of that?" the headmaster asked Indrek.

"I don't know," replied Indrek.

"Of course you don't know," said the headmaster. "But did you answer him, when he asked you the questions?"

"No," said Indrek matter-of-factly.

"You see," said Ollino to Mr Maurus. "Molotov isn't so crazy after all."

"Why didn't you answer?" the headmaster asked Indrek.

"I didn't understand the question," said Indrek.

"Why didn't you study then?"

"I couldn't."

"Why, Mr Maurus is asking you," said the headmaster, raising his voice.

"Somehow nothing stuck," Indrek said.

"What do you mean?" the headmaster said in amazement. "You've managed up until now, and then suddenly nothing stuck. It's not as if you've come here from St. Petersburg or Moscow, there are boys from those towns who come to see Mr Maurus complaining that nothing sticks. Everything should stick with an Estonian boy, absolutely everything, otherwise he isn't a true Estonian boy. And the ones who come to Mr Maurus from distant places pay Mr Maurus money, but you don't pay anything. Solotarski got zeroes too, but he's got honest decent parents who pay for their son, he can get zeros if he wants to. The rules are very clear in Mr Maurus's establishment: pay and live with zeros if you like, but when Mr Maurus pays, you have to get top marks."

Now that the matter seemed to be turning personal, Ollino thought it better to leave. This allowed Mr Maurus to talk more freely, "Tell me the truth now: it must be some girl who's making you get zeros. You're a tall boy, the girls must be straining their necks to get a look at you. And whenever some girl looks a tall boy in the eye, then all his maths marks end up as zeros. Mr Maurus is an old man; you can't deceive him. Tell me, is there some girl involved?"

Indrek said nothing, so the headmaster continued, "So it's some girl then. A girl is always sure to drive a boy crazy, you heed my words. That's why you should never look into a girl's eyes. Why did young Greek men have to keep their eyes on the ground when they walked down the road? So as not to end up looking some girl in the eye and going crazy, that's why. And you must never look at a girl from behind, because you'll see her ponytail and her hips, and you must never cast your gaze on them, because they'll drive you crazy too. That's just how girls have been created. But a poor boy won't go crazy at Mr Maurus' place. Here you can pay your money and go crazy, or if you don't pay, then you have to be in full possession of your senses. You understand?"

And so the headmaster reproached and instructed Indrek

in his fatherly manner. But the very next day he had to repeat his exhortations, in an even more serious tone, because news arrived that Molotov had run away with one of his students, his very own flaxen mane, who belonged to the wealthiest circles in town. Only now did it become clear why he had so desperately wanted to receive his wages when he was last at the school.

"That man is certainly crazy," said Mr Maurus to Ollino.

"He's just in love, not crazy. Who could have believed it, Molotov falling in love?" Ollino said.

"In love or crazy, what difference does it make," Mr Maurus said with a wry grin. And it was hard to disagree; Molotov's madness soon became the talk of town, and the best evidence of this madness was the letter which he had sent to the flaxen mane's parents by way of apology. The general thrust of the letter was that while he, Molotov, might be a socialist and a swine, he nevertheless loved their daughter, because she had amber eyes. But since they, being decent people, would never have willingly let their daughter be with a dolt like him, then he did what he had to do, because there was nothing else he could have done; because their daughter was such an angel, that he simply adored her, and because he was such a dolt, so he and their daughter were going to be dolts together.

Hearing all this, the first and only thought which came to Indrek's mind was the following: "It looks like integrals and differentials don't help that much, in fact there's nothing much that helps."

A pained and uncertain smile formed on Indrek's face, from which it was hard to tell whether he was glad of this discovery, or whether it was fate's final blow.

Chapter 36

Indeed it would not be long before fate delivered another blow, but in a way which Indrek could never have predicted. During the holidays a telegram arrived which set the school abuzz. True, there wasn't much left to buzz, because most of the students had gone home, but Indrek still had the feeling that the place was buzzing. That same day Mrs Malmberg left on the evening express train, heading south. News had come via Ollino that Miss Ramilda had fallen seriously ill while at the sanatorium, some sort of setback in her recovery. And then, a few days later, Mr Maurus appeared in mourning attire, and the evening German-language newspaper carried an obituary for Miralda Maurus.

Mr Maurus came downstairs to the front room – he'd started coming down so often that no one, not even Mr Maurus himself, knew exactly why he was doing this – but down he came, and he stood by the large table with his hands in his pockets, his gaze fixed on the street outside, where snow was falling. Indrek was standing at the other end of the table. The two of them stood there, and Mr Maurus started speaking in a tone which suggested that he might have been speaking to himself; either that or he was giving Indrek some teacherly advice.

"There were seven of us, three brothers and four sisters, and our parents lived to an old age and didn't lose their faculties as they aged. But me, I'm going to be driven crazy by my one and only daughter, so much more fragile am I than my parents. Our Molotov went crazy too, and you should watch out as well, make sure you don't go crazy over that girl who got you zeros in maths. An old man like me is allowed to go crazy, the Russian can too if he wants, but you're a young Estonian lad and you shouldn't go crazy over a girl. So look after yourself, I tell you. The main thing is not to think about it too much, because as soon as you start thinking about it, you end up going crazy. If you think to yourself, it's not me that's crazy, it's everyone else, then it's certain that you're crazy. It's far wiser to say: I'm crazy, but everyone else is still in full possession of their faculties; that's the wiser option, and that way you don't end up going crazy so quickly."

Indrek looked at the headmaster, who appeared to be talking to himself, his old eyes focussed on the snowy street outside, and he saw not the headmaster or Mr Maurus, but just some grey-haired old man who had lost his footing as he stumbled down life's path. Indrek would have liked to tell the old man that he was suffering too, and that one and the same young girl was the cause of both their suffering. But he didn't say a word, he just listened in silence to the distressed old man's ramblings and told himself, "No, nothing helps, neither integrals nor differentials, nor even old age."

A few days later Indrek got a letter. Mr Maurus had seen it arrive, and so he asked Indrek.

"Who is writing to you from Germany?

"Some relative," said Indrek, and he blushed bright red. Or he felt that he had blushed, because he was ashamed that he had to lie about Ramilda, when she herself had so loved the truth.

"What are they studying there?" the headmaster asked.

"Electrical engineering," said Indrek.

"Electricity is a good thing," said the headmaster. "Electricity is a very good thing; it's just like lightning. But you have to be careful with lightning, it can kill you. Lightning can easily kill you, and never at the right time. You should remind your relative of that."

Mr Maurus smiled at his own joke. He made jokes like that now and again, and Indrek was used to them by now.

But the letter which had given Maurus the opportunity to crack a joke went like this:

My last letter didn't come out right, please burn it. If I'd thought it over a bit longer, then I never would have sent it. It was terribly false. And terribly clever, don't you think? That letter was much cleverer than I am myself. Now I'm writing to you plainly and straight from the heart. I'm writing to you honestly and frankly, like a friend to a friend, because I feel that we are friends.

I promised to send you my address, do you remember? Of course that was just empty words. But you know that without me having to tell you, because it must be clear to you by now what the problem is. I could have told you in spring, I really should have told you, but I didn't want to, I wasn't able to, because you wrote me such a fine reply about donating me some of your blood. If only you could have guessed how much joy that letter of yours gave me! My joy would definitely have brought you joy too, only you couldn't have known that. Now that joy comes to you a little late. Joy often comes too late. Sometimes I think that we are born and we die too early, too quickly, joy never has time to reach us. Sometimes joy and happiness dance in front of us, sometimes behind us, but hardly ever hand in hand with us.

You have no need of a letter like this, but I'm not writing it so much for you, more to comfort myself. It helps me feel that I'm not completely alone, that I'm still alive. Because when death comes, we're very much alone. But even when we're alone, thoughts come to us, and so we're not completely alone. Doctor Rotbaum tells me every day: "Miss Maurus, it's best for you not to think, not to get too bogged down in your thoughts, it's bad for your health. People often die simply because they get too bogged down in things." That's what doctor Rotbaum tells me.

Of course you don't know exactly who this Doctor Rotbaum is, it's the first time you've heard his name. He's a man in the prime of life, and he resembles Jesus Christ a little in appearance; he's a bit like that Jesus on the church altar where the old pastor mused about eternal life. Do you remember which one I mean? I told you about him one time. He mused about a perfectly rounded eternal life, didn't he! That's the eternal life of those Germanified Estonians for you. That's the kind of man Dr. Rotbaum is, and he's now my object of sympathy or rather I'm his object of sympathy. Of course you can't know what I mean by that. In any case, it's a beautiful and profound thing, and if I'm not able to convey that to you, it's because of my limited writing skills, not because the thing itself isn't beautiful and profound.

Dr Rotbaum performs the role of the Good Samaritan in this place. Although he only does so with the young ladies, because they're in greater need of his services – at least that's the view here. The thing is that if a decision has already been taken about someone – if you understand what I mean – once the decision has been taken that someone will be left alone, which is the first stage of that great, eternal being alone, the preparation and familiarisation stage so to speak, then Dr. Rotbaum soon appears, because that's when his work begins. He visits once, then again and then a third time, until the sympathy starts to grow, the solace, the comfort, the yearning, the love. Dr Rotbaum and I have now reached the stage of yearning, which means that the sympathy, the solace, and the comfort stages have already been completed and that love awaits us. Whenever Dr Rotbaum comes to see me he says, "I started to feel a yearning for you, Miss Maurus." And if my smile happens to reveal any doubts, then he says, "It's true, I really did feel a yearning for you. Of course it's wrong for me to say such a thing to you, because you're now experiencing a period of crisis and my attention might disturb you, or unduly arouse you, but please believe me, I can't do otherwise, I simply have to tell you." And then he looks straight at me with his big brown eyes, with an expression which is a little sad, and he touches my hand, he comforts me: "but not to worry, we've overcome such difficulties before, we'll overcome this one, we're sure to, and then happiness awaits us. There are so many possibilities for happiness to be had in this big wide world, so many possibilities for two people to be happy, especially when they feel such yearning for one another, the kind of yearning which I felt for you today." That's how he talks to me, and that's how he must have talked to dozens of us by now. And although I know he's lying, it still makes me feel good when he lies like that, even if he does look a bit like Jesus Christ. But do you think it's possible that wonders can be performed with lies like that? Do you believe that lies can work wonders? I think they can. It once happened, when I first arrived here. There was a Russian girl here, aged eighteen or nineteen, bed-ridden, and Dr Rotbaum paid a visit, telling her about his yearning. And that Russian girl took him seriously, just like many others have: she started to believe in a greater happiness together with our very own Jesus, I mean with Dr. Rotbaum. She started to believe in the big wide world, where there are so many possibilities for two people to be happy, and she recovered from her illness, she started to get better. She took on the role of Jairus's daughter in our sanitorium. And you know what happened next? Our Jesus abandoned Jairus' daughter, and then Jairus' daughter took her own life. It was terrible, simply awful!

... But nothing like that could happen to me, because I don't take Dr Rotbaum's fine words about yearning too seriously. I listen to him, and I pretend that I believe him, and it works so well. I feel an amazing sense of inner calm. And just think: Dr. Rotbaum wants to deceive me, but in fact I'm deceiving him. He wants to comfort me with his lies, but in fact the reverse occurs: I'm comforting him. If he knew it, he would go crazy with rage. Every day I see how incredibly happy it makes him to believe, ever more surely, that I'm taking him seriously. He rejoices in his heart, because he believes he can be victor over death, over the pain of death, the sadness of death. And whosoever is victorious over the sadness of death is victorious over death itself, because, it seems to me, death is nothing more than that great sadness.

Once you've overcome that, then you've overcome everything. And I believe that I will soon overcome it, with Dr Rotbaum's help of course, but a little differently from how he and everyone else here thinks. Of course, Dr Rotbaum's view is that if a young girl falls in love, then she forgets about the approach of death, if not entirely, then almost entirely. But his belief in love or death, the way he plays with the idea of death through love, or death from love, it only makes me laugh. Because I'm not nearly as naive as everyone here thinks. And I'm not as naive as you think I am either. In general, that's the biggest mistake men make, considering us young girls to be naive. Although I can no longer call myself a young girl – after all, what kind of young girl can I be when Dr. Rotbaum comes to see me every day to talk about his yearnings – and so I'll let you in on a secret, which might come in handy later in life: young girls are never really naive, although they can often be pretty silly. I've never been naive, for example, although I have been silly, and I'm still a bit silly to this day. I've watched my father's and aunt's silly ways since I was a babe in arms, and I've been able to do so without them noticing, because it was in my interests to do so. And I've managed to get what I wanted with my own wily ways. People turned out to be naive enough that they thought me naive, while I was pulling the wool over their eyes. That's young girls for you. Girls tend to grow naive as they get older, but not me, I won't live to see those days, thank God.

… Last time I broke off before I'd finished, because I grew weary. And then Dr. R came to moan about his yearnings. I looked at him as alluringly as I could, and believe it or not I could see quite clearly that he has started to believe, ever more strongly, that I believe him. But I don't think anything of it, because I know very well that he's only playing. I'm very good at telling the difference between real and feigned feelings, because I've seen the real thing once before. Do you know where that was? Do I need to tell you? It was at home, in the main room downstairs, near that table covered in the

423

black waxed cloth. Outside, the sun was shining so brightly and the first green shoots had started to appear between the paving stones, so tender and so fragile that I even started to pity them – that was when I saw it. It was last spring. But that's enough about that. I wonder, could Dr. R ever look at me, in the way that a certain person looked at me back then? Could he make the same kind of gesture, which someone made by that black table? Could he utter the same words? Of course he couldn't. Maybe he's simply not capable of being with me in that way, of talking like that, of being silent with me like that. It's true, sometimes I find myself wondering whether he is capable of it at all. Of course I can't ask him, because he has no way of knowing himself, only some other person could know. But how can I find that other person, so as to ask them? I'm sure he's not capable, no he's not, otherwise how could he feign it like that? But if he is capable of something like that, and yet he knows how to feign it too, then he really is almost a Jesus Christ, his self-sacrifice knows almost no bounds.

In any case, over the last few days he's toned down his play-acting a bit, and every time he leaves I find myself wondering when he'll be next be back. And so my days pass – in play. There's only one thing I fear, namely that one fine day my aunt will burst in and then the game will be over, and the serious days and sad nights will start. Only today Dr R. asked me whether I've told them back home that my condition has temporarily – only temporarily mind you – got a little worse, and I told him that I had. "You don't think you might have worried them unduly?" my object of sympathy asked me, "because there really are no grounds for alarm." That's what he said. And what about me? I had no plans to tell or not to tell my aunt, because I don't even want to see her face. Right now, there would nothing more difficult for me than a familiar face, a sympathetic gaze. Here, I'm surrounded by complete strangers, and that's so soothing, so comforting, because you can be quite sure that you mean nothing to them. In any case, they are used to cases like mine. There's only one assistant here who sometimes gets on my nerves, you won't believe what she once did: she stopped by my bedside – I've got my own room, so it was only the two of us there – she stood by my bed, looked straight at me, and said, "Madam, I feel so sorry for you." "Why?" I asked. "You have such beautiful eyes," she replied. "And that's why you feel sorry for me?" I asked in amazement. "Yes," she said, "because when I think to myself that someone who has such beautiful eyes will never…" "Stop it," I interrupted her. "It's not I who has beautiful eyes, but you. And since you have beautiful eyes, it seems to you that everyone else has beautiful eyes too. Anyone who truly has beautiful eyes is unable to see the beauty of other peoples' eyes." That's what I said, and I really believed what I said. But do you know what she wanted to tell me? She wanted to tell me that I'll never get married. You understand: Dr. R. declares his love to me almost on a daily basis, but I won't ever get married. But there is one thing I would like to know: do I really have beautiful eyes. Are they just a little bit beautiful? What do you think? It would mean so much to me if you found them at least a little bit beautiful. Because beauty is what remains, everything else fades. The spirit fades, the intellect fades, but beauty doesn't, it persists. Because once someone has seen and known true beauty, then they absorb the beauty they have experienced, and thus beauty persists, when all else is lost. Isn't that divine? What persists is that which never truly existed and what is lost is that which did in fact exist. And so if you've seen just a little bit of beauty in my eyes, then that beauty will live on in you. It makes me so happy to know that!

… I feel that some kind of change has come over me. Not the same as the change which overcame that Russian girl, who our Jesus raised from the dead, and who then took her own life, but something quite different. I've started to cough terribly, to cough up phlegm. It started a while ago, but it seemed it wasn't much to worry about, that there was still time left, until one day I realised that the time had already come, the moment which had to come was here. I was so upset that I had to speak to my object of sympathy. And of course, I gave the game away a little, because up until then I had pretended that I understood nothing, and then suddenly all this fear and anxiety came out. But my sympathy remained perfectly calm, and as I listened to him talking, explaining things to me, I regained my self-composure. Trying to comfort me, Dr. R told me, "Now, the time has come, the moment which had to come, which I've been waiting for so eagerly (he used the word 'eagerly' and that must have been the only sincere word he's used throughout the whole time he's been with me, because he really was waiting for the end to finally arrive). The organism gathers strength, the liver exerts itself, it drives the infection from the wounds, and then the process of recuperation begins. That's the normal course of an illness. Sometimes it happens quickly, sometimes more slowly. It depends on the organism's stamina and resilience. Of course it's partly a question of temperament. The hot-blooded patient's recovery is hot, which means it's quick and energetic, the cold-blooded recovery is cool, which means it's slow, it's purely a question of character. Based on my experience you belong to the hot-blooded category, which explains the heated reaction to the hostile attacks. But please don't worry: everything is proceeding exactly as it should, everything is going fine. Just have patience, a little more patience! Hot-blooded people sometimes have that problem, that they don't know how to suffer, but suffering in patience is the start of serious life, and great suffering is the start of a new life."

And so he soothed me with sweet lies, and for the first time in my life I realised what a wonderful thing lies are. They are so wonderful that if they didn't exist they would need to be invented. And I'm convinced that God created lies when he created the world. He created them when he created man, because otherwise man wouldn't have been

426

able to cope with life. He wouldn't have survived! And you know what I think? Even Jesus Christ must have had to lie now and again, otherwise how else would he have been able to comfort people. Until now I hadn't understood that, I would never even have guessed it, but now I do. Just think what would have happened if Dr. R. had spoken the truth to me. If he had looked me straight in the eye and said, "This is the beginning of the end. Just suffer patiently a little longer, and then you'll be dead, well and truly dead." Even if he'd looked out of the window as he said it, it would have been pretty terrible. I'm sure that if you were able to look out of my window some time then you'd understand how terrible it would be to say something like that to a person. Just think – the day dawns, the sun rises and shines on the mountain tops, on the distant peaks, it shines on every single mountain top, because every one of them has its own face, and it is as if someone were stepping down from the skies wearing delicate pink shoes, and they descend the mountains, they descend, coming ever closer to mankind, so that all of mankind could also share in this wonder, and they walk, in their dainty pink shoes – to think of that and yet to know: you will never see it again! I would definitely have thought that, if Dr. R were to have spoken to me about it. I would have thought that because I've looked at those mountain ranges and peaks so many times that I can even see them when I shut my eyes, I see them as clearly as if I were standing by the window alongside Dr. R. Ever since I've been unable to go there in person, I often close my eyes – sometimes at night time too, when I can't sleep – I close my eyes and I see those mountains and I think to myself: there's nothing wrong, the mountains are there and I'm lying here in bed. I'm lying here, and the mountains are lying there, in almost exactly the same way, the only difference being that I can see them but they can't see me, because they have no eyes. Just think: I can see them with my eyes shut, but they don't even have eyes to shut. If only you knew what a comfort it is to me to think that,

427

at night, with my eyes shut! And during the daytime too. Divine!

... Today our Jesus spoke with me about love, today for the first time. This means we must have reached the final stage. Now only death can follow. For as soon as Dr R. speaks with anyone at this place about love, it means death will soon come. In that way you could say that he fulfils the role of God, because those whom God loves also await death: he calls them to his side, as if God lived in the kingdom of the dead, as if he were dead himself. Dr. R. took my left hand, stroked it, and asked me respectfully: "Am I allowed to kiss it? No? Please forgive me my daring, my shamelessness. You just have such beautiful fingers, they are almost translucent." He held my hand like that for a while as he spoke. But it seemed as if it wasn't my hand but someone else's, someone who was lying there with me, or inside me, and that if anyone were to touch me, they would in fact be touching that other person, who is now with me always, or inside me. And I thought to myself: there he is, that gentleman doctor with Jesus's eyes, and he's talking to that other person about love, but only a couple of days earlier he was talking to me about his eternal yearnings. Yes, he spoke with me about his yearnings. But it's good that he doesn't speak to me about love, but with that other one instead, because that means I can lie here in peace and I don't have to listen to him. That other person can listen, the one who is already with me. Of course the gentleman doctor can't yet see the other one, he can only see me. Anyway, it's impossible to see the other one, they can only be sensed. You can see a person's shadow, but you can't see that other one, it's finer, it's nobler than a person's shadow – that is why it can't be seen. The time will come when they can see it, but by then I will be lying with my arms folded across my chest.

... For the last few days I haven't dared put my arms on my chest, although it wasn't long ago that I did dare, because then it didn't occur to me that it's not decent to put your arms there. It was only today that I came to that conclusion, and it happened like this: I put both my arms across my chest and let them lie there for a while. But then I started to find it hard to breathe, so I decided to lift both my arms. I lifted my right arm, but when I thought about lifting the left one, I suddenly felt that I couldn't, I couldn't find the energy. And so my arm remained lying on my chest. So what, I thought to myself, soon or later that's where it will end up anyway. And so that left arm stayed there. It weighed heavily on my chest, because my chest has grown rather weak, bear that in mind. And do you know how long that arm rested there, pressing against my chest? Until Dr. R, the god of this place, came and lifted it, because he wanted to stroke it while he spoke of love. And then I said to myself: very well, Dr. R came today and lifted that hand from there, but what if he had never come? What would have happened then? How long would that arm have lain there? Could I have called the assistant and said: be so kind, take that arm off my chest, it's so terribly heavy? Could I have done that? I fear that I couldn't. Best for that arm to stay lying there for ever, if it comes to it. Of course my situation isn't so hopeless, because I've still got my right hand, which I'm using to write, and I could also use it to lift my left arm from my chest, couldn't I? But then what happens if the right arm stays there resting on my chest? If both of them end up there, the right and the left? I can't help thinking about that; I wait for that moment, and I think about it, I'm almost eager for it to happen. There's one thing which I regret more than anything: I won't be able to write to you anymore. Writing to you is my only true comfort, my joy, my distraction. I have started to use a pencil, which is easier, less effort to write with. Dr. R. brought me his refillable pen, but it was hard to write with, I couldn't manage it. I went back to using a pencil. You know what kind of pencil? A really thin one, because it's lighter for me to lift.

… I didn't finish my last letter. What I wanted to tell you is that if you don't get any more letters from me, you'll know what the problem is. You'll know that I wanted to write, but I couldn't, because my hand fell on my chest, and stayed lying there. It's terribly strange to watch one's own hand, lying here, but not moving at all. Suddenly I felt that I love that hand. I felt for the very first time that I love that hand which is lying like that on my chest. And do you know why? Because of the words which it wrote on the sheet of paper, and the words which it will still write. Because I have the feeling that it will write more. It will rest a while, and then write some more, because it knows that is what I want. What I want to tell you is how terribly grateful I am to you for the words which you said to me last spring, when we were standing there by that long black table. Have you ever thought about the fact that when we stood there we were probably closer to each other than we have ever been? I often think about that. And I've thought it just as often: what a shame it is that I didn't realise that back then. I suspected it, but I didn't want to truly know it, because if I'd have known it as I know it now, then we could have stood even closer to each other. But I'm indescribably grateful for what we had. And I know that for sure only now, as I commit these wretched lines to paper.

… Today I feel happy, today I feel almost deliriously happy, because all of a sudden I have this powerful, heavenly feeling that I might be loved. Do you know what that feels like? Have you ever felt anything like it? Have you ever believed so strongly in yourself that you could have that feeling? I feel it today. And I think to myself, that spring will come, the birds will come, and they will sing and build their nests, the flowers will bloom, and give off their scent – the scent is a flower's song, is it not? – and I am no longer here, but the one who loves me is walking in the sunlight and thinking of me, and that way I will enjoy next spring, the one after, and the one after next. Maybe not a great deal, but a little bit at least! A tiny little bit! For even if love dwindles over the years, something of it remains. Oh yes! I almost forgot! When spring comes, then the girls start selling flowers by the stone bridge. Sometimes there is a crowd of children there, all of them trying to sell you something, begging you to buy something from them. But there's one child amongst them – skinny, with large, serious eyes, grey and almost blue – and that one never begs you to come to her, she just stands there and looks straight at you, so that you go to her and buy something from her without saying a word. That one's my flowerchild, that's what I call her in Estonian. Just imagine! Flowerchild! You must buy something from her next spring, because I will no longer be here to do so, and otherwise she will lose a customer. If you want you can tell her that the lady with the wide-brimmed hat, the one with the white veil, won't be buying flowers anymore, that you're buying them in her place.

Dr. Rotbaum tells me that love makes people beautiful, but that probably doesn't apply to me, because I'm growing more and more ugly by the day. You wouldn't recognise me, even if I came walking down the road towards you. You wouldn't recognise me if you were all sitting round the dining table, and I came downstairs to join you. And so as to save you from having to imagine what I look like now, I'm sending you a picture. It was taken when I still didn't know that I was loved, but now that I feel that I am, I want to be loved just as I am in this photograph. I'm sending it to you in place of the mug handles; I'm sure you still have them somewhere. You can throw them away now. The mug handles marked the beginning, the photograph marks the end. That's just how our relationship is. I would be so happy if you agreed that the end is a little more beautiful than the beginning. So I'm sending you this photograph with that hope in mind. I was planning to send a lock of hair with it, but in the end I chose not to, because my hair is so horrible now: strands of it stick limply to my skull, as if they were covered in grease. It's so horrible! I'm sure that my hair is dead already, they told me that at our place a person's hair dies before they do.

Today Dr. R. spoke to me about myrtle and a veil. I'm sure

that must mean something, his words always mean something. In any case, I feel my arms moving towards my chest. If only you knew how awful it is to have to write that to you! But it's even more awful not writing about it, that's why I'm writing this now. Please forgive me for this, and everything else I might have done. I can't help feeling that I've only wronged you, that I've hurt you, and that knowledge torments me. But then I comfort myself with this thought: if I feel that I could be loved, that someone might love me even after I die, then I can't be such a bad person after all. Can I?

… At long last I told them the truth, I told them that I haven't written home, that I don't want to see my family. Nor do I want to see you: remember me as I am in that photograph. I'm afraid they'll send a telegram home. So what! It can change nothing now. Even if you gave me all the blood in your veins it would no use to me now. That's for the best, that's how it should be. Inevitability is for the best, the surest way now.

… This is probably the last time that I will hold a pencil in my hand, or maybe the penultimate time. Last time I signed the letter, because soon nothing more will be left of me than a hollow name. So I put my name at the end of this letter, like a scented flower. If only I knew which name had a more pleasing scent to you, whether Ramilda or Rimalda, Radilma, or Ridalma, or Darilma or Diralma, Dalmira or Dilmara…

Chapter 37

And that was the end of the letter. Indrek turned the last sheet over several times, he went through all the sheets and read them again and again, standing there in that cold classroom where he had hidden himself away, but he couldn't find the promised signature anywhere. Where could it have got to, Indrek asked himself, as if confronted with a riddle. But there were no riddles here, what had happened was the most natural thing in the world: Ramilda had died before she managed to sign the letter. Ramilda had thought that she could treat death just as she had treated Dr Rotbaum, the Jesus Christ of the clinic, but it turned out that death wasn't having it. It might be possible to pull the wool over Dr Rotbaum's eyes, but death had pulled the wool over her eyes: it promised to give her until tomorrow, or the day after tomorrow, but it came on that very day, it came when it was least expected, when even Dr. Rotbaum hadn't expected it.

Death strikes you down like a bolt of lightning. But what did Mr Maurus have to say about that lightning bolt? He said that lightning never choses the right moment to kill you. Death is just the same. It comes for you when you're still young, it takes you when you've just started to believe, maybe for the first time in your life, that someone loves you, that you might also be capable of loving someone: it takes you before your time. But it doesn't stop at that, this premature death is in itself premature, meaning that the prematureness reaches the second degree, as if death knew all about mathematics. But then death is the truest of all mathematics, it probably beats love, even if Molotov didn't know it. He was relying on equations and logarithms, he believed in integrals and differentials, and yet he came a cropper. That was why he ran away with his flaxen mane, after all, what more is there left for a "decent and honest" man to do once he's come a cropper? There's nothing left for it but to flee. But if you're in possession of that true mathematics, the mathematics of death, then you'll never come a cropper, then there's never any need to run away...

Indrek wasn't sure how long he spent in that cold classroom, alone with his letter and his thoughts, but it must have been quite a while, because when he finally got up from the table, his limbs felt numb, and his teeth were chattering, either from the cold or something else. In any case, when he'd pulled on his coat and put on his hat, and was out in the yard, about to go through the gates, Jürka told him that it was almost lunch time. Which meant that he must have spent several hours in the classroom, because the letter had arrived just after ten, and lunch was always between two and three. That was how Indrek worked out what time it must have been, not as it happened, but only later, when he looked back on the day's events.

Outside, it was cold and windy, and it was snowing – fine flakes of snow, as fine as grains of sand, not enough to settle. The snow was waiting for warmer weather, Indrek thought to himself. Snow abhors the cold – he added, shoving his hands into his coat pockets and heading off. Where to? He didn't know, he had other things on his mind, preoccupying him. Anyway, what did it matter where he went, on a cold day like today the main thing was to keep moving.

After walking for a while, he found himself somewhere on the edge of town, on an exposed stretch of road with a harsh wind blowing straight into his face, causing it to turn bright red and sting painfully. The pain made Indrek stop in his tracks and take in his surroundings. The first thing which caught his attention was the forest the other side of the open field. "I should be able to find shelter there," he said to himself, making a straight line for the trees, without bothering to look for a road or footpath. He waded through the snow, which became deeper and deeper as he approached the undergrowth at the edge of the forest, until it reached up to his knees, in places almost up to his waist. The snow slipped up Indrek's trouser legs and into his rubber boots, where it melted, forming rivulets of icy water which trickled down to the tips of his toes. Reaching the cover of the first large pine tree, he sat down on its exposed roots, which were free of snow, and pulled off his boots emptying each of them in turn. Once he'd finished that and put his boots back on, he took his handkerchief and used it to fasten his left trouser leg around the top of the boot. As he tied the last knot, he recalled that it was the same handkerchief which he'd had in his pocket the previous spring, when he'd been afraid that Ramilda wanted to hold his hand, and he'd had nothing to wipe his sweaty palms on, because the handkerchief was so dirty that he hadn't dared to take it out of his pocket. But today it was clean, and so he could use it to tie his trouser leg to the top of his boot.

Those were the thoughts that went through Indrek's mind as he tied up his trouser leg. But then he noticed that there was something strange about one of the branches of the tree he was sitting under; it was smooth and straight, and looked like an outstretched hand, with the fingers splayed. He had the feeling that he'd seen that branch somewhere else before, that very same branch and that same pine tree. Yes, that was right! There'd been a tree just like that back on the Vargamäe marsh, maybe it was still there, only back then that branch had still been so slender that it wouldn't have borne a person's weight. There was a wide grassy knoll under that tree, with a flax plant growing on it; Indrek had plucked some stalks from it to make a sun dial: two upright stalks, then when the shadow of one fell on the other it meant it was twelve o'clock. That was all he needed to tell him it was time to take the cattle and go to have lunch. That branch back there couldn't have held a person's weight, but this one looked strong enough. It might bend a little if someone were to hang from it, but it would bear the strain, it wouldn't snap.

Indrek stood up and stretched his arms up towards the branch. He couldn't reach it. What if he jumped? He tried, but his fingers didn't even brush against the branch. Then he decided to climb up onto the clump of roots and jump again. This time his fingers made contact, but he couldn't get a proper grip. He jumped again, he jumped several times, as high as he could, as if it were really important for him to grab hold of that branch. Eventually he succeeded, and then he hung there for a while, suspended between heaven and earth, one trouser leg fastened to his boot, the other still loose. As he dangled there a strange thought came to Indrek. He realised it was strange as soon as it came to him, because it went something like this: what would it feel like to hang himself from this branch, just to try it out, if only for the briefest moment: did he have anything on his person he could use? Not that he seriously planned to go through with it, but just for the sake of seeing if it were possible, if he should happen to feel the desire to do so.

As he hung there, Indrek realised that he had nothing with which to make such an attempt, because he had no belt, nor did he have a proper pair of braces, all he had was some sort of brightly coloured woollen cord – probably once stocking garter – which had performed the role of braces, stretched across his back at a crooked angle, but it wouldn't hold his or anyone else's weight. And it was so short that if he were to tie it round the branch, then there wouldn't have been much length left over – not much use for anything. Maybe a dog could grab hold of it with its teeth, and hang there. Yes, a dog could do that, he thought, remembering how they had once put a rope round one of their dog's necks, and how it had grabbed hold of it with its teeth and then held it while the loop had closed round its neck. Indrek could see that dog clearly now, with a noose around its neck, holding on to the rope as tightly as it could with its teeth.

He let go of the branch and fell feet first into the deep snow; there was no point hanging there if he didn't have anything he could use to make the attempt. As he stood there for a while in the spot where he had fallen he remembered that one of his trouser legs was still unfastened, meaning that snow had slipped into his boot again. He sat down on the root of the pine tree, pulled off his boot, and emptied it of snow a second time. Then he had a think about what he could use to tie up the other trouser leg. He rummaged through his pockets, but found nothing. He undid his overcoat, then his jacket, and checked the linings of both of them, but they were both sound, there was no loose material he could rip out to use. But then he had a good idea: he undid the handkerchief which he'd used to fasten one of his trouser legs, and tore it in half. "That's for last spring, for not letting Ramilda hold my hand," he said to himself. "You were the one who came between us with your dirtiness, so now I'm going to rip you in two, just like the veil which they tore in two at the temple. You remember that? It was after Jesus had died on the cross, remember. And now it's your turn, because someone has died again. You understand, you filthy, ragged handkerchief, that someone has died again? Two thousand years ago Jesus Christ died on the cross, and now death has come to the world again. And every time that death comes, something must be torn."

Indrek finished tying up his trouser leg and stood up. "Now I can continue on my way," he said to himself. He headed straight for the forest, because the cloudy winter day looked like it might break into rain any moment, and twilight was falling. As he went he gradually increased his speed, as if he were in a hurry to get somewhere in time, as if he was afraid he might be late. But in fact it was only because he felt the cold; it was cold enough to make him shiver.

At that moment, Indrek realised that his coat and his jacket were still unbuttoned. "How could I not have noticed?" he asked himself. As he started to do up the buttons, he realised his hands were frozen, they were already quite stiff. "Where are my gloves?" he thought, and started to check his pockets. Indrek stood there and searched for a while, trying his trouser and waistcoat pockets in the hope he might find the gloves there; there wasn't anywhere else they could be. He tried to remember if he had been wearing his gloves when he had crossed the field in that driving wind, but he couldn't be sure. He set off at a brisk pace, doing up his buttons as he went, because he didn't want to hang about. He turned up the collar of his overcoat, shoved his hands deep into his pockets and went on his way.

The forest grew thicker and darker as he got deeper into it, he stumbled on twigs underfoot, branches lashed his face and almost knocked his hat from his head, but Indrek carried on. How long he walked, he wasn't sure, but eventually he spotted a light. It was a pretty ordinary red light, the kind which would shine from a farmhouse window on a winter evening. "Farm," mumbled Indrek, "because here in Estonian we have farms behind the forest, and forests behind the farm. But not in other countries. In Germany a Superman sits behind the forest, and behind Superman's back there's a forest, where the dinosaurs feed, sixty *süld* tall, thirty high; they eat everything, including Superman. That's what it's like in Germany."

Indrek stopped under a thick fir tree and looked at the light in the distance. Then he sat down on the snow, leaning his back against the trunk of the tree, his eyes still fixed on the light. To the left of the light the sky was glowing, it must have been the play of the northern lights, or a distant dawn, either that or something was ablaze. "What could it be?" Indrek asked himself. But he didn't try too hard to answer his own question, because he already felt a pleasant weariness seeping into his limbs. Soon he would have been overcome with drowsiness, and he would have fallen fast asleep, if a thought hadn't suddenly struck him: "It must be the glow of a town there in the distance. Towns glow at night like distant fires."

438

Indrek opened his eyes and got up, feeling a shiver run down his spine. He set off again, not towards the glow of the town, but aiming straight past it. The snow was now falling thick and fast, and it no longer felt rough against his face. Indrek strode across the open fields, the wind battering him as he went. Now and again he cast a glance towards the distant glow, as if he was afraid it might disappear, or that he might get too close to it. And so he went on his way. After a while he came to a deep snow drift, piled up along a fence, and he waded through it, until he reached a road, which he chose to walk straight across. He crossed several roads like that, continuing across the open field, as if he were searching for something, or was afraid of coming across people. But eventually he came to another wide road with deep ditches either side and high edgings, and he felt that he no longer had the strength to cross. Stumbling through the deep snow, he tried to scramble up and over the ditch, but he fell back down. He tried again, but he couldn't manage it, so he just lay back on the snow, the blizzard blowing across him. He lay like that for a while, but when he felt the icy snow melting on his face, he sat up and opened his eyes wide: there, right in front of him he could see the glowing lights of the town.

Indrek tried to stand up with his hands still deep in his pockets, but he fell forwards into the snow. He tried again, and this time managed to stay on his feet, and started walking down the road in the direction of the glowing lights. He walked for quite a while. At first his legs didn't want to follow the road, it was as though they were under the influence of some sort of sleeping drug which made them limp and heavy. He slipped and stumbled through the deep snow, until eventually his feet found firmer ground, and he could make his way onwards. Here, in the outskirts of town, he encountered other people, coming down the path towards him. Some of them walked straight past, but he collided with others, especially the women, because they wouldn't make way for him. "Women never make way," Indrek thought to himself, as he veered into the middle of the road. There he found himself on a bridle path with coachmen shouting at him. But he paid them no heed and just trudged onwards. Eventually Indrek came to a triangular town square, a single coachman and his horse sitting in the middle, exposed to the blizzard – both of them were hunched forwards, and from a distance they looked old and wretched. Indrek found himself feeling intense pity for them. He couldn't help sitting down on the nearest step and breaking into tears, tears of pity for the old coachman and his nag, sitting slumped in the blizzard.

Indrek sat on the wooden steps, and after a while he forgot all about the coachman and his horse. But then when he eventually stood up he saw that they were both still there, slumped under the lantern. So he went straight up to the coachman and took a seat in his carriage. As soon as the coachman turned around in his seat and asked him where he wanted to go, Indrek recognised him. Without saying another word, Indrek got up from the carriage, left the coachman and his horse where they were, and fled as if he had just come face to face with a murderer. The coachman yelled something after him, he even gave his horse a flick of his whip, but its legs must have been stiff from the cold, because all it could do by way of response was twitch its ears and tail. By the time the coachman had got his horse to budge, Indrek had already disappeared into the blizzard, mumbling to himself as he went, "Shit school, no decent clothes, no nothing!" Thanks to that vile old man and his nag, Indrek had sat on that step for so long that he had started shivering all over. If he were still out there on the open field with the glow of the city in the background, he would have shown them how to get warm, but now there was nothing for it but to go home, otherwise he would have no chance. By now his vision was blurred, his head was spinning, his legs were buckling under him, they refused to bear his weight.

"Pile the clothes on top of me," Indrek said to Vainukägu,

once he was safely home and in bed, "pile on whatever you can get your hands on, otherwise the cold will take me."

And so the pious Mr Vainukägu piled the clothes on top of Indrek, and he went beyond the call of duty, because God had made him resourceful too. God had given him the desire to be a shepherd of human souls, but he had also given him the wits to understand that the soul could only be shepherded through the body, and that it could be shepherded just as well by pressing trousers as through reading prayers, even better in fact. And so when Indrek started moaning about how awfully cold he was, Vainukägu ran to the nearest chemists' and came back clutching powders of some sort. He also managed to procure a kettleful of hot water from somewhere, and Indrek took some swigs from it, as far as he was able to. Meanwhile, Vainukägu fussed about around Indrek's bed, straightening things up, tidying up here and there, until everything was spick and span.

"Don't you worry, the cold won't beat us," Vainukägu said. "We'll get the better of the cold, as long as nothing else comes our way."

And they did get the better of the cold, but Indrek's fever lasted for a good few days. It wasn't severe enough to kill him, but it definitely wasn't going to let him eat anything, or get up out of bed. So he had to stay put. And when he was finally well enough to sit up on the edge of his bed, he felt his energy reserves were depleted, and that his bones were poking out of his flesh at strange angles, and they somehow felt lighter, as if they were hollow inside. "Just like the bones of birds," he said to himself, feeling his hard shins.

Chapter 38

And so the holidays passed, and the school started to buzz with activity again. The current students came back to resume their studies, and new ones arrived to start theirs; as was well known, the doors of Mr Maurus' establishment were always open to newcomers. Indrek walked about in a daze amidst the hubbub and commotion. But it was better than the long silence of the holiday period. At least there was something to distract him now, to stop the same thought from pounding away in his head. It was the thought which he'd had under the pine tree, which he somehow couldn't manage to resolve for himself. It was as if there were some obstacle in his mind, something hard and tough, which stretched this way and that and wouldn't let the thought pass. It was only a stroke of good fortune which eventually spared Indrek from that incessant thought.

There was an old professor who taught astronomy – he was tall and thin with tired, deep-set eyes which would light up when he got onto the subject of the parallax and light years. Then his old bones were suddenly so full of energy that bits of chalk went flying in all directions as he wrote or drew pictures on the blackboard. He knew no greater pleasure than to gather the students together late at night, stand with them under a starry sky, and explain it all to them scattering learned terms and references left, right and centre. And what did the students do with all these figures and terms? They stood there yawning, either from boredom or from the cold, no one was sure which. But then the old man took them to the observatory, sat them down back-to-back, and showed them the disk of the moon, the breadth of which it would be possible to measure in *süld*. And with that, he won the students' hearts. With that frozen moon he even won Indrek's heart, which was still so sensitive, like an open wound, raw and bloody. It was wonderful to listen to the old man, to learn how mind-bogglingly huge the universe was and how impossibly miniscule that lump of rock called planet earth was in comparison. But what then was man, if planet earth itself was no more than a speck of dust, a spot of dirt? Indrek had no idea what the significance of man could be, if the earth was so tiny. Did the old professor know himself? Maybe he knew the meaning of mankind, although maybe even he didn't know. He stood too close to man, so he couldn't really know much about him. If man was situated at least as far from us as the moon, so that we could watch him from the observatory through a long telescope, watch him while lying on our backs, then maybe we could know something about him, about who man really is. Otherwise it was impossible.

Once when the students were up on the hilltop, sitting in a circle around the professor, the glittering lights of town dotted higgledy-piggledy below them, the shining starry infinity above their heads, the professor started talking to them about the Milky Way and the nebulae, which were only distant milky ways themselves, or so he assured them. He filled his explanations with talk of tens of, hundreds of and thousands of light years, but he did so as if the distance between the stars was little more than a couple of hours stroll across the universe. He spoke of stars which were heading at insane speed straight for us, and others which were speeding away from us just as fast. And it sounded as if he felt sorry for the latter, because at some point they would disappear into the infinity of the universe, and then there would only be one star left in the sky. Maybe mankind would still exist on planet earth, maybe he would have extended his range of vision a thousand times, but he would never find those lost stars. Man would live on, but the star would be dead. But who can prove that the stars we see still exist? It takes hundreds or thousands of years for the light of the stars to reach us. Do you realise what that means? the professor asked them. It means that if some distant star was born at the same time as Jesus Christ – because stars are born and die just like people – then it's possible that we will see its light for the first time today or tomorrow evening, or maybe only ten or one hundred or a thousand years from now. And if some distant star died with Jesus Christ, then it's possible we'll see its final glow today, and by tomorrow it will have already been extinguished, it's final ray of light having now reached our planet. But it's also possible that it will arrive ten, one hundred or a thousand years from now, and thus we still see stars which have not in fact existed since the death of Christ. In that way thousands or millions of stars might move around our universe which we can't yet see, whereas we can still see thousands or millions of stars which no longer exist. Which means that the whole of the Milky Way is nothing more than an optical illusion…

The professor stood there tall and thin surrounded by his students with the collar of his worn overcoat turned up and his hands in his pockets, because the night air was biting cold. Eventually he fell silent, appearing to be lost in thought. Indrek, who was standing right in front of him, took the opportunity to ask a question, "Professor, if the universe is so immeasurably huge and if there are nothing but stars, formations of stars and milky ways all over the place, then where is heaven?"

The old man raised his head and looked upwards, forming a sad smile with his frozen lips.

"I've been searching for over thirty years and I still haven't found it. I'm an old man now, but you're still young, now you must search, maybe you will find it."

He was still surrounded by his students as he said that, tall and thin, slightly stooped forwards, as if he found it hard to stand upright.

As they walked back down the hill, Indrek found an excuse to separate himself from the rest of the students. He felt the need to be alone for a while, to think things over without having to worry if his thoughts were going to be interrupted.

"So, there's nothing there," he said, when he'd got way from the others. "There's nothing else besides stars, stars and more stars. But if there is no heaven, then where is God? Where is he? Does he even exist?"

In fact Indrek had long suspected that there was no God, but now he was completely sure. That was the only explanation. Otherwise, the recent events of his life could never have happened as they had. That was the reason. Now it was all clear. Otherwise, Ramilda could have lived, because who else had the right to live if not her. But if there were nothing more than stars up there in the sky, it was all clear. If even the stars died, then how could humans withstand death? Only their light persisted, shining on for a little while longer than Ramilda's name or her memory...

Indrek walked alone under the starry sky in the cold night air, muttering senselessly to himself. And then when the other students had gone to bed, he sat down at the table and started to write. Now he simply had to write, he couldn't stop himself. This was to be his first contribution to the student journal which Pajupill had started the previous year, giving it the title "Truth" and the motto "The truth, the truth, nothing but the naked truth". The journal was supposed to combat moral degeneration, promote literature and learning, and give the students the opportunity to put their intellects to the test. They could write in Russian, German, or Latin. Indrek had read some of the other students' efforts, now he wanted to give them something to read.

The next edition was expected to generate something of a scandal, because Solotarsky was planning to ride across it astride his dinosaur, Vellemaa, who was already at university, was going to take on Superman, and Indrek had his sights trained on God himself. Indrek was the most determined of them all, and he had his reasons. He sat writing through the night, full of passion as he committed his determined words to paper. And if God himself had approached him as he was writing, put his hand on his shoulder, and said, "Young man, are you not afraid of sinning?" then Indrek probably would have replied in all honesty, "No dearest God. I'm not scared of anything now, because nothing worse could happen than what has already happened. Go to Vargamäe if you wish, and talk to them about sinning, but leave me in peace, because I know now that there's nothing more than stars up in the sky, stars, stars and more stars. There's no heaven up there, we must acknowledge that. And everything which exists is mortal; just as it is down here on earth, so it is up above, please remember that, dear God."

That's what Indrek would have said, if God had put his hand on his shoulder in the middle of the night. But God didn't do that, and so Indrek had no need to say anything. He just carried on writing, drawing on the wisdom he had acquired from everything he had read or heard or experienced in his life so far, with the aim of destroying Him who must see and know everything. As he wrote he became more inspired and even got completely carried away, until eventually he had no qualms about giving his creativity free reign, "I shall be the first in Estonia to deal you the fatal blow. I shall be the first who dares to cry for all to hear: You do not exist, there is nothing more up there than stars, stars and more stars! There is only the infinity of space, where the light of dead stars dwindles. If you do exist, then bring the dead stars back to life, return to the faltering light its mother, its fountainhead. Turn a wilted flower into a fresh one, make a new person from a scented signature. Do it, if you exist, if you can hear me! But I know that you won't. Because you didn't create this world, nor any others, you didn't create man, that was evolution, which started with the dinosaurs. You stand back and let thousands and millions of stars fade into oblivion. Why? The only ones you allow to die are those who should have lived. Why? There is only one answer: you don't exist, you have never existed, and you will never exist.

You never brought Lazarus or Jairus' daughter back to life and you will never bring anyone back, not even the most beloved of them all, however much we believe in you or pray to you. You never will…"

Indrek grew more and more emotional as he wrote those words, until eventually he slumped face down on the table. If God had now put his hand on Indrek's shoulder and said: "Young man, I'm going to bring all the dead stars back to life, I'll return all the dinosaurs to planet earth, if only you promise to believe in me," then Indrek would probably have told him, "Dearest God, what am I supposed to do with your stars and dinosaurs? I have no love for either of them."

When Indrek finally went to bed, he slept more soundly than he had in a long time.

The next morning he woke up feeling physically and mentally refreshed. And that was for the best, because further trials awaited him.

It only took a couple of days following the appearance of the latest edition of the student journal for Indrek to be summoned by Mr Maurus, whom Indrek found waiting for him downstairs in the main room with Mr Ollino, and some of the other students who had written pieces for that edition.

"What's this?" asked Mr Maurus, pointing at the copy of the journal lying on the table.

"That's our journal," Indrek replied.

"What do you mean, our?" asked the headmaster, trying to sound as calm and businesslike as possible.

"The students'," said Indrek.

"Who wrote this?" the headmaster asked, pointing at an article titled "God and Man."

"It was me," Indrek replied.

"Very well," said the headmaster. "If you wrote it then you can read it to us now, from here," he said, pointing to a passage marked in red.

Indrek focussed his eyes on the text, but he immediately realised that he couldn't read it, he wasn't capable of reading it, because he felt ashamed. He hadn't been ashamed as he wrote it, but now he was. The feeling was so unfamiliar to him, so strange, that he felt paralysed. At night he'd felt inspired, creatively satisfied, now he just felt shame and embarrassment.

"Read it," the headmaster instructed harshly, "we're waiting."

"No," Indrek replied resolutely, taking a few steps back from the table.

"Then you read it, Mr Ollino, because we would all very much like to know what this tall chap Paas has written."

Ollino picked up the journal and started reading:

"Your days are numbered...."

"Who's this 'you'?" the headmaster interrupted.

"It's Jehovah," Ollino said.

"That means God," the headmaster explained. "Let's keep that in mind. Now please continue."

"Your days are numbered," Ollino resumed. "Dinosaurs roamed the planet, then came man, and now there are no dinosaurs. So now it's man's turn, but soon Superman will come. First there was Apis, the holy bull, then Zeus came along, and so the bull is no more. There are still bulls, it's just that they're not holy anymore. Zeus stayed around for a bit, but then along came Jehovah, and now there's no sign of Zeus. So, Jehovah was here, but then came science, and now so I ask you this: where is Jehovah now? I'll tell you where he is, he's gone to the same place as the dinosaurs. Heed you that, men and women of Estonia, sons of the Fatherland."

"That's enough," said the headmaster. "Now read out that other bit."

There was another fragment of text which had been marked in red. Once Indrek had read it to himself, the headmaster came to stand right in front of Indrek and asked, "Do you admit to writing that?"

Indrek hesitated.

"I'll ask you again, was it you that wrote that?"

"It was," Indrek replied.

"You're out of your mind!" yelled the headmaster, now in

a fiery rage, and he slapped Indrek across the face. It was so unexpected, so swift, that Indrek didn't have time to shield his face, nor to answer like with like; his thoughts were elsewhere, as they had tended to be recently. And so Indrek just stood there in front of everyone, his face burning red. It was too late for him to defend himself, or to pay Maurus back in kind, too late, as it always seemed to be for Indrek. But meanwhile, Mr Maurus was waving the hand he'd struck Indrek with in front of his own face, the fingers splayed wide. Then, eying the students over the top of his glasses, he shouted, "This man is stark crazy! He's the first truly crazy person in Mr Maurus's decent and respectable establishment. There have been some half-crazy ones, of course, but this one is totally crazy. He got zero in mathematics but he's one hundred percent crazy himself. And he's decided to take on Mr Maurus's holy bull and Jehovah. He wants to be famous, he wants to win fame in Estonia for killing God. You understand? The first to murder God! He could at least have gone for the devil instead. But no, he doesn't touch the devil, he goes straight for God, as if he couldn't get to the devil otherwise, first he has to despatch God. Paas wants to make Mr Maurus famous, but Mr Maurus doesn't want to be famous for killing God, because he knows that he can't go up against God. Mr Maurus is an old man, he knows very well that God will tell the school inspector, the inspector will tell his director, the director will tell the procurator, the procurator will tell the minister, and then the minister will tell the tsar that Maurus wants to kill God. And then the tsar will tell the minister, the minister will tell the police chief, and the police chief will tell the gendarme that they're practicing deicide at Mr Maurus' place. Now you tell me, can old Mr Maurus go up against the tsar, and his police chief and the gendarme? So that's why our lanky Mr Paas, along with his hunger for fame, will have to take himself elsewhere. Let him go some place where there's no tsar and no religion. Mr Maurus will stay here in Russia, under the merciful wings of the Russian eagle, because a true Estonian loves the tsar and his eagle."

Maurus carried on in that vein until he had eventually calmed down a bit. Then he turned to face Indrek and asked, "How quickly can you get your things together?"

"Half an hour," Indrek replied, having had time to think things over as the headmaster was speaking.

"Let's say one hour," said Mr Maurus, "then you'll be just in time for the evening train, if you want to go home."

"I'm not going home," said Indrek.

"Of course you're not," said the headmaster, "because back there they know very well that God is alive and well and in very fine fettle."

While Indrek went to gather his things and put them in his case, or tie them up in his knapsack, Mr Maurus continued speaking to the students.

"Mr Maurus simply cannot allow for anyone to live in his house who has designs on God's life. If that person were to come and say, 'Respected Mr Maurus, I have a yearning to be a murderer, and so I would like kill you,' then I would let him remain under my roof for that night, because he's hardly likely to get round to killing old Mr Maurus in one night. But if that person wanted to kill not Mr Maurus but God himself, who has assigned Mr Maurus as headmaster here, then old grey Mr Maurus would put his fists up. Because who else is going to protect God, if not Mr Maurus himself? Would Mr Koovi do it? No, he wouldn't. He'll just say something in his lazy Russian way: 'Me and him never served together, why should I protect him.' Would Mr Ollino defend God? No, not him, he would just say: 'My God is still alive, what business do I have with any other Gods.' Would Sikk do it, given that he's such a strong lad? No, he wouldn't do it either. He would just say: 'There are stronger ones than me, let them do it.' And Vainukägu? He would just say: 'No, someone else can do it, I haven't been confirmed yet.' And so on. And so who is left? Mr Maurus himself, because he has served God, he's been confirmed, and if it's necessary to make a stand for God, then he's ready to do battle with a bear if needs be, or even Old Nick himself. That's the kind of man old Maurus is."

Indrek went to see Mr Koovi to ask if he could keep the book he'd borrowed for another day or two, and Mr Koovi took the opportunity of sharing his thoughts with him, "I've told you before, don't mess around with God or eternal man, because you'll lose touch with reality. You already know, you can see with your very own eyes what we have here: poverty and wretchedness. Will God or some eternal man come and tidy up this mess? Of course they won't! We have to help ourselves, and help our fellow man too. That's our holy duty, if we want to remain human. You get it? That's why we have to learn to feel compassion for those who are in trouble, otherwise we can't help them. In any case, what about you, what are you going to do now? You would have finished here in spring, but now everything's gone to hell. If you still want to try your luck, then I'll do what I can. It's a shame that Molotov is no longer with us, he could have helped you with mathematics. A woman had him away. Women and gods, they're the real evil spirits bringing us down."

With that Koovi had finished his speech. But Indrek didn't agree with him, especially where women were concerned. And he was pleased about that: "If I have a different view from Mr Koovi, then I can't be so wretched after all," he thought to himself. And with that happy realisation he fastened a rope around his chest, and tied up his knapsack, so that he would be able to carry them comfortably, one in front, and one behind, on his back.

Indrek had already started to put on his coat when the headmaster asked everyone else to leave the room, and the two of them were left face to face: "Do you have any money?"

"I have," said Indrek

"How much?"

"Forty-three kopecks," said Indrek.

"Now you've really taken leave of your senses," said the headmaster, but he said it in a way that suggested he was joking. "You've only got forty-three kopecks, but you still want to kill God in Estonia. But where are you going to get your money, when God is no more, it's not as if you're going to get by on forty-three kopecks."

"I'm owed some money for lessons," Indrek said.

"How much?"

"A little over a rouble."

"That's still not much," said the headmaster.

"I'll give some more lessons," said Indrek.

"What do you get for one lesson."

"Fifteen for one of them, twenty for the other."

A few moments passed while Mr Maurus peered over the tops of his glasses at Indrek, who was standing in front of him ready to depart, wearing his long, grey, homespun coat, his galoshes, and holding his hat in his hand.

"You're an idiot," said the headmaster, now in a more serious tone of voice, but in such a way that Indrek didn't take offence, but rather felt flattered. "You're planning to go to battle against God and his son with such a small sum of money! *Warten Sie ein bischen*,"[52] he said, rummaging in his pockets, producing a jangling of coins. Then he turned around, as if he was in a great hurry, and headed upstairs. Indrek was left alone, head hung despondently, wondering whether he should wait for the headmaster or not, and at that moment, somewhere in one of the back rooms, someone started singing a song which the count had taught them, and which had still not been forgotten: "The priest had a puppy". That put paid to any last doubts that Indrek had. He picked up his box and his knapsack, and started to leave. Mr Ollino appeared from his room and watched Indrek go without uttering a single word. Indrek opened the front door, causing the bell to tinkle, and at that moment he heard the headmaster's footsteps and voice, sounding as if it might be calling him. But Indrek paid no attention, he just went on his way, his chest knocking against the doorway, straight out into the snowstorm. Soon he heard the doorbell tinkling

---

52 *Warten Sie ein bischen*: "Wait a minute"

again, and the headmaster's voice, calling his name, but Indrek pretended he hadn't heard. And yet Mr Maurus didn't stop; Indrek could hear his voice approaching. Before long he heard a sound like someone playing the bagpipes, and at that moment a hand grabbed hold of the corner of his chest, and he heard Mr Maurus shouting, right next to him now.

"Why don't you listen, when Mr Maurus calls your name! Mr Maurus is an old man now; he can't run anymore! You'll be old yourself one day."

Those words had a strange effect on Indrek. He suddenly remembered his father's bent fingers, gripping the rungs of the ladder. He remembered wretched old Voitinski and unhappy Schulz. And so he stopped and turned around. The headmaster was standing without his hat on in front of him, his grey locks of hair matted by the wind. With his left hand he was holding his nightgown closed as the wind tried to blow it this way and that, with his right hand he was trying to shove something into Indrek's coat pocket.

"Hold it in your hand, otherwise the wind will blow it away. Anyone who wants to go up against God needs at least five Russian roubles. If Mr Maurus were still young, then he would come too, for he's a rebel at heart, but Mr Maurus is old already."

Having said that, he turned round and headed back to the front door, walking with the loping gait of an old man, while Indrek watched him go.

When the doorbell announced that Mr Maurus was back inside, Indrek propped his chest against a fence and stood there for a while, as if he was having a rest or mulling something over. Gradually he let his case slide downwards until it had reached the ground, then he put his knapsack on top of it, and sat down, as if he were indeed tired already. He sat there, thinking over the events of the last few days. But it wasn't real thinking, more like daydreaming. Somewhere in his thoughts there was some old coachman, someone with a red beard, then someone with a smiling face, sat next to him, pressing their knees against his leg, someone in the snow, behind a gate, the first kisses of trembling lips, shoots of grass poking up between cobblestones, a tabby cat, swallows, mug handles, and something else, someone else. But he didn't need to try too hard to think about that, because it was fresh in his memory anyway. It was as if nothing else was real in his life apart from the person he was trying not to think about. Somewhere he saw Mr Maurus' grey beard flashing past, his eyes peering over the top of his glasses. And there was some-one else standing behind him, who was greyer than Maurus, but when Indrek tried to look closer, he disappeared along with old Maurus. "We're sure to meet again one day," Indrek said, as if he wanted to comfort himself, or as a warning to those who had disappeared too soon.

But his hopes were not to be realised, for he would never see Mr Maurus again. He didn't even repay his debt to him, just like all those others who had eaten at Mr Maurus' table for years, who had studied at his establishment. So much for Mr Maurus.

As far as the other one was concerned, the grey one stand-ing behind Mr Maurus, that was another story: Indrek was likely to meet him again, maybe as soon as this evening. But the strange thing about him was that you never really knew when you would meet him. It was only in hindsight that you realised that it had indeed been him.

It went like this: as soon as Indrek sat down on his chest, mother Vaarmann appeared, heading out through her back gates to shovel snow, because she was sure that it would stop falling soon enough. When she spotted someone sitting out there on his chest, she came closer to check who it might be. She recognised Indrek straight away, "Mercy me! Mr Paas! What are you doing here?"

"I'm resting my legs," said Indrek.

"But where have you come from?" mother Vaarmann asked in surprise.

"From Mr Maurus' place, where else."

"But that's right here," Mr Vaarman said in amazement. "And where are you going?"

"To Old Traat's place," said Indrek.

"That old red beard died ages ago," mother Vaarmann explained. "He died because he was too fat, like all the old men. The fat is what kills the old ones. They live so well that they die from their fat."

"Then I don't know where," said Indrek. "Somewhere," he said, getting up from his case and slinging his knapsack onto his back.

"But what's happened?" mother Vaarmann asked.

"Mr Maurus threw me out, that's what," said Indrek.

"Well then come and stay with us, until you've found somewhere better, it's just me and Tiina now," said mother Vaarmann. "Go inside and join her, I'll come soon."

And so Indrek passed through the gate to mother Vaarman's house, together with his case and his knapsack, and then he groped his way downstairs into the cellar rooms, where Tiina greeted him enthusiastically.

"Mother is always telling me that you'll never come to our place again, but see, you did come," she said. "I always tell her, just wait and see, he'll come. And now it turns out that I was right, not mother."

"Where's Molli?" asked Indrek.

"Don't you know?" Molli asked in surprise. "Molli made herself some new lace-trimmed shirts and moved in with that fat Russian. That's where she is now. She's not yet betrothed, but the ring is ready, and that's enough to make mother cry all the time. Molli goes to our church, but the Russian goes to his Russian church, and now he wants Molli to belong to the Russian church too, then he'll ask her to marry him, and put the ring on her finger. Molli is learning the Russian faith. Mother says that it can't be so bad, now she has two chances of gaining salvation, either with our faith or with the Russian faith. Me and mother have only one way, but Molli has two ways, so she's sure to. If not one way, then the other."

455

A little while later mother Vaarmann came in herself and changed the conversation to the subject of Miss Maurus, hoping for Indrek to provide a detailed account of her death, in particular of the funeral. Unfortunately, Indrek couldn't do much to satisfy her curiosity.

"I always used to say it, I don't know if Miss Maurus is going to die soon, or whether it's because she looks so fine and so proud, and that's what I like about her so much. When she came home in the spring, I stood on the street and watched her, as if I were seeing her for the last time. And it turned out I was right – she died all alone, far away in a foreign country, where she had no one, no friends or relatives to keep her company. So that's what happens to those fine and proud ones, if God so wishes."

"If God so wishes," said Indrek in a mocking tone, because mother Vaarmann's words irritated him.

"How else if not by God's wish," mother Vaarmann confirmed. "Just like my Molli, she had to move in with that Russian, no rings or nothing, they just started living together. I was against it at first, she was too, but that's the way it had to be. God had decided that was the way it must be, he'd had his say."

"God doesn't exist," Indrek said.

"What crazy talk is that?" mother Vaarman said fearfully.

"It's not crazy talk, it's true," Indrek said. "Elsewhere in the world they've known that for ages, because they have better education, and higher standards of justice, but here in Russia we've fallen behind the times. Once everyone is educated, they won't believe in God. That's what I told Mr Maurus, and that's what I say to you, and to everyone else, because it's the truth."

"Well fancy that, there's no God," said mother Vaarmann, before adding: "But Jesus Christ definitely exists."

"No, there's no Christ either," said Indrek, showing no mercy.

"That's just empty prattle," said mother Vaarmann, sticking to her guns. "Let God not exist if that's how it has to be, but we can't do without Christ: otherwise who is going to bring us salvation?"

"Just think for yourself," Indrek said, "how can the son exist without the father? Christ's father was God. If there's no God, then there can't be any Christ either, there's no holy spirit, and no devil either."

"That's just the lies which clever people tell us stupid folk," said mother Vaarmann. "There is a devil, and Jesus Christ exists too, it simply can't be otherwise."

"There's no devil nor anyone of the sort," said Indrek. "There's no heaven or hell, there's only the stars, and emptiness."

"What's that blue thing up there then?" mother Vaarman asked, refusing to back down.

"That's the air, it's pure air," Indrek explained. "And the purer the air, the bluer it is, so there's no heaven up there at all. And if there's no heaven, then where is God? Where is he, if there is no heaven? You think for yourself."

"Well it doesn't necessarily follow, that just because there's no heaven, then there's no…"

"There's no heaven, that much is certain," Indrek interrupted, and started trying to explain what the old professor had said about heaven, but he couldn't, because at that moment he heard a whimpering sound coming from somewhere nearby.

"Who's crying over there?" he asked, looking at Mother Vaarmann. "Is that Tiina? Why is she crying? What's wrong with her?"

He got up from his chest, and went through to the other room, where he found Tiina, laying on her back on a pile of old toys and rags, sobbing pitifully. Indrek looked over his shoulder in the direction of mother Vaarmann, as if to ask for her to help.

"What's wrong with her?"

"Don't you see for yourself?" said mother Vaarman, replying with her own question.

But Indrek couldn't see. So he approached the unhappy

young girl, kneeled down in front of her and patted her head and slender midriff, which was heaving violently

"Tiina, why are you crying, what's wrong?"

Before she could answer, Mother Vaarman came close and said, "Don't be silly, Tiina, don't you believe what Mr Paas tells you. God does exist, Jesus exists, and the angels exist too, and you will get better, but only if you believe, only if you truly believe."

Only now did Indrek realise what the problem was, and he stared blankly and despondently first at mother Vaarmann, who was comforting her child, and then at Tiina herself, who was still sobbing. And then, just as if he was an old professor who hadn't found heaven after thirty years of looking, he slumped down onto his knees, right on top of the heap of rags, and his eyes filled with tears. As he looked at the child with her wretched, twisted legs, Indrek saw another figure before his eyes on the freshly turned black earth, next to the potato plants. At that moment her legs had looked just the same, poking out from under her coarse-clothed, muddy skirt. Back then Indrek hadn't been able to do anything more than rush towards those legs, and burst into tears, cry his heart out – and it had helped a little. Then he forgot all about his fiery rage, and the hat he'd thrown into the potato patch, and he thought only about the person who was lying there so wretched on the earth.

And now again he had no choice but to stop thinking about himself, all the opinions he'd been airing and try and comfort the one who needed his help. Full of compassion, he dropped down in front of the sobbing child and spoke with a trembling voice, "Mother is right, Tiina, mother really is right. God exists, Jesus Christ exists, God's angels live, they're all alive and well."

"Now you're lying!" cried Tiina like an animal in pain, her voice wild with despair. "God is dead, Jesus is dead, the angels are dead, all of them are dead, and I will never recover! I'll be a cripple forever".

"No you won't, you won't," Indrek said. "You'll definitely get better, because God exists, and he will send his angels. He'll send a whole legion of them, one of them is sure to be able to mend your legs. He'll send so many of them, that one is sure to help. Anyway, I lied about God, because he's caused me so much pain, that's why I lied about him, and about his angels too. I wanted to get my own back on them, that's why. But God exists, he definitely exists. And to make sure you believe me, that he really does exist, and that I'm not lying now, I'll tell you one thing: you wanted me to wait, remember? For me to wait until you get better. Now I will wait, I promise you that in Jesus Christ's name. And of course I wouldn't wait for you if I didn't expect you to get better. You'll definitely get better, if I'm waiting for you. And I will be waiting."

"Will you really wait for me?" asked Tiina, lifting her head.

"I will," said Indrek. "I promise you that."

"And you won't take yourself a wife?"

"I'll be waiting for you to get better. And you will get better, you believe it!"

Tiina flung her slender arms around Indrek's neck, and Indrek put his arms around her small frame. Then, kneeling on the rags, he pressed Tiina tightly against his chest, and she asked him for assurance again, "Will you really, truly?"

"Really truly," Indrek told her.

Tiina hung from Indrek's neck for a while, as if she couldn't bear to let go. Her tears and laughter, pain and joy melded into ecstasy. And then, she discovered she was resting on her knees. She yelled out in excitement:

"Mother, mother! I can stand on my knees! I can stand without any help!"

Now she let go of Indrek's neck as if it were burning hot, and she threw her long, slender arms up towards the ceiling, shouting, "Mother, look, I'm standing!"

"My dear child, whatever has come over you?" mother asked in a worried voice, and she rushed up to Tiina and grabbed hold of her hands, as if she were afraid she might fall.

"Help me up, mother" said Tiina, "help me, I'm going to get up, I'm going to stand, I'm sure that I'll be able to stand." Mother Vaarman helped her daughter up on to her feet.

"Now let go of me, mother," said Tiina, "let me stand on my own two feet, just watch me stand on my own."

But Mother Vaarman couldn't bring herself to lift her hands from her daughter, fearing that she would fall, and when she eventually did let go, she kept her arms outstretched in a half circle around Tiina.

"Mother, take your hands away completely," Tiina said.

"Heavens above, you've finally got better! Tiina, you're going to walk!" mother cried, seeing her daughter stand on her own two feet.

And yet Tiina still couldn't walk on her own. She tried, but she couldn't. Only when mother held her by her hand could she manage a few steps. But that little was enough to bring such joy to her mother that she couldn't restrain herself from grabbing hold of her daughter, pressing her against her chest, and hugging her, hugging her with all her might, until she had almost suffocated her. Tiina just managed to force out a few words, "Mother, I'm terribly tired now, put me to bed please."

And as soon as her mother did as she asked, Tiina fell asleep, a happy smile on her face.

Now so much happiness and joy filled that stuffy cellar room that mother Vaarman might well have choaked on it, if she had not been able to go and share the news with Molli and anyone else who she happened to come across. That's what she did, flinging a large rug around herself, and hurrying out at great speed, as if the place were on fire.

And so Indrek was left there kneeling in the middle of the room, and at that moment he didn't care where he was. He felt as if his whole life had been turned upside down, as if everything was mixed up, in disarray, like a heap of rubbish. Just recently mother Vaarmann had defended Jesus Christ, but now she had gone out of the door like a shot without mentioning so much as a word about him, as if he existed only for those who were in need of grace and redemption. But what grace and redemption could you want when your daughter was already standing on her own two feet! For Tiina's sake, Indrek had decided to keep his doubts to himself, and now he was kneeling there in the middle of the room, as if he were bowing humbly before the very authorities he had doubted. But there was one thing which filled him with gladness: he had overcome his preoccupation with himself, thanks to that sobbing girl. He had forgotten his sadness and pain, he had let go of the truth which he felt in his heart of hearts, in order to comfort that wretched, unhappy child. What more noble act could he conceive of? God himself couldn't do anything nobler, if he did indeed exist, and someone were to bow before him, praying imploringly.

That's what Indrek thought to himself as he sat there in the middle of the room, while Tiina lay asleep in bed, smiling.

461

Translators' Biographies

Chapters 1-18 of this book were translated by Christopher Moseley, and chapters 19-38 by Matthew Hyde. Vagabond Voices would like to express our immense gratitude to **Matthew Hyde** for taking on the second half of the translation at very short notice and **Alan Teder** who at the very last minute came in and very generously gave his time and experience in sorting out some queries that had arisen over the first half.

Matthew Hyde is a literary translator from Russian and Estonian to English. His translations have been published by Pushkin Press, Dalkey Archive Press, Words Without Borders and Asymptote. In 2018 he was shortlisted for the John Dryden translation competition and the Estonian Cultural Endowment translation prize. His writings have appeared in Europe-Asia Studies, In Other Words, and Asymptote. Prior to becoming a translator, Matthew worked for ten years for the British Foreign Office as an analyst, policy officer and diplomat, serving at the British Embassies in Moscow and Tallinn, where he was Deputy Head of Mission. After that last posting Matthew chose to remain in Tallinn with his partner and son, where he translates and plays the double bass. He recorded an album of his own compositions with leading Estonian jazz musicians, Nordic Blues, available on Bandcamp. For Vagabond Voices, he has translated Rein Raud's *The Death of the Perfect Sentence* from Estonian and Andrei Ivanov's *Hanuman's Travels* from Russian. He is currently translating Volume IV of *Truth and Justice*.

Christopher Moseley is a translator from Estonian, Latvian, Finnish and the Scandinavian languages. Originally from Australia, he came to Britain to study Scandinavian languages in 1974, but since then his main interests have slipped eastwards to Finland and the Baltic countries. After 19 years' service at the BBC, he became a freelance translator and editor in 2005. He is the author of Colloquial Estonian and co-author of Colloquial Latvian for Routledge. He has translated novels from Estonian by Indrek Hargla, Andrus Kivirähk, Ilmar Taska, and for Vagabond Voices A.H. Tammsaare's *I Loved a German*.

Remember the Translator!

Vagabond Voices continues to celebrate translations and its translators. It is proper that translators are occasionally invisible (particularly when the reader is busy suspending disbelief), as their task is to present the authors and not themselves to the reader. But the actual words are not the authors' but the translators', and it is also proper that the reader recalls the presence of this intricate and generous craft.

www.vagabondvoices.co.uk/think-in-translation